THE
CRASH

CARA KENT

The Crash
Copyright © 2023 by Cara Kent

All rights reserved. Without limiting the rights under copyright reserved above, no part of this publication may be reproduced, stored in or introduced into retrieval system, or transmitted, in any form, or by any means (electronic, mechanical, photocopying, recording, or otherwise) without the prior written permission of both the copyright owner and the above publisher of this book.

This is a work of fiction. Names, characters, places, brands, media, and incidents are either the products of the author's imagination or are used fictitiously. The author acknowledges the trademarked status and trademark owners of various products referenced in this work of fiction, which have been used without permission. The publication/use of these trademarks is not authorized, associated with, or sponsored by the trademark owners.

PROLOGUE

A CURL PINGED FREE FROM THE TIP OF HIS WIDOW'S peak, rebelling against the rest of his gel-slicked crop of graying hair. Roland had tried every product under the sun to tame it. He'd even resorted to an ill-advised chemical relaxer in his vainer days, but no matter the method, his cowlick refused to conform.

When he was a child, his mom called it his Superman curl. The affectionate nickname had appealed to his comic-book-loving sensibilities, but as a bullied preteen, he felt far from heroic.

He was marked as an easy target from the moment his mom dropped him off on his first day of middle school in plain sight of all his new peers. She'd lovingly called out after him through the open window before abandoning him to the playground piranhas.

To make matters worse, he had been forced to wear ill-fitting hand-me-downs and coke bottle glasses—the latter of which were nothing like Clark Kent's debonair frames, no matter what his mom told him. He had looked around for potential new friends. Socially confident from his home schooling and positive interactions with neighborhood children, he had absolutely no idea that his new peers smelled fresh blood in the water. From then on, he became their prey, and a cyclical routine of defeat and resurgence began.

Six months in, when the schoolyard attacks came to a violent head, he decided to take control of the only thing he could. In the bathroom, while his mother slept, he'd snipped the errant tuft of hair down to the scalp with a pair of safety scissors. It didn't help his self-esteem or the bullying, and his mother cried for days over the bald diamond on his forehead.

Thirty-eight years later, his mother was dead, his looks had vastly improved, and his curl had grown back dozens of times over. He'd embraced it a long time ago, and today—as he confidently flew over his kingdom, back from the dead after fifteen years—he finally felt as super as she'd told him he was.

He marveled at the town's exponential growth. Urban sprawl was taking hold, new suburbs spiraled out from the bustling center of what was once a rustic timber town, and strip malls joined them to serve the growing population.

From day one, he'd seen its potential; and though he was pleased to see it rise beyond the naysayers' expectations, he was also disappointed he couldn't take total credit for its subsequent development.

There's more to do, he assured himself. *Plus, you got the ball rolling.*

He knew it was true and that his once-faithful flock would be overjoyed at his unexpected return. Not only had he funded businesses and improved the local school, but he'd also turned a quiet town into a credible society with a drive-in theater, community gardens, trivia nights, fishing competitions, ghost story night hikes, a consistently active recreation center, and so much more.

Sure, he'd racked up some considerable debt, but looking down at it now, all the struggles he'd endured felt worthwhile.

THE CRASH

Glenville, Washington was no longer a place for old, lonely hunters to come to die; it was a rural sanctuary teaming with life.

Admittedly, he was relieved to see that some parts had remained the same. The white steeple of the 1960s-style Baptist church, in which he'd been married, pointed up at his plane as if to alert the community to his return. The town hall, too, had stood the test of time, its red brick and majestic white columns visible even from eight thousand feet above.

Guiltily, he had to admit that he was most excited to see that Dottie's Diner remained unchanged, complete with the statue of a retro waitress statue holding a stack of pancakes. Their fried chicken and waffles, which were the best he'd ever had outside of Texas, would make for a perfect reward after his apology tour was over.

Apologies, Roland thought, swallowing hard, his mouth somehow dry and pooling with saliva simultaneously.

He knew that most would be happy to see him, but he owed a lot of people explanations, and as he lowered the plane, nearing his destination, concerns grew that he wouldn't be applauded for his resurrection. He pictured himself in the stocks, being pelted with rotten vegetables by his citizens, while the people he loved the most glared at him from the sidelines.

He'd tried to take the edge off his anxiety with his usual medicine, but it wasn't working in the usual fashion. His heart pounded in anticipation and nervousness and fear.

He'd had panic attacks before, mainly as a child, but this one was particularly severe. Worried it might be a bad omen, he contemplated heading onward toward Seattle like he was supposed to, but quickly dismissed the thought as silly superstition. If he'd learned anything in his time, it was that life didn't dress itself up as a black cat, broken mirror, or solitary crow before biting you in the ass; it just went right ahead and sunk its teeth in.

He took a deep breath in, held it, and exhaled. It didn't help the pain, but after fifteen long years, he had earned his life back—and no severity of headache, sweatiness of palms, or rapidity of breath could deter him from what he deserved.

Roland continued to lower the plane, feeling worse with each foot dropped, and he found himself feeling suddenly ill-prepared for how quickly his reconciliation with Glenville was going to arrive.

CHAPTER ONE

THE DETECTIVE

It was the official opening of Sherwood's beer garden; the complimentary champagne glasses were generously filled, the cut ribbon was lying on the floor, the speech had been made by Bobby Sherwood himself, and Heather was hiding from the sun behind a plastic menu. The freshly spray-painted chair was sticky on her bare thighs thanks to her regrettable decision to wear bike shorts, but the weather was too pleasant for anything to shatter her contentment.

She hemmed and hawed over the impressive array of lunch options, much to the dismay of Gabriel's growling stomach. One growl was so loud she swore she could feel the rumble. Amazed by the power of his teenage-boy-type hunger, she peered over the edge of the menu and barked a laugh at the disgruntled expression on her partner's face.

Having tortured him for long enough, she forced herself to make a choice. To the surprise of herself and Gabriel, she opted for the charred sprout salad. It sounded delicious and healthy, but considering the half-price opening day discount on the 'Big Boy Bacon Bonanza' cheeseburger, choosing a bowl of greens was an awe-inspiring display of willpower.

She laid the menu down on the repurposed wine barrel with a smug grin, basking in the cheers of her cholesterol-free arteries. She raised her glass of cheap champagne, her expression as sunny as the weather.

"Cheers!" she exclaimed, and Gabriel hesitantly clinked his glass against hers.

"Why are you in such a good mood?" he asked, suspicious of her unusual state of being.

"I think it's the runner's high."

Gabriel widened his eyes, taking in the slightly damp edges of her tank top, and glanced under the table at her beat-up sneakers that were at least a decade old. "You ran here?"

"Yup."

"Isn't your place like three miles away?"

"Uh-huh. I made it in forty minutes. Not quite a ten-minute mile, but I'm getting there."

"Who are you, and what have you done with Heather?"

Heather rolled her eyes at the cliché phrase. "I woke up one morning a few weeks ago and decided I didn't want to spend the next twenty-five thousand days of my life hungover and out of breath."

"So, this isn't anything to worry about?"

"Why would it be? It's just running, Gabriel. It's good for you. Maybe you should try it."

Her sentences were warning hisses before the lashing, increasingly defensive and condescending. She didn't mean to be, but her words refused to soften no matter how she held her lips.

Gabriel looked at her with a bleeding-heart doe-eyed expression that made her drop her gaze to the table. She wished she could take the last part back. Cardio was the last thing

Gabriel needed, having dropped so much weight over the past three months.

"I know it's good for you, and I'm glad you're happy. I was just thinking that *maybe* you're staying super busy so that you don't have to think about—"

Kindly but firmly, she cut him off with a gesture. "I'm fine. Really."

"Okay. Sorry."

She could hear the air rushing out of him as he deflated and looked up to offer him a small smile and wave off his apology. He returned the expression, but neither could maintain eye contact for long.

Needing something to do with her hands, Heather rummaged in her fanny pack for a pack of cigarettes and looked around to check that smoking was okay. It seemed to be, judging from the clouds of smoke billowing above most of the mismatched tables and colorfully painted chairs, so she lit up.

She rolled her shoulders and closed her eyes as she inhaled, the sun's warmth lapping at her exposed skin. It was a nice hiatus from the gray bleakness of winter, which was due to return come Monday. She was almost at the point of meditative when Gabriel broke her tranquility. She could always tell when he was staring. He was like a little kid in a grocery store, eyes boring into you from their shopping cart seats. She opened her eyes and found him gawking at her in slack-jawed disbelief.

"What?" she asked, her laugh flecked with faux irritation.

He gestured at the nicotine patch on her arm. "I don't think Nic-Quit will ask you to be their spokeswoman anytime soon."

She raised her hands guiltily. "I know, I know. But life is all about balance. I ran here, I chose a salad instead of the Mega Bacon Heart Terminator 3000, and in exchange, I get to enjoy a couple of glasses of champagne and a cigarette."

Gabriel snorted and stole one from the pack. Heather's face fell. Her guilt for getting her friend hooked on her most unhealthy vice was insurmountable, but she offered him the lighter all the same.

"Maybe I need to give this balance thing a try, because whatever you're doing is working. You look great." Gabriel smiled broadly, but his sweet expression slowly faltered as the compliment hung in the air.

"Oh, so you're saying I looked like crap before?" Heather meant it to sound jovial, but it emerged strangled, and her compensating chuckles sounded more like chokes.

Gabriel flushed, his ears and cheeks turning a vivid copper color as blood pumped frenziedly beneath his golden complexion. "Of course not, I—"

"Kidding!" Heather squeaked, not sounding at all convincing.

"Oh."

His obvious embarrassment made her feel queasy and Uncomfortable Silence pulled up a seat at the table. They both resented its frequent presence, but neither knew how to ask it to leave. Conversation had become difficult between them since Alice Warren's funeral eleven weeks ago. It wasn't quite as bad as pulling teeth, but it was comparable to plucking weeds from between driveway slabs. Monotonous, repetitive, practical. It was coworker small talk, and Heather hated it.

She didn't know why she couldn't take the compliment. Aside from the purple eye bags she hid behind her favorite aviator sunglasses, even she had to admit that she could see the improvements in her countenance.

Her skin was clear, her body toned, and her lengthy, raven-black hair, which had always been her favorite feature, had become enviably lustrous. Gene had said her ponytail had "grown thicker than a horse's tail" the last time she saw him. She wasn't sure if it was a compliment or a neutral observation—it was hard to tell with her former boss—but she thought about it on her daily runs as it swung to and fro from shoulder to shoulder.

Amber Horton—dressed in bedazzled daisy dukes, wedge-heeled sandals, and a red gingham shirt fashioned into a crop top—sidled up to the table, saving the pair from suffocating speechlessness. Her nine-month-old baby, Savannah, was sleeping happily in a sling on Amber's chest. Heather had never been the type to coo over babies, but she had to admit Savannah was a particularly adorable—and wonderfully quiet—one.

Amber was Bobby's new girlfriend and Glenville's newest resident. She and Savannah had moved up from Texas together a couple of months ago and had happened to walk into Sherwood's, suitcase in hand, at the same time as Heather was drowning her sorrows in a pitcher. The two women had clicked, despite being polar opposites, and Heather spotted an opportunity to orchestrate a whirlwind romance for the famously lonely Bobby Sherwood. She wasn't usually very interested in other people's relationships, but she also liked putting puzzles together, and this two-piece one was easy to solve.

Amber was also the mastermind behind the beer garden, food serving, interior renovations, and Bobby's clean and ironed clothing. Witnessing the transformation of the infamous dive was what Heather assumed it must have been like to watch Michelangelo paint the Sistine Chapel over plain plaster. Sure, she'd liked the dingy darkness and drunken lock-ins, but a salad in the sun was a pleasant alternative to punishing her liver.

Speaking of punishing my liver, Heather thought as Amber placed a fresh frosty pitcher of beer in the center of the table, the smell of her fake tan and tropical-scented body spray attacking Heather's senses as sun-damaged, freckled arms reached across her.

"Sorry, but we didn't order that," Heather said.

"It's on those guys over there," Amber said, pointing to a group of mechanics who worked at the Pacific Silver Auto Repairs.

Heather waved at the red-faced men, dressed in their usual uniform of faded flannels and worn-out trucker caps, and politely poured a beer. She didn't want to be rude, but she wished that the free drinks would stop flowing so freely in her direction. She hated saying no to people with good intentions, but eventually, she knew she'd have to. Not today, though, because she was determined that today was going to be a good day.

Heather raised her glass and took a polite sip, and the men began to enthusiastically chant, "Sheriff Bishop!" They egged each other on, growing louder and louder, and Heather wanted to sink into the ground. Amber, fortunately, noticed Heather's discomfort and told the men to knock it off, which they did so quickly, obediently, and with many apologies.

When the auto shop guys weren't hounding her on buying a better car, they were on her case about turning down being Glenville's next Sheriff. It wasn't just them; it seemed more than half of the town was rooting for her to take charge after she'd finally taken down Dennis Burke and solved the mystery of decades of missing hikers.

"The locals really don't like Tina, do they?" Gabriel whispered.

"It's hard to compete with someone who caught a serial killer, but civilians have no idea what actually makes a good Sheriff, and let me tell you, I wouldn't be one."

"I don't know. You..." Gabriel caught himself before offering another compliment. "You're probably right. I just think Tina can be a little... abrasive."

"Well, at least she can look after a whole department. I can barely look after myself. I guess it helps that she's—"

"A micromanager?"

Heather suppressed a grin, trying to be on her best behavior. "I was going to say it helps that she's got a type A personality."

"Oh, so a control freak? Gotcha."

Heather snorted despite herself. "She's doing a good job. She had big boots to fill. Gene had been the Sheriff for decades, and the locals loved him because he was chill. It's like when the cool, old teacher retires and is replaced by someone with something to prove and a stick up their ass. You go from blowing up stuff in science class to pop quizzes and having to do your homework. The latter will benefit you more in the long run, but no one likes being told what to do."

"So, you think Tina has a stick up her ass?"

"Gabe, are you even listening to me?"

"Yeah, yeah. You're being really nice about her, considering how she talks to you."

Heather bristled imperceptibly, remembering yesterday's incident by the water cooler. Tina had approached, her face painfully contorted into a vast grin that didn't quite reach her mascara-laden eyes. She'd started by complimenting Heather's complexion, and Heather had countered with a nice comment about Tina's new braids. Once the niceties were out of the way, Tina had lowered her voice and condescendingly "whispered" that she didn't think Heather was doing very well, and that she'd like to keep her on desk duty for another two weeks. She claimed it was mainly because they were swamped with paperwork, but Heather knew when she was being babysat.

Though it probably had a lot to do with her emotional outburst after discovering that Alice had died, Heather secretly believed she was being punished for being the public's clear favorite when it came to the position after Gene had retired in disgrace. The woman had worked in the department and vied for the position for too long to get Heather's secondhand scraps, and now she was out to prove herself at any cost, even if it meant keeping Heather on the bench.

"She's just trying her best," Heather said with a shrug. It wasn't a lie; Tina really was trying her best. Whether she was making Heather angry in the process was irrelevant so long as she kept the department running like a well-oiled machine. And for what it was worth, Heather had absolutely zero desire to be the sheriff. She'd moved to Glenville to get away from the pressure, not add to it. As far as she was concerned, Tina would be a fine leader of the department. She just wished Tina wouldn't take things out on her so directly.

"Well, the park is nicer, at least," Gabriel admitted. "No more broken glass, urine in the fountain, dog crap in the sandbox, or graffiti on the toilets. So, she gets a point for that."

"Yeah, and she caught the package bandit," Heather added.

"You pointed her in the right direction."

"Still."

The strange, uneasy silence settled between them again, and Heather stared at the kitchen door, waiting for food to materialize and give her something to say or do. She sipped her beer, and with a lower tolerance than she used to have, liquid confidence took hold as she reached the glass's halfway point. She opened her mouth, ready to broach a tricky topic, except Gabriel had the same idea.

"So, I wanted to talk to you—"

"I just wanted to say—"

She shook her head. "Oh, you go."

"No, you go," he insisted.

Heather cleared her throat awkwardly, her heart pounding. "I just wanted to say I'm s—what the hell is that?"

The distinctive of a plane engine rumbling shook the ground, and Heather looked around for the source. It didn't take long to locate it. Heather's blood ran cold like it had when she'd choked on a hard candy while home alone or swerved to avoid a deer too late. It was a sense of inevitable disaster, reckoning with your mortality, and paralyzing fear.

"Oh my god," she whispered, her heart ready to pop, as a small airplane plummeted straight toward them at an alarming speed, its engines roaring and screaming in the air.

It was going to crash right in the middle of Glenville, and there was nothing she or anybody could do about it except get out of the way. She jumped up just in time to grab Gabriel and a nearby Amber and threw them to the freshly mown grass. At the last second, as they fell, Heather remembered Savannah, but upon landing felt that the sling was empty, meaning the baby must be inside with Bobby.

Heart pounding, Heather covered her friends with her body, braced for impact. The other patrons followed suit, all of them knowing that if the plane hit the beer garden, they were all done for, flat on the ground or not.

The blow was worse than she feared. The sound was deafening, bone-shattering, sickening. It felt as if the power of it could turn her to dust.

When the screaming started from afar, she realized she wasn't dead and apologetically clambered off the other two. Looking around for casualties and fallout as she helped Amber to her feet, she braced herself for the worst, but by some miracle, everyone was okay. Shell-shocked, sure, but there was no trace of blood or rubble in the beer garden.

Once Amber was steady, she offered a hand to Gabriel, who turned it down, looking flustered as he dusted himself off and joined her in checking for damages. The two of them—no longer insouciant weekend beer drinkers but Detective and Partner once more—followed the harrowing screams around the side of Sherwood's and toward the chaos emanating from the main street.

THE CRASH

Heather braced herself for carnage but was instead met with fire and broken glass, the nose of the plane penetrating the front window of the last remaining laundromat in town. It, fortunately, wasn't open until the afternoon on a Saturday, so there'd be no innocent bystander casualties there.

Once everyone joined Heather in realizing that they were still alive, the shocked screams faded and were replaced with the sirens of incoming ambulances and fire trucks. Heather stepped toward the plane as the other emergency services approached, but Gabriel grabbed her arm to keep her safe from the molten hot danger zone.

On the other side of the blackened glass, she could just make out the slumped figure of the pilot, already charred and burning from the wreckage. It was evident to her that he was already gone, but her gut told her that he'd looked like that long before he hit the ground, and she waited anxiously for the jaws of life and EMTs to prove her theory right.

CHAPTER TWO

THE SON

B EAU LOOKED UP AT THE OIL PAINTING THAT LOOMED above the roaring fireplace. The infamous family portrait. He'd always found it eerie, the four of them set against a black void wearing their fanciest formal attire. The two children, of which he was one, sat on a velvet couch the color of freshwater pearls, their legs falling short of touching the ground. Their parents stood stiffly behind the antique piece of furniture, a distance apart, the background drawing a dark dividing line between the two contrasting halves of the painting.

On the right side, Beau's younger sister and father smiled broadly. Lucy was dressed in powder blue ruffles, and the family patriarch was garbed in tailored pinstripes, his black hair

THE CRASH

glossy and slick. They were picture-perfect, photogenic, even on canvas.

On the left-hand side of the painting, Beau's eight-year-old expression was hollow, as if staring through the artist and into another room. He reminded himself of Damien from *The Omen*, a little boy in an all-black suit, the starchy collar perforating the lower fat of his moon-shaped face. His mother looked similarly unhappy, her brown hair slicked into a small beehive and her tiny mouth tautened like the clasp on a drawstring bag.

Visitors often asked why she looked so dismal and would throw jokes around about uncomfortable shoes and crasser comments about it being her time of the month. Nancy laughed at them all—ever the gracious host—before deferring to her usual excuse about the painful pins in her hair.

But Beau knew the truth behind her pinched expression. Her vicelike bony grip on his tiny shoulder gave it away if only the drunken spectators had known where to look. He was a rotten child, as his mother had so delighted in telling him, and she had tried and failed to keep him still all day before resorting to holding him steady by force.

He'd never noticed her dour expression until others pointed it out as odd. Smiling was not something his mother did. In fact, he thought her incapable of it until he was old enough to be paraded about her dinner parties. Then he realized he was the only person who never saw her teeth in the context of kindness.

Beau wiped the trickling beads of sweat from his forehead with the back of his ring-covered hand and tossed his leather jacket over the back of the white couch. It was the warmest day in months, but if the calendar said it was winter, the fire would remain lit. His mother claimed it was because she ran cold, which always made Beau laugh for reasons beyond her or her guest's understanding. He wasn't sure what was so hard to comprehend. Surely, one glance at her painted portrayal was enough to understand the punch line.

He continued to stare at her unsettling depiction as the flesh and blood version clanked around in the adjoining kitchen. Next to the hearty, handsome man by her side, she looked like something from beyond the veil, accidentally captured by the paint as if it were a photograph. Her hands and body were nearly skeletal from constant dieting, and her long, angular features were shadowy.

She was the type of woman that people often referred to as handsome. Never lovely, warm, kindly, or even pretty, but ostentatious and striking. At least, that's what people said. To Beau, she was more like an egret, her sharp beak and talons pecking and puncturing the softer, weaker parts of him.

More than anybody else in the world, she got under his skin. As time passed, it became increasingly easy for her to worm her way in, and he suspected she took some sick pleasure in doing so. Often the arguments started with money, but today, as the smell of cooking fish wafted down the hallway, he realized she was opting for disrespect disguised as naïveté.

Beau had hated fish since he was a child. Maybe it was a psychological hangover from fishing with his dad and having to gut the foul, slippery creatures, or perhaps he was still traumatized from getting a bone stuck in his throat. Whatever it was, even the smell made him sick, so when his mother called him to lunch, he marched toward her, ready to raise his voice. It was going to be *that* kind of lunch. Not that any of their rare one-on-one attempts at socialization were pleasant, but there was a sliding scale of bad, and though he preferred to avoid the lower end, he was damned if he'd let this slide.

She didn't look at him as he stomped into the kitchen, and when he noticed his childlike stance, his hands clenched into fists, he unfurled them and cleared his throat. His call to attention didn't work, and she kept her back to him as she removed her apron and hung it next to the other five vintage floral smocks. He tried again as she plated the fish, but she remained undeterred.

"Set some plates and cutlery on the kitchen island, please," Nancy said, tipping the butter and caper sauce over the slabs of soft, white fish.

Beau gagged, his brutal hangover coming back to haunt him. They were so frequent he'd learned to endure them, but this was pushing him to his limits. He cleared his throat again, and Nancy banged the pot down on the stovetop.

"Do you have a cold?" she asked tersely.

"Mom, you know I hate fish."

Nancy froze and slowly turned, plates in hand. "Goodness. I totally forgot. I guess it's been so long since I've seen you, and you know I am getting old."

"You're barely fifty, and I've hated fish since I was a kid. You'd think it would stick eventually."

"I guess not, but it won't kill you to eat something that isn't made in the microwave."

Beau sniffed. "I'm not eating that. I'd rather die."

He regretted saying it, because as soon as he saw his mom's knuckles whiten, he knew what came next. Calmly, her posture perfect, she floated across the tiled floor in her impractically tall heels and dumped their lunches into the porcelain dogs' bowls.

"At least two of my sons will appreciate my cooking."

It took Beau a second to realize that she was referring to her two prize-winning Weimaraners. He raised his eyebrows in surprise as she whistled for the silvery hounds. This was a new development. As a child, the dogs were resented and lived outside full-time to avoid any specks of mess, but now they wore knitted Christmas sweaters and had their own bedroom. Perhaps Lucy going to college had affected his mother more than he'd realized, but he was too frustrated by her dramatics to pity her.

"You could have still eaten it," he grumbled.

"No, no. Clearly, my cooking isn't fit for human consumption. Maybe you should go and grab some burgers or whatever from Sherwood's instead."

"You hate burgers."

She made a show of smiling and waving him away. It was dismissive, but not of herself. "Oh, don't worry about me. I have plenty of *disgusting* food here, but you always get so moody when you're hungry. I'd rather you eat something from a doggy bag than take a tone with me."

"Oh, *I'm* the moody one?" Beau asked incredulously, perching on a stool at the kitchen island and sliding the silver, fully stocked liquor tray toward himself.

"Beau, for God's sake, it's not even two o'clock!"

"As if you don't have a side of gin with your breakfast in the morning."

Her mouth dropped open and then compressed into a tight line. "I do not."

"Then why is there fresh ice in the bowl?"

Nancy stuttered, struggling to think of a retort. She rummaged in her purse, pulled out her overstuffed wallet, and plucked a crisp twenty-dollar bill from its zippered lips. She handed it over, and Beau snatched it with a scowl.

"Go buy your *burger*, and don't come back. I've had quite enough of your company today."

"I can buy my own burger," he shot back, pocketing the paper bill.

"Of course, dear. That's why you called me up begging for money in the middle of the night only last week."

"I've sold a bike since then; I'm good for it."

"Excellent news. Seeing as you're good for it, you can pay me back some of the money you owe me. Oh, wait, you can't, because you have to buy a new bike to 'fix,' and the cycle repeats itself."

"I work paycheck to paycheck like most Americans."

Nancy scoffed, supporting herself with the island as if the conversation was sucking out her life force. "Maybe you should have higher aspirations than simply breaking even. Your sister is well on her way to becoming an architect."

"You won't be so happy with her when she has to move back in with you because she can't find a job." He knew he sounded petty and jealous, but it wasn't because of Lucy's corporate, pantsuit-wearing lifestyle; his envy was much older than that.

"She already has a paid internship, but I guess you wouldn't know that."

"I guess I wouldn't. I don't hear from the golden child much."

Nancy pinched the bridge of her nose and let out a long sigh. "Where does the money go, Beau?"

"What do you mean?"

"I give you a hundred dollars a week for food and whatever else you need; you earn a couple of thousand a month through the cars and bikes. You should be turning some kind of profit, considering you don't pay rent or utilities. So, where does it go?" She stared at his eyes, pale blue and bloodshot, and shook her head. "Are you high right now?"

THE CRASH

"Jesus! No! How could you ask me that?"

He watched as his outburst confirmed her fears. She straightened and handed him another twenty. "Consider that this week's allowance. Don't call me asking for more. I don't want to hear from you for a while."

He rolled his eyes. "What else is new?"

Beau got to his feet, stumbled, and swigged his half-full glass of twelve-year-old scotch. The liquor ran down his chin as he glugged, and his mother looked on in disgust at what had become of her child. He struggled to suppress a grin, deriving so much pleasure from ruffling her feathers.

"Please leave."

Finally, the closest thing he could compare to a smile crossed his face. "My pleasure."

He slammed the glass down so hard on the grey-veined marble that a crack formed in the side of the diamond-patterned tumbler. It had been one of his dad's favorite glasses, and now only two of the original set of four remained. Beau had, of course, been responsible for the shattering of the other one after it was apparent that his dad was never coming home. At least this time, it was sort of an accident.

For some reason beyond him, he tightened his grip until he heard a crunch, and a shard sunk into his palm. His mother began fussing at once, but not over him. She ran a tea towel under water and soaked the marble immediately, terrified of the copper stain that might form in some of the rough crevices.

Beau staggered to the sink, dripping blood along the floor, before running his hand under the water. He caught his breath and stared out at the town. He had to admit that it was a nice view up on the hill. He missed looking out at night and counting the dots of light, but not nearly enough to ever come to one of his mother's stuffy dinners.

He looked over toward Sherwood's, thinking about what forty dollars could get him when he spotted something out of the corner of his eye. He turned toward it, suddenly fearful, his animal instincts roiling as he heard the rumbling over the tap. His mouth fell open, but his breath caught in his chest. An airplane was careening downward directly toward the center of town. Worst of all, he recognized it. It was a 2001 Beechcraft Bonanza A36. His father's pride and joy.

CHAPTER THREE

THE DETECTIVE

Heather and Gabriel split up, taking on different sections of the town square to cover as much ground as possible to get the chaos under control. Deeply shaken by the unexpected event, Heather ambled between tasks, going through the motions of her job on autopilot. She corralled panicked onlookers and helped her arriving colleagues erect a barrier around the crash with the fervor of a pimply teenager working in a drive-thru. She knew she wasn't much of a help or comfort with her monotone voice and sluggish demeanor, but she kept pushing through, determined to be part of the team.

As she referred another traumatized civilian to the EMTs, she felt a hand on her shoulder and jumped. She turned and saw

Tina, the shorter woman's plump face wearing a mask of calm stretched thin over burgeoning stress.

Tina spoke, her head tilted, her mouth slightly downturned. She looked as if she were asking a question, but Heather couldn't hear what it was despite their proximity. Her ears were still ringing from the crash's impact, and the clangorous world around her—dominated by power tools, fire hoses, and hordes of unsettled people—further hindered Heather's ability to understand her boss.

Tina repeated herself, louder this time, nearly penetrating the barricade but not quite. Frustrated, her mask melting in the heat of the sun's glare, she reached out and shook Heather's shoulders vigorously.

"Detective, are you okay?" she asked, clearly more aggravated than concerned that her best and only detective was having a moment.

The shaking worked wonders, and Heather nodded, blinking rapidly. "Yeah, yeah. I'm fine."

"I think you need to sit down," Tina said, gesturing to a nearby bench.

Heather almost found it funny, being forcibly benched again, but honestly, she could do with a breather. Her adrenaline was crashing, leaving her fatigued and disoriented, and she could see it happening to those around her. They were like a bunch of toddlers waiting on nap time.

You look death in the eye, and instead of jumping for joy, all you want to do is surrender to unconsciousness. Go figure.

She meandered over to the wooden bench and collapsed onto it, finding that her ribs hurt terribly upon leaning back. She hoped she hadn't broken them in her attempt at heroics but feared the worst as she tentatively prodded her lower left side. She sucked her teeth, knowing she should get one of the EMTs to look at it, but she was too tired to line up behind all the shaky people desperate for silver shock blankets. Her injury could wait until after the big reveal.

A metallic creaking sound indicated that the moment had come, and Heather watched intently as they pried the plane door open now that the fire had been successfully extinguished. In its wake, the molten heat had riddled the body of the plane with holes, and in turn, hot, silvery puddles of goo ran past the firefighters' feet over the bumpy tarmac. The remnants of the once smart paint job—white with navy and burgundy racing stripes—had turned as dark and brittle as the glass that encased the body of the poor pilot.

The nervous onlookers pressed against the yellow tape as more people crowded in from behind, desperate to discover the pilot's fate and identity. Heather wished she was as optimistic as the crowd of nail-biters. They whispered to one another, and she listened to their hopes sadly, wishing she could make them look away before it was too late but knowing that would be an impossible task. If there was one thing people were sure to do, it was stare at a terrible accident.

"But remember in that movie, The Aviat—"

"I think I can see him moving—"

"They got in there so fast—"

Broken and garbled, the messages of hope hissed into Heather's ears. She sighed wearily. Sure, Howard Hughes had famously survived a worse crash in 1946, but his survival had been nothing short of a miracle. The damage to his shattered, third-degree-burned-body had been so bad that his heart had vacated the left side of his body and taken up residence in the right cavity. To survive such a thing was a one-in-a-million chance, and this pilot struck her as the type of man who was all out of luck.

Certainly, the firefighters had been quick, but if still breathing postcollision, the pilot would've inhaled a lot of smoke, which, as far as Heather was aware, could kill you in under five minutes. It took nearly that long for the emergency services to arrive and get the hose out.

And yes, he could technically be unconscious, but Heather knew a dead body when she saw one, and so did the EMTs, who stood to the side with a black body bag at the ready.

It didn't take long for the truth to be revealed as two large men in bulky uniforms emerged holding the limp, charred body of what appeared to be a middle-aged man.

Heather decided she had been catching her breath for long enough, and with Tina distracted by the wailing laundromat owners, she was going to be the first on the scene. She tried not to let the satisfaction show, but striding toward the body, her hand on the leather police badge wallet in her pocket, she realized how much she'd missed her job.

She didn't even need to flash her badge as she sidled up, thanking those already there for a job well done. The EMTs knew her well from the aftermath of the Dennis Burke case, and they stepped back to let her into the circle formed around the stretcher.

"Gloves," she said to the EMT demandingly before correcting herself. She wasn't a Seattle bigshot anymore, nor did she want to be. "I mean, can I have some gloves?"

The young EMT handed her a pair of latex gloves, and Heather snapped them on as she moved toward the deceased's face. He wore a terrified, open-eyed, open-mouthed expression that perturbed all who could see.

She inspected his head thoroughly, turning it from side to side and opening his mouth. This examination not only aided her theory about him dying in the air but also provided a probable cause of death.

There was congealed white powder coating the interior of his bloody nostrils, his lips were covered in foam, his skin was blue from asphyxiation, and looking at the back of his throat, it seemed likely he had suffocated via emesis. All signs pointed to a drug overdose, and the lack of bleeding from his numerous contusions and cuts implied that his heart had stopped pumping some time ago.

She noted all of this down in her journal and nodded at the EMT who zipped the body up, keen to remove it from prying eyes.

She turned and found Gabriel standing with his hands in his pockets, tiptoeing behind a wall of medical professionals, gawking like the rest of the crowd. Heather rolled her eyes, pulled her gloves off, handily throwing them into one of the medical waste cans in the back of the open ambulance, and gestured for him to come over.

"So, what do you think?" she asked.

"Was it a drug overdose?"

She nodded, trying to hide her pride. "That's my best guess. We'll see what the pathologist thinks."

"Cocaine?"

"Looks that way."

They both looked over at the plane as firefighters emerged from the doorway and beckoned Tina—who had finally rid herself of the laundromat owners—over. They whispered something; Tina raised her eyebrows up into her hairline and summoned her usual cronies. Dutifully the three men boarded the plane and moments later exited, arms laden with plastic-wrapped bricks of white powder.

"So, he got too high on his own supply and crashed? What a way to go." Gabriel looked at the body and shook his head at the awful sight.

"I guess so," Heather replied.

Gabriel furrowed his eyebrows and clicked his fingers. "Wait, I know this guy!"

"Wait, you do?"

"Yeah, he's—"

A piercing screech coming from somewhere behind them interrupted Gabriel. Heather whipped around sharply, stepping back from the body to see a bone-thin, elegantly dressed woman in very tall heels writhing in Tina's grasp at the barrier. Tina had moved quicker than Heather thought possible to restrain the spindly stranger. However, despite the taller woman's slender physique, she managed to fight Tina off; and as soon as she was past the tape, she was clattering toward Heather, Gabriel, and the body at full speed.

"Ma'am, you can't—"

Heather didn't have time to finish her sentence. She got up and moved toward her, acting as round two of the blockade, but as she did so, the woman tripped on some debris and flew into Heather. Heather caught her handily, a sharp elbow catching her in her injured ribs, but despite that, she held her ground as the woman clawed at her.

Maybe all that running is paying off, she thought as she easily held the woman back and watched as an out-of-breath Tina staggered toward them. The woman fell to her knees, sobbing, and Heather looked at Tina in confusion.

"Is it him?" the stranger whined, looking past Heather's hip toward the now zipped-up body bag.

"Who?" Heather asked, tapping her foot, and rubbing her arm where the woman had torn at her shirt in desperation.

"Roland! Is it him?"

Heather looked around at Gabriel, bewildered, and saw him nod. Heather had no idea who that was, but she knew she couldn't answer the woman's question based on a nonfamily ID of the body. So, she helped the woman to her feet with the help of Tina, who now looked as shocked as Gabriel, and guided her toward the dead man.

At the stretcher, Heather put a hand on the woman's shoulder, but she writhed away from the friendly touch. Heather understood and dropped her arm before nodding at the EMT, who unzipped the bag.

The woman next to her wailed, confirming the ID of whoever Roland was. It was the kind of noise a person only made when encountering the most terrible grief. It was painful to hear and even worse to witness as the bony widow draped herself over the body and clutched at the charred clothing. Heather quietly backed away from the heart-wrenching display of emotion, leaving the Sheriff with all the emotional fallout.

Heather reunited with Gabriel, who watched the woman unblinking as everyone did. "That's Nancy Ellis," he whispered. "She's married—or I guess she *was* married—to Roland Ellis. The mayor."

"The man on the slab."

"Yep."

Heather frowned. "I thought Kenneth Ward was the mayor? You know, Tina's brother-in-law." It was a fact that Tina would never let anyone forget and was partially responsible for her power trip. Between her and Kenneth, her family ran Glenville.

Gabriel shook his head. "He's been the mayor for the past eight years, but fifteen years ago, it was Roland. He went missing in 2008. Got in his plane, and no one ever heard from him again." He looked to his left and nodded to Heather to follow his gaze. Another person had ducked under the tape unbeknownst to anybody, clearly there to look at the body.

"Should we stop him?" Heather asked.

Gabriel shook his head, and they watched as he numbly—visibly shaking from afar—approached Nancy and Roland. He didn't comfort her but stared down at the body from a distance, his face porcelain pale.

Heather realized that he looked a lot like the man on the stretcher, with his black hair and pale blue eyes, but he also resembled the woman with his gaunt face, tall build, pinched mouth, and elegant long neck.

In style, however, they couldn't have been more different. He wore small hoop earrings and an eyebrow ring, his body was covered in tattoos, his hair was lank and greasy, and his clothes were covered in dirt and what appeared to be motor oil. If he'd recently taken a bath, Heather thought he might have been handsome—in an exquisite, alien-like fashion model sort of way.

Heather knew who he was long before Gabriel informed her that he was Beau Ellis, the only son of Nancy and Roland.

Beau approached Tina, loudly confirmed the identity of his father, and walked away toward the bench Heather had earlier occupied. He sat down hard, his face still expressionless, and lit a cigarette. He looked past the body, the emergency vehicles, and the crash to somewhere in the distance, approximately a thousand yards away.

"What's his story then?" Heather asked, intrigued by the obvious black sheep.

"He's got some issues. Barred from most places for fighting. Has some priors for assault, drinking, possession, that sort of thing. He lives in the woods and sells old cars and bikes that he fixes up. The only people who have anything to do with him are the guys at the auto shop. They sell his stuff for a cut because no one wants to deal with him directly."

"Did you go to school together?"

"Yeah, and he was just as difficult back then too. Spent most of his time in detention. Started smoking in middle school."

"Bullied?"

"Sort of. Kind of went both ways. Rich kid in a small-town school, tried to be 'hard,' but you know how kids are. He thought he was better than everyone but got the crap kicked out of him too."

"Did he get along with his parents?"

"No idea, but looking at him now, I'd say that's a firm no." Gabriel paused. "Why are you talking about him as if he's a suspect?"

"Maybe he is."

"Only if he forced his dad to snort coke telepathically."

"I don't know. It feels like there's more to all of this."

"It's a weird one. I'll give you that. But I think you'd be hard-pressed to murder someone when they're alone in a plane."

"Unless it was poison," she pointed out.

"As you said, we'll find out what the pathologist says."

There was something competitive in his voice, and something ancient and callous in her wanted to bet on it. Yet, as much as she wanted a free lunch, it didn't feel right, so she kept her mouth shut and concentrated on feeling empathy for the victim and his loved ones.

None of it came easy: the self-improvement, the working on her professionalism, and the sitting with her emotions. She'd spent so long pretending not to care. Being hardened to the horrors of her job was so much easier than what she felt as she absorbed Nancy's screams. Strip away the dark jokes and the dripping sarcasm, and all her armor was gone. It hurt a lot more than she expected.

She was lost in thought when Gabriel suddenly collided with her. Distracted by Nancy, she lost her balance and fell hard to the floor. Panicked, she reached for her gun and, fortunately, looked up at the still-standing Gabriel before aiming it. He looked down at Heather apologetically, his arms held fast to his side by a young red-faced girl in a strappy summer dress.

Heather cleared her throat and stood up, moving her hand away from her gun but adopting a sturdy stance as she glared at the young woman.

"Ma'am, I'm going to need you to leave the crime scene if you're not a family member of the deceased."

The girl—her mostly blonde hair twisted into two buns on either side of her head, pink streaks dangling at her temples—ignored Heather and looked up at Gabriel simperingly. "It's okay if I'm here, right baby?"

Heather answered for him. "No, it's not."

The girl shot her a similarly innocent look which only made Heather angrier. "I just wanted to check on my boyfriend. I knew he was in town today, and when I saw the plane crash, I was so worried." She tiptoed and whispered in Gabriel's ear, "You didn't answer your phone; I think you accidentally had it on silent again."

Admittedly this bemused Heather, but the longer she waited for Gabriel to lay down the law with his girlfriend, the more impatient she became with both of them.

"Well—" she addressed the girl, waiting for one of them to fill in her name.

"Briana," the girl chirped.

"Briana. There's not much more Officer Silva needs to do today, so if you'd like, you can both leave my crime scene."

"Your crime scene, huh?" Gabriel teased and escaped the bounds of Briana's arms. "Looks like Tina has you beat on that."

"I'm still the head detective here. Which means I'm swamped, so how about you two go have a nice day off?"

Gabriel's face fell, unable to gauge if Heather was genuinely mad. He eventually nodded and escorted himself and Briana off the premises. Despite her scraped palm, once the young couple's backs were to her, she couldn't help but smirk. At least there was someone else for Gabriel to hang out with, though she would be okay if she never had to re-encounter Hurricane Briana.

She noticed Beau staring at her out of the corner of her eye. The blood had returned to his face, and his haunted expression had twisted into amusement as he watched her dust herself off. She dropped the smirk, trying to look competent in front of the man whose father had just died brutally. She mentally cursed Briana for making the whole thing appear like a circus and decided she would give Gabriel a lecture the next time they spoke.

She turned toward Beau and offered him a slight nod of condolences, but he kept looking at her with a toothy grin, shaking his head as he lit a cigarette. She wanted to bow sarcastically like a royal jester for his majesty but narrowly refrained. It disturbed her how easily distracted he was from his father's body being zipped up in a bag, but she knew too well how differently grief affected people.

On the opposite end of the spectrum, Nancy had been subdued and wrapped up in what must be the last remaining shock blanket, still sobbing her eyes out as she took a final glance at Roland before they took him away.

Tina appeared at Heather's side as if by magic, chewing her lip as she watched today's terrible scene come to an end.

She didn't look at Heather when she spoke, but said everything Heather had wanted to hear for the past three months. "I'm going to put someone else on desk work. I need you to help me look into this."

"Of course. You got it."

"Thank you, Detective Bishop."

"Thank *you*, Sheriff Peters."

Tina nodded, not half as appreciative as she should be, staring at the ambulance as it drove away. The older woman's mind whirred behind her eyes, and Heather half expected smoke to spill from her ears. Her distant expression made it clear that Heather wasn't the only one who sensed there was more to this than a drug-fueled accident.

CHAPTER FOUR

THE DETECTIVE

While Tina supervised the removal of the plane and the deconstruction of the crime scene, she assigned Heather the task of taking statements. Heather wasn't entirely sure why one of Tina's minions couldn't do it, but she figured it must be a test of her emotional stability and people skills, and she intended to pass with flying colors.

She smiled sympathetically, used her most soothing voice, and chitchatted enthusiastically as she took statements from those who had been in the town center at the time of the crash. It didn't matter how off-topic they got; she never showed any exhaustion or impatience and kindly indulged all the talk of new grandbabies and missed dental appointments.

When she moved on to the laundromat owners, they yelled at her as if she'd been the one that nosedived into her place of business, but she didn't flinch, didn't falter as their anger escalated.

She apologized for the damages and suggested the town host a fundraiser to get them back on their feet. They seemed to like that idea, and Tina nodded approvingly in the distance. Imbued with a sense of confidence caused by a job well done, Heather turned toward Nancy and Beau and strode toward them, a picture of professional perfection.

However, as she approached them—Beau sitting lackadaisically on the bench halfway through a pack of cigarettes and Nancy pacing behind him—Tina rushed over and caught Heather by the upper arm.

"Do *not* interrogate them. They're not suspects, they're not criminals, they're a grieving wife and son," she whispered.

"Thanks for reminding me, Tina. I was just about to go cuff them."

"All I'm saying is that you seem a little on edge today, and I just wanted to make sure that you're on your very best behavior." Heather scowled at Tina, who seemed to quickly realize that she'd overstepped. "I'm sorry, Detective, it's just that Nancy Ellis is a very influential woman in town, and I don't want her kicking up a fuss at the station tomorrow."

"I promise I won't give her a reason to."

Tina paused thoughtfully. "Although, if you do manage to squeeze anything interesting out of them—"

"You'll be the first to know. But as I said, I'm just going to ask them a few questions."

"Of course, of course."

"Can I go now?" Heather asked, gesturing to her arm.

Tina quickly released her grasp and fixed a sweet syrupy expression on Heather, her deep dimples sunken. Heather rubbed her arm. "Cool, going to go talk to the witnesses now."

"Thanks, Heather, you're the best."

Heather looked up at Beau and Nancy and realized they had been watching the bizarre interaction between her and Tina the entire time. She prayed they couldn't lip read, but regardless of their abilities in that area, their belief in her as a police officer was undoubtedly shaken—undermined by the Sheriff before taking a statement. She might as well pack up and go home.

Thanks a lot, Tina, Heather thought as she walked over, trying and failing to sink back into the personable groove she'd dug.

Nancy joined Beau on the bench, and Heather felt her palms beginning to sweat as she reached speaking distance.

"Hello, I'm Detective Bishop; I'd like to ask you a couple of questions about the day's events if that's okay."

"Of course, it's okay," Nancy snapped. "That's why we've been waiting here for an hour instead of going home."

"I apologize for the wait. I didn't realize the other statements would take so long." Nancy tutted but didn't continue speaking, and Beau's gaze was firmly planted on the ground. "I'd like to start by saying how sorry I am for your loss."

"Thank you," Nancy replied tersely.

"So, Nancy—"

"Mrs. Ellis, please."

Beau finally looked up. "Just Beau for me. Mr. Ellis was my father." It was a joke, but nobody laughed, and Beau returned to staring at the leaf-covered ground.

Heather cleared her throat nervously. "Let's start with just before the crash. Where were you both?"

"We were inside my kitchen, having a lovely lunch." Heather noticed Beau furrow his brow at the word 'lovely,' but she pretended as if she hadn't. That was something for her notepad, not the report.

"Okay, so why did you head into town once the plane crashed?"

"Beau saw the plane through the window. We'd recognize it anywhere." Nancy blew her nose loudly as her voice caught. A second wave of tears was on its way, the flimsy dam about to bust wide open.

"Okay, so you saw the plane, knew it belonged to your husband, and came into town then?"

"Yes," Nancy said, taking a tone that implied Heather was profoundly stupid.

"And what happened to your hand, Beau?" Heather asked, gesturing to the still bleeding wound on his nonsmoking hand.

"Must've broken a glass when I saw the plane."

"Because you saw it about to crash or because of who it belonged to?"

He shrugged. "Both, I guess."

"Are we under arrest, detective?" Nancy asked sternly.

"Of course not, ma'am; I just wanted to see if you knew anything that could help us."

Nancy put a shaking hand on her chest. "Oh, God, there's going to be some sort of dreadful investigation, isn't there? Officers and reporters milling in and out, tracking dirt onto the floor. My husband's body laid up on ice for God knows how long. I hate to think of him in some sort of chest freezer, waiting on his funeral, stuck in purgatory. How am I supposed to have any closure?"

"I'm very sorry, Mrs. Ellis. I know this must be extremely difficult for you, but unfortunately, the nature of your husband's death means we have to investigate."

"Nature of his death? Didn't he crash?"

"He did, but we believe at this stage that he may have been dead before he hit the ground. We found drugs around his nostrils and a large quantity of the same type of narcotic on the plane."

Nancy pursed her lips, the grief replaced by red-hot anger, and though Heather was on the receiving end of most of it, she could tell from the furtive glances to the remnants of the plane that Roland was receiving some lashes too.

"Are you implying my husband was some sort of drug addict?"

"I'm not implying anything, ma'am. I'm just wondering if you can tell me anything about Roland that might help me wrap this up as quickly as possible."

Nancy sighed. "I don't know what to tell you; my husband was a good man and a virtuous one."

Beau shifted again at that, glancing up at Heather and looking her in the eye. It didn't last long, but Heather did her best to translate the silent exchange. Those icy eyes told her that Beau had plenty to say, but not here, not today.

Having put down quite enough chicken scratch, Heather pocketed her pen. "Of course, Mrs. Ellis, I don't mean to imply otherwise."

"I'm sure you don't, Detective."

"Well, that's all I need from you today, but I will be in touch soon. Here's my card should you need it. Again, my sincere condolences for your loss."

Neither thanked her, and both reluctantly grabbed the cards she offered. As embarrassed as she felt, she had to admit it was not entirely a fruitless endeavor. Beau's reactions and Nancy's defensiveness told Heather a lot about Roland. If she read between the lines, she could see a lot of domestic trouble, resentment, and a repressed knowledge of an unsavory habit.

Despite what she'd said earlier, she decided not to tell Tina about her theories until she had some evidence to wow her with. With any luck, Beau would make use of the number on her card.

Just as she was about to leave the scene, Heather spotted a swarm of cars and vans arriving on the no longer barricaded scene. They parked haphazardly along the street and emerged carrying boom mics and cameras. The journalists had arrived.

Heather ran toward them, trying to keep them away from the Ellis family as they made their escape. Before she could even blink, they began holding out microphones to her, speaking over each other, and putting her on live TV without her consent. To her immense surprise, as someone who'd been on TV many times before, she began to panic. She clammed up, unable to even choke out, 'No comment.'

A gentle hand grabbed her shoulder and pulled her back from the rabble. "Detective Bishop is a very busy woman. She does not have time to answer your questions today."

Heather turned to see Gene Wells wearing his sternest expression. She'd never been more relieved to see her former boss wearing such an expression, and felt at ease as he guided her away from the cameras and whistled for another officer to take her place.

"You alright, kid?" he asked, his voice so gruff she could hardly understand him.

"Yeah, fine. I just hate when everyone's talking at once."

"You'll get used to it if you keep getting yourself involved in cases as big as this one." He looked over at the destroyed laundromat. "Jesus, what a mess. Roland was always... eccentric, but really takes the cake."

"Eccentric? How?"

"Tell you what, you come by and pay Karen and me a visit for lunch tomorrow, and I'll tell you everything I know about Roland Ellis. And believe me, as the Sheriff, I knew plenty."

For a brief second, Heather swore she smelled booze on the old man's breath, but told herself she must be imagining things. She blamed it on an alcohol-based mouthwash, scared to think about Gene drinking himself to death in the daytime. The Warren case was haunting him even more than it was her. She got to be the hero of that story; how must being the secondary villain feel?

"Alright, I'll come over. You know I can't resist Karen's cooking."

"Good girl. Now, how about you go on home, and I'll handle Tina. It looks like they're all about done here anyway."

Heather looked around at the officers turning away the journalists, the diminishing crowd, and the piles of rubble, and realized Gene was right. Even Tina, the notorious busybody, stood absently around, looking for some way to busy herself.

"All right, I'm out. See you tomorrow."

Just as Heather turned her back, Tina called after her. "Detective Bishop! Come by the morgue tomorrow afternoon to see what the pathologist says. I need my best detective with me on this."

More like your only detective, Heather thought bitterly as she offered a friendly wave. She turned back to the darkening street, suddenly bone-tired and beyond sore. She rubbed her ribs again, and though they felt better than they had, she was immensely regretful that she'd chosen to run into town today.

CHAPTER FIVE

THE SON

"Jesus, Beau, what are people going to think?" Nancy asked, gesturing to the photographers and reporters loitering around at the foot of her driveway. Two officers sat in a patrol car, ensuring that nobody crossed the threshold onto private property, but it provided little comfort to Beau or his mother. The cameras still flashed despite the gossamer barrier that the sheer curtains provided, and the primly dressed reporters still called out their names as if the repetition would eventually break them.

"What are you talking about?"

"We're going to be all over the news. Photos and videos of us at the crime scene and hiding in the kitchen."

"So?"

"Well, look at me! I'm a mess! And don't even get me started on you. Looking so bored with it all, as if your father crashing a plane into town wasn't worthy of your attention. Sitting there, smoking away with your tattoos and your face doing that thing I hate. People are going to think you hate your father."

"I do."

Nancy inhaled and fiddled anxiously with the still-sparkling engagement ring that hung about her clavicle from a thin silver chain. Beau tried to remember if she'd been wearing it earlier but came up blank.

"You take that back," she hissed, near tears again.

"Come on. I know you hate him too. Don't forget I'm not a reporter or one of your rich friends. I'm your *son*," he sneered. "I lived with you in this house for two decades. I've heard you crying in your room, I noticed the tension in your voice when you've been forced to talk about him, and I've seen how you look at that painting when you think no one's watching."

"Admittedly, I am still furious with him for abandoning us, and I don't know if I would have ever forgiven him for that if given the opportunity... but no, Beau, I don't hate him."

"Okay, fine, but I do."

She scoffed. "You're being a child."

"Because I have the balls to admit it?"

"You have no idea what you're talking about."

Nancy was becoming increasingly hysterical, and Beau knew he should drop it, but he was like a dog with a meaty bone when it came to his mother. He just couldn't leave it alone.

"You're not in charge of my feelings anymore. I can hate whoever I want. Maybe I hate you too."

Nancy didn't react in the way Beau expected. There was no gasping, crying, or other dramatics. Instead, she became very still, her expression stony. When she finally spoke, her voice was lower than her usual cadence, and she moved her mouth as if each word weighed heavily on her tongue.

"Your father would be so disappointed in you if he could see you now. I bet he's rolling up a storm in his grave right now."

"You mean in his chest freezer?"

"Beau," Nancy said through gritted teeth. "I know you must have a lot of feelings right now, but you need to mind your tongue. Around me, but especially around the police and the press. It's important that we preserve your father's legacy and don't taint his good name."

"You mean his legacy of abandoning his family to probably go live on some tropical island for fifteen years?"

"You know this town thought of him as a saint. Why would you ruin that for all those good people?"

Beau sneered. "He's not Jesus. Well, I suppose they both 'died' and resurrected, so maybe you're onto something. Shame that Dad botched the return part."

Nancy crossed her arms and pursed her lips.

"Seriously, Mom, do you really think his local legacy is anything other than being 'that guy' who mysteriously disappeared? Most people thought he was dead, if they thought about him at all."

"Oh, they knew he wasn't dead."

"How?"

"Because I told them he was still alive."

Beau froze, horrified. "Mom, what are you talking about?"

"Oh, don't look at me like that. I just mean when you really love someone, you just know if they're alive or dead. You can sense it. I hope that you'll find that out for yourself one day."

Beau pretended to wipe his forehead. "Phew. And here I was thinking you were talking about something real."

Nancy withered, the fight draining away, and returned to fiddling with her ring. The tip of her long, pointy nose was pink from blowing it, her face was streaked with mascara, and her always perfect bouffant was deflating. He hadn't seen her this unkempt for fifteen years, and knowing that he was partially responsible was dragging him down into a dark hole.

"I *am* talking about something real. And now that our connection is severed, it feels like a piece of me has died. I honestly don't know how I'll go on without him."

"You'll live. You have for the past fifteen years. What's the difference now?"

Nancy looked up at Beau in broken disbelief, her mouth agape at his callousness. She looked so old, sad, tired, and broken, and it stung him like a slap. For a second, he worried that he was the problem in their relationship, the reason for their suffering, but he knew that a couple of pills and a fifth of whiskey would soon wipe that fear away.

"Go home, Beau."

Only too glad to oblige, Beau turned and left the house without saying goodbye. At the bottom of the driveway, he ignored the mob of reporters—or vultures, as he preferred to call them—and spoke to the officers.

"Just heading home."

"Sure thing Mr. Ellis," said a chirpy young officer who'd been on the scene earlier.

Beau narrowly resisted making the same joke as he had done earlier, but it hadn't felt right then either, so instead, he gave the friendly officer a one-finger wave goodbye.

Mr. Ellis was my father, he thought to himself as he sat down on his bike and rode off into the dense, dark forest.

The burgundy and cream RV came into view, its walls coated in a thick layer of ivy and rust. It hadn't moved in at least two decades as far as Beau was aware. Bobby Sherwood's shady uncle, who had long since passed away, sold it to him for three thousand dollars, including the plot of land. It was a dream come true for a then twenty-year-old Beau, determined to evade his mother's crushing grasp; and even now, it was the only place he was truly content.

He parked, threw his helmet to the grass, collapsed in the worn-out fabric deck chair, and put his feet up on a rusty paint bucket. It had been the longest day of his life thus far, and his body ached worse than it did after losing a fistfight or falling off his bike. He wanted to sleep, force the day to end, and move on to the next, but something inside of him was buzzing, and he knew that the electricity in his veins would never let him sleep. His tired legs began to bounce, and he shifted uncomfortably, suddenly hot and irritable.

THE CRASH

Once again, he threw off his jacket in frustration before jumping to his throbbing feet and stepping inside his unlocked RV. He searched for something to take the edge off his jitters and palpitations and spotted an orange bottle full of circular white pills and the dregs of a bottle of whiskey. He knew the combination would make him drowsy, so he washed one pill down with a big glug and then swallowed the rest for good measure.

He soon wanted more and remembered the bottle under the bed that he'd been saving for a special occasion. The cost gave him pause as he ventured through colonies of dust bunnies to find it. Though he quickly decided that if his dad dying in a freak plane crash wasn't reason enough to open a bottle of green label, what was?

He drank, and for a brief moment, it worked. It cured the horrors of his day and removed the pain from his body. However, after his seventh shot, his father's contorted face returned to him in grisly flashes. The glassy eyes, the blue tinge to his skin, and the mouth open in a permanent scream were burned into his retinas as if he'd stared at the sun. It was everywhere: behind him in the mirror, printed against the darkening sky, peering out from behind nearby trees. Beau had never felt afraid of his father before, but he was covered in a fearful sheen of sweat as he continued to drink in the hopes of passing out.

It didn't work; his tolerance was too high to let him keel over after only a quarter of a bottle. So, instead, he resorted to the television—a tiny box from the early nineties with picture quality bad enough to rival his ancient radio's sound—but neither trashy reality shows nor nature documentaries could distract him from the ghoulish visions. So, he turned off the TV and decided to replace the cold, aged version of his father with the man he remembered.

Beau rifled through a drawer, pushing stray pills, empty packets of cigarettes, and mouse droppings out of the way to uncover a pile of developed photographs. It had been a long time since he'd ventured to the bottom of this drawer, and when he reached the photos, they were stuck together and yellowing.

He peeled them apart from the pile one by one, trying to remember the context of each one. His memories were hazy, but as he looked at the photos of him and his dad—on his birthday, riding bikes, petting the family dog—he felt nothing but warmth for the man who'd raised him. He'd been a good dad, or at least he tried to be. He remembered birthdays but forgot about Little League games. He bought takeout but burned everything he tried to cook. He did funny voices when reading bedtime stories but only read the ones he enjoyed. There were ups and downs, but Beau could clearly remember now that he was great when he was around.

He smiled, feeling better for having looked at the photos until he flipped to the next one. All the warmth melted away, and he was once again overwhelmed with rage. It was a picture of *her*. He tore it up into at least twenty pieces and let it join the other debris on his filthy floor. How could his dad have abandoned him and left him alone with his mother and the golden child? He knew how much they hated him, how ostracised he was.

Beau wanted to cry—a rare occurrence for him—ruminating on the happy life he could have had if only his dad had stuck around. It would've been one thing if he'd been dead all along, but the fact that he was out there alive this whole time and clearly never gave a damn about his family was too much to bear.

Glancing out the window, he spotted the one car he'd always refused to sell despite the many offers. It was a pristine 1965 Ford Mustang Convertible in baby blue, and it had belonged to his father, though it spent much of its time under a tarp in the garage. After his dad's disappearance, his mother—not caring about the rarity or worth of cars—had gifted it to Beau on his sixteenth birthday. He'd looked after it well, rarely driving it and keeping it sparkling clean. It looked brand new, as if it were still sitting in the dealership's window in the mid-1960s.

Beau had loved that car for a decade, but all of a sudden, he couldn't stand the sight of it. Stumbling, he moved to the front door and grabbed his baseball bat. He kept it there just in case one of the numerous people with a problem came knocking. Sometimes they did, but he hadn't needed to use it before now. It was pristine and polished, just like the car. He slammed

THE CRASH

through the RV door with his shoulder and ran toward the vehicle at a full, drunken tilt with the bat raised high.

First went the mirrors, then the windows, and then it was the body's turn to be beaten to a pulp. He relished the feeling of the fiberglass buckling under his blows, the sound of the chrome pinging loudly into the woods. He hit it until it was totaled and his arms felt like they were going to drop off. His most prized possession was reduced to a smashed-up junker, and he couldn't help but laugh hysterically at what he had done. The damage was so severe that fixing it would take months and money he didn't have, but he was too high on adrenaline to care. He howled like an animal and beat his chest until the high wore off.

And then he looked upon what he'd done in a fresh, somber light and collapsed to his knees, the damp grass soaking through his jeans. It was the only thing his father had left him, and it was ruined beyond recognition.

Beau thought to take the bat to his own body, but instead, he dropped it in the pile of glass and skulked away to drink until he couldn't feel anything anymore.

CHAPTER SIX

THE DETECTIVE

HEATHER WOKE UP GROGGY, HAVING SLEPT THROUGH all of her alarms, but she was grateful for having slept at all. She couldn't remember the last time she'd gotten a solid eight hours of sleep, and the shock was only exacerbated by the fact she'd expected to stay up all night. Roland's awful expression had haunted her when she'd first entered her dark house, joining the litany of terrible waking nightmares she'd collected throughout her career. Yet, as soon as her body hit the couch, she was out like a light.

She wished she felt refreshed, but there had been too many hours lost in the past week for eight to fix all the damage. She needed at least twenty more to recover, and she considered

THE CRASH

playing hooky until the events postcrash returned and the day's appointments stacked up in front of her. She checked the time, groaned, and struggled out from beneath her dogs, much to their displeasure. In sync, Fireball, Beam, and Turkey grumbled, stood, stretched, yawned, and circled before collapsing into the blanket's furrows.

Heather looked at her three freeloaders with jealousy and reluctantly ventured to the bathroom to get ready. It was freezing in her house; she could feel it in the porcelain tiles through her fluffy socks and see it on the frost-coated window. The brief spot of sun that had lit up her life yesterday had been extinguished by tragedy, not to be seen again until after Christmas. The sun wasn't even up yet, but without checking the weather app, she knew it would be a bleak, gray day.

She showered and was thankful for the heated towel rack when she emerged. Heat fading fast from rough cotton, she rushed toward the bedroom that she so rarely occupied and rooted through her wardrobe for something nice to wear to Gene's. Her usual athleisure or work clothes wouldn't do, not next to Karen's funky ensembles. So, she opted for a pair of skinny black jeans and a roll-neck cream sweater, pairing it with zip-up ankle boots. She always felt strange not wearing work clothes and struggled to find a visual identity outside of work. It was all slacks and button-ups there; practical, authoritative, and bland. Outside, she wasn't even sure what colors she liked or what suited her. It was an untapped world and another thing on her list of skills to learn.

She sat at the last occupant's vintage vanity table, pulled her hair into a ponytail, and applied some moisturizer, sunscreen, lip balm, mascara, deodorant, and perfume. Each day she did this in the same place, in the same order, with the same brands and application methods. She realized, smiling at her reflection, that she finally had one of those enviable morning routines instead of rolling out of bed and hoping for the best.

She knew she'd never get bored with the repetition now that it had arrived. She was fascinated by monotony. Watching those satisfying viral videos of things being made in factories scratched all her anxious itches after long days. She longed to sit by a factory conveyer belt, tasked with one specific job.

Blushing the cheeks of baby dolls by the hundred days in and day out seemed like a dream come true compared to her career choice. It was almost meditative, whereas her daily life often felt like free-falling from an airplane and unsure if she had packed a parachute.

She knew, of course, that she couldn't do anything else. She was born to be a detective, but it was nice to fantasize about herself in a parallel universe, living a comfortable, quiet life. She also knew that the grass was always greener on the other side and that working on an assembly line would soon make her desperate for a bit of danger. Contentment was a myth, in her opinion, and humans were all just vying for a slice of each other's pies.

Take Tina, for example; she'd been increasingly desperate to take over as sheriff as each year passed, something she made evident to all her peers. Her hard work was the foundation of her mutiny, as was her befriending the cops that disliked Gene the most. Then came the suggestion portion; she'd spend many work-drink get-togethers talking about how much her father loves being retired. She could throw a party, she'd say, and Gene could spend so much more time with Karen and their grandchildren. He could even go fishing as much as he wanted! It sounded terrific to Heather, and she joked that she'd retire tomorrow if she could get the same deal; but one look at Gene's droopy expression, and she knew that he'd never let go of the job unless forced, just like her.

And then he was forced, more or less, as the staggering incompetence of his years of mismanagement of the Dennis Burke case came to light. Tina finally got the job she'd been after for so long. At least someone was happy with the situation.

Heather pictured herself forty years down the line, wrinkled like a prune, sitting in some dark wood office in some hick town. She'd have dozens of killers caught under her belt, subsist solely off of coffee and cigarettes, and piss off all the new blood who wanted her old ass out of their way.

She'd had this vision a lot during her career, but it felt different this time. It used to be her goal to morph into a crotchety, old badass like something out of the western movies her dad loved so much, but now it felt less like ambition and more like

THE CRASH

an inevitability. She looked at herself in the mirror, noticing her tired eyes, and wondered if fate could be changed.

She had no idea, and she was too tired to try today, so she moved on to her next destination and brewed her coffee in the kitchen by the low light of dawn. She cracked a window despite the cold and lit a cigarette. She had at least forty years to quit if she was going to alter fate, and today didn't feel like the day to do so. However, for the sake of maintaining her balancing act, she followed her coffee and cigarette with the remnants of a green smoothie and a bowl of granola.

While eating at the table, she searched the internet for her local forensic medical center, as Tina had mentioned meeting at the morgue. It quickly dawned on her that she was no longer in the city, and she unwillingly called Tina—who was allergic to texting and emails despite only being in her late thirties—to ask where the morgue was located.

"Hello, this is Sheriff Peters. How can I help you?" Tina asked in ignorance, her tone singsongy, even though Heather knew she knew that her smartphone had caller ID.

"Hi, it's Heather."

"Oh, good morning, Detective Bishop. How are you feeling today? You looked a little stressed out yesterday." Heather could practically hear the condescending jutting of Tina's bottom lip through the receiver.

"All good. Thanks. Turns out I bounce back from near-death experiences pretty well."

"Oh, goodie. So, you're still joining the pathologist and me today?"

"Yeah, that's why I'm calling, actually. Where is the morgue? It doesn't seem like we have any sort of crime lab here. I know we send samples to Seattle, but what about bodies?"

"Fortunately, we don't get too many dead bodies that need examining around here, but when we do, we send them to the local funeral home and get a pathologist to travel down from the city. Hey, I'll bet you've worked with this guy before. Does Dr. Julius Tocci ring any bells?"

Heather did indeed know Dr. Tocci, not just because he was the best forensic pathologist in the state but also because he examined all the victims in every homicide case that she'd ever worked. That was how they met and became friends. They hadn't spoken since Heather left Seattle, though he crossed her mind from time to time—especially on bad nights, because she knew he was probably the only other person out there unable to sleep for the same reasons she couldn't. It was a sort of silent bond, though she figured he probably thought very little of her with all the news-making homicides on his plate.

Heather cleared her throat, the blast from the past causing her mind to wander. "Yeah, I know him well. I worked with him for my entire career in homicide."

"Wow, that's great. I've heard good things." Tina's tone was forced, and Heather became aware that she might be jealous that Heather knew the specialist so well.

"Yeah, maybe I'll see if he wants a coffee after. It would be good to catch up."

"Hmm. That doesn't sound very professional, but I suppose it wouldn't hurt. After all, it's always good to have a wide array of friends."

Heather wasn't aware she was asking for permission and hated the saccharine tone Tina adopted when not-so-secretly irate, but she also derived some degree of sick pleasure by winding her boss up.

"So, what time are we meeting Dr. Tocci?"

"He'll be done with the autopsy at five."

"So, I'll meet you at 4:50 at the funeral home. Can you text me the address?"

"Sure, but let's make it 4:55. I don't want him to feel rushed."

Heather frowned, unsure as to why they were squabbling over such minute details. "Fine by me."

"Great. Oh, and send Gene my regards at lunch. Tell him I have some tomato plants with his name on them. My greenhouse has been going so well I'm just inundated with the things."

"Will do. See you later, Tina."

"Goodbye, Detective Bishop."

Heather drummed on the table with her short, strong nails before pacing across the sticky linoleum in her boots, staring at the contacts page on her phone. She hopped up onto the counter, swinging her legs as she scrolled. When she reached T in the alphabet, she lit another cigarette and pressed the 'send message' button.

Hi, Julius, it's Heather Bishop. I don't know if you still have my number, but I just wanted to let you know that I'm the lead detective of the Roland Ellis case, so I'll be at the funeral home this afternoon. I'm available for a coffee if you're in town for a few hours afterward. No pressure.

She sent it before she could talk herself out of it but quickly regretted it when the message was marked as read and a three-dot typing bubble appeared. She waited anxiously, but after five minutes, no message arrived, and the bubble burst. She tried not to overthink but suddenly dreaded their reunion. They both carried bad memories for each other, and meeting for the first time in years at a funeral home with a body between them was probably the worst way to reunite.

Stomach churning, heart pounding, she decided to head over to Gene's house early for a welcomed distraction, giving each sleeping dog a kiss on the forehead on her way out.

CHAPTER SEVEN

THE DETECTIVE

Heather arrived at Gene's and Karen's house holding a bowl of potato salad—laden with bacon chunks per her dad's recipe—and a small carton of eggs from her neighbor's chickens. She figured that's what you were supposed to do as an adult invited to lunch, though she still wasn't sure about the dos and don'ts of these sorts of things. Her ex-husband was the one who'd memorized the unspoken rules of polite society, and she'd relied heavily on his guidance. He was the sort of guy who knew which fork was which at a fancy restaurant and what the difference between black tie and formal was.

She wished she'd retained more of what he'd taught her, but his hand-holding had made her complacent, and when you're young and in love, you never anticipate them letting go. So, here she was at thirty-two, unsure of what clothes were fashionable, what was acceptable to bring to a potluck, and whether 'no gifts' really meant no gifts.

Not that you've been invited to a potluck in Glenville, she thought, *or any party for that matter.*

She knocked on the door, and Karen opened it so quickly that Heather wondered if the woman had been waiting eagerly on the other side. Karen was grinning from ear to ear, staring at Heather in disbelief as if an angel had turned up on her doorstep. In almost complete opposite fashion to Gene, Karen had an incredible knack for making everyone feel special.

She shook her head as she held out her arms for a hug. Her roots were silver and longer than usual, but the rest of her frizzy perm was a vivid henna red. It was swept back off her forehead with her signature knitted headband that matched her tasseled indigo poncho. Her wide linen pants were dirty at the hem and on her knees from where she'd been gardening, and her feet were blatantly bare.

Karen was among the few people Heather enjoyed hugging, so she accepted the offer happily and didn't even pull away when it went on for too long. She smelled like patchouli and pine, and everything about her was soft. Eventually, they broke apart, and Karen clasped Heather's cheeks in her liver-spotted hands.

"Well, hello, beautiful! Don't you look great?" She turned her head toward the interior of the house. "Honey, the supermodel is here!"

Gene grumbled something unintelligible as he made his way out the back door. Karen rolled her eyes as she turned back to Heather. "He's happy you're here."

"I know."

"But you know who's going to be even happier that you're here?"

Heather knew the answer and braced herself. Karen removed her hands from Heather's cheeks and whistled with her fingers. Soon the skittering across hardwood could be heard, and the two decrepit little mutts skidded around the hallway corner toward the front door. They practically coughed up dust as they yapped their lungs out, and when they finally reached Heather, they began to maul her ankles with their mostly toothless gums. This never seemed to bother Karen, who was blissfully unaware of most of life's unpleasantries, so Heather had simply learned to wear boots when visiting.

Ignoring the dogs, Heather handed over the potato salad and carton of eggs, and Karen looked as if she might cry over the offerings. Her bangles clattered as she wrung her hands.

"I'm so proud of you!" she exclaimed, hugging Heather once again. "You know how much I worry about what you eat; I'm so glad you're finally learning how to cook."

Heather laughed sheepishly. "It's only potato salad; I've got a long way to go with everything else."

"Oh, don't be modest. This is a big step; it'll go perfectly with the salmon I'm making." They separated once more, and Karen stepped back and beckoned Heather inside the dark, cluttered house.

It was like a lot of old people's homes. Piles of newspapers, books, and family photos lined the walls, and various trinkets and porcelain figures covered most surfaces. It was undeniably clean—every adorable piece of ceramic had been recently dusted—but the hoarding problem was undeniable.

It made sense. The pair had lived in the same house since they married in 1975. That gave them plenty of time to acquire a lot of stuff; and with four grown kids—who'd left most of their childhood belongings behind in their time capsule rooms—clutter was inevitable. She dreaded to think what their attic looked like. Probably filled with plastic tubs and garbage bags of decorations, just like her parent's basement was. It was fascinating compared to her home, whose remnants of history belonged entirely to someone else.

She thought again about who she'd be in forty years and wondered if the house she would share with that special someone would one day look like this one. Would it be filled with old pictures of her, newer ones of her children, and brand-new ones of her grandchildren? She'd never given much thought to children before, but she would be thirty-three next year, and it had begun to occur to her that making the decision was no longer miles away.

She used to think she would be a terrible mother—she still did, considering how badly she'd burned the tandoori chicken the night before—but for the first time, she thought that could change in the coming years.

She approached the fireplace mantel and looked at the picture of a little girl with white-blonde hair. She smiled at the Wells' youngest granddaughter, but something flashed into her mind's eye that she didn't want to look at. She took two quick steps backward, her eyes clenched. A little hand stuck out from under a basement door, mottled by coagulation and illuminated by fluorescent tubes. It was a hand she dreamed of often.

Maybe she wouldn't be a bad mother, but could she handle being one after seeing what she'd seen?

"Heather, are you all right?" Karen asked, at her side in a flash.

Heather blinked away the image, slightly dazed by its power. "Yeah. Of course."

"I'm going to fix us some lunch. How about you go talk to Gene in the garden?"

"Okay, sure." Heather turned, still a little shaky, and caught sight of the cupholder in the La-Z-Boy recliner that Gene so often occupied. The big plastic hole contained a half-full bottle of bourbon. She knew Gene liked to drink—that was no secret in Glenville—but she'd never seen him drink straight from the bottle before. Her gut churned as Karen followed her gaze and offered a sad smile.

"He's been looking forward to seeing you; you should come by more often," she said softly. It wasn't a question or an invitation. It was a request.

"I'd like that."

Karen's smile widened, and she tilted her head to the back door. "Go on now. Lunch will be ready in half an hour."

Heather ventured down the hallway, mindful of the piles of tools, bags of soil, old clothes, dog beds, and bags of clothes going to charity that had been there since four visits ago. She reached the ajar back door with its little stained-glass window and pushed it open to reveal the most fantastic garden she'd ever seen. It plunged her into Technicolor like Dorothy in the Wizard of Oz, making the rest of the world look like a drab, sepia wasteland in comparison.

Surrounded by a white picket fence, the garden spread about half an acre, and it was difficult to know where to look first. There were the fruit trees—lime, lemon, orange, cherry, plum, and apple—in the far-right corner and bushes sporting berries in a row along the right fence line of the square plot. Heather often said that they'd ruined supermarket fruit for her, and they'd laugh as if she were joking, but she was dead serious.

At the center of the haven was the deconstructed rainbow of flowers in their enormous circular bed. Peonies, tulips, roses, ranunculi, irises, sunflowers, daffodils, pansies; these were Karen's passion, and she often provided Heather with bouquets on her way out the door. The sunflowers were beginning to die, which added to the bleakness of the winter weather, but she knew they'd come back taller and sunnier than ever next year. She supposed that was the best part about all this bounty; there was always something to look forward to throughout the year.

Gene was over on the left side, digging in the moist soil around the impressive vegetable patch. The remaining post-Halloween pumpkins were large, as were the surrounding squashes. Much of the rest was hidden underground, but the lush leafy greenery was still pleasant to look at, if not as visually breathtaking as the flower display.

The old man was shakily unearthing yellow onions and enormous Yukon gold potatoes and sorting them into baskets. Without calling out to him, Heather grabbed a pair of gardening gloves and quietly joined the digging, kneeling in the dirt despite her freshly washed jeans.

He didn't look over at her, but she saw crinkles form by the corner of his eyes. "Hey, kid."

"How's the harvest?"

"Good, considering the time of year. Guess that's global warming for you. At least it's good for something."

Heather hummed thoughtfully as she unearthed a particularly sizeable—perhaps even award-worthy—potato and placed it in a wicker basket.

THE CRASH

"I don't know how you keep all of this alive. I only have one house plant, and it hates me," she said.

Gene chuckled. "My kids didn't get the green thumb either. Requires too much patience, which you young folks don't seem to have enough of."

Heather didn't feel that young, but even she had to agree. With the dawn of next-day delivery, takeout apps, streaming services, and social media platforms, instant gratification was the way of the future. She couldn't remember the last time she finished a jigsaw puzzle, stuck to a new arts and crafts hobby, or cooked a meal that took longer than forty minutes to prepare. It was all go, go, go in the Bishop household.

Great, more bad habits to break, she thought. *Thanks a lot, Gene.*

She looked around the garden and asked, "Do you have any seeds I could have? Something good for beginners?"

"Oh yeah, tons. You got good soil?"

"I have no idea."

He shrugged. "I guess you can only try. I couldn't cook an egg or grow a weed before I met Karen. I was downright hopeless, and you don't strike me as hopeless."

"You sure about that?"

Gene looked at her as if to say, 'Take the compliment, kid.' So, she did. It was the nicest thing he'd ever said to her, and it struck her dumb as she sat with it. Gene didn't seem to mind. He preferred the quiet.

Once the potatoes were all piled up, Heather leaned back on her haunches and dusted the dirt off. "Tina wanted me to tell you that she has some tomato plants for you."

Gene sucked his teeth. "God, that girl gets my goat."

Heather laughed, taken aback by the admission though she already knew as much. "You don't like tomatoes?"

"It's not that. Go look in the greenhouse."

Heather did as she was told and walked toward the little glass house. Inside were some healthy pepper plants on one side and a cluster of brown, withered tomatoes on the other.

She re-emerged and called out to Gene. "What happened?"

He shrugged. "I just suck at growing tomatoes. Always have and always will. And Tina damn well knows it after I invited her over for dinner once she got the sheriff job. I was trying to be polite to the new head honcho, and well, look what that got me."

"Maybe she's trying to be nice."

"Yeah, maybe," he grumbled. "I'm glad you can see the good in people."

"I have to try really hard to. It's honestly exhausting," Heather panted, half-laughing, half-choking up.

"That's the job. You see regular, everyday people do the worst shit imaginable. The mailman abducts a little kid, the delivery driver does a hit-and-run, and the butcher serves up stray cats. And these are normal, local people with families, neighbors, jobs. Heck, most of 'em even go to church. Once you realize that anybody could be bad, it's hard to trust anybody to be good. You even start to doubt the ones you love. Maybe your son comes home late with blood on him the same night a girl goes missing in the park. Worst of all, you can't switch it off, not ever."

"You trying to get me to quit?" she asked.

"Nope. I don't have enough breath left to waste on that. But a piece of advice: any optimism you have left, hold on to it."

"Alright. I will."

"Good. Now you've listened to my lecture, let me tell you about Roland Ellis before Karen finishes lunch."

Heather had almost completely forgotten about Roland Ellis, despite the dramatic events of the day before, and she sat down hard in the grass and pulled her notepad out of her beat-up leather satchel.

"Alright, so how well did you know Mr. Ellis?"

"Pretty well. When you're sheriff, it's your job to know everybody, especially the bigshots and the scumbags."

"Was Roland Ellis a scumbag?"

"No, but he was the kind of big shot who dabbled in that territory."

"In your opinion, off the record, do you think he was a good person?"

Gene thought hard. "The people in town certainly thought so."

"But you're not so sure?"

"As I said, when you're in this line of work, sometimes you see what other people can't."

Heather looked down at her notes. "You called him eccentric yesterday; how so?"

"He was a real friendly guy. Put this town on the map. So, of course, everyone around saw him as this magnanimous Great Gatsby type, but I saw him for what he was: a real odd duck. But, like Gatsby, only a few people were privy to that side of him. I remember getting roped into whiskey and cigars with him and a few other big players in town at the time, and he asked us if we'd ever been with a pro or dabbled in drugs."

"A pro, as in a sex worker?"

"Yup. Big grin on his face looking me right in the eyes as he said it. Asking the sheriff if he'd ever... it showed me a different side of him. Thrill-seeking. The other guys laughed, thinking it was just a big joke, but I knew he was serious. I don't know if he was looking for blackmail to alleviate his own guilty conscience, but it was weird. After that, I always kept an eye on him, and when he flew off and never came back, I was about the only person in town who wasn't shocked."

"Were you shocked that he came back?"

"Oh yeah. I thought he was long dead. The cocaine was less surprising."

"Was he a user back then?"

"No idea. Not for sure. But I knew a lot of rich guys who were. Guys he was real 'friendly with.'"

"Where do you think he's—"

"Lunchtime!" Karen called from the doorway, putting an end to the interview.

"Another time," Gene whispered. "Karen doesn't like when I talk about work."

Lunch was filled with pleasant small talk as they indulged in succulent salmon. The potato salad was also spooned out heftily onto each plate and received multiple compliments from both

Karen and Gene. Heather had never received compliments on her cooking before, aside from sarcastic ones from her ex-husband about instant noodles and bowls of cereal.

Despite feeling embarrassed by Karen's enthusiasm, she tried not to shy away from the kind words. She thought this must be how it feels to have grandparents—her biological ones were either dead or far away in India and England—and she wondered if they saw her in a similar light. The idea made her chuckle. She and Gene's relationship had come an impossibly long way since he'd stepped down. Gone was the tempestuous employee-boss angle, and replacing it was a growing, almost familial bond that seemed to serve them both well. She was surprised to find herself becoming attached to the cranky old bastard.

Once lunch was over, Heather hugged Karen goodbye and waited as Gene tottered down the hall into the backyard for something he wanted to give her. She'd forgotten all about the seeds until the packets were in her hands. Radishes, carrots, and beets. Good beginner vegetables, he promised her, even for someone with a brown thumb.

The moment she was through her front door—covered in dirt and with hours to spare—she headed to the backyard to rip crusty dead plants from the raised bed by the concrete patio strip and plant the seeds she'd been gifted. She followed the instructions on how to space them and watered them thoroughly before sitting back, lighting a cigarette, and admiring her handiwork. She had to admit… she wished they'd sprout right away, but she was glad that she had something to look forward to.

CHAPTER EIGHT

THE DETECTIVE

HEATHER ARRIVED A FEW MINUTES BEFORE THE agreed-upon time and saw Tina's brand-new, utility model Ford Police Interceptor parked in the driveway behind the shiny hearse. Gene had been only too glad when that thing had rolled into town and saved him from giving up his pickup truck, but Heather found the SUV—designed for city violence and high-speed pursuits—to be a bit ostentatious. Primarily as the "Sheriff" written on the side of it was definitely a custom job.

Sometimes Heather thought to remind Tina that she was a temporary sheriff, hurriedly thrust into the role by county executives, but thought better of it. She was still haunted by the time she reminded Gene that he was the sheriff of the smallest county in Washington and had lived—by the skin of her teeth—to regret it.

She also knew that saying it would be an unsatisfactory endeavor. Tina didn't care that she was a stand-in. It allowed her to get her foot in the door and prove her worth without needing the votes of her constituents. Then, come general elections the following November, she'd have worked her way into the hearts of the county and comfortably maintain her seat for a full term. Unlike the occupants of Glenville, Heather had no problem with Tina being sheriff for the next five years or more. Though she admittedly thought it tacky to order a taxpayer-funded, personalized sheriff-mobile on week one of her takeover.

Heather gritted her teeth and cursed under her breath, but it wasn't the flashy car that was making her angry. Tina had conveniently parked halfway between the hearse's rear and the driveway's mouth, leaving no room for Heather. This left Heather with only one dire option: to parallel park on a busy road.

Despite her sweaty palms, she succeeded without any disasters and, after a fleeting celebration, found something else to be irritable over. Even from a distance, she could see that Tina wasn't in the driver's seat, leaving only one place she could be—inside the funeral home with Dr. Tocci.

So much for not wanting to rush him, Heather thought, picturing Tina standing by the body, looking at her watch, and loudly sighing. She'd make some underhanded comment about unreliable employees or Heather's time management skills, and Dr. Tocci would nod as if he cared.

Smelling a setup, Heather slammed the driver's door hard, her jaw aching.

Eyes on the ground, she strode across the street and only paused when her feet landed on a cushy, two-toned striped lawn. She looked up at her destination, and her tight jaw fell slack. Hands on her hips, she whistled long and low at the mansion before her. The sun above the roof was blinding her, but not wanting to look away, she retrieved her aviators from her shirt collar and put them on.

THE CRASH

She'd never seen anything like it. At least not in Glenville, which was dominated by shoddy 1960s starter homes and exorbitant lakeside estates. The Ellsworth Family Funeral home—as the hand-painted wooden sign, written in perfect cursive, informed her—was an enormous gothic revival mansion painted a strange shade of pistachio with hunter-green architraves and lattice.

The sign also said that it had been established in 1894, and considering it was older than the town itself, it was in remarkable condition. Which made sense considering it was the only funeral home for thirty miles.

Two young men holding large pairs of shears were trimming the impressive topiaries and rose bushes on either side of the narrow pathway, and they waved as she approached the porch. She waved back and noticed that they were identical twins, an observation that would not have typically perturbed her but only added to the strange energy that the house radiated. She felt silly but grew increasingly uneasy as she approached the iron knocker.

She rapped and rapped again, the second round's force creating more of a booming effect, and finally, a lock clicked, and the door creaked open. A man, who was approximately one hundred years old and a towering six-foot-five, stood on the other side. Dressed in a crisp, old-fashioned suit, he was as cadaverous as the bodies he attended to: his eyes were milky, his skin was sallow, and when he smiled, his receded gums made his teeth look like yellowed piano keys.

"You must be Detective Bishop," he croaked, stepping to the side of the door and beckoning her inside with the sweep of his lengthy arm.

"I am. Nice to meet you. I'm assuming you're Mr. Ellsworth."

"I *am*," he enthused, seemingly surprised she picked up on his name despite all the signage. "Foster Ellsworth," he clarified. "The grandson of the original owner."

She stepped inside, the smell of mothballs hitting her and the pink sculptured carpet squishing beneath her feet. Lots of the interior was a similar shade of dusty pink, but great swathes were also mission brown and umber. The floral wallpaper combined all of the above with some splashes of green that matched the exterior paint. It clearly hadn't been updated in at least six decades, and much of it seemed far older than that. The side table sported a fringed lamp and a rotary phone next to a series of framed pictures arranged haphazardly on top of the doilies.

One photo facing Heather's direction featured two young men, one extremely tall, dressed in old-fashioned bathing suits at Coney Island. It was accompanied by a porcelain urn bearing the name Ernie Walsh. The dates read 1928-2013, meaning if Mr. Ellsworth was the tall man in the picture and thus the same age as the man in the urn, he would be roughly ninety-five years old.

A hundred wasn't too far off, Heather thought, giving herself a point for her stellar guesswork.

"Would you like some tea, Mrs. Bishop?"

"Heather, please," she said, flinching at the title he'd applied. "And no, thank you, I should probably join my colleague."

"Ah, yes. Sheriff Peters. A woman in charge at last," enthused Mr. Ellsworth. "I'm hoping she'll make some much-needed changes in this town."

Heather found herself quickly warming to the man and, on any other occasion, would've eagerly joined him for tea. The very old always had amazing stories to share, and someone who had been an undertaker for more than twice her lifespan would undoubtedly have his fair share of grim and fascinating tales.

"Yes, Sheriff Peters and Dr. Tocci. Where might I find them?"

"Down in the basement," he creaked, his voice reminding her awfully of classic horror movies starring Christopher Lee and Vincent Price. It was stately and timeless, suiting his home and place of business perfectly.

He pointed to a small wooden door with a tiny key twisted in the lock before creeping away into a side room. She could only see a sliver through the doorway, bordered by velvet couches and thick, shirred drapes with swooping valances. The whole place was like stepping back in time.

She made her way to the little door, expecting it to be like the rest of the house, dusty and haunted by ghosts in corsets and bustles, but it was much worse than that. At the top of the stairs, she was met with fluorescent white light, tiled walls, and plastic-covered steps. It stank of chemicals, embalming fluid and bleach taking her back to a place she tried daily to escape. It didn't matter what other horrors she saw—Alice Warren pinned and bloody, Dennis Burke still grinning with a hole in his head, or Roland Ellis permanently screaming—none compared to the Paper Doll Murders. Instead, they compounded it, twisting memories into a monster with more limbs and faces.

Tina called out from down the stairs. "Heather, is that you?"

There was no turning back now. "Yeah, it's me. Sorry I'm late."

"Not late at all; in fact, I only just finished up my report," replied Dr. Tocci, sounding a little irritable, perhaps over Tina's very early arrival.

Aside from the scolding tone, Julius's voice was velvety and a pleasant mixture of accents: a little bit of Italian, a sprinkle of English, and a whole scoop of American from the past few decades as a permanent resident.

It was warm and familiar, and though it took her back even further to the darkest days of her past, it provided the same comfort as it did back then. Lured by it, she descended the stairs, praying her shaky knees wouldn't give out.

The morgue came into view at the bottom of the stairs, and her stomach lurched like it did when she smelled vodka or saw someone eating a California roll. The past was coming back to haunt her, but this was much worse than a hangover or a case of food poisoning. The white tiles, the stainless-steel bench tops, the tools on the wall, the metal drawers in the walls for the bodies, and the slab in the middle. It had been a long time since she'd been in a morgue. Seeing a body on the scene was somehow different because her mind was protected by adrenaline. It was so quiet and clinical here that she could hear her own blood pumping.

Roland Ellis had been sewn back up and cleaned—embalming equipment at the ready for their departure—and for that, Heather was grateful. She wasn't squeamish per se, but she was better with photos than the real thing. Tina was dressed in scrubs, and Heather wondered how much she had seen. It was hard to tell from the woman's neutral expression. None of it seemed to bother her, but Heather knew her own brown complexion must be turning ashen as she approached the body.

Julius Tocci winked at her, imperceptible to Tina, and removed his gloves to pat her on the back between her shoulder blades. After he hadn't replied to her texts, she was nervous about things being awkward between them, but she should've known better. Julius had never once been cold to her, not even during the case's worst moments.

He was dressed in white, as she was used to, but he looked different than she'd last seen him. Three years ago, he'd been dark-haired and swarthy, and though his skin remained tanned and speckled with moles, his lashes and brows were the only hair that was still fully black. His hair was still dense and curly, but the gray was new, as was his impressive beard that had never been there before. His tiny, oval-shaped spectacles were also new, and he moved them onto his head as he turned to face Heather.

"Heather. How are you?"

It was how he always opened a conversation, and she relaxed despite the eerie setting.

"I'm looking forward to getting out of here, to be honest," Heather muttered, trying not to look at Roland, though his mouth had fortunately been closed.

He chuckled. "Me too."

"I have a lot of paperwork to do, so I, too, am looking forward to getting out of here," quipped Tina with none of the warmth of the other two. "So, let's discuss the findings. Dr. Tocci here was gracious enough to let me watch the ending of the procedures, so I think I have a pretty good idea, but we need to clue you in as lead detective, of course."

Julius's sweet nature vanished for a blink that only Heather seemed to notice as Tina mispronounced his last name as 'toochie,' but he said nothing as he lifted his clipboard and addressed the room.

"Mr. Ellis suffered a contusion to the temporal area as well as minor breakages in the ribcage, left zygomatic, and central mandible."

"Would any of those have been fatal?" Heather asked.

"It's unlikely."

Heather peered at the body. He looked to be in good shape. She could see the facial breakages, but they weren't any worse than the results of a drunken fistfight or minor car accident.

What stood out as odd was also that he possessed a singular tattoo on his right bicep. It was old, softened, and spread around the edges, but it stood out among the rest of the unmarked flesh. It depicted a strange-looking bird with a sharp curved beak and double crest atop its head—something Heather had never seen before. Underneath the bird was a sentence written in Spanish. *Las águilas arpías volarán para siempre.* Heather noted it down in her notebook but had no idea what it said. Languages had never been her strong suit, and her Spanish was basic at best even with Gabriel's help.

The Spanish, combined with the cocaine, gave her a good idea of who Roland had been hanging out with and what he'd been doing with such a high quantity of narcotics in his plane. But the question was, which side of the border had he been operating on?

"So, it was the drugs?" Heather asked. "Cocaine?"

"While Mr. Ellis was heavily intoxicated to the point of overdose, his actual cause of death was acute cyanide poisoning."

"Cyanide poisoning?" Heather repeated, nodding as Dr. Tocci said it.

He looked at her fondly. "You always were clever. You should've been a doctor."

"I knew it. I knew he was poisoned," Tina added confidently.

"Well, clearly, this case is in good hands with the two of you," Julius said.

"Do you know how he ingested it?" Heather asked.

"Obviously, it was the cocaine," Tina said, an unspoken 'duh' tacked onto the sentence.

"I would say that is very likely, Sheriff Peters, but unfortunately, I won't have an answer for either of you until the lab has finished examining the drugs."

"Either way, someone poisoned him," Heather muttered, staring down at the y-shaped incision on Roland's pale, hairy chest.

"That, I'm afraid, is where my expertise ends. I can tell you that he died from cyanide, but I'll have to leave the mystery-solving up to you. I'll send you the full report as soon as I can."

"Is his body okay to be released to the family?" Heather asked. Julius nodded. "That's all I need from him."

"I'll call Nancy," Tina chimed in. "I know Nancy pretty well."

Keen to adjourn, Heather happily agreed and quickly led the group toward the stairs. At the top, she flinched when greeted by the towering figure of Mr. Ellsworth. She'd almost entirely forgotten about the funeral home and all its antique splendor.

"Cup of tea, anyone?" the old man asked, his eyes twinkling.

Heather turned and looked at the other two, one who looked receptive and the other who stomped past her toward the door.

"Not today, I'm afraid; I have far too much work to do. Detective Bishop should be available though," sniped Tina.

Heather straightened and looked toward Mr. Ellsworth kindly. "I'd love to join you for some tea. Julius?"

Julius, ever lovely, with no bad bone in his body, addressed the elderly man directly, craning his neck. "I'm dying for a cup of Earl Grey."

Mr. Ellsworth chuckled. "You're in the right place for both, my boy. Please make yourself at home."

Looking positively giddy, Mr. Ellsworth pushed open a heavy, wooden swing door into what must be the kitchen, and Heather beckoned Julius toward a large doorway into what she thought must be the living room.

Upon turning the corner, she realized she was wrong. Sure, there were couches and a coffee table, but most of the room was occupied by an array of polished, high-end coffins, all of which were open to show the lavish interiors.

"Whoa," she sputtered. "Check these out."

Julius waltzed into the room, looking amused at his surroundings. "When I die, I want Mr. Ellsworth to handle it. If he's still alive."

"Oh, he definitely will be. I think he'll outlive us all."

Julius chuckled, his back to Heather as he investigated the coffins. "I wish my place looked like this. It would be very on-brand for my line of work."

THE CRASH

"Come on. Your house looks like something out of a sci-fi movie. Smart home everything. Organic everything. Minimalist everything. This place would make you nuts in one hour. The town too."

"Well, I've already been here for a few hours, and I'm not nuts yet."

"A day then."

He chuckled silently and slid his eyes over to her. "What about you?"

"What about me?"

"Have you 'gone nuts' since I last saw you?"

"I'd like to say no, but isn't the main symptom of insanity thinking you're sane? So, I'll let you be the judge."

Julius looked her up and down. "So, far so good."

Mr. Ellsworth arrived in the room with a silver tray sporting a teapot, three cups, a bowl of sugar cubes, and a saucer of milk. Heather and Julius politely sat down on the pink loveseat and ceased their banter, thanking the man thoroughly for his offerings. Mr. Ellsworth looked delighted as he poured the tea with a deft and practiced hand that didn't shake despite its stiff joints, blue veins, liver spots, and tufts of silver hair.

Once everyone was served, he took the armchair opposite and looked down on them fondly as if they were a couple of adorable babies. She supposed their age gap was even larger than that of her and a newborn. Julius, too, even with him being ten years older.

"Do you enjoy your work, Mr. Ellsworth?" Julius asked as he gratefully sipped his sugary tea.

"Foster, please. And oh, yes. I have lived a life worth living, helping the dead along. My dear friend, Ernie, used to call me a death doula. Helping the deceased get through to the other side as painlessly as possible. I always liked that."

"Perhaps you should rebrand," teased Julius, and both Heather and Foster smiled.

"Ah," the old man croaked. "What a sign that would be. What about you two? Do you enjoy your jobs?"

"Not half as much as that, but I don't think I can do anything else," Julius spoke for both of them, knowing that her answer would be much the same.

Foster's face dropped, and he placed his tea carefully in his lap. "Why not? When you help so many people?"

"I think it's the ones we couldn't help that haunt us," Heather explained.

Foster nodded thoughtfully and slurped loudly. "Well, I hope you know they're all eager to thank you on the other side. They know it's not your fault."

Heather felt a lump form in her throat. "I hope you're right."

"Of course, I am. You two help catch monsters and bring justice to the innocent. I don't think there's any more honorable position than that."

Heather smiled and tried to take a sip from her tea, but the tiny cup trembled and clanked against her teeth as she looked at the ceiling and tried to resist tears. She wasn't someone who cried, but the combination of the basement, the plane crash, the lack of sleep, and the words of sincere support—from both Gene and Foster—had pushed her to her brink.

Foster didn't seem to notice as he looked happily around at his coffin display room, but Julius, ever perceptive, noticed and quickly slurped down his tea. He pulled out his phone and faked a groan.

"I'm terribly sorry, Foster. I hate to be rude, but I've just received an urgent message that I'm needed in Seattle. So, I'm afraid we must say our goodbyes."

Foster nearly leaped to his feet. "Of course, I'm sorry to have kept you. You have much better things to do than drink tea with an old man."

Julius stuck out his hand, and Foster clasped it in both of his. "Well, we certainly don't have anything *nicer* to do than to drink tea with you. Thank you for the delicious Earl Grey," Julius said.

"This has been wonderful, but I hope I never have to see you again, Doctor," Foster said, referring to the nature of Julius's visit. "But, Detective, if you're ever in need of tea or medical expertise, please give me a call. Sheriff Wells, and Peters, too, think of me as a bit of a kook, but when it comes to the dead, there's no one who knows more than me."

Heather gave a quick, appreciative nod. "Thank you, Foster. I'll see you soon."

Knowing she was telling the truth, Foster seemed to glide toward the front door and waved cheerfully as they walked down the long path. Only once they reached the curb did he shut the door behind him.

Once he was out of sight, Heather's tears vanished. There was something strange about the funeral home. A power of sorts emanating from all the death within its walls. Foster, too, was an overwhelming presence, and she promised herself that she'd visit soon before it was too late. She'd force Gabriel along too; Foster would like him, if not quite as much as the highly charismatic Julius.

Julius touched her in the same spot again, between her sore shoulder blades, and kept his eyes tactfully away from her increasingly blotchy face.

"What a lovely man," he said.

"Yeah," she squeaked out.

Julius looked at his watch. "Fancy a proper drink?"

CHAPTER NINE

THE DETECTIVE

Heather took Julius to Sherwood's because it was open, cheap, and, fortunately, had not been demolished by a plane. She declared it her favorite place in town as they exited their cars and immediately regretted it. Julius was the type of man, much like her ex-husband, who enjoyed the finer things in life. He knew all the most exclusive spots, the best chef's tasting menus, and which wines to pair with fancy cheeses.

However, unlike her ex-husband, he didn't mind slumming it on occasion. Not that Sherwood's was exactly slumming—at least not anymore—but it was hardly worth a Michelin star, like the places Julius usually occupied. Still, he complimented the retro decor as they walked through the bar, saying it reminded him of being a student, and greeted Bobby enthusiastically as he ordered a beer for him and a glass of red wine for Heather.

She'd forgotten that a rich merlot used to be her drink of choice whenever she felt emotionally fragile. She'd hardly drank it since she'd last seen Julius, and the nostalgia of him handing her a large glass in a dark bar after examining a body was so potent it nearly knocked her off her feet. Despite having reached the comfort portion of their old routine, she couldn't tell if it was a good feeling to be back in it, but at least it gave her a quick trip to Seattle without spending a cent.

They wandered through to the beer garden, where Julius looked around approvingly and chose them a seat on an outdoor two-seater couch. It was overcast but warm, and after two sips, Heather reclined and pulled out a cigarette.

"You still smoke?" Julius asked.

"You don't?"

"No, not for a year now. I'm getting too old for it."

"You're not old."

"You should tell my ex-wife that. She left me for a twenty-five-year-old guy who works at one of those trendy start-ups with a foosball table and beanbags."

Heather tried very hard not to laugh. "Man, I'm sorry."

"It's fine. It's been two years now, but I think that's what did this." He gestured to his graying hair.

"It suits you. You finally look old enough to be the best in the biz."

Julius chuckled. "Thank you. You know I have tenure now. Officially a senior staff member."

She whistled. "Wow, maybe you *are* old."

"At least my students take me seriously now."

Heather snorted. "That's probably because they all have crushes on you."

Julius looked uncomfortable with the prospect. "Well, at least they're coming to class. I just wish the people I met at bars would want to sleep with me instead of eager twenty-year-olds."

"They probably do. You've always been oblivious to that kind of thing. Remember the receptionist who worked at the forensic center?"

"Oh, God, don't remind me," Julius groaned.

"She even bought you roses on Valentine's Day."

Julius buried his head in his hands, and Heather laughed. It was so easy between them. That was Julius's gift. The man had probably seen more dead bodies than Mr. Ellsworth, and yet he was effortlessly charming, always in a good mood, and polite to a fault.

He recovered from his humiliation and changed the topic. "Foster was quite a character. I liked him."

"Me too. I'll admit, he creeped me out at first. I think because of the house and—"

"What he does for a living?" Julius asked, eyebrow raised.

"No, no, I mean—"

"I'm just teasing you, Heather. It's a natural reaction. Do you know how many times I've been dumped after a first date for explaining what a forensic pathologist does? Death and all its disgusting intricacies make people uncomfortable, and when you work with it, it spreads to you like an infection. They can smell it on me, they can smell it on Foster, and I'm sorry to tell you, but they can smell it on you."

"Is that why she left?" Heather asked, making a reckless jump over the usual boundaries of catch-up chitchat. Julius, always an open book, didn't seem to mind. He polished his spectacles with his jacket lining as he thought about the question.

"Yeah, I think so. I don't know for sure, but yeah. I know I brought my work home too often. I'm sure you know the feeling."

"Yeah, we barely made it through my first major case, and the Paper Doll Case really kicked the chair out from under us."

"Yeah." Julius rubbed his face. "I'm in my forties, I've been working in pathology for over twenty years, and that's the worst case I've ever been involved with. You know, I still dream about it."

"Me too," Heather responded, putting her drink on the table with a shaky hand.

Julius pushed his glasses back atop his curls again and turned his body toward Heather. He touched her shoulder briefly, a gesture of understanding, not flirtation, his always-present smile wiped away. Looking into his eyes was like looking into a mirror, and she hated what she saw. Knowing that someone else out there has the same nightmares as you should be comforting, but she didn't feel comforted. She felt seen as if he'd flayed her skin off and exposed her bones to the public.

Clearly feeling the same, Julius broke their psychic link and took a bitter gulp of his martini. "This is why people like us shouldn't get married," he declared as if stating a fact.

Heather was taken aback. "You really think that?"

He shrugged. "I don't think anyone can understand us in the way we want to be understood, and in return, we relentlessly terrify them. You're confining a person to a prison of anxiety. Day in and day out they're asking themselves what-ifs. What if Heather gets shot in the line of duty? What if a serial killer targets my family? What if my husband got a secret vasectomy after seeing something so horrible he can't bear to be a father?" His stare gave weight to the last question, and Heather sat with the confession for a moment, her chest tight with sadness for her friend.

"It is a lot of baggage to put on another person's shoulders," Heather stated.

"It is."

"But I still think there's hope. My old boss, the last sheriff, has been married since before *you* were born, and Foster and Ernie—whatever they were—seemed pretty happy."

Julius looked at her fondly as he had done earlier, but his dark eyes were full of pity. "When did you become such an optimist? It's not like you."

"I've hit a few bumps in the road. Decided to do better."

"I know you were always fond of a drink. Even when you were married to—"

Heather interrupted. "I've been better, and I've been better. If that makes sense."

"Are you optimistic because you're seeing somebody?" Julius asked.

Ten years ago, Julius asking about her love life would've made her heart flutter to the point of bursting. She'd been obsessed with him after meeting him in the hallway of the forensic building. She was green, but he didn't treat her like a child. After sharing a coffee, she formed an all-encompassing infatuation. His intelligence, charm, looks, and dress sense were magnetic, but he was married and wasn't the adulterous type. Nor was he the type to sleep with a twenty-two-year-old rookie. She was more of a protegé to him, much as Gabriel was to her now; putting herself in Julius's shoes, she could see why he never acted on her obvious attraction to him. It was a very different situation now, but her heart was too tired to drum up any interest.

"No, it's just the dogs and me. What about you?"

"Just me and a big apartment. You should come and visit. People in Seattle miss you."

"Yeah, maybe. I don't get up to Seattle much outside of work. I like the quiet life."

"Well, it definitely is quiet. Cute thought. Quaint."

More drinks arrived at their table, and Heather could feel herself slipping into old habits, so she nursed her wine while he took big sips of his cocktail. The vein of addiction that ran through her profession was starting to frighten her now that she was getting some distance from her own vices.

"Did you ever go visit him?" Julius asked.

"Who?" Heather responded, terrified he was going to bring up her ex-husband.

"The killer," Julius replied, bringing up the only person she wanted to talk about even less.

Heather shook her head fervently. "No. I can't. I've thought about it, and I just can't. I can't even Google him. I see his face, and I just fall apart."

"I did. Visit him, I mean. I was the only person on the visitor log. It was awful; he was awful. You know, in some of these true crime documentaries, it's like they're a 'normal' guy and a monster part-time? This guy is a monster full-time—like just an inhuman freak, twenty-four-seven, every day of the week."

Heather didn't want to hear it. She had enough nightmares about him without new source material. Pretending she hadn't heard him, she said, "So, this Ellis case is weird."

Julius nodded enthusiastically. "Very weird. Extremely high level of cyanide toxicity. I've seen laced drugs before and plenty of poisoning victims, but this was off the charts. The amount of cocaine in his system was also something. The two components were really fighting to kill him first."

"Do you think it was murder? I know you can't legally say, but off the record, in your professional opinion?"

"All I'll say is that it would be a very strange way to kill yourself. Especially while flying a plane." Julius leaned toward her. "Do *you* think it was murder?"

Heather realized people were out in the beer garden with them and lowered her voice to near lip-reading levels of volume.

"I think there's more here than meets the eye. I've been hearing things about this guy, and my gut tells me..." she drifted off, remembering when she'd last talked about her gut at Sherwood's with Gabriel.

"Your gut tells you what?"

"That there's something big going on here. Something I need to keep pursuing."

"That's good. Go with that. As long as I've known you, your gut has always been right."

"It tries its best."

"So do you." Julius swills his drink around. "You know, I have some cold cases with your name on them if you want to come to Seattle. Everyone I know has given up on them, but I think your gut might be able to help steer us in the right direction."

"I'll think about it."

Julius shrugged. "Maybe I'll just send you the boxes, just in case you want something to occupy your time."

"Sure, send them my way, and I'll try to take a look, but I won't make any promises. I've got enough going on around here."

"Of course." Julius finished his drink and checked his watch. "I'm afraid I really have to go back to Seattle now. I think I've made my driver hang around for long enough. Do you need us to take you home?"

"No, I'll get Bobby to give me a lift."

Julius put his drink on the table and stood. "Stay in touch, Heather."

"I will." He seemed to be waiting for something, so she stood and hugged him.

He held her close and whispered, "Take care of yourself and get some bloody sleep. You look like you're on the verge of collapse."

They pulled apart. "I'll try my best."

"I know you will. You always do. See you soon, Heather."

Once he was gone Heather fell backward onto the couch and wondered whether she would see him soon or whether it would be another few years. She wasn't sure which option she'd prefer, but after the intensity of their catch-up, and the nature of their reunion, she was leaning toward the latter.

CHAPTER TEN

THE SON

BEAU WOKE UP ON THE FLOOR, HIS HEAD SPINNING AND his nose filled with crusted blood. More hungover than usual, his memory of the previous day was mostly black. The plane crash was still there in vivid detail, as was taking a baseball bat to his dad's car, but all the conjoining moments were gone.

He worked up some strength and peeled himself from the filthy ground. Bits of dirt and grit were stuck to his face, and as he wiped them away, he saw that his hands—slender but calloused and covered in scars—were bloodied. His knuckles were busted, the blood congealing and turning scabrous. He assumed it must've happened after going several rounds with the Mustang, and he wondered if he'd gone back outside for a KO with his fists. It certainly felt as if he had.

He spotted the orange bottle of Valium. It was lying on its side, white circular pills scattered across various grimy surfaces. He plucked one of them up from the carpet, rubbed it on his T-shirt, and swallowed it with a sip of room-temperature water. It would take the edge off soon enough, but while he waited, he lit a cigarette, grabbed a bag of birdfeed and a can of cat food from under the bed, and shuffled outside.

He kicked the door open, hands full of animal food, and jumped down into the dirt. He sat on the step into the RV, shook the bag, and tapped the tin against the metal rim of his seat. It didn't take long for a fluffy gray cat with one eye and a matted coat to skulk out of the trees.

"Hello, Sid," he said to the mangy creature, peeling back the metal lid and dumping the fishy goodness into a plastic bowl. Once Sid was near enough, Beau reached out and scratched the creature's head. It was a dangerous feat considering half of the pale marks on Beau's hands and arms were from Sid's claws, but the occasional payoff was worth the risk.

While Sid was distracted—eating slowly due to his flat face and missing teeth—Beau poured the bird seed into the feeder and sat back on the step of his RV to watch the wildlife as he smoked.

Chickadees, goldfinches, swallows, sparrows, and Beau's favorite—the red-breasted nuthatch—gorged themselves silly on the food, and Sid, who luckily preferred his high-quality wet food to such little, bony birds, joined Beau in watching the chaotic flitting.

Beau did this every day when he woke up and sat for at least an hour to watch them eat. It had become his version of watching TV. Sid was a tense drama, the birds were a competitive reality show, and when the squirrels turned up, they were a sitcom. He barely needed his little box when he had so much entertainment around him. His sister said, last they spoke, that he was turning into a hermit. She was frustrated that he didn't know anything about the world, so they had nothing to talk about. He didn't watch modern movies, binge the hot new streaming series, or read books. He didn't endlessly scroll on social media, go to exciting places, or meet new people.

He wasn't offended that he thought he was boring, the feeling was mutual, but she was wrong that he didn't know anything. He knew how to cook a can of beans in twenty ways and navigate the woods without a compass. He knew which cat food made Sid's stomach hurt and which liquor made his head hurt. He knew how to break a man's nose using only his palm and which cuss words upset his mother most. He knew what he was and was content with it. It wasn't like he was trying to become a prominent city architect in a high-rise. He was more than that; he was unique, a vagabond. He was Dean Moriarty, a free spirit, untamed by the rules of society. When he tried to explain this to his sister, she'd called him a bum, and that was the last time they'd spoken.

He sighed loudly with relief as the benzo kicked in and leaned back on his elbows as he smoked hands-free. Even though the animals were beginning to dissipate, and the bashed-up car was begging his attention, the medicine held him together at the seams.

The Mustang was in worse shape than he'd remembered, and it would take a lot of repairing to get it back to where it was. Maybe he'd take it to the scrapyard instead. Either way, he needed the eyesore off his lot.

He thought he'd feel better for having done it, that it would provide some catharsis, acting as a substitute for the punches that belonged to his dad. It didn't. There was no moment of power, realization, and healing, and now he was as banged up as the hunk of junk.

He checked his alarm clock and saw that it was late afternoon already. He'd slept all day, which explained why Sid was glaring at him. On the upside, it also meant it would be a respectable time to start drinking at Sherwood's. He was trying to be better about drinking in public, so he'd devised some new rules: nothing but beer before five, no shots after ten, and never start before midday on a weekend. It was mainly to stay on Bobby's good side; no need to piss off the one alcohol supplier in town who'd still serve him.

He'd never really worried about Bobby banning him before; the man was a pushover, but his new girlfriend Amber certainly was not. She'd really turned the place around, and Beau hated her for it. Or at least, he tried to; Amber was hard to hate due to her cutesy Southern charm and country-singer-style outfits. He also couldn't deny that the woman could cook a mean burger, and her chicken wings were the best he'd ever had. The place smelled better too—not that it was hard to improve upon the scent of piss and cigarettes—but still, he had to hand it to her.

Beau looked down and saw he was still dressed in what he'd worn yesterday. So, after wiping some blood off his leather jacket and gargling mouthwash, he was ready to head into town. He waved goodbye to Sid, who was licking the empty bowl, and rode away toward town. He wondered if Sid had a home. He liked to imagine him sneaking out, ruining his freshly groomed coat on the thickets, just to get an extra meal and escape the affection of his overbearing family. Twin flames. That's what he and Sid were.

———

He pulled up around the back of Sherwood's, and Amber watched with her hands on her hips and a glower on her face as he revved his engine repeatedly before parking. He grinned wickedly as he removed his helmet and shook his hair out. She rolled her eyes and turned away to walk inside, likely to complain about him to Bobby. He found himself a seat at a small, wobbly table, but upon noticing the detective from yesterday at the table next to him, he moved a table away and shifted his chair around so his back would be to her. He needed a drink before enduring another line of questioning.

Beau had no idea why she seemed suspicious of him. It wasn't as if he could've forced his dad's plane to crash, but he'd half expected her to grill him for an alibi, which he fortunately had. He'd been with his mother attempting to have lunch for an hour prior to the crash. Just before that, he'd stopped off to sell a bike to the guys at Pacific Silver, having come straight from Dottie's, where he'd enjoyed an extra-large, All-American Breakfast Combo, knowing he was about to pick up a decent chunk of cash. He could've told the detective all of this if she had asked, but she wasn't an idiot and knew it was a dumb question. Still, he knew something was bothering her and was keen to find out what it was.

Today, her guard was down; even with the bike revving, she hadn't noticed him. It was the man that was with her; he was distracting her. He was older than her, graying, with a big nose and a generous amount of head and facial hair. He wore a watch worth more than Beau's RV, an unbuttoned navy suit jacket with matching slacks, a pristine white button-up, and dad-style faux retro sneakers at the bottom of the fashionable outfit. This implied he was often on his feet, but he didn't look like a cop... more like an affluent inner-city professor or a specialist at a private hospital. Maybe a plastic surgeon. Going under the knife would explain Detective Bishop's good looks, Beau thought, glancing over his shoulder as subtly as possible.

Maybe I should be the detective, he thought, self-satisfied.

"Ahem," Amber interrupted his rubbernecking with a loud throat clear. Her hands were on her hips, and Savannah was asleep in her sling as usual. Beau didn't care much for babies, but at least she never cried, just stared at you with her big, blue eyes.

Beau looked up at her, looking as amiable as possible. "Hi, Amber. How are you today?"

"I've been better. About fifteen minutes ago, in fact. Before your stinking, deafening bike rolled up."

"Aw, give me a break. My dad just died."

Something clicked behind Amber's hazel eyes, and she clasped a hand to her mouth. Beau nearly laughed as she softened into a pile of mush before his eyes. He'd never seen anything like it. She began stuttering, her ears turned bright red, and she looked toward the doorway for backup from Bobby. It was a microcosm of mortification. Beau let her suffer by looking glum, but he didn't hold it against her. She was probably so worried about her and her baby getting squished yesterday that it'd slipped her mind who'd really died. It wasn't like she knew his dad anyway.

She composed herself but forced an unfamiliar smile. "I'm really sorry for your loss, Beau. Drinks are on the house. Lunch too."

He realized that he might be able to collect freebies from around town for at least a week and beamed up at Amber, genuinely thankful but intentionally smarmy.

"Thank you, ma'am," he replied, impersonating her Southern accent. "I'll have the buffalo chicken burger with blue cheese."

"And the drink?" she asked, batting her eyelash extensions, the lids covered in sparkly blue that had clearly been applied with an acrylic-laden fingertip instead of those fancy brushes his sister used.

He checked the time and stuck to his first rule. "Just a can of beer for me."

"All right, you let me know if you want anything else."

"Thanks, doll," he drawled, refusing to drop the southern twang.

She looked at him funny, a slight cock in her neck as she examined his face. Whatever she was thinking about—likely slapping him upside the head or dragging him by the ear to the parking lot—she soon snapped out of it and clomped toward the kitchen.

He watched her as she went, her toned calves sticking out the bottom of skinny white capri pants. He mentally flogged himself for looking, but his eyes followed her toned posterior—as his mother would've said—and shapely hips as they swayed to and fro in a mesmerizing fashion. There was something about the way she moved that was familiar to him, and he continued to observe her alluring gait until she was out of sight. The penny dropped. After months of it bugging him, he finally knew who she reminded him of.

Pamela.

Pamela, too, had been curvy, blonde, southern, and full of fire. That was his dad's type of woman. The kind of girls he grew up with in Texas before he decided to climb the ladder by marrying—as his paternal grandfather had said—a rich shrew who was built like a plank of wood and wouldn't know fun if it bit her in her nonexistent ass.

THE CRASH

If his dad had landed safely, he'd have spent a lot of time at Sherwood's hitting on Amber; of that, Beau was confident. It made sense why his mother hated Amber so much. She reminded her too much of Pamela, her most significant source of jealousy. She wasn't used to trailer trash one-upping her—not with her class, education, and money—and yet even with all of that, she couldn't make her husband want her more than bottle blondes from Podunk towns.

He remembered when his dad had first hired Pamela. They'd all been sitting around the dinner table, talking about school—which Lucy was exceeding at—and when it came Roland's turn to talk about his day, he'd unveiled a bottle of champagne. Beau watched as his mother went from excited to irritated when the cork hit the ceiling and left a dent, but at least she was still hopeful for good news.

"What's the special occasion?" she asked.

"I finally have enough money in the budget for a personal assistant, which means I can spend more time with my wonderful family."

Beau looked at his mother again to gauge her reaction and saw that she remained calm and collected, likely picturing a young go-getter, fresh out of business school and looking to get into politics. She thought it was a waste of money and worried that Roland was spending more than he was earning, but him being around more did sound nice. At least, that's what Beau could glean from her raised brow and slightly upturned lips.

"Her name's Pamela Bennet," he said. "She was just a real gem compared to the others I interviewed. Phew, some of those wannabe politicians just had no personality. All work and no play makes for a damn dull assistant." Roland laughed at his own reference, as he often did, but Nancy didn't join him. She was already busy striding over to the kitchen island and opening up the family laptop. After some furious typing and clicking, she spun it around, revealing a high-angle, over-saturated, revealing selfie of a young makeup-laden blonde holding a beer bottle.

"*This* is your new assistant?"

"Yes, that's her!" Roland exclaimed with an oblivious chuckle, his wife's anger not yet dawning on him. "See what I mean about fun? Though I've got to say, she's nothing but professional on the job."

Nancy slammed the laptop screen, which made the other three flinch. Roland's jolly expression darkened, and he frowned as he filled two champagne flutes with the expensive liquid.

"Did she have a good resume, at least?" Nancy hissed.

Roland shook his head. "No, she worked at some local drive-through in Texas, but she's been struggling for work since moving up here."

"Why did she move up here?"

"Hated the heat. Aren't we lucky? She's cheap too."

"I'll say."

"Come on, honey, have a drink! You'll like her when you meet her."

Beau hadn't known if it was the raise of the glass, the saccharine smile, or the photo of Pamela burned into her retinas, but Nancy then picked up a small dessert plate and hurled it like a frisbee toward Roland's head. It luckily missed, and he could see that she was relieved it did. Roland, however, was far from tranquil. He was wide-eyed and stone-still as he stared at his wife of a decade in broken-hearted disbelief. He then turned to his children with the kindest expression he could muster and told them to go to bed quickly, shut their doors, and put their earplugs in.

Once they had—flouting the earplug rule as usual—the roaring began, as well as more plate smashing. Who was doing the breaking? He never knew. He liked to think it was his mother, but he knew full well that his father also had the capacity for violence.

It was only years later that Beau acknowledged that his father had likely found Pamela online in some sort of chatroom for sultry southern belles or Texan escorts and offered her the job. He'd hoped the theory wasn't true, but there wasn't any other explanation for their paths crossing.

The conversation next to him cut through his memories.

"Are you optimistic because you're seeing somebody?" the professor asked the detective, laying it on in a thick sticky layer. The guy turned Beau's stomach.

These big city assholes think they can get any girl, he thought. *How about you stick to your students and big city bimbos and leave our locals alone?* If he were drunker, he would've picked a fight, but today he forced himself to listen and sip at his beer.

"No, it's just the dogs and me. What about you?"

"Just me and a big apartment. You should come and visit. People in Seattle miss you."

Detective Bishop hesitated, clearly not into this old weirdo at all. "Yeah, maybe. I don't get up to Seattle much outside of work. I like the quiet life."

Beau nearly laughed at the rejection. She needed someone young and fun like him, not some boring old guy who lived in a lonely, glass-walled apartment. Those places were like cages. Forcing you to earn thousands of dollars, never taking time off, so you could look out at the city while sitting alone in your million-dollar penthouse—that's not what Detective Bishop wanted; he could smell it. She needed excitement. She was too young and hip to settle down. Beau bet she knew how to ride a motorcycle and shoot a moving target with her eyes closed.

He realized he'd been fantasizing, inarguably lonely himself, and missed some of their conversation.

"So, this Ellis case is weird," the detective whispered.

"Very weird. Extremely high level of cyanide toxicity. I've seen laced drugs before and plenty of poisoning victims, but this was off the charts. The amount of cocaine in his system was also something. The two components were really fighting to kill him first."

Beau froze. Cyanide? He'd thought a lot of things—injuries, heart attack, overdose—but never poison. It was an impractical way to kill someone—that was for sure—and if it was a murder investigation, maybe he would need that alibi after all.

"Do you think it was murder? I know you can't legally say, but off the record, in your professional opinion?"

"All I'll say is that it would be a very strange way to kill yourself. Especially while flying a plane." The man leaned into her, seconds away from stretching and putting his arm around her. He could see that she was getting tipsy from the red wine, giggly even. "Do *you* think it was murder?" he asked, practically waggling his eyebrows.

He noticed Detective Bishop look around the garden, and though his sunglasses and ballcap protected his identity, they began to speak so quietly he couldn't hear a word. Frustrated, Beau picked himself and his table number up and went inside to become comfortably numb.

CHAPTER ELEVEN

THE DETECTIVE

Heather woke at dawn after a fitful sleep, and before brushing her teeth, brewing a coffee, or even pulling on pants, she opened her laptop that was precariously balanced at the foot of her bed. The autopsy report was still open and as dense and thorough as it had been the night before. Despite this, she reread every section twice as if the answers to her impossible questions were buried in Julius's messy handwriting.

They weren't, and she knew it. She rubbed the back of her neck and began to pull at the hairs as she continued to read, but nothing emerged. She'd never been involved in a case where she knew so much and so little.

She knew that Roland died of acute cyanide poisoning—and forensics had confirmed that the cocaine in his nostrils was laced—and that his heart had burst due to the poisoning. She knew what the locals thought of him, what his family was like, and that he had likely been down by the border smuggling drugs for the cartel. In a typical case, these details would lead her to a nearby killer lurking in plain sight, but everything felt so far out of reach. Why would someone poison him? Why would they use cocaine? Why was he flying over Glenville? Why did he disappear fifteen years ago? Why would a mayor join the cartel?

She had a list of whys as long as her arm, and she had no clue how to answer them without a motive, suspects, or knowing where he'd been for fifteen years. Usually, with a homicide, there was a gunshot or stab wound that could be traced back to a particular weapon or a crime scene with fingerprints, hair samples, or even calling cards. More importantly, the suspects would be local and in her jurisdiction.

Frustrated that the light of dawn wasn't shedding any new light on the autopsy, she got up and strode into the living room.

The dogs all barked at the creaking floorboards but soon fell back asleep once they'd realized the intruder was their owner. She hardly registered their howls, her hands on her hips in her oversized T-shirt, her hair an untamed creature after having fallen asleep right after showering.

Her eyes ached as she looked at her trusty corkboard. It had helped her solve many difficult cases over the last ten years and was riddled with pushpin and thumbtack holes. Until last night, it had sported photos of the Warren and Burke families as well as a photograph of Luisa Silva's forest monster. Today, those faces were replaced by those of the Ellis family, and Beau's mugshot stared back at her with bloodshot eyes. He'd been busted for possession of cocaine two years earlier, but it was less than half a gram, so he got a slap on the wrist and sent home. Heather pinched the bridge of her nose and closed her eyes. She was close to something, but she wasn't sure what.

Moving back through the house, she knew she needed to change gears to get over this hill, but she was out of ideas for activities. Gabriel hadn't replied to her numerous texts about a brainstorming session, Gene and Karen were with their grandkids, Foster would be too busy with preparing Roland's body for tea, and she'd already had enough of Tina for the week. So, short of driving to Seattle, she was out of socialization options, which left exercise or errands. While pondering this, she padded into the kitchen for breakfast, opened the fridge, and found her answer.

Aside from some half-eaten meal prep containers, out-of-date milk, condiments, and a carton containing one egg, it was completely bare. She hated grocery shopping. Back in the city, her ex-husband was in charge of grocery shopping and cooking, much like he was with cleaning and their social lives. Heather often thought back to that time and wondered what she brought to that relationship other than being irritable and overworked. Something must have made him stick around for so long, but she had no idea what it was.

As grateful as she'd been to him at the time, now she resented those who had coddled her into a life of toast and microwave meals. She knew, really, that there was no one to blame but herself.

She shut the fridge, already overwhelmed. How did people know what they needed or would cook beforehand? She never knew what she was going to cook before she started, and even then, she always ended up hungry for something else.

She could've just ordered takeout and continued to stare at her corkboard until her headache became a migraine, but she glanced at the stack of recipes and cookbooks her parents had sent and decided it was time to be an adult. Armed with reusable carrier bags and a disorganized list of ingredients required to make her favorite family recipes, she got into her car and drove to the store.

Her confidence dissipated as she wandered aimlessly through the overlit and unpleasantly chilly store. Her shopping cart had a crooked wheel, and her list was confusing and out of order, forcing her to return to specific sections of the store over and over again. The certain specialty items on her list sent her on a wild goose chase around the small, rural store, and when she asked a teenage cashier where the tamarind paste and ghee were, he just stared at her blankly as he chewed on a large wad of gum.

Just as a breakdown was upon her, someone tapped her on her shoulder, and she spun around to see the crinkly-eyed and kindly Luisa, who pulled her into a rib-crushing hug.

"Heather! I didn't know you shopped here!"

"I don't, really," she wheezed, the power of the hug squeezing all the air out of her lungs.

Gabriel's mother released her and frowned at Heather's panicked expression. "Are you okay, *conejito*?"

"I have no idea what I'm doing," she admitted, gesturing to her overfull cart.

Luisa furrowed two perfectly drawn-on eyebrows and began pulling fruits and vegetables out of the cart and laying them on the side. Finally—leaving tomatoes, onions, garlic, and bell peppers in the cart—she held a bag of sweet potato in one hand and zucchini in the other.

"How often do you cook?" she asked, arms teetering up and down like a balancing scale.

"Maybe two nights a week. I cook enough for leftovers."

"Okay, so pick one; otherwise, the other will rot."

"Okay, um, I'll go for the sweet potato."

Luisa nodded and put the sweet potato in the cart. "Don't overstock. Only buy what you'll cook in the next two weeks, or else it's a waste of food and money."

"Great, I'll keep that in mind."

"Let me look at your list."

Heather reluctantly handed it over and watched as Luisa's lips curled upward. "This... is the worst list I've ever seen."

Heather hung her head. "I know."

"Didn't your mother ever teach you to do this?"

"Oh, she tried, but I resisted."

"Hmm. Sounds like my eldest daughter." Luisa flipped the piece of paper over and wrote a bullet-pointed list in neat block print. She pointed at each of them. "Vegetables, fruit, meat, dairy, frozen, and pantry. Break it down like that, so you're not pinballing around the store. And keep it simple if you don't know how to cook. You can leave the..." she squinted at Heather's handwriting, "squid ink and black garlic for when you learn how to make a decent spaghetti."

Heather sighed with relief as Luisa removed more things from her cart. Though the exchange made her miss her mother, she was now eternally indebted to this wonderful woman.

"I think you just saved my life."

Luisa laughed but shook her head. "No, just your wallet and your fridge. Consider us even for catching the Glenville Forest Monster. I've been sleeping again thanks to you, my little Nancy Drew." She paused and frowned again. "And what about you, *mi amor*? Are you sleeping?"

"Here and there," Heather said, her voice strained.

Luisa squeezed her upper arm affectionately and pulled her hand back in surprise. "Oh, look at you! A regular G.I. Jane over here."

"Yeah, I've been getting into running and a little lifting."

"Well, if you're going to be doing all that, you need to be sleeping and eating. Come over tonight. It's been too long since you've been over. I'm making goat birria, which I know you love."

"I'd love to," Heather said. "Also, which rice?"

"Basmati," Luisa said sternly, as if there was no other option. Heather shrugged and added it to her compartmentalized cargo. Slightly delayed, Luisa realized what Heather had said and clapped enthusiastically before pulling her into another hug. "Oh, I'm so excited. We bought good champagne to celebrate Martin's promotion to head of the timber mill."

"Oh, that's great! Tell him congratulations for me."

"You can tell him yourself. I'll get Gabriel to pick you up so you can have a couple of glasses."

Something about Gabriel's name made Heather shift uncomfortably, but she didn't let it show. "I don't want to be a pain. I'm happy to walk."

"A young woman like you walking alone at night? I don't think so."

Heather wanted to remind her that she carried a gun and was trained in combat, but thought better of it and accepted the offer. "All right, tell him to text me when he's on his way, and thank you again. I better get this stuff back to my place before it defrosts, but I'll see you later."

"Of course, we look forward to it. You know you're always welcome, Heather."

They parted as Luisa moved toward the butcher's section, and Heather rested her weight on the shopping cart handle as she idled toward the checkout. She did love going to the Silvas for dinner. Their cooking was out of this world, and they never failed to make her laugh or get her wine drunk. Their love filled a hole in her life—like with Gene and Karen—that being far away from her family had left, but she couldn't help feeling guilty. She felt underserving of most people's love and adoration, but Gabriel was Luisa and Martin's son. Their precious youngest child. And Heather had taken him out to that shack in the woods and put him in a situation where he had to put a bullet in a serial killer's head. She should've protected him, and now all she could do was keep an eye on him and make sure he didn't end up like her; all the while, his parents praised them both as heroes.

She paid for her groceries, slung her six recyclable bags over each shoulder, and drove home, already anxious about the impending dinner.

CHAPTER TWELVE

THE SON

THE NARROW DOOR, NESTLED BETWEEN TWO LARGE, barred windows, buzzed as Beau entered the pawn shop. The neon lights were turned off, but he could still read the list of offerings: *Pawn, Buy, Sell, XXX, Gold, Diamonds, Loans.* Cash only, of course... just how Beau liked it. He rummaged around in his jacket pocket for the dark blue velvet box and offered the owner a small wave.

The man, whose name Beau had never caught, stood and opened his arms wide. He had a smoking stogie between his lips, filling the room behind the bulletproof glass with thick, pungent smoke. The man put the cigar down into a glass ashtray and greeted Beau with an accent he'd whittled down to either being Hungarian or Romanian. He stood up from behind the counter, stogie burning in a glass ashtray, filling the room behind the bulletproof barrier with a dark cloud of smoke.

"Beau, my friend! How are you doing?"

"I'm doing okay, considering."

"Ah, yes. The plane." The pawnbroker mimicked a plummeting plane with thick, ringed fingers.

"Yeah, the plane. Did you see it?"

"No, no. I was asleep upstairs. Had no idea until a bunch of people came by to buy engagement rings and take out loans for tropical holidays." The pawnbroker chortled. "Death makes people want to live, I suppose."

"I suppose," Beau said, unable to relate to the premise.

"Ah, where are my manners? My condolences. It's very sad. Mr. Ellis was a good man."

"Thank you."

"My father is dead too. A long time now. You will get over it."

"I'm sure I will."

"So, what have you got for me today? It's been a long time." The pawnbroker pouted like a put-out girlfriend on a forgotten anniversary.

As soon as Beau placed the box on the counter, the slot in the glass slid open, and his mother's diamond Tiffany & Co necklace was gone.

The pawnbroker oohed and aahed as he checked the necklace in the dim ceiling light and under the special UV lamp. After a lot of tapping and staring, he nodded, delighted.

"It's not often I see real diamonds," he said. "Very nice necklace. I can give you twenty-eight hundred for it."

"Come on, let's call it three."

"Fine, fine. We can do three, but that's as high as I can go." He paused, looking at it in awe. "Am I going to see Mrs. Ellis in here tomorrow to buy it back?"

Over the years, Beau had stolen bits and pieces from his mother to sell for much-needed cash. She'd gotten so adjusted to him doing this that she visited the pawn shop several times a week to buy back her own items. It was an exasperated game they played, but none of the previous objects had been this costly. There was a mother-of-pearl-handled hairbrush, a por-

THE CRASH

celain figure of a cat, an old painting of cows in a field, and other trinkets. Each was worth a few hundred dollars, but this was worth far more. He'd been saving it for a rainy day and figured grieving his murdered father was the perfect opportunity to splash out.

"I don't think she even remembers it. I stole it thirteen years ago. Been holding on to it."

"Good, good, because she's one scary lady. I'd probably end up selling it for two and losing money." The man laughed heartily again, phlegm rattling in his throat as he counted the cash.

Beau's phone began to ring, and he apologetically stepped back from the counter and exited through the front door, leaving the pawnbroker holding a wad of cash.

Beau lit a cigarette and looked at the caller ID. Speak of the devil, and she shall appear.

"Hello?" he asked.

"Beau?" came Nancy's crackly reply.

"Yeah, it's me."

"I can barely hear you. Where are you?"

"In town."

"Where in town?"

Beau looked around. He was on the outskirts, which explained the poor reception. The closest other structures—other than run-down houses belonging to the older, drunker, and poorer Glenville occupants—were the Black Bear Motel and the Fishmonger's. He opted for the latter for his lie.

"Why in Heaven's name would you be at the Fishmonger's?"

"Needed some fish."

Nancy soughed, already irritated. "I'm just calling to tell you that your father's funeral is on Saturday. They've released the body back to us."

"Burial or cremation?"

"Burial. Your father hated the idea of being burned."

"That's ironic."

"I suppose it is," Nancy replied tersely. "Though apparently, he wasn't alive long enough to know about the fire. Sheriff Peters informed me that the official cause of death is—"

"Acute cyanide poisoning."

"How did you know that?"

"I overheard the detective discussing it with some professor-looking guy at Sherwood's."

Nancy clicked her tongue. "I hope she's not going to be some sort of loudmouth spreading gossip all over town."

"I doubt it. She seems professional enough. Besides, what do you mean by gossip? He died of cyanide poisoning; that's a fact, not gossip."

"Your father died in a plane crash," Nancy said sternly. "No one except for us and the police needs to know anything different about that."

"But—"

"Repeat after me. My father died in a plane crash."

Beau sighed and relented. "Dad died in a plane crash."

"As I said, it's our duty to uphold your father's legacy, so I think it would be in everyone's best interests to omit certain aspects of his final moments."

"Like all the cocaine?"

"Yes, like that."

Beau tsked. "Good luck with that. They made quite a show of removing it from the plane."

"Then we tell them he was set up. A fall guy, or whatever they call them. They were going to kill his family if he didn't. Something like that. Who knows? …maybe it's true."

Beau didn't even bother trying to debate or entertain the idea. "Is there a will?"

"Yes, I was getting to that. As it turns out, Roland kept his bank account open the entire time he was missing, and whatever he's been doing this whole time—"

"Moving and selling cocaine."

"—has been very lucrative. I get half, and you and Lucy split the other half."

He scoffed bitterly. "How much is that?"

"I loathe to tell you because I know you'll just spend it on slowly killing yourself, but your share is seven hundred and forty thousand dollars."

Beau's jaw dropped, he felt faint, his hands grew shaky, and he could not hold his phone. It felt like a dream, and he was waiting to wake up. He was so overcome that he almost didn't respond. "Are—are you fucking kidding me?"

THE CRASH

"Don't spend it all in one place," his mother said dryly, her face likely twisted into a grimace over the usage of her second least favorite word. "And, Beau, don't tell *anyone* about this. Especially the detective. If she asks, we'll say he left us a pittance. A big inheritance makes us look suspicious."

"It's not like you need the money."

Nancy didn't respond.

"Wait, I thought you had loads of money from when Pop died?"

"I did, fourteen years ago, but the world is expensive, as are college tuition and mortgage repayments."

"Maybe you're right about not telling the detective," Beau replied, suddenly suspicious of his mother. He knew it was ridiculous, and the detective would be an idiot for following up on either of them, but he also knew if anyone could pull off a murder this complex, it was his mother. And as she'd steadily revealed over the last forty-eight hours, she had plenty of motive.

"I'm always right. Now, the funeral. Saturday at the church. Wear a suit. Write a speech. Be there before midday."

"I am not going to make a speech."

"Yes, you are. Your sister and I are going to. Can you imagine how strange it'll look if you don't?" She was clearly doing something else and highly distracted, slamming drawers and rummaging through papers.

Trying to find some happy memories for speech inspiration? Beau thought, bemused by the obvious panic.

"Okay, then I'm not wearing a suit," he said.

"Beau, you know how important image is."

"I'm not—"

"The next words out of your mouth better be 'not going to let you down' or so help me God," she snapped.

"I—"

"If you arrive and you're not in a suit, I will have you turned away."

He sighed. "Fine, when do I get my money?"

"In a few weeks. How about you just sell another bike?"

"Fine. Whatever."

"See you Saturday."

He hung up, his irritation with his mother quickly buried by a spring-green rain of dollar bills. He could be anything he wanted to be with that amount of money. He could put a house on the land, open his own business, and travel across the country. He thought money would feel like a cage, but with the number of doors opening, he realized he could buy the keys to the coop he didn't even know he was trapped in.

As he reopened the pawn shop door, he wondered if that was how his father had felt. Maybe his need to spread his wings was why he never returned. Beau grabbed the cash, thanked the pawnbroker, and for the first time, saw how close the apple had fallen from the tree.

"Don't spend it all in one place," the pawnbroker said to Beau's back.

The man's tone was the opposite of his mother's, though he was just as serious. Unfortunately, unlike the six-figure windfall, Beau was about to blow his three grand in one fell swoop. It would all be worth it to see the look on his mother's face when he turned up in a high-end tailored suit.

The tailor was only a block away, and Beau whistled as he walked, filled to the brim with joy and confidence. His pockets were full, his bank account was going to be fuller, and he was going to be somebody.

He barged into the dark little building in the same manner he imagined his father may have done, and a tiny old man in the corner, crouched by a sewing machine, looked up at him. Beau's jolly demeanor faltered as he swore he saw fear flash across the man's face and a tremble in his expert hands. They'd never met before, and Beau stepped forward awkwardly, smiling as kindly as he could.

The man relaxed and smiled back, his circle-shaped face consumed by wrinkles. He shakily got to his feet, put on his chain-held glasses, and approached Beau. The lenses enhanced his eyes four times over, giving him the appearance of a little mouse or an inquisitive owl.

"Roland Ellis?" the old man asked, clearly delighted.

Beau shook his head. "No, I'm his son."

"Ah, of course. You're much paler than a ghost. To tell you the truth, I first thought you were a ghost."

"No ghosts here, sir, just the descendant of one."

The old man faltered. "Roland is dead?"

"I'm afraid so. As of two days ago."

"Oh, dear. I can't remember the last time I saw the poor fellow. I assumed he must've started seeing a competitor."

"Don't take it personally. He was missing for fifteen years before he died."

"Ah, well, that explains that, I suppose." The old man adjusted his glasses. "He did mention he was going on a trip, but I'm so old, I forget these things. It was with his young lady friend. Paisley? Paige?"

"Pamela."

"Yes, that was it."

CHAPTER THIRTEEN

THE DETECTIVE

Heather was on her knees in the kitchen reorganizing her freshly stocked pantry when Gabriel knocked on the door. She knew it was him because he'd texted her ten minutes ago telling her he was on his way. Still, the sound surprised her, and a jar of pasta sauce slipped from her grasp as she stood. She caught it with her other hand before it hit the ground, and she was thankful she hadn't been drinking to calm her nerves.

She didn't know why she was feeling nervous. She loved the Silva family, and when she'd seen Gabriel on the day of the crash, things had been good between them, or at least better than usual. Walking to the door to greet him, she thought about feigning sick, hacking up a lung, and pretending she couldn't go to dinner. Then she thought of Luisa—who'd saved her at the grocery store—and how disappointed she'd be if Heather didn't make it.

She opened the door and restrained herself from fake sneezing in Gabriel's face. To her surprise, the person who would've received the unpleasant action was Briana, whose sincere cheerful expression dissipated when she looked Heather up and down. Heather wore a plain white T-shirt and blue jeans, which she'd thought appropriate until she saw Briana's 1950s-style dress with a heart neck and an A-line skirt. It was parrot red, covered in roses, and beautifully contrasted with her new chocolate brown dye job.

Heather rarely cared about being underdressed, not even when she accepted a televised award back in Seattle dressed in an ill-fitting button-up and gray slacks with the tag hanging off the belt loop. It wasn't her job to be beautiful, nor did she have anyone to be attractive for. Yet tonight, as a pretty girl, likely ten years her junior, looked her up and down, she was transported back to high school. Suddenly, her eyebrows were too thick, the hair on the back of her neck too tufted, and her clothes too frumpy.

She shook it off, telling herself that she was much too old to hold on to being unpopular in school, and addressed Briana amiably. "Hi, Briana. Are you joining us for dinner?"

It was a stupid question, and the face Briana pulled expressed that she thought so too. "Yeah. I go to dinner with Gabriel every Friday."

"Right. Is Gabriel with you?"

"...Yes. He's in the car."

"Great. Let me get my coat."

"No rush," the girl said, scoping out the unorganized, distinctly unchic household over Heather's shoulder. She sniffed, clearly smelling wet dogs from the earlier walk in the woods, and Heather moved as quickly as possible to shut the door.

The ride to the house was awkward, with Gabriel barely acknowledging either of the passengers. Heather knew he was a nervous driver, but he seemed to be waiting for someone else to speak, but nobody did.

After an excruciating eternity, they arrived, and Luisa was already waiting in the doorway, waving the champagne around.

"Heather, will you do the honors?" she called out loudly, and Heather, taking her opportunity to remove herself from third-wheeling hell, bounded from the still-moving car and popped the cork with ease, much to Luisa's delight. Martin applauded from somewhere inside at the bang, and Heather stepped inside the cozy home, foam running over her hand.

The house—warmly lit and smelling divine—put her at ease as she waltzed into the kitchen dining area and greeted Martin with a cheer. He gestured to the six champagne flutes, and she filled them to the top leaving only dregs in the bottle. Despite being burned out on socialization, she was determined to be the best dinner party guest she could. Though she made herself no promises that she wouldn't do a little investigating in the meantime.

After serving the champagne, she was told to sit and enjoy herself. She chose a seat in the middle but was quickly ushered by Luisa into the chair at the head of the table. She tried to resist, but Luisa was unusually strong, and she eventually gave in and collapsed atop the thin, terracotta-colored cushion.

Eventually, the two youngsters sidled in, smelling of smoke, and Heather once again felt a pang of guilt for inflicting nicotine onto Gabriel as her superiors had done toward her. Luisa made a face, and Heather was glad to have smoked and then showered before coming over.

Briana seemed tipsy already, and she could sense Gabriel's agitation as she haphazardly lowered herself into the seat. She wondered if he was always like that to Briana or if having his boss around made him self-conscious. She hoped he knew her calculated judgment and analytical behaviors weren't targeted at colleagues' romantic interests. Being a decade older than Briana, Heather didn't much care for her. She'd been cocky at that age, too, before adult responsibility took its toll. So, there was no judgment being passed around, but if she said it out loud unprovoked, it would sound as if the opposite were true; so, all she could do was cast polite expressions in her best friend's direction until the food was served.

Once the food was on the table, Luisa and Martin sat on either side of Heather. It was evident they weren't much interested in Briana's ramblings about her job at the gas station and how much she hated her coworkers. Nor were they interested in their son's minor inputs about his tedious desk work and how he and Heather had been saddled with piles of paperwork for months. What they wanted to hear about was Roland Ellis.

"I can't discuss the ins and outs of an open investigation, not even in exchange for amazing food," Heather teased.

"Of course, we understand," Luisa replied, suddenly flustered.

"But I actually do have something I want to ask you."

"Of course," Martin and Luisa replied in sync, eyes wide and eager.

"What did you think of him?"

Luisa put a hand on her chest. "Oh, we adored Roland."

"We did," confirmed the mostly silent Martin.

"He did so much for this community. He helped Dennis—" she cut herself off. "He helped get the timber mill up and going again. Which gave Martin the job that bought us this house."

"He did."

"We have the drive-in theater, thanks to him. And he opened up the community center where I have my knitting club. Oh, and the pool! He was the best mayor a little town like this could ask for. He knew all of us by name, well, I guess the town wasn't very big at the time, but still. What a man..."

Luisa looked dreamy as she remembered the contributions of the handsome, generous man whom Heather had only had the pleasure of meeting the corpse of. It was sad, she thought, how much was stripped away in death.

She glanced at Gabriel and found that he was staring at her. They made eye contact for the first time all night, and his sober gaze told her not to mention the drugs or the poisoning. If most of the town thought he'd died in a freak crash, it was for the best, for now.

"He sounds amazing," Heather responded, adhering to Gabriel's warning. She bit into the delicious meal and tried not to laugh when she spotted Briana chugging ice water. It was spicy, just as Heather liked it, and she admired the girl's tenacity to keep going.

"Oh, he was," Luisa said, lost in thought, her food untouched. "You know if he'd have been mayor when all those hikers went missing, he would've done something about it. He was just a lovely, lovely man."

Heather could tell Luisa was about to start crying, so she had the thought to change tact. "These birria tacos are amazing. You know, I never really thanked you for helping me at the store earlier. Maybe next time I'll have to try this reci—"

Briana interrupted with a slam of her glass on the table, having just swigged the entire thing. Another glass of ambiguous, half-drunken cocktail sat by her plate. "My mom says Roland was a real shit," she slurred. To make matters worse, she burped after the fact, and as Gabriel cringed, Luisa stifled a gasp, looking toward her husband with watery eyes.

Heather didn't want to encourage the conversation, based on how the other three were reacting, but as a detective, she felt she had no choice. "How did your mom know Roland, Briana?"

"She was a secretary in the office." Briana paused thoughtfully and took a big drink of her cocktail. "Actually, she was more like a sex-cretary." She giggled at her own joke.

The others recoiled, but Heather kept pushing. "So, she was having an affair with Roland?"

Heather felt Martin and Luisa staring at each side of her face as if an alien had inhabited her body; she attempted to reassure them through sideways glances. She hoped it came across that she was only doing her job.

"No, but he paid her more when she wore tight skirts and unbuttoned her blouse down to her cleavage. He really liked the ladies, if you know what I mean."

"That can't be true," Luisa interjected, but it didn't stop Hurricane Briana, whom Heather was weirdly warming up to despite her lack of tact. She admired brutal honesty in the face of adversity.

"She used to take us on vacation with that money, but she got married and pregnant again, and the bonuses stopped coming."

"Did he have his eye on anyone else? Anyone other than Nancy?" Heather asked, leaning forward over her plate and reaching for her notebook that was still at home. She caught sight of Gabriel and reeled it in.

Briana finished off her drink. "Oh yeah. There was all sorts of talk. Bastard babies. Girls stowed away in lake houses. Who knows what was true? But that man got around, that much I know for sure."

Luisa clapped her hands loud enough that everyone flinched. "How about dessert?" she asked despite no one having finished the meal. "Let's all have dessert. Would you like some wine, Heather?"

Luisa loudly scooted her chair out, brought Heather a full glass of wine in less than a minute, and then returned to the kitchen to busy herself.

Heather maintained eye contact with the now-drunken Briana, who turned herself toward Gabriel and informed him in a loud whisper that she needed to go to bed. He did as she asked, leaving Heather and his parents to a mild-mannered dessert session, where they, fortunately, managed to move away from the discomfort of the prior conversation by discussing Heather's parents, Sima and Adrien.

Just as she polished off her mango sorbet and glass of wine, Gabriel rejoined them, reassuring everyone that Briana was asleep. He said she was apologetic for her behavior and that her new medication, mixed with alcohol, had gotten the best of her. Heather could tell he was lying and that he was the only sorry one of the pair; but it appeased his parents, so she kept her observations to herself.

Shortly after her glass was refilled, Gabriel invited her out into the garden, and she gladly joined him at the glass table on the veranda. He offered her a smoke, and after a couple of drinks, she couldn't resist. She could tell he was drunk, too, from the way his eyes kept wandering.

He shook his head, his curls bouncing, and fake cried as he buried his head in his hands. "Mamá is going to kill me tomorrow once Bri goes home."

"She's a piston, that girl," Heather said with a smirk. "A real firecracker."

"Don't I know it?"

"Are you happy?"

"Sometimes." He lowered his voice. "She keeps trying to pick out my outfits."

"Hey, you need all the help you can get," Heather teased.

"You're one to talk."

"Maybe I should let her style me too. I have no idea what to wear outside of work."

Gabriel chuckled. "Me neither. I don't know how she does it. She looks like she's on the set of a TV show every day of her life."

Heather paused, thinking about the little bits of Spanish she'd heard throughout the day. "Hey, do you speak fluent Spanish?"

He raised an eyebrow. "*¿Venga ya? ¿Estás de coña?*"

"I assume that's a yes."

"My parents still test me all the time."

"Do you know what *las águilas arpías volarán para siempre* means?"

He frowned. "Harpy eagles. *Las águilas arpías*. The harpy eagles will fly forever. Why do you ask?"

"It was tattooed on Roland's arm," Heather replied, googling harpy eagles and finding a match to the bird depicted. It was a South American bird, the national bird of Panama in fact, found from Mexico all the way to Brazil and parts of Argentina, but was rapidly declining in population thanks to deforestation.

"Do you think he was involved in some gang stuff?" Gabriel asked, his voice still hushed.

"It's looking that way."

"What would make a well-to-do mayor fly off to join a cartel?"

"That's what I keep asking myself."

They both leaned back in their chairs to smoke, drink, and think; and even more than the answers she'd obtained tonight, Heather was glad to have her partner back. Even if it was only temporary.

CHAPTER FOURTEEN

THE DETECTIVE

It hadn't been long since Heather had last sat on the back row pew of the Glenville Baptist Church, waiting for a funeral to start. She'd been at the service for Alice Warren—digging her nails into the arm of Gabriel's jacket as she tried not to cry—only three months ago. It had been a predominantly warm affair, filled with kindnesses and humorous stories, but bitter anger emanated from those left behind, and some of it had been aimed at Heather. Seeing Paul kiss the top of baby Holly's downy head, tears streaking his cheeks before shooting a hollow look in Heather's direction, had nearly been enough to make her leave. Nonetheless, she endured without fleeing or weeping because she'd been too late for Alice and did not deserve the pity of those who were busy grieving.

The funeral for Roland Ellis was the complete opposite of that. It was busier than Alice's funeral, with many people having to stand for lack of pews toward the back of the church, but no one was crying. Instead, they were murmuring in groups as if at a town hall meeting. Most weren't even dressed in black, and the front doors remained open as people filtered in and out.

Only the Ellis family attempted to maintain proper conduct and sat rigidly in their expensive black outfits on the front row. Heather couldn't see their faces from the back row but saw Nancy occasionally bring a handkerchief to her face. Whether it was for show, she couldn't say.

She'd hardly recognized Beau when he walked in because of his freshly cut hair and very expensive-looking suit. He cleaned up well. She knew he was a striking man, but she was surprised by how well he suited elegance and how easily he could polish his rough edges into something touchable. Yet, as he looked around with disdain, she felt a face as pretty as his would be better served on someone else. His personality suited broken noses and scars, but instead, he looked as if he'd been plucked out of a gothic Victorian romance novel.

She wondered if he was a ladies' man like Briana had inferred about Roland. Beau wasn't nearly as conventionally handsome as his father—or men like Paul and Gabriel—but he had a cool, loner vibe with his shaggy black hair, motorcycle, and ripped skinny jeans that Heather knew some young girls must go nuts for. He certainly wasn't her type, but he was an intriguing character, and she looked forward to talking with him in more detail.

Lucy, whom Heather had yet to meet since her arrival two days prior, sat prim and proper, her legs crossed and shoulders back. Her model-like frame—which she and her brother clearly inherited from their waifish mother—was clothed in a strappy black jumpsuit that showed off a lot of her porcelain skin.

Heather had caught a glimpse of her as she walked in and took to the central aisle like a catwalk. Her hair and makeup looked as if they had been professionally done, meaning she knew she wasn't going to cry. Heather also noted that her bag

THE CRASH

and shoes were designer, and her tiny button nose—that was so unlike that of the rest of her family—was evidently the work of a high-end plastic surgeon. This led Heather to wonder: Why was one child so wealthy and the other so poor? Was it favoritism, or had Lucy simply made her own success? She certainly carried herself in a way successful people did. Her posture was good but not overeager, like it didn't really matter what people thought of her.

Nancy, on the other hand, was stiff as a board, and Heather had noticed how her eyes darted before she'd covered them with sunglasses. The crowd and attention made her nervous like she was preparing for something to go horribly wrong. What that hypothetical disaster might be, Heather wasn't sure. She'd seen all kinds of crazy stuff happen at funerals. Embarrassing speeches, fist fights, secret family members showing up. You name it.

Heather looked around, seeing if she could spot any sad-looking women Roland may have secretly romanced, but there were no melancholy faces, just neutral ones waiting for everyone to get on with it.

Eventually, the priest arrived at the pulpit and spoke into the microphone. "We gather to celebrate the life of Roland Ellis. He was a brilliant man who loved his community and was loved in return. He changed the face of Glenville for the better; for that, we owe him many thanks. I have to wonder, how many of you would be here today if it wasn't for the improvements he made to this town. What a man."

It was an oddly personal introduction, and Heather glanced at Gabriel, who seemed to be thinking exactly what she was. From speaking to Luisa and Martin, it was clear Roland had a spell cast on the older members of this town, but as Heather looked around at the nodding, graying heads, she realized just how powerful it was, even all these years later. How far did their love stretch, she wondered? Was it possible that one of them, or all of them, helped him disappear or even turned a blind eye to whatever illegal enterprises he'd become involved in? Suddenly, the answers to her endless questions didn't feel very far away at all.

"He was survived by his beautiful wife, Nancy, whom we all know and love, and his accomplished children, Lucy and Beau," continued the priest.

Heather heard someone snort with laughter at the last bit, which rang through the room. Beau stiffened but didn't turn around. Easily secondhand embarrassed, Heather felt Gabriel tense up beside her. She looked at him with a grimace. There were definitely more unpleasantries to come.

The priest cleared his throat awkwardly. "I believe some of Roland's colleagues would like to speak first, and then the family will read what they have written."

The priest took a seat, and a man from the left side of the front row took the stage. He was Roland's accountant, which immediately pricked Heather's ears though he had little of interest to say. She didn't know what she expected; it wasn't as if the man would admit to tax fraud or money laundering after at least thirty years in the business, even for an impudent anecdote.

He was followed in succession by Roland's gardener, maid, ex-business partner, campaign manager, and a long list of other employees and colleagues. Their speeches were almost identical, word for word, as they gushed about him with sincere tenacity and love. He was an excellent coworker; a kind employer; and a funny, generous, loving, enthusiastic, apparently perfect man.

They each had an anecdote to differentiate them: he rescued my dog from being run over, he babysat my triplets, he ran my abusive husband out of town—and though none of it revealed anything untoward, Heather was intrigued with the man's heroic virtues. Had she judged a book by its cover—or a man by his corpse—she wouldn't have thought him half the gentleman he apparently was or used to be.

Then it was the family's turn, and a very old woman, too shrunken to spot from the back row, was helped to the stage by Nancy. The woman looked out at the large audience and shook her head in disbelief. "I never thought there'd be anyone here except for me, Nancy, and my grandchildren," she said in a croaky Southern accent. "I've never been up here before; I always made Roland come down to Texas to see me instead. I thought he was making everything about this place up, and I was happy to let him lie to me instead of disappointing me with the truth. I'm glad to see I was wrong."

She wheezed a laugh. "Y'all are looking at me like I'm crazy, but know I'd look back at you the same way if it wasn't for my cataracts." A polite titter of laughter rose from the audience. "You see, my son was a very difficult boy, and up until today, I thought I'd raised him all wrong. I blamed myself for him running off like he did and abandoning his family. Though I'm not quite sure how you people reconcile who you knew with who he ended up being, at least I now know that there was good in him after all. Thank you for that. A mother should never outlive her children, but now I'm glad I have, so I can die without the guilt of being a bad parent." She took another look around the now stunned-silent room before being escorted back to her seat.

The energy in the room was very different after that. Murmuring arose from the edges, and it only worsened when the next speaker in line—Beau—refused to move. His mother whispered fervently in his ear, her body twisted toward him, the nails on her right hand digging into his right shoulder. A disobedient child in a man's body was about ten seconds from receiving corporal punishment. It was unpleasant to witness, but Heather couldn't stop staring. Soon the judgmental murmurs reached Nancy, and she relinquished her grip and smiled as she took to the stage with a piece of neatly folded paper in hand. Her speech was even more peculiar than her mother-in-law's.

"Roland and I have been married for twenty-five years, which sounds like a long time. You might wonder what my secret is, and I'll tell you, it's having your husband go missing for more than half of it."

She didn't pause for laughter, of which there was none anyway, and continued to read at a manic pace but flatly, much like a child being asked to read a paragraph in English class.

"He gave me two wonderful children and had a beautiful house built for me which I still occupy, and I still have many fond memories of him. While I do not know this man, the one in the coffin, I once loved who he used to be, and I am sad to lose him in the process of losing this stranger. What a tragedy this is for our town and our family. Thank you for being here and sharing your stories."

It was unpleasantly silent afterward, and Lucy quickly hopped up onto the stage with a warm expression and a confident, enthusiastic speaking voice. Her speech was the longest and clearly well-rehearsed. It was all about her childhood memories, the funny things her dad used to do and say; and frankly, Heather thought, it was the only normal eulogy of the entire bunch, townspeople included. The weird part was, once Lucy stepped off the stage, her smiley mask vanished, and she returned to bored neutrality.

By the time the hymns and prayers were done, Heather was feeling claustrophobic, and as soon as the doors were open, she was the first one out the door with Gabriel hot on her heels. She inhaled the cool afternoon air as if it were her first breath after suffocation. The fresh relief it brought was bliss. Then it passed, and she ruined the effect by lighting a cigarette.

"That was weird," Gabriel said, joining her.

"No kidding. Everyone in town loved the guy except his own family."

"I guess you never know what goes on behind closed doors. Plenty of people in town liked Dennis Burke too."

"Yeah." Heather inhaled and exhaled deeply and spotted Beau in the shade of a tree doing the same thing while his mother and sister shook the hands of the attendees by the arched doorway. She wondered if he'd even written a speech.

He caught Heather's eye, and she nodded at him. He gestured back, and a corner of his mouth quirked up for a second as if relieved to know he wasn't invisible… though he might as well have been. Not a single soul approached him, and every passerby in the crowd went so far as to give him a wide berth. She was about to break the mold and offer her condolences and perhaps a cigarette when the journalists once again descended

THE CRASH

on the scene. They got to him and the Ellises before she even had a chance to stub her smoke out.

It immediately turned into chaos, with Nancy yelling, Beau shoving, and Lucy threatening legal action. Heather was glad to not be the only police officer on the scene. Tina and her faithful cronies ushered pushy microphones away from the family members, and as fights began to break out between incensed locals and camera-wielding predators, arrests were made. Gabriel, being one of the strongest on the force, was quickly roped into tackling and handcuffing, and though Heather tried to join in, all the action was taken care of, and she was pushed to the outskirts of the skirmish.

"Got a light, Detective?" came a voice from behind her.

She turned to see Beau, surprisingly unscathed and not under arrest, holding out an unlit cigarette in her direction.

"Yeah, and you can call me Heather," she replied, reaching around in her pockets. She offered the lighter, but he put the cigarette between his lips and leaned forward for her to do the honors.

He inhaled as the cherry glowed red. "Thanks."

"You're welcome, and my condolences."

"God, I hate that word. Condolences," he muttered. "I've been hearing it so much it doesn't even sound like a word anymore."

"I understand. Words are weird. I once worked a manslaughter case, and by the end of it, I couldn't stop saying mans-laughter."

Beau chuckled. "I think I'll call it that from now on. Gives it a dark, cosmic twist."

"So, how are you holding up?"

"Weirdly, I'm doing about the same as ever, somewhere in between crappy and not bad. What about you?"

"What about me?" Heather asked.

"You looked pretty shaken up from the crash."

"Yeah, I guess I was. Slept like a baby after though—for once." Heather had interrogated enough suspects to know that just a tiny bit of personal, relatable information about herself was enough to get most people to open up.

"Yeah, I haven't been sleeping either. Not unless I grab a drink first."

"Yeah, Sherwood's definitely used to be my version of a sleeping pill. Trying out melatonin and exercise instead."

"Gross. You can pry whiskey from my cold, dead hands."

"I might have to if you keep drinking that bottom-shelf swill at Sherwood's."

Beau grinned, bemused. "I didn't know I was talking to a top-shelf girl."

"I'll have you know I'm very classy."

Beau looked her up and down. "Yeah, maybe if I squint."

Heather raised her brows and scoffed. "Well, you've got me beat today. That is a nice suit."

"Don't look so surprised. I'll have you know I have great taste. My music collection alone will blow your mind."

Heather's smile lines deepened. "Oh yeah? Who's your favorite band?"

"I'll tell you if you come over to my place. Then you can check out my record collection."

Heather faltered, taken aback by Beau's undaunted flirtation. Was he actually trying to pick her up, the detective in charge of his dad's case, at the deceased's funeral? She tried to sputter out an answer, realizing she may have taken the banter too far. "Beau, I—"

Beau winked. "Don't worry, Detective. Strictly platonic, though I'll have you know I'm a hot item around these parts."

Heather exhaled and shook her head. "Yeah, I'm sure."

Beau snorted and lit another smoke. "What, you don't believe me?"

Heather looked around. "Where are all these ravenous women, then?"

"Women, Detective? That's very presumptuous in this day and age."

Once again, Heather faltered before realizing he was messing with her.

He smirked. "Maybe I only like city girls."

She had to give it to him. He was smooth. "Alright, I'll choose to believe you've got a dozen lovers on the go in Seattle. But only because you're having a bad day."

"Hey, if you really want to make my day better, come have a drink with me at my place."

"Beau, I really shouldn't. It's not professional."

"What about if it's on the record. I'll let you ask everything you're clearly dying to ask, and you can record the whole thing for all I care. All you have to do is hang out with me for an hour."

"I have..." she was going to say 'plans.' Gabriel was going to be coming over to her house for a little brainstorming session. She was going to tell him all about Mr. Ellsworth, meeting Julius again, and what exactly killed Roland Ellis. However, when she turned around, she saw him canoodling with Briana, and when they laid a sticky, open-mouthed kiss on each other, Heather spun back to Beau, her mouth deeply downturned in disgust.

"Have you become the third wheel?"

"A little bit, yeah," she chuckled, watching Beau raise his eyebrows as the kissing likely intensified.

"You want to make them jealous? Put on a little show? I showered today; I promise."

Heather rolled her eyes. "I'm good, but I appreciate the offer."

He shrugged. "I'm always here if you change your mind. Just make sure you bring the baton."

"While I must decline your generous offer of a passionate night—"

Beau howled with laughter, attracting looks from funeral attendees and the remnants of journalists. Heather tried and failed to shush him. "A night of passion! I was just going to give you a smooch. I didn't realize you were so forward, Detective."

She ignored his faux scandalization but felt a blush crawl up her neck. "—I will take you up on that drink. Only I am there as a professional, on the clock, and *not* as a friend."

"I'll take what I can get. It's this or drinking alone because I am not going back to my mother's for the wake. I can tell you that much for sure."

The word mother took Heather aback. She knew Beau had an upper-class upbringing, but his inelegant and informal manner made that easy to forget. He had a working-class accent, some might say, so the word mother stuck out like a sore thumb and sent a chill up Heather's spine. She realized how grateful she was for her relationship with her mother, as strained as it was at times.

"All right, I'll meet you if you give me the address."

Beau shook his head, his cigarette between his lips sprinkling embers. "You'll never find it with a GPS or a map; you'll have to follow me."

"Sure. I've had enough of hunting for houses in the woods for a lifetime."

Something serious, even close to empathetic, crossed Beau's face before the impish boyish expression returned.

"Race you," he said and jogged off toward his motorcycle.

Heather walked after him but was stopped dead by a strange feeling. She shuddered as if someone had walked over her grave and turned left very slowly to see a cameraman filming in the middle of the church's front lawn without any reporter accompanying him. She supposed he could've been trying to capture the setting, but something about him seemed off. He was sun-wrinkled and leathery, with many old, blue tattoos and a spiky crop of receded, thinning hair. He wasn't dressed as well as the others either. His clothes looked ill-fitting and starchy, as if they'd just been bought from Walmart today.

Heather followed the direction of his camera and found that it was trained like a sniper on Amber in her black miniskirt and blouse. He wasn't a cameraman—not a real one—she realized, and stormed over to the suspected pervert.

"Sir, can I see some identification?"

"Huh?"

"Which news station are you from?" The man looked confused, so she repeated herself, gesturing around at the lack of news trucks and reporters. "Who do you work for?"

"I..."

"If you can't show me identification, you will have to delete that footage and vacate the vicinity immediately."

The man still looked blankly at her but pressed some buttons on the camera and turned the screen toward her. The footage had been successfully deleted. She nodded approvingly, and the creep began to retreat into the alley beside the church.

Once he was out of sight, Heather made her way to her car where Beau was waiting for her revving his bike. She tried to

THE CRASH

match his enthusiasm but felt distinctly unnerved by the interaction. She glanced at Amber, who was blissfully unaware, and decided to put the file of the creep away instead of mentally shredding the exchange. Men like that were always worth keeping tabs on.

CHAPTER FIFTEEN

THE SON

Beau was putting Heather's driving skills—and her 1977 MK1 Ford Granada in mission brown—to the test. He didn't actually want to lose her to the forest, curving roads, and unexpected forks, but it was a fun game to see if she could keep up with the athletic metal musculature of his 2002 Harley-Davidson Road King. Beau knew both vehicles like the back of his hand, having worked on several Granadas, so he assumed it must be Heather's tenacity powering the car. He laughed in surprise as she deftly made the 90-degree left turn and was somewhat sad when the RV rolled into view because it meant their game of chase was over.

THE CRASH

He pulled up, and she parked at the end of the dirt road before the clearing, clearly keeping herself at a distance and ready to retreat.

"You drive like a maniac," she shouted, stepping out of the car.

"I could say the same about you."

"That's because I was following you!"

"You could've stopped if it was too much for you."

"Clearly, it wasn't." She seemed angry, but he could see past it to the self-satisfied adrenaline junkie. He could also tell that it was something she denied herself. She had to be responsible and reliable, and she knew that thrill-seeking was a slippery slope for someone like her. He'd looked in the mirror often enough to spot an addictive personality when he saw it. His problem, unlike the detective, was that he never denied himself anything.

"Well, you certainly handled yourself and lived to tell the tale. In exchange, I'll let you ask me five questions and do my best to answer them truthfully."

"I'm going to ask about your dad. Is that okay?"

Beau shrugged. "Why wouldn't it be?"

"We were literally just at his funeral."

"Well, considering my memory of him has been rigorously jogged, I think it's a great time for an interrogation."

"I'm not here to interrogate you."

"Sure, you're not. I bet you have your gun in your belt and a tape recorder in your jacket."

Heather opened her jacket and spun around, revealing an empty leather holster and a small notebook in her interior breast pocket. "You were half-right," she said.

"No gun?"

"Do I need it?"

"Not with me, but I'm going to guess you don't need to in general. You look like a woman who can handle herself."

She ignored the compliment and walked past him, looking around at the cars, particularly the ones surrounded by broken glass. She approached it with interest, her sturdy leather boots crunching over the debris.

"1965 Ford Mustang Convertible?" she asked.

Beau was stunned and struggled to speak. "Yeah… how did you know that?"

"My dad is obsessed with classic cars. He actually has a scale model of this one. Though his is in… better shape." She looked at him and opened her mouth before closing it again.

"You clearly have something to ask. So, ask. That's what I brought you here for."

"Will it count as one of my five questions?"

"Honestly, the five questions part was bullshit. You can ask me as much as you want while I'm still sober."

"All right. Was this car your dad's?"

Beau applauded her, drumming one palm with the fingertips of the other hand. "Astute observation, Detective," he answered in a posh English accent.

"Well, it was pretty easy to figure out. The others are in such great condition; it seems weird that the most expensive car here has clearly gone toe-to-toe with a crowbar."

"Baseball bat," he corrected her, grinning smugly. "I thought you were supposed to be some sort of detective?"

"You fix cars—a crowbar was the obvious choice, but on closer inspection, the dents are the wrong shape."

"Maybe there's hope for you yet," Beau taunted.

Heather ignored him again and walked over to the row of cars he was working on. She pointed at them one by one and correctly identified the year, make, and model. Beau was impressed. He'd initially invited her over because she was the only person in town that would come—but also because he was as curious about her and his dad's death as she was about him. However, as she moved onto the bikes and performed the same feat again, she spun around, her ponytail shining in the dappled sunlight, and Beau admitted he was genuinely glad for her company.

"Was I right?" she asked.

Beau swallowed hard. "Yeah. You got them."

He looked at her, taking in the details and layout of her face in a way he hadn't before. She was obviously good-looking, anyone could see that; but he now realized just how beautiful she was. Elegant and dainty, with high arched brows, full lips, defined bone structure, and upturned brown eyes. Her nose was slightly Grecian, with a bump in the middle section, which pulled her features together and tied her face up with a bow. Her body was slender, toned, and athletic, but he tried his best not to gawk at it, knowing that her observant eyes would catch him looking.

"So, how about that drink?" she asked, keeping it professional by removing her notepad.

"Yeah, sure."

He led the way toward the RV's entrance, and as he pushed open the unlocked front door, he heard Heather shift uncomfortably behind him on the leaf cover. "You leave your home unlocked?"

It must be a police officer's worst nightmare, especially one who catches serial killers, but Beau chuckled. "You'll soon realize that I have nothing worth stealing."

"What about you? Got any enemies?"

"Oh, yeah, plenty, but I figure if they wanted me dead, they would have done it already."

He stepped up into the RV and headed left into the cab where the seats had been swapped for storage and a box fridge. Heather headed straight toward the dismal living area and sat on the squeaky couch he'd picked up from the side of the road. At least the blankets on it were clean, though he was suddenly aware of how messy and musty the place was. While Heather flipped through her notebook, he covertly picked up some dirty clothes from the floor and cracked a window.

He poured them both a double whiskey into mismatched glasses and walked toward Heather who was giving him a strange look. It was somewhere between anger and pity, and Beau didn't like it one bit.

He threw his hands up after placing the drinks on the windowsill. "I know—I know. It's a shithole, but not everyone can afford to buy some house in the suburbs."

Heather shook her head and pointed at the side table. There was a baggy of cocaine with some remnants at the bottom and a line on a CD that he'd forgotten to snort. His blood ran cold. It wasn't his usual pick of poison, especially considering his dad's death, but he'd needed courage for the funeral.

"Are you going to arrest me?"

"No, but I will if you don't flush it."

He did as he was told without protest; it was such a tiny amount, and his usual dealer—a shady guy in a town over—said he'd have more in stock in a couple of weeks. Beau could easily wait that long. There was always booze to tide him over. Still, actually seeing it flush away stung just a little bit. That line would have gone down real smooth after his father's funeral, and for the first time, he regretted inviting the detective into his home.

He sat opposite her on the narrow bed after sheepishly returning from the bathroom. "Sorry about that."

"Like father, like son," she commented, half joking, but immediately screwing up her face in regret. "Sorry."

"You're not wrong. We were alike in a lot of ways."

"Oh yeah?"

The questioning had commenced, and he held up his side dutifully. "Bad with commitment. Bad with money. Bad with addiction. Bad with women."

Heather quirked a brow. "Oh yeah. Girlfriend trouble?"

"I've never been with a woman for longer than a week, so girlfriend trouble isn't exactly how I'd describe it."

"Why is that? Can't hold 'em down?"

"Total opposite. I've never found anyone I can stand for longer than that. Maybe I need someone more interesting. Like, someone who solves murders for a living."

Heather scoffed. "Are you seriously hitting on me after your dad's funeral?"

Beau shrugs. "I guess. What else am I going to do, cry?" His tone was sarcastic. "Plus, you ruined my fun, so now I really am out of options."

"Maybe you should find better ways of having fun."

"I can think of some better ways," Beau replied suggestively.

"You hit on me again, and I'll leave," Heather replied sternly.

Beau raised his hands in defeat. "All right, I'm sorry."

"Really though, maybe you should get some help with the drugs. I know people. I can write down some numbers." She pulled one of her cards from her jacket, flipped it over, and looked up at Beau questioningly; she clicked the pen hovering above the blank surface.

He bristled, his expression darkening. "I don't have a problem. I just like to have a little fun now and again."

"That's not what your file says."

"Oh, you did a background check?"

She recoiled, and he realized he'd become very rigid, his hands balling into fists. He was already taller than her, even more so considering the height advantage the bed had over the couch. He unfurled, took a sip of his drink, and offered a smile of apology to encourage her to continue.

She did, but her eyes stayed trained on his hands until he picked up a cigarette, each hand too occupied with a vice to be dangerous. She cleared her throat and returned to looking him in the eye. "Of course, I did. That's my job."

"Am I a suspect?"

Heather paused. "Who's asking the questions here?"

"Detective, be fair."

"I don't know."

"So, it was definitely murder."

"Unless you think your father would intentionally commit suicide while flying a plane, yes."

"My dad was way too self-obsessed to kill himself."

She gestured. "There you go then."

"Well, I'd have been hard-pressed to murder him considering I would've had to know where he was to poison him."

Heather tilted her head, underlining scribbled notes from prior days. She sighed, repeatedly tapping the pen's tip on a blank spot. "That's the thing, I have no proof that you didn't know where he was. I think it's unlikely, but you could lie, and I'd be none the wiser. That's why I never rule out the improbability until it becomes impossible. When I was investigating Dennis Burke, I even had a 'forest monster' on my list of suspects because there had been sightings of one. I don't believe in Bigfoot or anything like that, but I still kept it up there."

"I admire that, but it really wasn't me."

"I guess we'll see. Why didn't you speak at the funeral?"

"Didn't have anything nice to say."

"That bad?" Heather asked.

"He was good when he was around, never yelled, never spanked, but the problem is he was barely ever around. And then he left me, abandoned me with my mother until I moved out at twenty."

"Why do you think he left?"

"Well, considering what I caught him doing with his assistant, I'd say he ran off to screw her in some faraway country. Or maybe Texas. That's where they were both from originally."

"Your dad was having an affair?"

Beau blinked rapidly; he was near speechless. "Has nobody told you this?"

"Not for sure. There have been whispers, but most people struggle with speaking badly about your dad."

"Well, I can tell you that he was one hundred percent, undoubtedly sleeping with Pamela Bennett; and on the day he left, she was with him. They both got into the car together—I watched them—and drove to the airfield, where they abandoned the car in the middle of nowhere. So, either she got on that plane, or she became another forest monster."

Heather scribbled furiously in her notepad. "So, where's she? Does anybody know?"

"Nope, but I bet you'll find her. She was never far behind Dad. Followed him room to room like a puppy with separation anxiety." Heather nodded, looking a little stressed as she continued to make notes. Beau sipped his drink and chuckled. "Hey, take a breath. No need to worry too much. This is way easier than your last case."

She paused and looked up. "How so?"

"Well, my dad is already dead, so there's no one to save. History can't repeat itself, you know?"

What was supposed to be a moment of light-hearted deprecation went down like a lead balloon. Every feature on Heather's face hardened, and she slammed her notebook shut. Beau stood, stumbling over his words, trying to explain himself, but it was too late. Heather was already leaving. He attempted to beg her not to leave him alone right now. It was getting dark inside and outside of his head. He was sorry. He'd fix it. He needed a friend.

A panic was consuming his body that he wasn't familiar with, and everything he tried to say came out jumbled. Heather

THE CRASH

was already out the door by the time he uttered a coherent "Please."

"Thanks for the drink," she said coldly, referring to the untouched beverage, and slammed the RV door behind her.

Beau stood dumbfounded for a long time, his lip trembling and his buried emotions bubbling up toward his throat. Thunder rumbled in the distance, and he prepared himself for a very bad night.

CHAPTER SIXTEEN

THE SON

BEAU HAD SLEPT POORLY. EVEN THOUGH HE'D BECOME suitably drunk, he tossed and turned, thinking about Heather. Usually, he didn't care about awkward situations or hurting feelings because, as far as he was concerned, everyone he met was either an asshole or a moron, and most of the time, both. He didn't have friends and avoided the public unless he was looking for a fight, but Heather was different. She was intelligent, pretty, and funny. They had a better back-and-forth than Federer and Nadal, and there was something in him that wanted her to like him. Of course, he managed to irreparably blow it.

THE CRASH

"Stupid, stupid," he said, remembering the final blow of their conversation, and covered his face with a pillow in an attempt to suffocate himself.

As tempting as it was, he knew he'd lose his mind if he laid in bed all day feeling sorry for himself. So, powered by the manic phase of a sleepless night, he bounced out of bed, determined to make it up to Heather. He brushed his teeth, flossed for the first time in months, groomed himself, and put on some clothes that didn't stink of booze, cigarettes, or body odor. It was a difficult task, but worth doing. He knew he had to be presentable and sober to make the apology count.

Just as he was about to head into town, with the hopes that she'd be milling about somewhere, he received a text that filled him with dread all over again.

Dinner with Lucy and me tonight. Here. Formal. 7pm. Don't be late.

Family dinners were always dreadful affairs, but the ones eclipsed by funerals were brutal. Beau shivered at the thought of them all dressed in black at the long table, a fire flickering behind his mother's back and casting her into shadow. All the scene was missing was a raven to make it Poe-worthy.

Unfortunately, Beau also knew he had no choice but to attend. He knew he could theoretically say "no," but his mother had enough dirt on him to bury him ten times over. Drug-related secrets, mostly, that she kept from the police. Whether she'd ever utilize any of it, and embarrass herself in the process, he didn't know, but he didn't want to jump into the grave to find out if she'd grab the shovel.

There was also the added anxiety regarding the massive inheritance. He wasn't sure how it all worked, but until the money was completely and firmly in his bank account, it was an intangible dream that could easily be shattered by his mother's hands. So, for now, he was on his best behavior.

Beau arrived late and drunk, almost falling off his motorcycle to the dismay of Nancy, who stood in the doorway, her apron on and her hands on her hips. He hadn't found Heather, but he had found a bottom-shelf bottom of whiskey at Sherwood's with his name on it. It had passed the time gloriously, and he staggered up the pathway between the beds of flowers, unapologetic in his stance and with a big grin on his face. He wrapped his mother up in a hug, but she did not return the gesture.

"You're late," she hissed, wriggling free of his grasp. "And you smell like liquor."

"So nice to see you too, mother," he replied, still grinning, removing his arms, and shoving his hands into his pockets. He swayed and leaned against the side of the doorway.

"Did you drive here drunk?" she asked, looking at his poorly parked motorcycle.

"Just getting the party started."

"Jesus. Get inside before the neighbors see you."

"All right, all right." He thought it was nothing the neighbors hadn't seen before but staggered into the house all the same.

At the end of the hallway stood Lucy in a similar position to her mother. The only difference was when he neared, she opened her arms and welcomed the embrace.

"You've gotten tall," she said as if it had been years since they'd seen each other. He was twenty-six and knew he hadn't grown that much since the Christmas shortly after he'd turned twenty-five. She smelled like sandalwood and vanilla, and her clothes looked even more expensive than their mother's. He wondered how much an internship could possibly pay.

"I guess."

"Even taller than Dad." She backed away and looked him up and down. "God, you look so much like him."

He knew he didn't. Aside from the hair and the eyes, his genetics were all from their mother. Really, it was Lucy that looked like their dad, with her short face and conventional features.

"I guess," he said again, the booze hitting him hard now that he was relaxed.

THE CRASH

"I've missed you," she said, but it sounded insincere. She was just good at knowing what to say.

"You too."

"Come on, let's sit down and catch up while Mom finishes dinner." He'd forgotten she called her that. Mom. It sounded foreign. Too warm by half.

"Sounds good."

"I've opened a bottle of red. One of Dad's good ones from the cellar."

Beau didn't usually drink wine, but wasn't one to say no to any form of booze. He walked through to the dining room with her; his mother still stood in the doorway, her presence looming. Once they were safe inside with the heavy wooden door shut, he heard her heels click down the hallway back into the kitchen. He just prayed she wasn't making fish again.

The fire crackled in the dining room as it did in the living room, and he and Lucy took their usual seats—Lucy in the middle with the doors to her back and Beau at the end to the right of his father's seat. The proximity to his father's chair at the head of the table had allowed them secret dinnertime conversations as a child, and it still provided some comfort all these years later, as if he were still being shielded from his mother.

In a surprisingly unclassy move, Lucy sipped perilously from her full-to-the-brim glass. Weren't all the big shots obsessed with health smoothies and getting drunk off of one fifty-dollar old-fashioned? Lucy grinned at him, her lips stained purple, and she filled his glass up to a similarly full degree and dangerously slid it across the table. He, fortunately, looked at her in disbelief.

"Mother would've killed you for that."

Lucy's eyes glinted dangerously. There she was, his sister, the secret terror, the thrill seeker. He wondered if her life in California was as dull as he thought or if she had some dark secrets to keep the Ellis recklessness satiated. Maybe her day-to-day was exactly the same as his—work, party, sleep—but just of a more expensive variety. Perhaps she was drinking old-fashioned, but ten of them, and maybe she was doing blow, too, but the good stuff. Or maybe, this was the only place she could be who she really was because Beau was the only person alive whose opinion she didn't care about.

Beau wished the feelings were mutual, but unfortunately, Lucy was one of the few people in the world that he was desperate to impress. Typical sibling rivalry stuff but tragically one-sided. What did Lucy—twenty-two, beautiful, talented, successful, wealthy—have to be jealous of her older brother about?

It had always been the case. She had been the perfect golden child who'd easily attained perfect grades and was popular with her classmates, whereas Beau had been a dropout waiting to happen from day one. He didn't know why he was the way he was, or if he did, he didn't like thinking about it. A shrink would probably tell him it had something to do with his parents and how he was the only sibling old enough to remember all the fighting and their dad's disappearance, but Beau didn't know about any of that. He thought it was more likely he came off the assembly line wrong.

Lucy raised her glass and gulped it down, and Beau tried to copy her but quickly became nauseated and swapped to sipping while she drained the bowl and smugly poured herself another. She was becoming competitive, and he couldn't help but join in the games. He burped and gestured for her to pass the bottle. He caught the bottle, brought its lip to his, and tilted his head back to chug. Merlot was not a chugging drink, but he forced himself to drink at least two glasses worth before he put it down.

When he did, his mother stood in the doorway, cutlery in hand, and his sister silently applauded him. He poured the rest of the bottle into his glass and slid it over to Lucy, who did not catch it in time, resulting in a stupendous smash against the hardwood floor.

Pretending as if nothing were amiss, Nancy laid out the cutlery next to the already set bowls and left her rowdy, overgrown toddlers to return to the kitchen. Beau burped again and waited for round two, but Lucy didn't pour another drink. She tilted her head, amused as if watching a dog perform a beloved trick for the millionth time. Beau knew he'd been had. Lucy knew he'd get competitive and drunk; all the while, she stayed pleasantly tipsy and watched the catastrophe unfold. He raised his glass and nodded.

Touché, he thought. He had to hand it to her; she really was a master of manipulation.

Nancy returned with a large tray. At the center was a roasted chicken accompanied by roasted potatoes and grilled Brussels sprouts. Beau could go without the latter, but he'd eat it all the same. Even he couldn't deny his mother's prowess in the kitchen.

She sat back while they served themselves before putting tiny portions of each food on her own plate, but just as the kids were about to dig in, she stopped them by tapping a fork against her empty glass. For a moment, Beau thought she might be about to ask them to say grace—something he'd refused to do since his early teens—but what she said chilled him to the bone.

"Today, we remember your father. A wonderful father and husband and a local hero. Roland, we love you, and we'll miss you forever."

Beau was so drunk he'd almost forgotten about his dad's death, and he was also too drunk to deal with it right now. Nancy raised a glass to the empty seat next to Beau, and for a horrible second, he swore he could feel his father next to him, his breath wafting in his direction. He looked out of the corner of his eye, half expecting to see some shadowy figure, but all he saw was an oak chair and emerald green upholstery.

"Come on, raise a glass to your father," Nancy repeated, sounding a little desperate.

Reluctantly, they raised their glasses—one also empty, one overfull—to the empty chair and glanced nervously at each other as they turned back to their mother.

"Since when did you love Dad so much?" Beau asked, slurring a little already.

"You have wine around your mouth."

Beau wiped the dark red away on the back of his hand. "You've hated his guts for the past fifteen years. What's changed?"

"Nothing's changed. I've always loved your father. I've just been a bit frustrated with him, is all."

"A bit frustrated?" Lucy laughed. "You've done nothing but bitch about him, and now that he's dead, he's a hero and the love of your life? And then you expect us to follow suit even though you raised us to hate him too?"

"I did not."

"Yes, you did. You're a hypocrite," Beau interrupted. "And an actress. All of this, even in private, is for show. I wonder if you even put on an act for yourself, alone in your room, looking in the mirror and forcing tears. The perfect widower and her flawless husband who definitely didn't die while on a drug smuggling run." His tone was mocking, and even Lucy looked taken aback.

"I, I—" Nancy stammered, veins bulging in her forehead. Whether she was going to sob or scream was anyone's guess.

"And don't even get me started on the affairs," he doubled down. "You're going to sit there and tell me you have no ill will toward the man who screwed and ran off with his assistant and left you alone with two kids? Not to mention the babysitter, the cleaner, and his friend's wives. Why can't you just admit he was a shitty father and husband for what he did to us?"

"Yeah, Mom, all this stuff coming out about him is really tarnishing my career. He might be family, but he's still hurting us from beyond the grave," Lucy added.

Nancy opted to cry. "He may not have been perfect, but he was your father, and you should show some respect. You'll never see him again; don't you understand that?"

Beau shook his head slowly in disbelief. "Oh yeah, I know it. More than that, I'm glad. He fucked up my life, and frankly, I'd like to shake the hand of whoever poisoned him and then punch him in the face for killing the bastard before I got the chance."

Nancy looked aghast, and even Lucy paled. "You don't mean that, Beau."

"I fucking do. I wouldn't have poisoned him, though. I would've..." Beau tapped his chin as he thought. "I would've hanged him from the beams in his foreign motel and made it look like suicide. Wait. No, not embarrassing enough. Oh, I know—make it look like erotic asphyxiation! Or maybe I should've tracked him down with a gun and shot him through the head. A bit boring, I know, but guns are easy enough to get your hands on, and I'm a good shot."

"Beau!" Nancy gasped, pained as if she was the one shot.

THE CRASH

"How would you have killed him, Lucy?" Beau asked, ignoring their mother and delighting in the haunted look on his perfect sister's face. This was a competition of extremes she'd never win.

"Beau," Lucy said, echoing their mother, her eyes wide and frightened. "Dad sucked, but don't say things you can't unsay. And don't blame people for your bad choices. Our childhood wasn't perfect, but there's always a choice. You don't have to be a mess."

Beau's fun was over, and he was no longer hungry despite having eaten no more than two bites. He sipped at his wine, sinking lower into his seat as he looked between Lucy and Nancy, who busied themselves with their food. Whenever they did risk a glance at Beau, they looked as if they were calculating how much of what he said was true. Did he have the potential for murder, and were either of them next? If they'd asked him aloud, he would've told them that every person on the planet has the capability to take a life when pushed hard enough.

But they didn't ask. They just sat there in terrible, awkward, stilted silence.

CHAPTER SEVENTEEN

THE DETECTIVE

The conversation with Beau had been enlightening even if it had ended unpleasantly. Heather worried she'd overreacted to his comment at the end by storming off. There was much more to learn about the Ellis family, and it wasn't professional to break so easily. She was much sturdier in actual interrogations, but she'd been too friendly with Beau, treated him less like a suspect and more like a personal acquaintance, and gotten her feelings hurt in the process.

She hardly blamed Beau, as inappropriate as he was. The comment was accidentally cruel, not designed to maim, and it made her realize how much healing she still had to do after the Warren case. She loathed seeing police psychologists, but

THE CRASH

she considered asking for a referral. It had been mandatory for Gabriel to go, considering he killed a man in the line of duty, and he had nothing but praise for the woman he ended up talking to. She must've done something because he seemed to be handling things a lot better than she was—either that or he'd become a master at masking his instability.

Heather didn't really care for Briana, but she was glad Gabriel had a support system in her, his parents, and mental health professionals. She hoped he was reaching out to them if he needed help. It was unusual to ask for help in her profession, which led to a variety of sad outcomes, as the high rate of suicide and alcoholism indicated. So, it was nice to see someone break the cycle, and she hoped she'd be able to follow his footsteps along the unbeaten path.

She wished she could be there for him too. Regardless of the awkwardness that had formed between them, he was still her partner. Deciding to be proactive about their relationship, especially after having warmed to each other after dinner with his parents, she decided to invite him over to help with the investigation. She'd learned a lot via Beau, and her corkboard was starting to take shape, but she needed someone to bounce ideas off of. More than that, she needed the company of someone her own age. She loved going to see Gene and Karen, but she missed having a buddy to drink some beers with.

He responded to her text immediately and enthusiastically, giving her hope for their bond reforming. He was over within the hour, bringing two large boxes of chow mein and a six-pack of beers, just like old times. The dogs had clearly missed him even more than she had, and he threw himself into his favorite groove on the couch as if he had never left.

Maybe it's all in your head, Heather thought, but sadly, she knew it wasn't. That was the thing with shared trauma and all its aftershocks. Sometimes you bonded, and sometimes you drifted apart. In the first instance, you feel that person is the only one who understands you in the entire world. Or, on the flip side, they remind you too much of all that went wrong. Usually, Heather was a drifter, but she didn't want to drift, not from Gabriel. Julius had reminded her of how much drifting sucked.

How much of his friendship had she missed out on by offering him nothing but radio silence ever since leaving the city?

Gabriel sat on the couch, slurping up noodles and nodding while Heather pointed to each pinned photo on her board and gave him some background. She told him about the four members of the Ellis family: Beau, the black sheep; Lucy, the golden child; Nancy, the cold mother; and Roland, the seemingly perfect father. She also showed him the photo of the tattoo Julius had helpfully sent over and listed her theories about Roland's possible locations for the past fifteen years.

Gabriel knew most of it already, considering he'd grown up in Glenville and talked to Tina frequently, but when Heather mentioned Pamela leaving with Roland that day—repeating Beau's joke about her running off to be another forest monster—Gabriel's eyes widened.

"What if she didn't go with him? What if she's buried in the woods, and he took off because he'd killed her?" he asked.

He really was shaping up to be a fine detective, but Heather shook her head. "Way ahead of you. As soon as Beau told me about the abandoned car at the airstrip, I called Gene, and he sent me his log of forest sweeps. They did one the day after Roland and Pamela disappeared, and there were no signs of foul play or a body."

"All right, so she definitely went with him. But what if she killed him?"

Heather paused. She hadn't thought of that. All she'd thought about was where Pamela was now, not whether she was a suspect. But it made sense. She'd likely been with Roland, wherever he'd taken off from, and it was strange that she hadn't tagged along for the trip.

"It's not a bad idea. Print a picture of her to add to the board."

"On it," Gabriel said, sliding a brand-new laptop out of his bag, a significant improvement on Heather's ancient beast. He looked up at her as it booted up. "Do you think he was planning to land in Glenville?"

"Hard to say. His low altitude prior to the crash implies that he was, but maybe he was just already dead."

"Jesus. This case is nuts."

"You're telling me."

THE CRASH

"Just so I'm clear, it was definitely murder, but we have no idea where he took off from, who was with him, or who did it?"

"Yup, except it was *probably* murder, technically," Heather clarified, putting a lid on her pen and sticking the last of the sticky notes to the board. She sat heavily on the couch, cracked a beer, and opened the top of the chow mein. It really did feel just like old times.

"I mean, I know the family seems suspicious. But if he was down in Mexico, smuggling drugs, it was probably someone he was running with, right? Seems a little out of our jurisdiction and a little—"

"Impossible to solve?"

"I was going to say tricky, but impossible works too."

Heather groaned and sunk into the armchair in the corner. Then she sat bolt upright and looked back at the board. "Pamela is a good lead though; you're right. Maybe if we find her, we can find out what Roland has been up to all these years."

"I've just Googled her to get you that photo, so let's see what she's been up to." Gabriel typed for a few minutes, clicked around, and his eyes widened, flitting back and forth as he rapidly read. "Huh."

"What is it?" Heather asked.

Gabriel beckoned Heather over, and she joined him on the couch. It was an article with a smiling blonde woman who looked strangely like Amber. Her name was Pamela Bennett, and she'd been found dead eighteen months ago in a seaside villa in Valle de Bravo, Mexico. She'd been shot in the gut and bled out from her injuries and remained a Jane Doe until a local police officer, who happened to be up in Texas, had seen Pamela's picture on the news and had invited her family down to identify the body. She was then transported back to her hometown of Grapevine, Texas, where she was laid to rest.

Heather blinked slowly at the article, rereading it over and over again, her noodles going cold on the coffee table. Neither spoke for a long time until Heather asked, "Do you think Roland killed her and fled?"

Gabriel struggled to find the words. "I don't know. Maybe. And someone found out and killed him? Maybe one of her family members?"

"Do you think they would've known that Roland existed? If so, why haven't they reached out? He's been all over the news."

"This is crazy."

"Yeah. Now we have two insane murders to solve."

"At least we now know that he was definitely in Mexico." He paused, looking at the article. "Unless Pamela's death is completely unrelated to him. Could've parted ways years ago."

Heather stood and paced around, nursing her beer with one hand and her thick mane of hair with the other. Neither action satiated her, so she opened her living room window and lit an increasingly rare cigarette, perching on the arm of the couch.

"Was the villa rented or owned? Can you find out?" she asked.

"It was purchased in 2011 by a man named Dallon Riles."

"Dallon Riles. Dallon Riles. Dallon Riles." Heather chewed on the name before jumping to her feet again and writing the name on a piece of paper. She continued to write while Gabriel continued to search.

"Found her on Facebook," he said. "Her last post was in 2008, just before they absconded. Talk about ancient history…"

"Dallon Riles is an anagram for Roland Ellis!" Heather exclaimed. "He was the owner of the villa!" It felt like a eureka moment, but Gabriel was still buried in the laptop. Heather clicked at him. "Hello? Did you hear me?"

Gabriel slowly looked at Heather. "You're going to want to see this."

She sat beside him, her cigarette having gone out for lack of puffing, and looked at Pamela's old Facebook page.

Pamela was standing with her arm around a man outside of the Texas State Penitentiary. They were both smiling, his mouth filled with teeth. He was tan and muscular with a greasy slick of black hair and a large, ropey body covered in tattoos. The photo was from 2005, and the caption read, "Happy release day, Francisco. I'll love you forever! Pam xoxo."

Heather nodded to Gabriel, who was already on it. It didn't take long to find a list of Franciscos released in 2005 from Texas State Penitentiary. Luckily for Heather and Gabriel, there were only three. One was sent away for sexual assault, the other for armed robbery, and the last one, Francisco Medina, had gone away for drug trafficking.

"You got a theory?" Gabriel asked, gleeful to be a part of emerging leads.

"I think Pamela was the bait, and she lured in a big fish, ready for Francisco to reel in," Heather said. "Go back to that photo and zoom in on his arms."

Gabriel did as she instructed, but the photo turned into grainy, mushy pixels after zooming in. A tattoo on his right bicep looked like an image with text underneath, but whether it was the same as Roland's was impossible to say.

They also googled Francisco Medina, but nothing much turned up. A few Spanish articles about his arrest that Gabriel translated, and then nothing after his release. It was a dead end for now, but Heather was going to bring all of this to Tina and her contacts in Seattle, and together they were going to get out of this maze.

She cracked another beer and offered one to Gabriel, who was now deeply absorbed in his phone despite their numerous revelations. He looked at the beer and shook his head sheepishly.

"Sorry, Briana wants to meet up."

Heather lowered the beer, closed his laptop, and handed it over. "Understood."

"This has been good, though, really good. Call me if you find out anything else or want to talk about the case. It feels nice to be useful again. Desk work sucks."

"Will do."

After some awkward goodbyes and farewell dog pats, Heather lit another smoke and opened her laptop. She had a lot of printing to do and a metric ton of notes to make. It was going to be a long night, but weren't they all?

CHAPTER EIGHTEEN

THE SON

Beau was sitting in the dining room at his parents' home for the second day in a row, only this time, he was alone—aside from the ghost of his father and the two silver dogs sitting patiently to his left. They were drooling over the steak he'd made himself. It wasn't particularly good and was probably better suited for pedigree dogs, but he wasn't about to waste free Wagyu even if it was overdone and underseasoned. He was just glad it wasn't burned, unlike most of what he made on the camp stove in the RV.

Much to the horror of his relatives and ancestors in the photographs and paintings on the walls, he served his steak with some shoestring fries, onion rings, and ketchup. Though to his credit, he did pair it with a lovely red wine stolen from the cellar. One swing and several misses, according to the foodies of the Internet, but his crime against beef didn't stop him from enjoying the taste as he warmed himself by the fire in his mother's seat.

Even the dogs couldn't deter him from his relaxation session with their incessant dribbling. He didn't mind dogs, though he was more of a cat person. He had to admit they were exceedingly polite. So, when his mother decided to head up north to her favorite wellness spa, he was happy to volunteer to dog and house sit—for a decent paycheck, of course, as his inheritance money wouldn't be in his hands for another three weeks, according to the executor of his father's estate.

Eyes closed and mouth full of a particularly succulent bite, Beau hardly registered the creaking noise at first. It was an old house, after all, and that made it particularly noisy. However, when the second creak came, he reluctantly opened his eyes and looked around the dining room. He hadn't bothered with the overhead lights, thinking the candle in front of him and the fireplace behind him were enough. He realized he was wrong as he stared at his father's chair. It was almost completely swallowed by shadow, and this time he wasn't entirely sure if there wasn't a dark figure occupying it.

Come on, man, you're jumping at shadows, he thought as he swallowed his bite, eyes fixed on the chair.

He hadn't expected the house to be so creepy, but it made sense when he thought about it. In his entire life, he had never been there alone at night. Maybe because his mother didn't trust him, but someone else was always around no matter what. Sometimes it was staff, sometimes Lucy, but almost always it was Nancy, watching him with an eagle eye.

He'd hoped Lucy would still be here. He wanted to talk about their dad; she was the only person who knew him like he did, even if she had a more favorable view of him. Unfortunately, Lucy had friends and a social life, so she was up in Seattle for the night at a twenty-first birthday party. Beau wasn't even sure he'd had a twenty-first birthday party, though Lucy's had indeed been something to behold. Or at least it seemed that way from the professional photos he'd seen on social media while using the library computer.

Thunder struck, and one of the dogs bolted under the table. The weather had been getting progressively worse, and though Beau pretended not to, he still held on to his childhood fear of storms. He leaned to the side to look at the poorly hidden, quaking animal. He could relate and held out a hand for comfort. The big scaredy cat pressed his head into Beau's palm, and the other braver dog decided to take the opportunity to lick his hand.

"Ew!" Beau grumbled, but as thunder struck again, the windows rattled, and the house groaned, he was secretly grateful to have their companionship. He was so glad, in fact, that as he became full—his stomach used to subsisting on scraps—he cut the last of the steak into two and offered it to the animals. They ate it gratefully, the frightened one even slinking out from his hiding spot.

"Come on, boys, let's go watch TV."

The word boys got them wagging, and they enthusiastically followed him down the dark hallway and toward the drawing room, as his mother called it. He couldn't remember when it had gotten so dark. It always crept up on him in the winter, and forgetting where the light switches were, he used his tiny flip phone's screen to guide the way.

At the front door, just as he was about to turn right toward a night of Sons of Anarchy and expensive whiskey, a flash of lightning flickered on the other side of the windowed front door. He froze, momentarily and irrationally terrified that Roland's charred silhouette would be on the other side, his jaw hanging low because of the screaming. Of course, there was nothing there, but it didn't stop Beau from looking over his shoulder as he entered the living room.

Once his heart rate had settled, Beau made himself comfortable, nestling into the expensive lounge set and pressing a button to turn the seat into a recliner. The dogs hopped up next to him even though they weren't supposed to, but they kept their distance, and he felt comfortable as he sipped his drink, turned on the TV, and pulled the toggle on the vintage lamp on the side table.

THE CRASH

His heart stopped. Once it started going again, he laughed, his hands tingling. He'd forgotten about the oil painting. He wasn't sure how, considering how often he thought of it, but it had caught him by surprise, his family's ghostly visages floating in the dark, staring down at him in judgment.

"Screw you guys," he spat, sloshing his drink around and looking away from them.

He focused intently on the screen, and after pressing play, he tried to focus and patted the closest dog to calm his nerves, but he couldn't shake the feeling of being watched; and every time he'd glance in the direction of the painting, he'd see his father's face and remember how he looked in death. Blue-tinted, afraid, high out of his mind, scorched. It frightened him, his heart pounding despite his reassurances, but it also irritated him. His father looked so judgmental, wondering what had happened to his chubby, adorable little son, who hoped to be a baseball player or a rockstar.

"*You* happened, you absent asshole."

Unable to take it any longer or concentrate on his show, Beau put his drink on the coffee table and ran at the painting with a war cry. He jumped up and tore it from the wall, hook and all. The missing strip of wallpaper was a problem for Morning Beau, the hard-done-by Jekyll to his Hyde.

Then he marched upstairs with determination, not even caring about the dark, the storm, or the bumps in the night. The dogs dutifully followed him, their nails clicking rhythmically on the stairs and hallway floor as Beau neared his father's office door. When he reached it, he tried the knob, expecting it to be locked. Instead, it creaked open, a tiny golden key twisted in the keyhole. He wondered if his mother had ventured inside after Roland's demise.

Beau stepped inside and shivered from the cold. It reeked of dust, dampness, and decay. The books on the shelves had likely gone to rot, and the dark red carpet was lifting at the edges. He was sure it was a haven for spiders and other creepy crawlies, and he dumped the painting on the floor, keen to make his exit, but the door, blowing shut in the wind, stopped him. It felt like divine intervention, so he turned on the light instead.

The office was grand but cozy with burgundy walls, leather furniture, a huge oak table, oil paintings of dark forests and glistening lakes, and an impressive collection of nonfiction tomes about history and business.

For reasons beyond Beau's understanding, he felt drawn to the chair behind the stately desk. He sat, spun, and wondered if he should build an office when constructing his new home. There wouldn't be much purpose for it, but he'd never felt manlier than with a massive slab of oak laid out in front of him, a stuffed barn owl to his left, a sepia globe to his right, and an array of fountain pens before him.

Intrigued by the room he had never been allowed to enter as a child, Beau began to rifle through the drawers. He wasn't sure if he was being guided by a higher power or whether Heather had worn off on him, but for some reason, he knew he would find something meaningful.

He quickly found what he didn't know he was looking for. A hidden drawer—a trick he was familiar with—was carefully covered by a stack of tedious paperwork. Inside the secret slot was a baggy of cocaine, a black-and-white printed leaflet for a Mexican realty company, and a series of Polaroid photos of Pamela. The latter was the only one that shocked him. He'd seen his father and Pamela whispering sweet nothings, but to see tasteful but explicit photographs of the woman was too much evidence for his liking. Sure, it finally confirmed every theory he'd ever had about the two's love affair, but something about the slap-in-the-face confirmation sent him reeling.

He poured out some of the cocaine and pocketed the bag and leaflet with the intention of giving both to Heather. Offering up cocaine would show strength of character, and she didn't have to know he'd sampled some of the goods.

He chopped up some lines and snorted them by pressing his face close to the wood that still smelled like beeswax polish. The drugs smelled funny and didn't seem to have the instant kick he was used to. For a few panicked moments, he worried that this, too, was laced with cyanide; but then he realized, after fifteen years, it had likely just expired. He pulled the baggy from his pocket and saw a strange brownish hue. He didn't know much about pharmacology, but he could bet that meant it was

THE CRASH

no longer potent. He rubbed some on his gums to no avail and cursed under his breath. Disappointing, but at least it wasn't fatal.

He liked being in the office, but he could see his breath, so he turned to look at the fireplace. To his surprise, it was full of fresh firewood and kindling, but he didn't have to look far for an explanation. Atop a table in the corner that accompanied a recliner was an empty of sherry glass and a pile of papers. Beau wheeled himself over and saw that it was a pile of overdue bills, and each one was covered in water droplets. With gut-churning realization, he knew his mother had sat in this room recently, crying her eyes out over the debt her husband had left her in.

Beau knew he could use the drugs and the photos to hurt her, but something in him resonated with the woman, abandoned by a man who was always so full of promises. Roland had ruined both of their lives, and there was no need to drag her name through the mud any further. Beau knew he was embarrassing enough as a son and that his mother's determination to not tarnish Roland's name had been less about the man himself or the town that loved him so much as it was about self-preservation.

In a rare act of benevolence, Beau lit the fire, gathered up the photos, removed the bag of drugs from his pocket, and cut the painting out of the frame with a knife. He put the images and drugs atop the picture, rolled it up, and threw it all onto the flames. It burned satisfyingly, and he watched as the inferno devoured the dark parts of his family's past. Once it was done and the fire ran out of steam, he left the cold room to return to the dogs, drinks cabinet, and TV. As he cozied up beneath a blanket, he looked up at the blank spot on the wall and noticed a weight he hadn't realized he'd been carrying was absent from his usually aching chest. Sinking beneath the comfort of the blanket, Beau took his first deep breath in years.

CHAPTER NINETEEN

THE FATHER

2007

66 "ARE YOU SURE YOU'RE READY FOR THIS, HONEY?" Pamela asked, her blouse partly unbuttoned, revealing a lacy bra as she bent forward over the glossy desk. Roland was dumbstruck, trying to remember how to speak English as she let her hair down and shook out the curls. Over the past few months, she had transformed herself into some sort of 1950s pinup girl, and he loved that the makeover was entirely for his benefit. The big blond hair, the pointed pumps, the stockings with the pinstripe, the

THE CRASH

skintight pencil skirt, the red lipstick. She was the Marilyn to his JFK, and he'd never been happier.

When she straightened up, she looked at him quizzically and, seeing his slackjawed expression, giggled and blew him a kiss. In her soft, manicured hands, she held the silver tray that usually housed Roland's fountain pens. His Sailor, Caran D'Ache, Waterman, Visconti, Aurora, and prized Montblanc pens had each been replaced by slender white lines. Three for him and three for her.

He didn't even care where she'd put his collection. They could be in the fire for all he cared because, right now, it was all about her. She sidled up to him, kicking off her heels as she went, hips swaying to the jazz playing quietly from the record player in the corner. Her dimples deepened as she got close, the flattering amber glow of the firelight enhancing her already extraordinary beauty.

Roland craned his neck and glanced at the calendar on his computer screen. It was 10:30 p.m. on Monday, June 5, 2007. The kids were both indeed asleep, Nancy was visiting her sick father in Portland, and he had no meetings scheduled for the following day.

"Ready as I'll ever be," he said, flashing Pamela an election-winning smile.

Pamela perched on his lap delicately, held up the tray, and placed a rolled-up one-hundred-dollar bill in his hand. Roland looked at the money and chuckled.

"Couldn't have used a one?"

"You gotta do this right. It's all about luxury, baby."

He loved her accent. It sounded like home dipped in honey. That voice of hers could convince him to do just about anything. Not that he often needed convincing.

"All right. So, three each?"

"I like your enthusiasm, but let's start with one."

He looked up at her, pulled her in for a kiss, and then snorted the nearest line. The high was almost instant. Pupils blown, reality shifted, heart pounding. He looked at Pamela in wonder as she snorted her own line. She even made that look pretty, he thought, and when she looked back at him, she clapped a hand over her mouth, muffling a raucous laugh.

"My God, look at you," she whispered.

"I feel amazing."

"I bet you do. This is the good shit. Best in the world."

"I had no idea you lived such a sexy, dangerous double life," he growled in her ear, the scent of hairspray and perfume filling his nostrils.

Pamela laughed. "I don't know about sexy, but it certainly is dangerous."

"That sounds exciting."

"Oh, baby, you have no idea."

This was a whole new side of Pamela. She'd been a dutiful assistant, a little quiet at first but sweet as pie, and when their relationship had shifted into unprofessional waters, things had still been a little tense at first, even if the sneaking around was fun. Pamela had wanted more, and Roland hadn't known how to give it to her. Buying her her own place in town helped to satisfy her demands, but it also gave him a place to escape to. He hung his hat there three nights a week, and though she couldn't cook or mix a cocktail to save her life, the warmth of her love was better than anything his wife had ever made.

After a year together, she'd revealed her darkest secret. When she'd sat Roland down with a solemn look on her face, he prepared himself to hide their love child from his wife, but instead, Pamela told him something he would've never guessed in a million years. She was running drugs across the border for her ex-boyfriend Francisco Medina. Roland hadn't believed her at first. His Pamela? A drug mule? No way. However, the more detail she revealed, the more convinced he became. It turned out that being cute was the perfect cover for crime; nobody ever questioned a pretty girl in a dinky car with a suitcase full of bikinis.

For years this had been her life, sending money to her family, buying designer clothes, living in upscale rentals all over America, and passing it all off as a girl who just loved to travel. Roland had admittedly wondered about her frequent trips out of town but had never put two and two together.

Pamela had been taken aback by his unwavering support of her crimes, not realizing that Roland had sniffed out an excellent business opportunity. One that would be a game changer.

THE CRASH

His other businesses were doing okay, though he'd never been great at the profit side of things—but this Francisco guy? There was a man who knew a thing or two about making money. Despite everything Roland had built in Glenville, including his family, he couldn't deny that Mexico was calling his name.

"I want in," he said, out of the blue, picking up the bill again and going in for line two. His heart was pounding in his ears, and he wanted to speak faster than his mouth would move.

"What do you mean you want in?" Pamela laughed. "You want to move drugs? Roland, baby, you're the mayor of Glenville; you have a family. You can't have both."

"What if I don't want both?"

"Come on, you don't mean that. That's the drugs talking."

He couldn't tell if she was right but knew his life lacked something. His biggest thrill was sneaking around with his personal assistant, and as great as that was, he needed more than that if he was going to feel satisfied on his deathbed.

"Think about it, Pammy. Being a mayor is the perfect cover. I invent a business opportunity down in Mexico that gives us an excuse to go down there for meetings. My wife barely asks questions, and no one else would, that's for sure. We could use my plane, rent a vacation home to give Border Patrol a reason for visiting, and then we move the drugs back up to America and drop them off wherever Francisco wants. It'd be easy. No one would ever suspect a guy like me. A *mayor*. I'm a very well-respected man with no ties to drugs or crime of any kind. I could even be at home most of the time and use the money to save up for my kids' college funds and help out around town. It's the best of both worlds."

He was out of breath once he'd finished, and Pamela looked at him in awe before shaking her head. "No, you can't. I won't let you. You'll get caught. Eventually, everyone always does."

"Pammy, it's perfect," he insisted. "We can be together in Mexico. You can even live there full-time if you want. I can live two lives, just like you. In Glenville, I'm a family man and a dutiful mayor, and in Mexico, I'm wild and free."

She smiled, but it didn't quite reach her eyes. "I don't know."

"I don't even have to be a resident to buy property down there. My buddy has a whole empire he bought up to rake in the tourist cash. We could even rent the place out in the meantime, make even more money."

He could see her warming to the idea, her smile widening. She snorted another line and threw her hair back when she came up.

"I think you're nuts," she said.

"I might be nuts, but you have to admit it's a great idea."

"It's a dumb idea... but if you're really in, I can talk to Francisco next week."

"Oh, I'm in, baby; I'm *all* the way in."

Roland snorted the last line from the tray and tackled Pamela onto the carpet. Despite her protests, she squealed and jokingly fought him off before grabbing the sides of his face and kissing him passionately. When they pulled away, he looked down at her, picturing the exact same scene but on the beaches of Mexico, and knew he'd never been surer of anything.

CHAPTER TWENTY

THE DETECTIVE

HEATHER PULLED UP TO THE CURB THAT BORDERED THE Silva family's front yard and parked when she saw that Gabriel was not outside waiting for her. She couldn't blame him for wanting to hide inside. The mowed lawns of Glenville suburbia were crunchy underfoot with frost, and the adjacent street gutters, sidewalks, and roads were slick with ice. The morning air, too, had lost its baby teeth sometime in October, and its brand-new incisors, canines, bicuspids, and molars packed a forceful bite.

Warming her hands against the dusty A/C vents, Heather repeatedly yawned, her eyes watering from her lack of sleep and the aggressive blast of dry heat. After mere seconds, she turned it away, feeling her lashes and brows begin to singe. Burt at Pacific Silver had fixed it for free, but she feared it worked a little too well post-restoration.

She beeped her horn and continued to wait for Gabriel, but when he still didn't emerge from the lightless house, she took the opportunity to recline her seat and close her eyes. She was just resting them—as her dad would say—but jerked awake shortly after as a car backfired across the road. With unfocused eyes, she looked at the analog dashboard clock. It had been fifteen minutes since she'd arrived, and there was still no sign of Gabriel.

Heather lowered her window, hoping to hear the boiling of a kettle or the thumps of Gabriel jumping down the stairs, but the world outside her car was completely silent aside from the merry song of early birds catching worms.

She decided to text him, thinking he'd likely slept through his alarm. It wouldn't be the first time. Knowing it was cold and he was accompanying her voluntarily on his day off, she sweetened the pot with promises of a complimentary breakfast at Dottie's before work. As usual, there was a lot to do today, but none so pressing that they couldn't stop for bacon and eggs first—even if doing so would lead to their age-old argument of crispy versus chewy and scrambled versus fried.

Gabriel read her message immediately and began typing. She scoffed, confident that she'd won him over. She looked over to the front door, expecting him to barrel out the door any second now.

Her phone dinged, and she looked down at her screen.
Gabriel: *Sorry. I'm already at Nancy Ellis's house.*
Heather: *???*
Heather: *I told you I was picking you up.*
Gabriel: *Totally forgot. Sorry.*
Heather: *I guess we can always get lunch after the interview.*
Gabriel: *No bueno. I've got plans with Briana. Maybe another time.*

Okay. See you in five, she typed but didn't send, frustrated by their return to weirdness. Why would he leave without her? Heather didn't believe for a second that he'd forgotten. It seemed like he couldn't endure being in the car or catching a bite with her anymore. Not sober, at least. Was that the only reason things had returned to normal at dinner? Because he'd been drinking?

The idea that her presence was so unpleasant he needed to socially lubricate made her feel queasy. She used to drink before her mother-in-law came over, and that woman had been a real piece of work. Heather knew she could also be a bit of a pill, but she wasn't a complete witch, was she?

Speaking of witches, she thought as she pulled up to Nancy's house. The wispy woman was waiting in the doorway, wearing a flour-coated floral apron covering a lemon-yellow tea dress and a glower that would make the devil quiver. Heather attempted to chastise herself for thinking hateful thoughts about a grieving widow, but as Nancy began to tap her foot impatiently, animosity won out in the struggle for moral order.

She parked behind Gabriel's car in the steep driveway and politely trotted toward the front door with a wave and a pleasant expression. Nancy's face didn't change, but Heather maintained the one-sided conviviality, even though Nancy's body language implied they might be doing their interview on the doorstep.

Heather craned her neck to look up at the angry woman. Nancy's color-coordinated stilettos extended her already ample height past six feet, and Heather's above-average five foot eight inches had never felt more insignificant.

"Good morning, Mrs. Ellis," Heather started. "Beautiful dress. A tad cold for it though."

"I have the fire going," Nancy retorted.

"Wow, that must be nice. I wish I had a fireplace," Heather admitted, shamelessly brown-nosing and looking over Nancy's shoulder to the roaring hearth in the living room.

Nancy sighed. "I suppose you want to come in, too, don't you?"

"If you don't mind."

Nancy didn't respond but stepped back into the hallway, allowing Heather to seek shelter from the elements. Heather rubbed her freezing hands together, feeling like an orphan in a Dickens novel—though she hoped Nancy might have something better to offer than gruel.

"Detective Bishop," Nancy whispered, looking over her shoulder. "Your partner has been here for half an hour drinking all my coffee from the cafetière and refusing to ask me any questions. I hope you'll be able to wrap this up so I can resume my day."

"Of course, Mrs. Ellis, my apologies for my partner," Heather responded, trying to keep the mounting fury from polluting her professional diction.

What was Gabriel thinking? Performing an interview alone without the lead detective was bad enough, but Mrs. Ellis was an interviewee that was way out of his league. Heather cussed Gabriel out in a fictitious argument that may have soon become a reality if it wasn't for the house's distracting grandeur.

There were oil paintings on the walls, presumably of Nancy's family, considering the features and statures of those immortalized in paint, and a red runner carpet that made up the backbone of the shiny floorboards of the hallway.

To her left and right, not unlike Mr. Ellsworth's home, were large doorways that led into even larger rooms. However, unlike the funeral home, these rooms had been brought into the twenty-first century by glossy white paint and classically styled yet clearly contemporary pieces of furniture. It was beautiful, but despite the crackling fireplace, the ostentatious layout and clinically clean furniture left her feeling cold.

Nancy eyed her suspiciously as she looked around, and Heather quickly reeled in her curiosity. However, the darker rectangular spot on the wall in the living room—where the bleaching effects of sunlight had clearly been blocked—specifically caught her attention.

She wondered what had inhabited that large, central spot. Such an inordinate piece of art was undoubtedly expensive and not easily parted with.

In a home so intensely kept up, its removal was clearly a recent act. Nancy did not strike Heather as the type to leave a tear in the wallpaper for long. This meant that the absent painting had likely been of Roland, but that also struck Heather as strange considering how much Nancy loved her late husband. True, her grief could be so painful that she couldn't bear to look at him, but as they walked along the hallways, Heather saw

THE CRASH

plenty of paintings of the woman's late father. Maybe the two were different kinds of grief. Heather had no idea, having neither a dead husband nor a dead father.

They rounded the corner into the kitchen where Gabriel sat contentedly at the marble island. The smell of the five sugars in his coffee announced his presence before Heather even laid eyes on his agreeable face.

He was wearing a white button-up and slacks, a far cry from his usual outfit, and she realized—with a degree of pride, her anger further fading—that he'd dressed up to impress Mrs. Ellis into spewing information. Heather had had a similar idea, and so she sat beside him, the two of them a visage of ironed clothes, smelling of shampoo and body wash. She was wearing off on him, and perhaps he wouldn't need her at all in a few years.

Mrs. Ellis looked at them, not with her usual scorn but a neutral acceptance, as if they'd passed the test to sit at her table. She was cooking something on the stove and returned to it, her back to them. It was a defense mechanism to hide one's face and keep your hands busy, but Heather didn't mind as long as she told the truth when she talked.

Heather cleared her throat and poured herself a coffee. "Mrs. Ellis, we don't want to take up much of your time, but we do have some questions about your late husband, Roland Ellis."

"Yes, I thought that was clear, Detective. I hardly thought this unexpected visit was a bid for my friendship. You hardly seem the type to vie for an invite to my parties."

The clothing only went so far, Heather realized. She was still lower middle class at best, and to the crème de la crème of Glenville, a well-put-together outfit and a detective badge only slightly elevated her from the people that mowed Mrs. Ellis's lawns.

"Yeah, you got me. I am not the dinner party type. Wouldn't know which fork to use," Heather affirmed, hoping her self-deprecation would amuse Nancy. It didn't.

"Well, ask away," Nancy snapped, a high-pitched note of manic impatience in her voice. "Mind you, I'm not sure why you or Sheriff Peters care about Roland. He's already dead; we know how he died, so what else is there to solve? Though, I suppose there's little more to do in a small town."

Heather remained agreeable, letting Nancy get her licks in. "You're right about that. Pretty boring around here most of the time."

"I'm surprised there's enough to do to justify there being so many of you. I hadn't even seen this one before." Nancy gestured with a thumb over her shoulder at Gabriel.

Gabriel crinkled his nose as if smelling something unpleasant. He wasn't so used to being disrespected. Being an officer of the law in a small town essentially made you royalty, but Heather was used to being spat on in the big city by all manner of people.

"You're right, ma'am. We do spend most of our time throwing winos in the drunk tank. But investigating your husband's death is far from a time waster for bored cops," Gabriel said dryly.

Nancy glanced over her shoulder, bemused by Gabriel's comment. "And why is that?"

Heather nodded at Gabriel and tapped in. "We know that Roland died of acute cyanide poisoning, but that means—especially when you factor in the large quantity of cocaine and that suicide seems unlikely—that we're looking at a possible homicide as well as several federal and state drug crimes."

Nancy froze. "Well, good luck arresting a dead man."

"We're not looking to posthumously punish Roland. We just want to know who gave him the drugs. Don't you want to know who killed your husband?"

"I don't know, Detective. Will finding that out bring him back? Or undo the fifteen years that I spent as a single mother? Or will it simply smear the name of a beloved man?" Nancy retorted, stirring her cooking ferociously.

"It might bring you some peace," Heather offered.

"I doubt that, but enough dilly-dallying. Ask your questions."

Heather sipped her coffee and braced herself. "What was your relationship with your husband like?"

"The same as most marriages. Filled with ups and downs. Roland was a big personality. He could make you feel like the sun rose just for you, and he could also make you feel like it would never rise again."

Heather scribbled in her notebook. "Did you argue a lot, or were the ups and downs more nonverbal?"

"A bit of both. Perhaps more shouting than silent spells, but not any more than any other couple," Nancy replied, scattering spices across the surface of what Heather had decided was a spicy pumpkin soup.

"What did you argue about?"

"The usual. Money, work, children."

"What about adultery?" Heather asked.

Nancy froze again and turned slowly to face Heather and Gabriel, her hands clutching the edge of the marble counter behind her. "Who on earth have you been talking to?"

"I'm not at liberty to say, but I will say that I have multiple sources on the subject. Enough to push me to ask such an uncomfortable question."

Nancy pursed her lips, seemingly unhappy about the entire line of questioning to talk but also unable to stop herself from talking. Heather had expected to be forcibly removed after the first question, but Nancy was more accommodating than expected. It might be the first time she'd been able to talk truthfully about her husband, considering her social standing, and Gabriel and Heather had adopted the role of therapists to this unwilling patient.

"On my end, it was," Nancy whispered eventually, returning to her soup. "As I said, Roland was a big personality, and a man like that attracts all sorts of people. Businessmen, women—"

"Criminals?" Gabriel asked.

Nancy threw another glance his way, this one less amused than before. "Yes, again, as I said. He attracted all sorts."

Heather looked between the two and chimed in, keeping the train on the tracks. "And what about Pamela Bennet? What can you tell us about her?"

"Pamela was Roland's personal assistant, as I'm sure you're aware. A tarty little thing that all the men in town were after. She could've ruined any marriage but sought to destroy mine. I suppose it's because my husband was the most eligible non-bachelor in town."

"And on the day Roland left, was Pamela with him?" Heather asked.

Nancy hesitated. "I think she must've been. My children always alleged that they saw them get into the car together, but I don't know for sure."

"So, they were having an affair?"

"I feel I've adequately spelled that out for you, Detective."

"Do you think he left to be with her?"

"All I know is that he said he had a business meeting. An opportunity in a state over. But I'd seen the bags he'd packed. Swim shorts, sunscreen, and enough clothes to last a month. I knew what was happening, but I was naïve. I thought if he got what he wanted with her occasionally, he'd be able to be with us for the most part. Sadly, it turned out that my parents were right about him and his ability to be a family man." She paused and glanced over at them. "Are either of you married?"

They shook their heads, but then Heather, trying to make Nancy comfortable, said, "I was. For a few years."

"So, then you know. Getting married young often ends as poorly as everyone warns you it will. I loved my husband. On the good days, he was incredibly romantic, thoughtful, funny, and, most importantly, a good father. Fortunately, for seven or eight years, the good days were frequent; but like most people, he had another side to him, and I'm afraid neither of us could satiate it forever."

"What about the drugs?" Heather asked.

"What about them?"

"Did you ever see him take drugs or ever see drugs in the house?"

"No, but he was often erratic, manic even. Full of big ideas. It was like he'd become a completely different person. I blamed the affair for invigorating him, but in retrospect..." she trailed off as she sampled her cooking.

"We think he might've been involved in cartel activity."

Nancy laughed coldly. "Well, that shows you the difference between Pamela and me. I made him into a politician. A mayor. I shaped him into a pillar of this community, and that succubus turned him into a gangster. If you're looking for a murderer, I would look no further than that wretched hussy."

"Pamela Bennet is dead, ma'am," Gabriel stated bluntly.

THE CRASH

Nancy brought a dainty hand to her throat before moving determinedly to the sink by the window. She looked out at the ash-gray sky and said, "Well, perhaps she turned his hand to worse things than drug smuggling."

"Mrs. Ellis—" Heather started, but Nancy interrupted, still fixed on the view from her hilltop home.

"I'm afraid I've become tired. Detective. Officer. Perhaps we can continue this chat another time if you allow me to schedule it into my calendar."

"Of course," Heather said, scraping her chair back and standing. Gabriel followed suit, and they thanked her for her time before leaving her frozen and white-knuckled in the kitchen. They let themselves out and closed the door behind them. Heather had forgotten how cold it was and missed the comfort of the fireplace, but she appreciated how the frosty air sharpened her thoughts.

The pair said their silent goodbyes as they climbed into their cars, and Heather knew that they were both going over all the questions Nancy had answered and the ones she'd opened up. The main one was... what had happened to Pamela Bennett?

CHAPTER TWENTY-ONE

THE DETECTIVE

Emerging from the station after updating Tina on her findings, Heather spotted Beau leaning against his motorcycle, puffing on a cigarette, the smoke emphasized by his condensing breath. He was staring right at her, so she gave him a reserved nod and continued toward her car. As she did so, he straightened and began to jog in her direction. Heather groaned as she heard him approach but turned toward him with the most neutral expression she could muster.

"Mr. Ellis, how can I help you?" she asked.

"Please don't call me that."

"Fine. What's up, Beau? Anything urgent? Not to be rude, but I have a date with the diner and some Canadian bacon."

THE CRASH

"Mind if I join you?"

Heather thought about it. "Yeah, I do, actually. I've had enough of talking to your family for one day."

"Yeah, my mother will do that to you."

"Yep," she agreed, her hand on the handle of her car.

He moved around to her door, seemingly trying to block her from opening it. "How about you sleep on it, reset, and meet me tonight? We could go to Luigi's, my treat."

"Beau..."

He threw his hands up and crossed his heart. "Nothing weird. Nothing romantic. I just want to say I'm sorry for the other day. It was a shitty thing to say, and I want to make it up to you."

He seemed genuine, and Heather was big on second chances for minor offenders. "Okay, I'll go to dinner with you on two conditions. One, I get to pick your brain about your dad, and two, you at least look at my addiction counseling contacts. You don't have to promise me you'll go to any sessions—just that you'll think about it and not throw the list in the trash as soon as I'm out of sight."

To her surprise, he smiled easily. "Deal."

He was eager, receptive, and definitely cleaner and soberer than usual. His clothes looked new and lacked the stock holes and frays of his regular ensembles. His hair, too, looked as if it had been washed and conditioned, and even his skin was glowing as if he'd just come from a spa. It made her wonder about his inheritance and the thought that maybe dinner was a good idea after all; Beau was more loose-lipped than Nancy at the best of times, especially when the setting was social.

"Great, I'll meet you there at seven," she said, trying not to stare at him in case he got the wrong idea.

"How about I pick you up?" he asked with a wink.

"No chance. I've seen the way you drive."

Beau laughed and began to walk away. "Fine. Have it your way. Seven it is."

Heather opened her car's driver's door. "Oh, and Beau?"

"Yeah?" Beau spun around eagerly.

"Don't bring me any damn roses."

Beau grinned. "I can't make any promises."

"Beau," Heather said sternly. "If you embarrass me, I'll leave."

"All right, all right. See you later, Detective."

Heather shook her head as Beau exaggeratedly skipped away toward his bike. He really did make it hard to hate him and was just about the goofiest criminal she'd ever met. It made her sad that he didn't want better for himself. In another life, he could've lived in a town that didn't hate him, and they could've been good friends. She told herself that it wasn't too late to help him turn it around—though from her experiences with the thousands of other Beaus out there, she wasn't entirely sure that was true.

Beau was late but seemingly sober when he arrived at Luigi's, which scored him some points and prevented the immediate derailment of what could be a nice evening. Heather's Breathalyzer confirmed his abstinence after he voluntarily and confidently blew into it. He smugly lit a cigarette after it showed up green, and she pocketed the device, happy to be proven wrong for once.

His appearance was even better than it had been earlier. He wore a suit nice enough to rival the one he'd donned for the funeral. This one was navy with a black button-up shirt undone at the collar. He'd even gone so far as to add a complimentary pocket square—maroon with a print of mustard-yellow flowers—and shiny, oval cuff links.

She leaned forward to inspect his wrists. "Those are white gold," she said. "Fourteen carats, if I had to guess."

Beau beamed at her and flashed the cuff links in the light of the neon window sign. "Good eye, Detective. How could you tell?"

"Worked on a homicide a few years back where a guy killed his mom for her jewelry. Turned out most of it was fake."

Beau whistled. "That's cold."

"No kidding. Yours is real though. Looks like it would've cost a pretty penny. Your dad's?"

THE CRASH

"Cuff links are new. The suit is his though. I got the tailor to bring it into the 21st century and snip off all the oversized nineties slouchiness."

"Looks great. I don't think I own anything half as fancy as that. Shame that the only place you can wear it around here is Luigi's."

"Maybe I'll run for mayor and wear a suit every day."

Heather chuckled. "Now that I'd like to see. What else did your dad leave you?"

"Wouldn't you like to know?"

"Yep, kind of why I'm here, actually," she cautioned, reminding him of their agreement.

"Jeez, okay. Put the claws away. Let's go in, eat some bread, and I'll tell you all about it." Beau strode toward the door and opened it for Heather. "You look nice, too, by the way."

Heather looked down at her white button-up, skinny blue jeans, and slightly heeled boots. She was underdressed for the fanciest restaurant in town but didn't want to give Beau any flirtatious ammo or the wrong idea.

"Thanks," she muttered and followed him inside.

Beau had booked the best table in the restaurant. Or so he said. It was a circular two-seater at the center of an isolated, carpeted island and could only be accessed by a small wooden bridge that crossed the encircling Koi pond. A bucket of champagne, a lit taper candle, and a complimentary bread basket awaited them as they sat down, and Heather began to worry that this outing was a big mistake.

The bow-tie-wearing waiter introduced himself as William, pulled out their chairs, and guided them into their seats. He introduced the champagne, plucking it from its ice bed and informing Heather that it was a 1990 Dom Pérignon Brut Champagne.

Nineteen-ninety was the year Heather had been born, and she wondered if Beau had chosen it because of that. She hoped not and decided that she was too nervous about the possibility to ask. If he had… was it something he thought was cute, or was it to show that he was just as capable of looking into her as she was into him?

She hoped it was just her detective brain talking, and she gladly accepted a glass, though it would be her only drink of the night. Sure, she could order a taxi, but keeping her wits about her was important, especially as she had a strong suspicion that she'd be driving a drunk Beau home. He may have been on his best behavior to start with, but he eyed the bubbling, golden liquid like a starving wolf looks at an innocent lamb.

"Cheers!" he exclaimed, grasping the glass hungrily.

"Cheers," Heather said, with half the effort.

He downed his drink, whereas Heather sipped hers, having been immediately proved correct about being a sober driver. She wasn't going to let him drive drunk under her watch, though she knew he must do so often when she wasn't around.

"I know you're apologizing, but it also seems like you're celebrating. What about?" she asked, hoping the answer wasn't hanging out with her. Once again, a pang of sadness hit her when she realized she might be the only person Beau could celebrate his wins with.

"I'm rich," Beau whispered loudly. "Dad, the amazing asshole, left me three-quarters of a million dollars. Though if I went to Australia, I'd be a millionaire. Could double my money over there."

Heather wanted to explain to him that's not exactly how it works but was distracted by her arising suspicions. She raised her glass and tried to seem unaffected despite the massive reveal. "Wow, that's amazing. I'm really happy for you, Beau. Did all of you get the same?"

"Nah, my mother got half, and Lucy and I split the other half. Not complaining though. He put her through enough. Surprised he didn't leave anything to Pamela. Maybe he did love us the most after all." He laughed bitterly. "More likely, he just had some Mexican bank account, and she got all of that."

"Why Mexico?" Heather asked, cocking her head, unable to concentrate on the menu at all despite multiple attempts.

"Oh, I forgot. I found this in Dad's office."

Beau reached into his pocket and handed over a crumpled printout of a real estate flyer from Valle de Bravo, Mexico. Heather looked at it and tried to veil her excitement over the confirmation that Roland had been—or at least had intended to be—there: the place where Pamela's body had been found.

Beau poured himself another glass. "Your expression is telling me that you already knew about that."

"Not exactly. Not for sure. Can I keep this?" Heather asked, already folding it up.

"Sure."

"Thanks."

"So, you already knew he was in Mexico? Detective, you've been holding out on me." Beau winked.

"I'd theorized about it, considering the cocaine and the harpy eagle tattoo, but I never had confirmation."

"The what tattoo? You really have been holding out on me."

"Beau, you know I can't tell you about an open—"

Beau cut her off harshly. "Detective, this is my dad. The guy might've been a bastard for running off, but I loved him when he was around. I deserve to know what's going on."

Heather couldn't argue with that. "Okay, fine. We can flip it just this once. Ask me what you want to ask me."

"The location on that flyer. It means something to you, doesn't it?"

"Yes," Heather replied, not revealing more than she had to.

"What does it mean to you?"

"It's where Pamela Bennet's body was found."

The game ended abruptly, and Beau slowly put his drink down, his joyful, frenetic energy ebbing away as realization took hold. "Oh, God, you think he killed her, don't you?"

Heather looked away guiltily. "I don't know yet. They found her eighteen months ago in a villa in that area under the name Dallon Riles."

Beau groaned and refilled his drink to the brim. "Please don't tell me that's an anagram of my goddamn useless father's name."

"I'm afraid it is."

Beau drank deeply from the slender glass and slammed it down again, this time so hard Heather was worried it might break. Beau rubbed his face and repeatedly combed his hair. Heather mentally willed him to not have a public meltdown or flip the table in her direction. He took a shaky breath in and managed to calm himself.

"Poor girl," he lamented. "I know she kind of ruined my family, but she was only my sister's age when they met. I really didn't think he was the type to do... that."

"We don't know anything for sure."

"But it fits?"

"It does, but it's not the only theory that fits. Have you ever heard of Francisco Medina?"

Beau shook his head quickly at first but then slowed, his eyes widening. "Wait. I thought I'd dreamed this—hell, maybe I did—but I remember playing hide and seek with her once, and she was taking too long to come find me, so I tracked her down and found her on the phone in Lucy's room. I listened in at the door and heard her speaking crappy Spanish, and I swear she said the name Francisco. I thought she was just talking about San Francisco at the time, but now..." Beau trailed off. "Do you think she lured my dad into a trap?"

"I really don't know, but it's a theory I have. Your testimony certainly helps support it."

"Jesus. This is crazy."

"Yeah. It is."

"I bet he killed her," he said bluntly as he topped himself up again.

Heather was taken aback, having heard this twice in one day from two Ellis family members. It was starting to look worse for Roland than it already had on the day of the crash.

"Why do you say that? Was he ever violent?" she asked, worried she was about to drown in a deluge of childhood trauma.

Fortunately, he shook his head. "No, never. But I don't think the man who crashed that plane was the same man that fathered me."

Heather was going to ask him to elaborate when the sounds of William's polished brogues echoed over the hollow bridge. He smiled at them, and they looked back politely as if they hadn't just been discussing the possibility of Beau's father committing a brutal domestic femicide.

"Can I take your orders?" William asked.

THE CRASH

Heather looked at the menu, realizing she hadn't absorbed any of it. Though, if Beau was now exorbitantly wealthy and buying, she thought she might as well splurge. "I'll have the lobster, please, and half a dozen oysters," she said coyly, handing the menu to William.

"Excellent choice, madam," William replied, clearly trying to put on somewhat of a European cadence despite clearly having lived in Washington his entire life.

Beau was fake aghast as he requested the chicken alfredo. Once William had also complimented Beau on his—claiming the alfredo as his favorite on the pasta menu—he theatrically placed napkins in their laps and journeyed once more across the noisy bridge.

Beau leaned in and breathily informed her, "Oysters are an aphrodisiac."

"Wow, I'd never heard that before," Heather said dryly, growing irritated with his drunkenness.

Beau leaned back, his brow furrowed. "Really? Yeah, there's been all kinds of studies... oh, you're joking."

"Yes, Beau. I'm joking. It would take a lot more than six oysters for you to see any action from me."

"How about twelve?"

"Beau."

"Sorry, sorry." Beau slapped the back of his hand. "I'll behave."

"Heather?" asked a booming voice. "And... Beau?"

Heather turned to see Bobby Sherwood and Amber Horton join them on their private island. Frankly, it was a relief to have some company only a table over, especially now that their cognizant conversation had turned into further attempts at flirting and was unlikely to return to anything informative.

"Don't worry. Nothing romantic going on here. Just going over the case," Beau clarified before Heather got the chance.

Bobby and Amber looked slightly confused to see the pairing regardless of context but soon shrugged it off as they took their seats nearby.

"Well, it's date night for us," Amber said. "Karen offered to babysit Savannah. I'd normally say no, but she's just so damn good with babies, and I don't get out enough. Especially with us running the bar too."

"Well, considering it's your night off, would you like a glass of champagne? I'm only having one, so there should be plenty," Heather offered.

"Oh, if you wouldn't mind," Amber said.

"Of course not," Beau replied, getting to his feet exuberantly and bringing the bottle over to the couple. He performed his best William impression as he spun the bottle around to show them the label and even poured it with one hand on the base like a high-end waiter.

Amber clapped in delight as he filled their glasses, and just for a moment, she noticed her and Beau make eye contact. Heather wasn't sure if he was trying to work his newfound moves on her or if he was just too drunk to control where his gaze landed.

He sat back down, and Amber sipped her drink for approximately one minute before she cleared her throat and reached around in her bag.

"Beau, do you have any cigarettes?" she asked.

"I do. I'll join you for a smoke. Champagne always makes me want one," he replied.

The two stood, and Heather nearly joined them, but something about their energy made her feel uninvited, so she stayed behind and watched as Beau held an arm for Amber. The woman took it happily, and the pair of them strode out of the restaurant, though they both turned and waved as they reached the double doors.

Bobby chuckled. "She had a few before she came out tonight. Deserves to let loose. Thanks again for the fizz."

"No problem."

"He's a good kid."

Heather nodded. "He tries to be."

"Ain't that what matters?"

"I suppose it is."

She smiled at Bobby, and the two made small talk while Heather kept a watchful eye out the front. It wasn't much use; it was much too dark to see either of them, much less read their lips. So eventually, she gave up and listened to Bobby's stories with her full attention.

They returned a couple of minutes later just as Heather and Beau's food arrived, and strangely, Heather noticed neither of them smelled of smoke. She knew she'd somewhat adjusted to the smell, being a smoker herself, but she could still tell when it was and wasn't there.

Beau, Amber, and Bobby chatted away while ordering drink after drink, and though Heather politely chimed in from time to time, her thoughts drowned out much of the conversation, and her stomach tightened so much that she only managed her oysters and requested a doggy bag for the rest.

Beau didn't seem to notice. He'd transitioned from champagne to whiskey a while back, and when he tripped on the bridge while attempting to go to the bathroom, Heather wrapped the event up and apologized to Bobby and Amber for intruding on their date. Fortunately, they didn't seem to mind, clearly enjoying some adult social time, and bid them enthusiastic good nights as Heather herded Beau into the back seat of her car, where he quickly fell asleep.

CHAPTER TWENTY-TWO

THE FATHER

2008

THEY PASSED THE BORDER IN THE BLINK OF AN EYE, AND despite Roland's anxieties, the plane didn't spontaneously combust, nor did anyone try to shoot them down from below. Nothing had changed aside from their time zone, and Roland let out a breath he didn't know he was holding. It was all going to be okay.

He looked at Pamela, who had been gripping her seatbelt the entire ride, and tried not to laugh at her scrunched-up expression. She hadn't told him she was terrified of heights until after they took off, and even that admission seemed to be

THE CRASH

an irrepressible reaction rather than information she was willingly offering up. That was just the type of woman she was: a lionhearted, boundary-pushing, comfort-zone-rejector. He was so proud of his partner in adventure, and he reached out a hand to squeeze hers.

"Nearly there now," he assured her.

She nodded, unable to open her mouth for fear of losing her breakfast but seeming to unwind with their destination in sight. She even looked pretty when she was green around the gills, Roland thought, and as soon as they unpacked and her stomach settled, he was going to take her out dancing and spoil her rotten. An electrifying fairy-tale life was what she deserved, and he was going to give it to her, no matter the cost.

If he couldn't live the dream full-time, he at least wanted her to be able to. He'd be a buttoned-up family man half the time and a bohemian drug runner for the rest; all the while, both parties he provided for would live in the lap of luxury. Though he resented providing for Nancy, at least the money would keep her out of his business. As long as the children were well-served, he could have his cake and eat it too. All she'd ever cared about was them; if they were content, so was she.

A small plane appeared behind them, closely following Roland's even smaller Beechcraft Bonanza. Before he turned on the radio to communicate with the other pilot, he knew it was Border Patrol. Though the man's tone was blunt, Roland didn't feel he was in danger of arrest as they approached the landing strip. It was like getting pulled over by highway patrol. All he had to do was meet the officer face-to-face and win him over. Despite frequently speeding, he hadn't been slapped with a ticket since his teen years. He owed it all to his generational gift of the gab, which he'd fortunately passed on to his daughter Lucy. It certainly worked like a charm on her mother.

He whistled a merry tune as they made the easy descent onto the dirt track. Pamela looked at him like he was crazy for being so calm, but he could see her desperation for danger burning brightly in her eyes. Once they came to a halt, she unbuckled and pounced on him, planting a big, wet, lipstick-laden smooch on his smiling mouth.

He pushed her off with a laugh as she tried to attack him with love, and she soon ran out of steam. Sighing with relief, she smoothed her skirt and reached into the glove box to retrieve her silver wedding band. She slipped it onto her dainty, pale finger and admired how the silver set against her ruby red nail polish. Roland had to admit that the new 'Mrs. Ellis' was a significant upgrade.

"You ready to give them a show, *hubby*?" Pamela teased, fluffing her abundance of blonde pin curls.

"I sure am," Roland said, putting on his sunglasses and planting a kiss on her pink cheek.

They exited the plane, Pamela in a powder blue dress and a wide-brimmed sunhat and Roland in a tasteful Hawaiian shirt and pressed chino pants. They waved excitedly to the armed officer, who looked them up and down, his expression softening. Just as they'd planned, they'd been immediately identified as harmless and vaguely idiotic American tourists.

They swaggered forward, passports in hand and movie-star smiles plastered on their faces. The man didn't mirror their enthusiasm, but he took and returned their passports within seconds.

"What is your purpose in Mexico?" the man asked.

"We're on our honeymoon," Pamela cooed, looking up at Roland and batting her eyelashes. She wiped the lipstick from his lips and giggled.

"Congratulations," the man replied flatly.

"Why, thank you!" Pamela exclaimed. "I said I was fine grabbing some dinner at our favorite steakhouse and going square dancing, but this one always has to spoil me."

Roland wrapped an arm around her and squeezed. "Hey, happy wife, happy life, am I right?"

The officer's serious expression finally broke. He smiled and gave a slight nod. "You certainly are, sir. Where are you two staying?"

"I actually bought a place nearby. Decided it was about time to buy an investment property. I have a copy of the deed right here."

The man looked at the real estate listing and copy of the deed and nodded approvingly. "Valle de Bravo. Nice area."

"I hope so."

"Now, you are aware you can only stay for 180 days before you need to obtain a Visa," the man warned them.

"Yes, sir, it isn't my first trip across the border," Roland said.

"It's mine, though," Pamela added. "I'm a homebody, you know?"

"Well, I hope you have a great time in Valle de Bravo," the officer said, eyes lingering on Pamela as he returned the papers.

"Thank you, sir, we will," Roland affirmed.

"Thank you!" Pamela shouted as she began to run back toward the plane, teasing Roland to catch her.

"You're a lucky man," the officer said quietly, shaking his head.

"Don't I know it," Roland replied. He nodded to the man, thanking him once more before taking off after Pamela at full speed.

As they pulled up to the modest villa—a Spanish-style three-bedroom with white stucco walls and a red roof—Roland spotted movement. A man emerged from behind the enormous leafy plant and accompanying terracotta pot that obscured the view of the front door. Cigarillo smoke hung about him in a thick cloud, and he raised the wannabe cigar to his lips as Roland observed his fingers and wrists dripping with gold. He bared a mouth full of matching gilded teeth and waved his smoking hand as if it were sporting a sock puppet. Roland didn't wave back.

The man was built like a wrestler with pumped-up biceps, pronounced pecs, and a thick, ropey neck. His hands were also oversized with large knuckles that reminded Roland of the knots on gnarled tree branches. His gaudy skintight outfit only emphasized this, and Roland felt more out of shape than he had in high school. However, that wasn't the end of the blows to Roland's self-esteem. Despite the stranger's leathery looks and evident middle-aged status, his hair was dense and grazed his muscular shoulders. More than that, it was combed back effortlessly as if it grew that way. Roland's cowlick tickled his forehead, and he glowered at his newfound adversary.

Before Roland could stop her, Pamela hopped out of the moving car and ran at the stranger who held out his satin-covered arms and tattooed hands, ready for impact. She slammed into him at full force, but he didn't budge an inch. Instead, he swept her up into the air and spun her around, exclaiming happily in Spanish. Roland nearly crashed the rental car as the man lowered Pamela to the ground and kissed her rosy cheeks. They were both enjoying their encounter too much for Roland's liking, and he rushed toward them, fanny pack around his waist, both hands trailing suitcases thunderously behind him.

The man turned and held his arms out wide as Roland approached. As much as he tried to maintain his scowl, the man's happy expression was infectious, and Roland's face twisted into something almost friendly.

Once close enough, Roland found himself engulfed in a powerful embrace. The man's arms were as strong as they looked—frighteningly so. He was definitely a man that wasn't to be messed with, so when he held Roland's face in his rough hands and playfully slapped his cheeks, Roland laughed off how much the impact stung. Then came the cologne-scented kisses for his own face, which both deceased and increased his unease.

Pamela sidled up to Roland and looped her arm through his. "Roland, I'd like you to meet Francisco—your new boss."

Francisco scoffed. "Boss. Psh. Such an awful word. I prefer your new uncle. Your new best friend. Your new confidant."

Roland liked what he was hearing and stuck out his hand despite having already hugged the man.

"It's nice to meet you," he said.

Francisco enthusiastically accepted the handshake. "It's nice to meet you too. I've heard many good things from this special little lady. Thank you for bringing her back to Mexico. It was getting dangerous for her to cross the border on her own."

"No problem at all. Thank *you* for letting me in on your enterprise."

"I can always use an extra pair of hands, especially if those hands are white and can drive a plane. Those border patrol *pendejos* won't look twice at you."

"Here's hoping."

"You'll take me for a spin sometime, right?"

Roland hesitated but saw Francisco's enthusiasm fading fast, so he quickly nodded and said, "Of course."

Francisco slapped him hard on the shoulder, the numerous rings striking bone. "Good man. I can tell this is the start of something beautiful. Now, I have something for you."

Francisco clicked his fingers in the air, and an imposingly large, bald man emerged from the driver's door of a black car parked on the street. Its windows were tinted too dark to see inside, but Roland knew it would be far more luxurious than his 2003 Kia Rio.

In contrast to the approaching man's threatening physicality and all black outfit, he carried colorful gift bags in each meaty hand with cartoonish animals printed on them. Roland suppressed a chuckle at the sight, though no one else seemed to find it remotely amusing, least of all the shiny-headed bodyguard.

"Oh, Francisco, did you get us presents?" Pamela gushed, her hands clasped together and her hazel eyes full of stars.

Francisco shrugged. "I couldn't resist. You know me."

The man handed the bags to Francisco, and in turn, Francisco checked the interiors and handed them over to the correct recipients. He winked at Roland as he passed it over, and Roland, taken aback, tried and failed to wink back. He hastily looked away as Francisco politely pretended not to have noticed the facial spasm. Roland was starting to become convinced that the man fed on the appeal of others, like some sort of charisma vampire.

Not wanting to be rude, he opened his present anyway and had to admit that Francisco was an excellent gift-giver. Inside was a wad of cash, a gift card to a local tailor, a coupon for sky diving, a pair of gold cuff links, a pack of *San Cristobal Monumento* cigars, a bottle of mezcal complete with a *gusano rojo* at the bottom, and an English to Spanish translation book. Roland opened the first page, and written in perfect handwriting was, 'Welcome to Mexico, my friend.'

He thanked Francisco with another handshake—this one heartier than before—and looked over to see what Pamela had received. Her significantly larger bag also contained a roll of pesos and a multitude of gift cards. In place of mezcal, she was given a large bottle of champagne and a box containing a set of crystal flutes. Next, she pulled out a bottle of Dior perfume, which Roland thought would be the clincher; however, nothing excited her as much as the sultry satin red dress, the powder-pink teddy nightgown, and the diamond tennis bracelet.

She clearly couldn't believe her eyes, and Roland was in the same boat, looking between her shocked expression and Francisco's pleased one. Buying lingerie for her was indeed a boundary overstepped, but seemingly Roland was in the minority with this unsaid opinion.

"This is too much!" Pamela exclaimed, jumping back into Francisco's arms.

"Nonsense. Nothing is too much for *la mujer más bonita en todo el mundo*."

Roland didn't know much Spanish, but he knew enough to tingle with a jealousy he'd long since forgotten about. Since he was eighteen, he'd been the handsome one, the one with money, the one that all the girls wanted. Now there was a bigger dog with a stronger bite and louder bark in the room, and all he wanted to do was mark his territory.

Roland pulled Pamela close to him around the waist once the hug ended and examined the pink number. "This'll look good on the bedroom floor tonight," he teased.

Francisco was unfazed, but Pamela froze up and pulled away, clearly embarrassed. Roland felt a pang of guilt for using the love of his life as some sort of sexist tug-of-war toy, but he couldn't help himself. Francisco seemed like a nice guy, but he knew they were both after the same thing, and it wasn't just drugs and money.

Francisco chuckled. "There are pamphlets in the bags recommending some of our finest local restaurants. Tell any of the staff Francisco Medina sent you, and I guarantee you'll have the most *delicioso* meal of your life at the best table in the house."

"Thank you, we appreciate it," Roland said, still holding Pamela firmly in his grasp around her soft middle.

THE CRASH

"Well, I'll leave you two to get on with your romantic evening. I hope I remembered your size," Francisco said, gesturing to the clothing with a golden grin. "I'll have a car pick you up in the morning at eleven."

Then he was gone, and Pamela twisted in Roland's arms, her mouth pouty but her forehead angry. She stroked Roland's freshly shaven face with the back of her hand.

"Don't be jealous. Francisco and I haven't been together in years. You're the only man for me," she whispered sweetly.

"I'm not jealous."

"Roland."

"I promise. I trust you."

Pamela analyzed his face for a long time and must've seen enough truth in it to relax in his arms. The pair kissed passionately on their new porch, and as Roland opened his mouth, he realized how intensely he'd been clenching his jaw.

CHAPTER TWENTY-THREE

THE DETECTIVE

Heather arrived bright and early at Beau's RV with two coffees, a glazed donut, and the intention of dragging him to an AA meeting at the local Baptist church. The sugary offerings from Dottie's Cafe were intended to soften the blow, and they also provided a blood sugar-boosting ladder out of hangover hell.

By the time they'd reached his RV the night before, he'd been so far gone she'd half-carried, half-dragged him from her car to his bed. Luckily for him, he was slender, but his gangly frame and height proved a challenge. Once she'd gotten him into bed, she'd stayed with him for half an hour to ensure he wasn't in danger from alcohol poisoning. She left him half-conscious and mumbling in the recovery position with a glass of water on the side table.

She'd had a restless night because of it, worrying about him choking on his vomit like his father had on his descent. She'd gotten up to smoke and pace several times and only managed a couple hours of light sleep before calling it quits and waking herself up with a cold shower. The mixture of the icy water and frosty temperatures were still working to keep her alert, but she knew it wouldn't last for long and drained the remnants of her coffee, wishing she'd bought two for each of them instead.

"There will be more at the meeting," she said quietly as she approached the RV door. "There's always black coffee at these things."

She honestly had no idea if he'd accept the somewhat forceful invitation but hoped that she'd be enough of a draw to at least get him into one of the plastic chairs. She also hoped he'd tag along for a two-birds-one-stone situation. Ever since the group had formed, she'd wanted to attend, but she needed a good excuse, not wanting people in town thinking their lead detective was an alcoholic. She wasn't, not really, but it was always good to improve her relationships with her vices, even if she wasn't ready to eradicate them completely.

Heather knocked on the unlocked door and called out for Beau but received no reply. A panicked meowing from under the RV startled her, and she looked to see a mangy, flat-faced cat crying up at her. She didn't know much about cats and wasn't sure if it was hungry or sick, but either way, the sounds unnerved her. She knocked again, and when she still didn't receive an answer, she entered the RV.

The pit in her stomach grew larger and heavier as she rounded the corner, afraid of what she might find. She was relieved to see Beau alive, but when he quickly pushed away from the table with a rolled-up note in hand, fury took hold.

"I didn't hear you pull up," he said, gesturing to the corded headphones he was wearing.

Heather pursed her lips. "Beau, please tell me you're not doing what I think you're doing."

Beau got to his feet. "No, it's not what it looks like."

"You've got a little something," Heather said, rubbing at her nostrils.

He mimicked her, wiping white powder away from his nose. He cringed as if doing so hurt, and Heather thought it served him right until his hand crept up to his forehead, and he screwed up his eyes.

"Ow, crap. Oh my god. That really hurts," he whined.

"Beau," Heather said, hesitantly approaching and setting the coffee and doughnut down. "This is your final warning. I'm going to have to arrest you if I see—"

Beau waved her off. "Yeah, yeah, sure. Jesus, is it bright in here, or is it just me?"

"That bad of a hangover?" Heather asked, looking around at the drawn curtains.

Beau moaned, his hands starting to shake. "No, no, no, I don't know. My head hurts so bad."

"Beau, sit down," Heather commanded, a waver appearing in her own voice.

He did as he was told, balancing on the edge of the bed with his head in his hands. Heather moved in front of him, looking around for something to ease his pain and catching sight of all the orange pill bottles—some empty, some full—and began to scan them for Tylenol or aspirin. There was nothing of the sort, and when he started to wretch, she pulled her phone from her pocket, ready to call 911.

"Jesus," she said. "Do you suffer from migraines?"

He shook his head, unable to speak. He continued to wretch and alternated between clutching his stomach and head. With each gag, his voice became raspier, and when he grabbed at his throat, his lips turning blue, Heather made the call.

Beau slid to the floor, suffocating as Heather informed the operator of their location and his symptoms, and when it finally clicked—the cocaine, the symptoms—she told the woman on the other end that he had ingested cyanide-laced cocaine.

They were on their way, but Heather and the operator knew full well that by the time they arrived, Beau would already be long gone. Heather dropped her phone to the bed and looked around the room in a panic for anything that might keep him tethered to life.

THE CRASH

He had every prescription drug under the sun, it seemed, except anything that would actually help him stay alive. She'd nearly given up—fallen to her knees to comfort him during his last breaths—when she spotted a bottle of poppers and remembered her advanced first aid training with poison control. Amyl nitrate, a key ingredient of the stimulant, was a popular cyanide antidote, even if it was of the recreational variety.

Heather reached for a cloth—an unused microfiber still in a plastic package with all the others—and smashed the little glass bottle. She poured the remaining contents over the soft blue rag, saturating the center, and held it over his mouth and nose. He watched her with panicked eyes, clearly afraid in his unwell state that she was attempting to put him out of his misery. He tried to squirm, but she shushed him and mimed an inhale. He relaxed as best he was able and breathed in the chemical. She continued to hold it there as she scooted around and placed his head in her lap. She stroked his hair as he continued to inhale and told him everything would be okay—though she made sure to omit the word promise.

She removed the cloth and was relieved to see a lack of foam at his lips and that the blue tinge was turning white. She left it off momentarily, leaving his mouth free to breathe the stale RV air as she reached for an old T-shirt. Tipping the glass of water she'd provided the night before onto it, she dabbed at his sweaty forehead and neck, cooling him down before giving him another inhale of the amyl nitrate. For the first time ever, she was grateful for the existence of illegal drugs.

His Adam's apple bobbed, and tears escaped in a flood from the far outer corners of his eyes. The saline ran over his temples and onto her lap to join the rest of the sweat and water. He strained to look up at her, his eyes bloodshot and lashes congealed.

When he spoke, his voice was hoarse. "Am I going to die?"

His ability to ask provided her answer. "No. Thankfully your bad habits saved you this time. Poppers? Really? What is this, a rave in the nineties?"

Beau chuckled weakly. "Thanks."

"Please don't talk."

Beau nodded and closed his eyes. Heather jostled him occasionally as they waited, ensuring he was still alive as she'd once done with her elderly dog whenever she'd slept too soundly. When the ambulance pulled into the clearing, siren blaring, he opened his eyes again but had grown scarily pale. Heather knew that the administered drug was only a temporary cure and that he needed urgent medical attention. She prayed to a god she didn't wholly believe in that the EMTs hadn't arrived too late.

She heard them getting the gurney ready, and just before they reached the front door, Heather asked, "Who sold you the cocaine?"

Beau swallowed hard again, clearly reluctant to give a name.

"Please, Beau. I'm trying to keep this town safe. I need you to tell me who did this to you."

He whispered something, his voice too hoarse to understand.

"What did you say?"

The door burst open, and Beau tried again.

"It was Amber."

CHAPTER TWENTY-FOUR

THE FATHER

2009

Roland held Pamela's hand and helped her down from the towering SUV. She wobbled on the curb, struggling to find her balance on account of her enormous eight-and-a-half-month belly throwing off her center of gravity. Roland helped steady her, but she brushed him off and readjusted her shirred sundress which was stretched to its breaking point.

She rubbed the baby bump absentmindedly as she watched Roland unload their luggage from the trunk but quickly grew bored and strode away toward the hotel lobby. Roland cringed as he watched her struggle in her six-inch heels. Why she was still determined to wear them was beyond him, but he knew better than to say anything. She'd been in a bad mood ever since they boarded the plane on account of the cramped seats and how much her back hurt. He sympathized. Really, he did. Both of them wanted her to be able to stay behind in Mexico, but they had no other choice. She was integral to this deal.

Roland wheeled their suitcases—hers an oversized Louis Vuitton monstrosity that weighed more than she did—toward the hotel lobby, quickly gaining on her as she struggled not to break an ankle.

He was nearly close enough to reach out and touch her when the mob of tourists parted like the red sea to let her through but then closed in on him when he attempted to use the same path. He watched as she reached the front desk and laid her palms on it as if she was near collapse already after mere minutes of standing. The concierge, a friendly-looking, middle-aged woman, immediately began to fuss over Pamela, and the show was in full swing by the time Roland pushed through the swarm of spectators.

"Oh my gosh, how did you know?" Pamela squealed in awe.

"You're carrying low and in the front. Same as I did for my boys. You're much bigger than I ever was though. You sure there's only one in there?" the woman remarked—somewhat rudely, in Roland's opinion.

"We're sure," Roland retorted, putting an arm around Pamela, who didn't seem to mind the roundabout compliment.

"Oh yeah, only one in here. He's going to be a big baby just like his dad was," Pamela said, grabbing Roland's hand and placing it on her extended abdomen. She looked up at him and flashed a dimple before resting her head on his shoulder. It was the first lick of sweetness he'd received from her all day, and it was all he needed to forget about the frustrations in getting to this point.

"When are you due?" asked the concierge.

"Three months," Pamela replied, and Roland repressed a laugh.

THE CRASH

It was her favorite joke to make at the moment, as it was evident to everyone, doctor of obstetrics or otherwise, that she wouldn't last three more weeks, let alone three more months. The looks on everyone's faces were a picture as they tried to picture just how mammoth their unborn child was going to be.

The concierge's face was particularly perfect as she uttered a quiet, "Wow."

"As I said, he'd going to be a big one," Pamela giggled.

The concierge nodded, wide-eyed. "Yeah, you might have a linebacker on your hands."

"Or a heavyweight champ," Roland concurred.

"Well, best of luck to you," the concierge said, looking Pamela in the eye with something resembling pity. "And here are your keys to the honeymoon suite."

The woman toyed with the word honeymoon while looking directly at Pamela's baby bump and the lack of rings on their fingers. This was another thing that Pamela thought was very funny. Roland found it somewhat embarrassing, but he figured he'd let her have her fun where she could, considering most other enjoyable activities were off the table.

In the luxury suite, Pamela stood barefoot—her feet pink and sore—and scrutinized her new body in the full-length mirror. She put her hands on the small of her back and massaged her aching muscles. Roland watched her do so from the foot of the bed and wondered what she was thinking.

"This is all Francisco's fault," she grumbled, voicing at least one thought about her condition.

"Mmm," Roland agreed half-heartedly, not wanting to talk about Francisco.

Pamela didn't get the message. "His ideas just always sound so smart when I'm drunk. And then, boom! This kind of thing happens."

Roland frowned. He'd had enough of talking about Francisco and his genius ideas when he was in Mexico. This trip to Portland was supposed to be an escape from their constant competition, but it seemed that jealousy could follow him anywhere—especially where Pamela was involved.

He approached the love of his life and tried not to think about Francisco—or, more importantly, her and Francisco—as he snaked his arms around her. It was a much more difficult task than it used to be, and he tried something he'd once done with Nancy and lifted the belly, alleviating the weight for a minute. It weighed a ton, and Pamela moaned with relief.

"How can I help?" he asked her.

"You can order us room service and a romantic pay-per-view movie and rub my feet while I take a bubble bath."

Roland frowned. "But what about our reservations? You have to book that place a month in advance."

"I know, but going out is so exhausting." She pouted, and Roland smiled, moving his hands to her shoulders.

"Fine, we'll get room service and watch a movie in bed."

"Thank you, honey," Pamela moaned. "Now, help me out of this damn thing."

Roland obliged and helped her out of her dress. After several ripped seams and a lot of struggling, she stood in her sports bra and bike shorts. Roland, who was kneeling on the floor, looked up at the protuberant silicone semi-sphere strapped to her body. It was jarring to see it uncovered, and clearly, Pamela, with her pinched expression, felt the same.

Their eyes stayed locked on the beige mass of synthetic skin as he undid the clasps and buttons at the back. She removed her maternity bike shorts that partly kept the fake belly in place and peeled it away from her flat stomach. She laid it on the floor with a thump and opened the compartment at the back to reveal several bricks of cocaine, all still in perfect condition. She shut the chamber, straightened up, and clicked her back with a moan.

The drugs—six densely packed bricks—weighed around fourteen pounds. So, not only did the contents weigh twice that of the average baby, but there was also the weight of the thick silicone to contend with. He noticed the straps had left red marks and contusions all over her back and sides and looked away guiltily.

THE CRASH

"I guess that's why you didn't want to go out to dinner," he said, grabbing a soft white robe and handing it over to her.

"Yep. Plus, I can't drink either with it on. Doesn't sound like much fun to me. I'm looking forward to having a break from pregnancy for a few hours."

"I bet actual pregnant women would love to be able to take the belly on and off."

"I don't know how they do it," Pamela said, shaking her head as she slipped on the robe. "I'm tired after only a couple weeks of faking it."

"Well, at least you'll never have to do it for real," Roland replied.

Pamela frowned at him in the mirror, the singular line on her forehead deepening. "What do you mean by that?"

Roland knew he'd stepped in it, but it was too late to retreat into safety. "You don't want kids, do you?"

"I don't know. I've always wanted to be a mom. Not right now, maybe… but one day. Do you not want kids?"

"I don't want *more* kids. You have no idea how exhausting it is. I want wild and free, not diaper bags and midnight feedings. I promise you'll hate it."

"Well, maybe you don't know me that well," Pamela countered, her lip trembling.

"Pammy, come on. I'm sorry."

"It's fine, honey. I'm just tired," she said quietly.

"Me too, come here." Roland patted the bed, and Pamela ran at him with a smile and bounced onto it before wincing over her aching body.

She snuggled up to him and asked, "You really don't miss being a dad?"

"Sometimes. But it's too late to go back to them now."

"You could go visit them tomorrow after the drop-off. It hasn't even been a year, baby. You could explain and apologize and maybe arrange more frequent visits."

"I don't know. Maybe."

"Think about it. I'm happy to go with you."

Roland laughed and shook his head. "Nancy would shoot me on sight if she saw you waddling along next to me."

"All right. I can wait in the car and send you supportive texts."

"As you said, I'll think about it." He kissed Pamela's forehead. "Now, how about we try out that jacuzzi?"

Pamela greeted the room service attendant with her belly back on and dressed in a white hotel robe. She greedily grabbed the bottle of chardonnay and twisted the cap off, and took a hefty swig directly from it.

The young man who had delivered it looked mortified and nervously handed the silver trays of food to Roland, who thanked and tipped the server. He shut the door and shook his head, pretending to be angry, and Pamela snorted, shooting wine out her nose. This only made her laugh harder and louder.

"Come on, baby! Don't be a party pooper. Messing with people when I look like this is too easy!"

"You sure are good at it," he replied, his serious façade starting to crack.

Pamela quickly sloughed the baby-shaped carry case and threw herself back onto the bed, wine in hand. Out of her pocket, she pulled out a small bag of white powder and grinned. She shook it in Roland's direction, and he joined her on the white sheets.

"A little present from Francisco for trying out the baby idea," she said. "Well, he doesn't know he gave it to me, but still."

Roland kissed her hard. "You're a genius."

"Oh, I know it. See, this is why we should have a baby. With my brains and your brawn, it would be unstoppable."

"You're starting to win me over. But you can't do cocaine if you have a baby."

Pamela dipped a long-nailed finger into the baggy, brought the bump to her nostril, and snorted. She hummed thoughtfully. "Okay, how about five more years of drugs and adventure, and then we settle down just a little bit?"

"How about ten years?"

THE CRASH

"Eight is the lowest I can do."

Roland held his hand out. "It's a deal."

Pamela shook it, scooped out another bump, and held it to Roland's nose. He inhaled, and she jumped to her feet—high enough to forget how much they hurt—and continued to drink from the bottle. She turned on the little radio on the bedside table, turned it to the country channel, and began to dance as Roland watched, enamored.

He almost forgot about the food but remembered when his stomach growled. He unveiled the luxurious seafood platter for Pamela and the steak and asparagus for him, but even crab legs and butter dipping sauce couldn't draw Pamela away from the dance floor.

Roland laughed at her as he dug in and shook his head as she beckoned him to join her. "No, no. You see, I love you way too much to subject you to my dancing."

Pamela paused. "I love you, too, baby."

A surge of cocaine hit Roland, and he shook his head slowly, realization washing over him. "No, like I really love you, Pamela. More than anybody in the world. I love you so much that I don't ever want to leave you. Not for one minute."

"What are you talking about?"

"I want to live in Mexico with you full-time. I want to change my name, leave my old life behind for good, and get married."

Pamela stopped dancing. "Are you proposing to me?"

He didn't even hesitate. "Yes."

"But you're still married."

He shook his head. "It won't be legal. But we'll be married in the eyes of God, which is what matters."

"What about your kids?"

"I'll send them money once we're set up. They'll be fine with Nancy. She comes from money. I was never a great dad anyway."

Pamela hesitated but then joined Roland in bed. "So, you're all in with me?"

"I'm all in, baby. I'm all yours… forever."

"I'm all yours too," she whispered, kissing him softly.

"Is that a *yes*?"

Pamela's beam lit up the room, and she nodded. "It's a yes. Of course, it's a yes!"

They kissed hard, clacking teeth as neither could stop smiling, and when they finally pulled away, they were half-crying and half-laughing.

"Come here," Roland said, dipping his finger in the baggy. Pamela did the same, and they linked arms and rubbed the powder on each other's gums before leaning in for a passionate kiss.

Too excited, Pamela broke the kiss and continued to drink and dance, and looking at her beauty, silhouetted by the moonlight, he knew that this marriage and these hypothetical kids would be different. He was going to be happy with her for the rest of his life.

CHAPTER TWENTY-FIVE

THE DETECTIVE

STILL SHAKING FROM SAVING BEAU'S LIFE AN HOUR AGO, Heather parked in Nancy Ellis's driveway without calling ahead for a second time. She knew the woman would be angry, but Heather knew delivering the news about Beau in person was important. She also knew that she was the one who had to do it.

Once again, as Heather excited the car, Nancy was already standing in the doorway—this time wearing a different floral apron over a mandarin-colored dress—with her hands firmly on her narrow hips.

Heather moved toward her apologetically, the approach made more awkward by her shuffling steps as she avoided slipping on the patches of black ice.

Nancy called out to her. "Detective, I know you're busy, but surely you haven't forgotten what I said about unexpected house calls already? I'd be more than happy to schedule something into the calendar—"

She stopped as Heather stood in front of her and looked up. Nancy placed trembling fingers to her ajar lips. Heather realized she must look as bad as she felt.

"Oh, God, it's Beau, isn't it?" Nancy asked.

Heather swallowed hard. "It is."

Nancy nodded frantically, looking around at nothing in particular. "Is he dead? Oh, God, he is, isn't he? Motorcycle crash, I'm assuming. I'm always telling him not to drink and drive."

"No. He's not dead, but he is at the hospital in a medically induced coma."

"Oh no. No. My poor Beau."

Nancy was quivering worse than Heather, and she was growing increasingly pale as she began to silently cry. Heather readied herself for the woman to come tumbling down to the frozen ground.

"I thought I'd come by in person to tell you," Heather said, her voice breaking.

"Thank you," Nancy squeaked, blinking rapidly and looking wildly at the white sky like a high-strung racehorse. Heather realized when she saw the glint that the woman was trying not to cry in front of her.

"You're welcome. I'm sorry to intrude."

When Nancy didn't respond, Heather began to back away, wanting to leave the woman to her grief, but halfway along the path, Nancy finally spoke.

"Heather, won't you please come in? I could use the company."

Heather turned back and saw that Nancy was finally looking at her, tears streaming down her cheeks. Heather turned on her heel and graciously accepted.

Nancy looked relieved as Heather approached, and as she moved to let Heather inside, her body hung slack, her joints

THE CRASH

almost too loose in her sockets compared to her usual rigidity. Once the door was closed, Nancy kicked off her heels against the wall as Heather carefully removed her muddy boots.

Nancy strode flat-footed along the hallway, her stocking-covered feet slapping against the polished wood. She was still elegant—years of etiquette lessons impossible to undo—but it felt like Heather was seeing a real person for the first time instead of an Operation Doorstep mannequin.

In the kitchen, Heather sat once again at the marble island as Nancy put the kettle on. She paced for a moment before joining Heather on the opposite side. She surveyed Heather coolly despite the occasional tear still escaping her red-rimmed eyes.

"Tell me what happened to Beau," she demanded softly.

"We went out to dinner last night, and he got really drunk, so I stopped by the RV this morning to bring him some coffee. He didn't answer, and when I entered, I caught him snorting a line of cocaine." This didn't seem to shock Nancy, so Heather continued. "Then he started getting sick. He was complaining of headaches and retching, and once he collapsed, I realized he was suffering from cyanide poisoning."

Nancy gasped, and more tears spilled out, though to Heather, they seemed born of confusion rather than sadness. Once she was able to, Nancy asked, "How is that possible? Did the same person who killed Roland try to kill him too?"

"I assure you we're looking into it, and I will contact you when we have the answers you're looking for."

"How in heaven's name is he alive?"

"I was fortunate enough to find some amyl nitrate, which kept him alive while we waited for the ambulance."

"You saved my son's life?"

Heather gestured yes, and Nancy began to shake again. Ignoring the whistling kettle behind them, she reached for the sherry in the middle of the island and poured herself a full glass.

"How am I ever supposed to repay you for saving my baby?" she asked.

Heather faltered, immensely surprised to discover that Nancy loved Beau after all—a secret so well kept that it seemed only Nancy herself had known it.

"Please, you don't have to repay me. It's my job to look after the citizens of this town. I'm just glad he's alive."

"Well, in doing so, you've saved me too. My children are my entire life. If anything happened to them, I wouldn't be able to go on."

Heather noticed that a small family photo was missing from the collection of memories lined up on the kitchen bench, leaving a gap in the row like a missing tooth. It had been a photo that included Roland. The rest were of the Ellis children and Nancy. It didn't seem like there was much to remove of him. More like a mole than a tumor.

"How did you feel about Roland?" Heather asked.

"What do you mean?" Nancy asked frostily.

"It seemed like he was your whole life when he died, and now I'm not so sure."

"You overstep, Detective," Nancy snapped.

"I know."

Nancy sighed and softened again. "I did love Roland, especially at the start. The problem was that he didn't love me. That knowledge wears away at a person. I held on to my love because he gave me my two children, and I made a promise before God, but it's been trying to wriggle out of my hands for a long time now."

Nancy, who Heather usually thought looked very good for being in her fifties, suddenly looked every day of her age and several hundred more.

Nancy continued. "Worst of all, he didn't love the children either, and *that* is unforgivable. If he did love them, he had a funny way of showing it, running off with a girl a decade his junior. Honestly, I'm starting to wonder if I only ever loved him because of the children and because I was expected to."

"Then why were you so upset when he died?"

"I think because it just seemed like another act of selfishness. He'd already put us through so much, and just when we'd gotten past it, he comes back and takes us all down with him."

"I'm sorry if I offended you, but before now, I didn't even think you liked Beau."

Nancy drooped. "I know you mustn't think much of me, Detective."

"Why do you say that?"

"Well, if you're as close to my son as it seems, I know you've heard a lot of unflattering things about me."

"He hasn't said much, but I've noticed your relationship seems... complicated."

Nancy scoffed. "That's putting it politely. I suppose it's what happens when your husband forces you to be the disciplinarian while he gets to be the fun one who comes home with presents. I've never been fun—somebody had to be the parent. And when he was gone, and I tried to be both mother and father, I failed terribly. They rejected any warmth offered because it was so foreign, so I just stuck with discipline because I didn't know what else to be."

"I don't like to speak ill of the dead, but it seems Roland really screwed you guys over."

"Yes, I suppose he did. Though, as in life, it seems that he still has his uses."

"Are you talking about the inheritance?"

Nancy cocked an eyebrow and sipped her sherry. "I suppose Beau told you about that?"

"Was it a secret?"

"Not exactly, but like winning the lottery, some things are best kept to oneself."

"You're worried about people asking for money?"

"Among other things."

Tension was forming between the two, and Heather cleared her throat. "So, what are you going to do with the money?"

The doorbell rang, and Nancy leaped to her feet. "That must be the renovators!"

"The renovators?" Heather frowned, looking around at the immaculate interiors.

Nancy looked very grave and nodded. "Oh yes. It may have a pretty face, but the foundations are turning to mush. There's so much water damage I'm surprised the ceiling hasn't caved in on my head yet. The inheritance from my father kept me afloat for a while and sent Lucy to college, but it wasn't enough to keep me going forever."

"So, this money is pretty life-changing?" Heather asked.

Nancy narrowed her eyes. "I suppose so. Especially for Beau. He can even afford his own hospital bills for once."

Heather compressed her lips into a tight line. "Well, I hope it brings you all happiness."

"Thank you, Detective, now, if you'll excuse me," Nancy tilted her head in the direction of the front door, where the bell rang again.

"Of course, thanks for your time."

"No, thank you ... for saving my son."

"I'll be in touch."

Heather escorted herself out and opened the door to see two burly men on the other side. She pushed through them, and they let themselves in, ready to tear down and build up the already stunning house.

Heather sat in the car, thinking about the inheritance. She hadn't realized that Nancy had also been flat broke.... nor that they resented Roland so profoundly. Would it be that farfetched that Nancy used the last of her money to hire someone to find and kill Pamela and Roland? It seemed absurd—conspiratorial even—but a large and desperately needed inheritance was undeniably suspicious.

It wasn't sitting quite right in her gut, but she never abandoned theories unless proven false by evidence or process of elimination. So, she drove home, trying to remember all that had been said by visualizing her corkboard and sticking several sticky notes underneath Nancy's sour-faced portrait.

CHAPTER TWENTY-SIX

THE FATHER

2014

A YEAR TURNED INTO TWO TURNED INTO SIX IN THE blink of an eye, and Roland hardly ever thought about his previous life aside from the occasional dream. He woke from a dream about Lucy and Beau in the same villa he'd bought years earlier. Beau would be seventeen and Lucy thirteen. He wondered what they were like, how their personalities had grown, and whether they looked more like him or Nancy now that puberty was in full swing. He could imagine Beau to be the spitting image of him. He'd been a chubby moon-faced kid, too, but it all turned to muscle around seventeen. Lucy, he thought, would look more like Nancy, but he hoped she'd get his nose and lips—not that he thought Nancy was ugly, but he knew which parts of him were superior to hers.

Pamela stirred in bed next to him. She'd been sleeping a lot recently. Naps, sleeping in, early bedtimes. She easily spent over half the day under a duvet with a sleeping pill in her system. He knew what was wrong. It was Francisco. Upon realizing that Pamela would never leave Roland for him, he'd turned cold. The pay was worse, the jobs were more dangerous, and Francisco took out his frustrations on his men in violent ways. With each beating, Roland and Pamela knew Francisco was picturing them on the ground, but they were too precious for him to hurt, so all he could do was inflict guilt on them instead. It worked. The responsibility was agony, and their adventurous life now felt like a prison. They were terrified to leave and terrified to stay. It was a catch-22, so Pamela visited her dreams as often as possible to escape.

What she didn't know was that Roland had a plan. Knowing that she'd be asleep for another couple of hours, he got up, cleaned the villa, and cooked them some breakfast. The smell of bacon eventually summoned her, and she shuffled into the kitchen, looking absolutely exhausted.

"Thanks for cooking," she mumbled, sitting at the table across from Roland.

He barely acknowledged her, his attention focused on his laptop. He clicked and typed, and Pamela narrowed her eyes while she ate.

"What's going on?" she asked. "I haven't seen you like this in years."

He spun the laptop around and showed her a five-figure bank account she'd never seen before.

Suddenly alert, Pamela looked around and whispered, "What the hell is that?"

"That is our nest egg. Tomorrow I'm going to withdraw it all, and we're going to run."

"Listen, honey, I want to get out even more than you do. But that's not enough money to start again. Sure, it'll tide us over, but we'll need to get a new car he doesn't know about. We'll need new IDs, new bank accounts, new debit cards, and new looks. That will cost a lot of money—never mind finding somewhere to live. Do you know how much houses cost?"

"We could rent."

"That's not the point."

"What is?" Roland asked, deflating.

"Tomorrow is just too soon. Let's give it a year, save up some more, and make sure that the plan is airtight. Francisco is smart. He won't just let his meal tickets ride off into the sunset."

Roland considered this for a second. "Okay. Deal. A year from now, to the day, we'll take off to some other unknown coastal town, buy a place on the water, get real jobs, and live happily ever after."

"What about moving to Florida? Or Hawaii?" Pamela asked. "He'd struggle to find us there, and then we don't have to worry about visas anymore."

Roland shook his head. "I'm all over the news in the States. Someone will recognize me. Here I can just disappear."

"Okay, so we'll stay in Mexico. You know I'm happy anywhere as long as I'm with you."

Roland frowned. "You're not happy here."

"That's because he's about one snide comment away from forcing me to marry him and shooting you in the head."

"He's not that unstable," Roland argued, not wanting to shatter his illusion of safety.

"Oh, you have no idea. He's much more dangerous than he seems."

"Then why did you bring us to him?" Roland snapped, taking an angry tone with Pamela for the first time in their relationship.

She looked wounded but brushed it off. "Because you begged me to. You wanted adventure. I warned you it was dangerous. You didn't care. Answer me this, honey: Have you had an adventure?"

"Yes."

"Good. Then I gave you exactly what you wanted."

He couldn't argue with that. "Okay, okay. Let's not fight. I just want to see you smile again. I miss your pretty dimples."

Pamela forced a tired smile. "What are you going to do for work?"

"I think I'd be a good waiter. You'd definitely be a good waitress. Imagine the tips you'd get."

Pamela hummed thoughtfully. "I think I'd rather teach children. Or maybe do something with animals. A vet nurse, maybe?"

He chuckled. "Well, you're right about us needing a lot more money if you're going to go to college."

Pamela looked out the window for a minute, deep in thought, then returned her gaze to him with a new light in her eyes. "What if I know how we can get enough money?"

"I'm all ears."

"One last job. We fly across the border. Except we're not going to see Francisco's contacts, we're going to see *my* contacts. Some guys that Francisco screwed over years ago that I've been keeping in my pocket for a rainy day. We sell the coke, take all the money, and fly on to wherever we're going next. Never to be seen by him again."

His eyes popped open wide. "You want to steal from Francisco? Are you crazy?"

Pamela giggled. "Maybe. But I think it's our only shot at starting over. One last job, and then we're set for life. A couple of million dollars will go far down here."

Roland felt his heart pounding, and he looked at Pamela the same way he had the first night he'd tried cocaine. She was a genius. His partner in crime. His lifeblood. She'd keep his heart ticking and adventure in their lives as long as the two of them drew breath.

"I'm sold."

"Are we really going to do this?"

"We're really going to do this," he confirmed.

A branch snapping sounded on the other side of an open window. Roland turned toward it with a frown and glanced at Pamela, who wore a similarly disgruntled expression. Roland put a finger to his lips, grabbed his loaded gun from the kitchen counter, and crept toward the front door to sneak around the side.

He pressed his back up against the house's front wall, took a deep breath, and turned into the alley, holding his gun out.

THE CRASH

"Freeze!" he called out, hoping he wouldn't find himself pointing his gun at a stray cat.

He was not. A man who worked for Francisco was cowering by their kitchen window and looked up at Roland like a frightened animal with his hands up. He was young, a new recruit with a wispy mustache and nervous energy. Roland didn't know his name, but he knew he was Francisco's step-nephew or second cousin once removed. Another addition to the endless list of distant relatives.

Roland turned off the safety just as Pamela rounded the corner and joined him at his side.

"Ask him what he's doing here," Roland instructed.

"*¿Qué estás haciendo aquí?*" Pamela asked.

"*Francisco me envió aquí para… para pendiente de ti,*" the young man stammered, his voice panicked as he raised his hands higher, shielding his head and face.

"What did he say?" Roland asked.

"He said Francisco sent him here to spy on us." Pamela put her hand on Roland's arm. "I think you've scared him enough. He's not going to say anything."

"Ask him how much he heard."

"Roland."

"Ask him."

Pamela sighed. "*¿Qué escuchaste?*"

The young man shook his head frantically. "*No escuché nada. Estabas demasiado lejos.*"

"*¿Estás seguro de que no escuchaste nada?*"

"*¡Sí! ¡Sí estoy seguro!*" the man exclaimed.

Pamela looked at Roland. "He says he didn't hear anything. He was too far away. Roland, honey, I know tensions are high, but you have to let him go. He's not going to say anything."

Roland shook his head sadly. "That's where you're wrong. The innocent ones always squeal. When I was a kid, I accidentally ran over this bully's cat on my bike, and even though my dorky, shy friend Ronnie—who was even more pathetic and hated than I was—promised he wouldn't tell, he ratted me out before the day was up. Weak people, like this sniveling scumbag, always seek out the protection of the strong. And Francisco is the strongest guy around. So, we let him go, and you can kiss living on the beach and rescuing sea turtles goodbye and say hello to kissing Francisco on the mouth with my ashes on your bedside table."

He was frightening Pamela, and even though the young thug couldn't understand a word of Roland's rant, he looked as if he might piss his pants in fear. Roland felt horrible, but he didn't lower his gun.

He pictured their future, playing fetch on the beach with a dog, lounging in the sun on the deck, blue skies, white sand, maybe some kids, a job that fulfilled him. Then he pictured what would happen if Francisco found out about their plan. All Roland could see was darkness for him, and Pamela dressed up to the nines cradling a baby that looked just like Francisco, her dimples gone forever.

Roland fired the gun.

CHAPTER TWENTY-SEVEN

THE DETECTIVE

"Y<small>OU READY?</small>" H<small>EATHER ASKED</small> G<small>ABRIEL AS THEY</small> looked ahead at the mountain range mural that Bobby himself had painted onto the front of the windowless brick building. The wooden sign that read Sherwood's banged against the wall behind it in the frigid breeze, and the double doors beneath blew open and shut in sync.

Gabriel nodded. "Are you?"

"Ready as I'll ever be."

"Maybe we're wrong about all this. It could be a big misunderstanding."

"It's not."

"Beau could've been lying."

"He wasn't."

"How do you know?"

Heather removed her sunglasses and looked at her partner with purple-rimmed eyes. "I just do. There's no misunderstanding. She sold him drugs, and he nearly died. That's it. She'll be lucky if they only charge her with possession."

Savannah cried out from somewhere inside the building, and Heather cringed. She was teething, apparently, which was causing a lot of strife for the whole family. The melancholic howls of a baby in pain provided an unpleasant soundtrack to the entire affair. Perturbed, Heather hesitated with proceeding until Gabriel patted her shoulder and gestured toward the doors. Shaking off the increasingly shrill shrieking, Heather gave the okay, and they moved in.

Heather closed the door hard behind her, causing Amber, who was behind the bar with Savannah strapped to her chest, to startle, which only made the crying worse. Once she recognized them, she grinned broadly and returned to her work.

"Well, ain't this a nice surprise?" Amber said, her eyes on the unpolished glasses before her. It was only when she finally turned to ask for their order that her good humor faltered. The gravity of her expression aged her before their eyes. The sun-damage spiderwebbed across her face, pronounced jowl lines formed a frown, and her eye bags looked like they weighed more than Heather's own.

There she is, Heather thought. *The real Amber Horton.*

"What's going on, Heather?" Amber asked, her voice wavering.

"Amber Horton, you're under arrest for the possession and distribution of laced narcotics," Heather said, gesturing for Gabriel to move behind the bar. "You have the right to remain silent and refuse to answer questions. If you give up the right to remain silent, anything you say can and will be used against you in a court of law. Do you understand what I've said?"

Amber looked at her blankly, clutching Savannah to her chest and removing herself from the harsh glow of the string of blue LED lights. Time turned back, and she transformed into a scared teenager getting busted for underage drinking.

"Laced narcotics?" she asked. "I don't know what you're talking about."

"Do you understand your rights?"

"Y—yes," Amber stuttered.

"Where's Bobby?" Heather asked.

"I don't know."

Amber backed into the shelves into bottles, knocking an open bottle of red to the ground. Savannah began to wail again, and the explosion of red spattered Amber's legs and looked exactly like blood.

Perfect, Heather thought. *That'll really freak out the townspeople.*

"Amber, calm down," she said aloud, looking around at the crowd of patrons. "I need you to give the baby to Bobby. Where is he?"

"Bobby!" Amber hollered. "Bobby, come here quickly!"

Bobby emerged from the store room, a wooden crate of bottles in his burly arms, and he looked at the scene with a slack jaw. "Heather, what the hell is going on?"

"Amber is under arrest. I need you to take the baby."

"Under arrest? For what?" Bobby spluttered.

Heather looked at Amber to give her an opportunity to explain herself. Amber was still gibbering, moving away from Gabriel and clutching her baby so tightly that it seemed like a smothering hazard.

"Bobby, will you please take the baby?" Heather asked impatiently.

"Sure," he huffed, moving toward Amber cautiously like a rabid animal, and carefully pried Savannah from her arms. He turned back to Heather and asked again. "What is she under arrest for?"

"Amber is under arrest for selling cyanide-laced cocaine to Beau Ellis."

"Is he...?" Bobby asked.

"He's in a medically induced coma," Heather answered darkly, unable to keep the rage out of her voice.

"Miss Horton, please stop struggling," Gabriel said.

"Cuff her," Heather instructed.

"Oh, you don't have to do that!" Bobby exclaimed, bouncing the screaming baby.

The cuffs clicked shut, and Gabriel adjusted them for Amber's small wrists. He led her out from behind the bar, her lower half covered in claret. Her knees buckled, but Gabriel kept her upright by her armpits and guided her toward the door. Heather followed them but was stopped by Bobby calling out to her.

"Heather," he said quietly, his eyes pleading as if that could possibly do anything to save his girlfriend.

Heather looked down at Savanah's chubby, red face and said, "I'll let you know when they set bail."

"Amber, can I get you some tea or coffee?" Tina asked, sickly sweet, as Amber sat in cuffs on the opposite side of the table from Heather.

"Just some water, please," Amber said, her voice trembling so badly it was hard to understand her.

"Of course," Tina said. "And Officer Silva, please uncuff Miss Horton before you excuse yourself."

Gabriel looked between Heather's glowering face and Tina's affable one. It was clear that he was expecting to sit in on the interrogation but then had remembered that Heather was not, in fact, his boss. Reluctantly, he removed the cuffs and himself from the room.

Heather wished they'd stayed on. Not because she believed Amber to be a threat but because she knew she was a flight risk. Just one question would likely send her running at the door, where they'd have to subdue her again. It was a waste of energy, but it was also Tina's funeral.

Tina beamed. "That's more like it. No need to treat you like a criminal without any evidence, isn't that right, Detective Bishop?"

Heather looked up from her chair at Tina's disapproving face and said coolly, "Victim testimony is evidence."

THE CRASH

"Not when that victim is Beau Ellis," Tina grumbled.

"How very professional of you," Heather retorted. "Using personal vendettas and judgments in a legal setting."

Tina faltered and, when she couldn't think of a reply, stomped out of the room to grab a cup of water from the cooler. Heather resumed staring at Amber in her absence, who had long since stopped trying to get on Heather's good side.

Heather wasn't like this—not usually. The bad cop. The aggressor. The type of person who likes to make their suspects feel small and panicked. However, Beau had nearly died in her arms this morning, and she wasn't in the mood to sugarcoat the situation.

Tina was similarly furious with Heather for her underhanded approach regarding the arrest. Tina liked to know everything that was going on in town at all times, and the fact she had no idea about Beau or Amber had humiliated her. As a result, she was throwing her weight around to regain her sense of power.

Heather felt somewhat guilty about her accidental unprofessionalism—she genuinely had forgotten about the chain of command in her state of stress—but she didn't have time for Tina to twiddle her thumbs about the arrest while more people potentially snorted toxic cocaine. With any luck, anyone else who had purchased it wouldn't be doing it first thing in the morning. So, at least, time was currently on their side.

Tina returned with water for each of them, shut the door, and sat beside Heather. She turned on the tape recorder and said, "Suspect name, Amber Horton, 31. Time, 11:43 a.m. on Friday the fourth of November, 2023. Suspect has forgone the option of having a lawyer present."

"Arrested on suspicion of knowingly selling poison-laced narcotics," Heather added coldly.

Ignoring Heather, Tina reached out and patted Amber's arm. "Don't worry. We'll get this all straightened out. Heather's just been unfortunately misled by a very unwell young man, who, I might add, is well-known for being a liar."

"But he's not lying about this, is he, Amber?" Heather asked.

Amber looked between the two, a deer caught in headlights. She stopped the back and forth and landed on Heather before screwing up her face. Heather resisted a groan. There had already been too much crying today.

"No, he's not," Amber squeaked. "He was telling the truth."

Heather leaned back in her seat, self-satisfied, as Tina's face fell. She knew she shouldn't be smug, but after half an hour of berating by her boss, it was hard not to be when proved right so quickly.

"Amber, why?" the sheriff asked, clearly devastated that a member of her precious book club and MLM Tupperware parties could do something so terrible. Heather almost felt sorry for her. The realization that you can't trust anyone—not even the most beloved people in your life—was a wake-up call she wouldn't wish on anyone.

Amber stuttered but failed to answer Tina, so Heather rephrased the question. "Why did you sell the drugs to Beau?"

"I don't know. Because he asked me?"

"Are you a drug dealer?" Tina asked, saying the word like a slur in a hushed tone.

Amber shook her head fervently. "No, never. I swear this is the first time I've ever sold drugs."

"I don't believe you," Heather said.

"Okay, there was this one time in high school that I sold some of my dad's pot to another kid and got caught, but that was like forever ago!"

"Amber," Heather said sternly. "I need you to tell the truth because if anyone takes this cocaine, they will die. It's still possible that Beau might die, so I need you to be honest."

"I swear, Heather. I swear this is my first and only time selling cocaine."

"So, you're not a drug dealer?" Tina asked, sounding immensely relieved.

"No. Someone gave me this cocaine as a gift, and Beau mentioned that his usual dealer over in Snoqualmie got busted when he was drunk. I needed money to fill a cavity and figured, what's the harm? He's going to get it somewhere—might as well be from me."

"And the cyanide?" Heather prompted.

"I had no idea it was laced—I swear. I never tried any myself. It's not my thing."

Heather chewed her cheek. "Well, no offense, Amber, but I'm having a hard time believing you, considering how his dad died. I'm starting to think you might've had a very big part to play in all of this."

Tina opened her mouth to defend Amber, but Amber stopped her. "I think I can explain how this has happened, but I warn you, it's a long story."

"Well, luckily, you're the only thing on today's docket," Heather stated, waving for her to continue.

Amber nodded. "So, around eighteen months ago, I was hanging out at a small-town motel in rural Texas next to a truck stop. I can probably find you the name of it when I get my phone back."

"What were you doing there?" Heather asked.

"Girls' trip," Amber replied a little too quickly. The right side of her mouth twitched, and Heather spotted her tell. Which, at least, meant she hadn't been lying thus far.

"Girls' trip to rural Texas?"

"Just a stop on our way to Dallas." She twitched again, but Heather let it go. Whatever she and her friends had been doing didn't interest her much. Plus, the mention of motels and truck stops told her everything she needed to know.

Amber cleared her throat, her skin turning ruddy. "Anyway, there was a little bar in the lobby, and my friends had gone to bed, so I was drinking alone and enjoying my time off work. Then this guy tapped me on the shoulder, and I was immediately pissed off because I didn't want some lonely schmuck waving his pecker in my face. But when I turned around, I see this handsome guy with beautiful eyes. He seemed a little down on his luck and desperately needed to lose the beard, but when he offered to buy me a drink, I accepted. We talked and drank, and then he bought more drinks, and he talked some more. I think this went on for like four hours. He was more than a little sad and looked like he'd seen some shit, but he was still sweet as could be. More than sweet, he was charming. In fact, he charmed the pants right off me."

"So, you slept with him?" Heather asked.

"Yep. And that one night alone was enough to make me fall in love. I begged him to take me wherever he was going, but it was never going to happen."

"Why not?"

"Because he was still in love with his ex. Talked about her constantly after we were done. Told me I looked just like her, but the laugh wasn't the same, and my clothes weren't right. Started to get real melancholy about it. He even called me by her name a couple of times during—"

Heather waved her off. "I get the picture. Let's get to the part about the cocaine."

"Right, of course. Well, three weeks later, I missed my period. Whoops. I pee on a stick, and those two little lines show right up, and I freak out. I was sleeping on couches and living in motels saving up for a trailer at the nicest local park, but I barely even had a job. But I decided to keep her and muddled along, not knowing where in the world her daddy was. Then, as fate would have it, I ran into him in Dallas five months later. He looked at me, and it just clicked right away. He was sorry enough, but not enough to stick around. So, instead, he offered me the only thing he could."

"The cocaine."

"Yep. A brick of high-quality Mexican cocaine. He said if I sold it, I could make enough money for the kid to go to college, so I took it, and I never saw him again until..." Amber drifted off.

"Until?"

"I saw him on the news six months ago. Some unsolved cases special. Fifteenth anniversary since he went missing. The documentary was crap, but I saw him, Roland Ellis, mayor of Glenville. Now, he'd told me his name was Dallon Riles, so of course, when I looked him up, nothing showed up; but when I searched his real name, I found his whole family. So, I devised a plan to move to Glenville and get to know his family. Tell them that he's alive, that he's a no-good drifter, and that Savannah is his baby. Then, in turn, I hoped they'd welcome me into their super wealthy fold."

"So, you came up here for a shakedown?" Heather asked.

"I wouldn't put it like that, but babies are expensive, and I realized I couldn't provide for her like the Ellis kids."

"So, does Nancy Ellis know?" Tina asked, recovering from her shock regarding Savannah's father. Heather had put two and two together long before the culmination and felt her smugness levels rise once more.

Amber shook her head. "No, not even Bobby knows who Savannah's father is. I got up here ready to tell her day one, but then I walked into Sherwood's, you introduced me to Bobby, and everything changed. He turned my life around so quickly that I didn't even need the Ellis family's money."

"Well, thank you for that enlightening story, Miss Horton," Heather said, her mind racing. "Now, the problem is that I have to take your word for this being a series of screwups and not something intentional."

"Heather, I'm not capable of murder. You know me."

There was no twitch anywhere on her face, and Heather knew she was telling the truth, but it didn't stop her mind from racing. "What if you *did* know who Roland was at the time of the conception, and you knew you could stand to make a lot of money if you played your cards right? So, you get pregnant on purpose. You lace his drugs with cyanide, you come up here for the shakedown, and await the massive inheritance to plump up Nancy's generous offerings."

"Heather," Tina said in a warning tone.

"Okay, okay. *Maybe* you didn't know that Dallon Riles was Roland Ellis, but what if Beau got drunk here, as he always does, and spilled the beans about the inheritance. So, then you took a gamble on the cocaine in your possession, also being laced, and gave it to Beau to bump him off in the hopes that Savannah will be gifted his cut of the inheritance?"

Amber looked devastated and utterly drained. She kept it together enough to retort, "That would mean I'd have to believe that Nancy would ever give me a cent. I thought she might before I met her, but not now."

Heather scraped her chair back, ready to leave. "It's a good point. The problem is I just don't know for sure."

"What happens now?" Amber asked, the shakes returning.

Tina took over. "You will be officially charged, by your own admittance, for possessing and distributing a Schedule II drug. However, everything else is a theory, so unless Detective

Bishop gathers some evidence to disprove your testimony, you will be released with bail once we set the amount. Then you will be expected to attend your court dates regarding your sentencing for possession and distribution."

"So, I'm staying here tonight?" Amber asked.

"Yes, you'll be staying in a solitary holding cell tonight and probably tomorrow too."

Amber nodded, and Heather furrowed her brow, noticing a faint glimmer of something in the woman's expression. Something she'd never have expected to be there.

"You look relieved," Heather said. "Why?"

"I don't know if you'll believe me," Amber murmured.

"Try me."

"I keep seeing this creepy guy around. He's tall and narrow with a big chin. Dresses in black most of the time. It almost feels like he's following me."

Heather remembered the day of the funeral. She'd been following Beau when she'd spotted the creep with the camera. The guy who slinked off into an alleyway after trying to take creepshots of Amber. Or so she'd thought. She felt a cold chill run down her spine and looked at Amber as she stood.

"No matter what you've done, I promise I will keep you and Savannah safe. I'll ask some of the guys to patrol Sherwood's and your house."

Amber opened her mouth to thank Heather, but the detective was already gone.

CHAPTER TWENTY-EIGHT

THE DETECTIVE

AFTER THE INTERROGATION, HEATHER DECIDED TO take fifteen. That quickly turned into an hour. This was because, upon sitting down on the bench outside, she soon found that one of Gabriel's cups of black coffee and a single cigarette would not be enough to revive her. It wasn't even one o'clock in the afternoon, and she'd already saved a life, made an arrest, and uncovered a litany of secrets. Three coffees and ten cigarettes later, she was awake enough to function and requested Nancy's presence for the second time that day.

She owed the woman an update and an explanation of all that had happened. Heather didn't have kids, but if her hypothetical son was in a medically induced coma because someone sold him poison-laced drugs, and the person that sold them to him was also was the mother of her children's half-sister, she would want to know about it.

Nancy arrived wearing flat shoes and donning her hair in a bun. She seemed subdued, and Heather realized she'd probably come straight from the hospital.

Heather greeted her warmly to little response and ushered her past staring eyes into the staff room. Nancy collapsed on the little two-seater couch, and Heather offered her a coffee. Nancy frowned at the smell emanating from the pot of charred sludge and shook her head.

"Fair enough," Heather said, sitting opposite her on a wobbly chair. "So, I called you in because we've made an arrest regarding Beau's poisoning."

"So, someone did try to murder him?"

"We're not exactly sure about that. The way she tells it, it was all a big mistake, but we're still holding her for selling him the drugs in the first place. Maybe it's attempted murder, maybe negligence, maybe neither. I'll keep you updated as far as legalities go."

"She, Detective? Who's she?"

"Amber Horton. Bobby Sherwood's girlfriend. She sold him the drugs."

Nancy sucked her teeth. "I always disliked that woman."

"Why?"

"Oh, I don't know. There's just something about her. Her accent, the way she talks to me, her dress sense..." Nancy trailed off and gasped. "Oh my God, I think it's because she reminds me so much of Pamela."

It clicked for Heather then that the ex Roland had been torn up about when he met Amber was Pamela and that when the two met, Pamela was already dead. He'd slept with Amber because she resembled his dead ex-girlfriend, and the reminder of her was too painful to stick around.

It was starting to become clear that the man had screwed over all the women in his life, and as suspicious as all of them were in different ways, Heather could not overlook the common denominator of destruction.

"Yes, she does bear a striking resemblance to Pamela. In fact, your husband thought so too," Heather said.

Nancy buried her head in her hands with a moan. "Please don't tell me that he slept with her too."

"Well, if what Amber says is true, they not only slept together but conceived a child together."

Nancy remerged and looked at Heather, her eyes hollow. "The baby?"

"Yes. Savannah Bennet is your children's half-sister."

Nancy straightened. "I think I will take that coffee now unless you have anything stronger."

"Not since Gene quit," Heather chuckled and stood to pour the lukewarm liquid into a novelty mug.

"It seems my husband can humiliate me, even from beyond the grave."

"I'm so sorry, Nancy," Heather said, reaching out to Nancy's shoulder as she handed her the coffee.

Nancy didn't pull away as she had when they first met and let Heather comfort her briefly before pulling away.

"I shouldn't be surprised," she quipped. "Really, I'm shocked he doesn't have more bastards running around. Perhaps he does."

"So, you really didn't know about any of this? Amber hasn't come around shaking you down for money or anything like that?"

"Certainly not. I've barely said three words to that woman. And it's not like I'd give her anything either."

Heather was beginning to see more and more truth in Amber's side of events. The aspect still up in the air was whether she knew the cocaine was poisoned when she gave it to Beau. Her face hadn't twitched, but Heather couldn't write off the theory based on a flicker of the mouth. Just as Heather was about to mention this hypothesis, Nancy fixed Heather with a pleasant expression. It was the one Heather imagined she saved for her rich friends at dinner parties, something normally inaccessible for someone like herself.

"Can I see her? Talk with her woman to woman?" Nancy asked. "After all, she did sleep with my husband. Maybe there's more she knows about where he's been."

"Of course, you can," said Tina kindly from the doorway. "Better to squash this 'beef,' eh? I don't think either of you means any harm, and she's in a terrible state. She probably has a lot of apologizing to do to you. I'm sure she feels just awful about Beau."

Heather glared at Tina for overriding her but said nothing. She looked back at Nancy and asked, "How is Beau doing?"

Nancy's mouth was drawn into two thin lines that curled up at the corners. The stretched, masklike smile did not reach her eyes. "He's stable, though seeing your first child and only son on a ventilator is just as painful as you might imagine."

It was evident to Heather that it would be a mistake to let Nancy see Amber today, but none of it seemed to dawn on Tina, who guided Nancy through to the holding cells with an ignorant cheerfulness. The main problem with Tina was that she wanted everyone to love her, especially people with as much community pull as Nancy and Amber. One was beloved among the working class, the other entrenched in the world of the wealthy. She wanted to solve the case but was clearly balking at the idea of involving two beloved women or treating them like suspects. After all, she needed the votes of the county to remain Sheriff.

Regardless of Heather's feelings, the three moved to the holding section, which comprised four private cells and two groups—all of which were rarely occupied, with the exception of local drunks and the odd unruly teenager.

Amber was sitting in the cell closest to the thick metal door that separated the cells from the precinct. It was old and could only be unlocked by a rung of large keys, which Tina hadn't yet mastered the order of. Heather watched Nancy as Tina struggled to find the right one. She was back to her usual rigid self and shifted her weight from the tips to the balls of her feet in impatience.

They finally entered and peered into the small circular window in the cell. Amber seemed calm, or at least less hysterical than earlier, but was clearly uncomfortable in her cold cell with her polystyrene cup of cold tea.

She looked at Heather and Tina hopefully, as if they might be announcing that she was leaving already, but then they

THE CRASH

parted to reveal Nancy, and Amber turned pale around the edges of her fake tan.

"Hello, Amber. I was just wondering if we could have a little chat," Nancy started. She then turned to Tina and asked, "Can I go in? I feel a little awkward hovering outside the door."

Tina looked to Heather, who shook her head. Ignoring Heather, she replied, "Sure, I don't see why not, as long as we supervise the conversation."

Nancy nodded, Tina unlocked the door, and Heather stepped back against the cold paint lacquered concrete, her arms folded. Nancy entered the room and sat on the bench opposite Amber.

"So, you knew my husband," she quipped. She didn't wait for a response before continuing. "And that child of yours is his."

"Yes, ma'am," Amber admitted, shrinking into herself. It was a foreign sight for the brash woman that Heather had once liked so much.

"Were you in a relationship?" Nancy asked, as Heather and Tina stayed silent.

"No. I wanted to be, but—"

"But? My husband wasn't interested in marrying some sort of truck stop floozy," she sneered with sudden cruelty. "Roland was a lot of things, and though he indulged in danger, he never liked his vices cheap."

Amber bristled. Her stance changed, and her fists clenched. "Is that why he left *you*?"

Nancy stood, and Heather expected her to stride out of the room, but instead, she opened her palm and swung hard. The impact of the slap was muted by the small, thick-walled room, but it still sounded like it hurt. Before Tina or Heather could move, Amber stood and attacked, grabbing a fistful of hair in her strong hands and yanking Nancy down to her level. The women shouted in rage at each other as Heather and Tina ran over to break it up.

"Why you—"

"How dare you—"

"Ladies, cut it out!" Heather bellowed as she wrestled Amber's flailing arms away from Nancy and forced them behind her back.

"I'm going to file for paternity, you trailer park bitch!" Nancy screamed as Tina pulled her out into the hall. "That daughter of yours is no child of my husband. You're just after his money, you goddamn grave robber!"

Heather, who had never heard Nancy speak like this before, nearly released Amber from her grasp in shock. It was evident that the pressure had gotten to both of the usually well-mannered women because they kicked and screamed obscenities, fighting against their captors, until Nancy eventually calmed herself enough that Tina released her vicelike hold.

"I'm fine," Nancy said, slicking her hair though it hung loosely from her now half-sized bun. "But I hope you prosecute this murderer to the full extent of the law. I'm sure she killed my husband, and I'm sure she intended to do the same thing to my son. Likely to claim money for her illegitimate bastard child."

"Come on, Mrs. Ellis," Tina said. "Let's go."

"I don't need you to remove me," Nancy replied, her voice high and strained. "I'm quite capable of leaving on my own."

She stalked away, and Heather left Amber with Tina in order to follow the woman through the station. At Gabriel's desk, she soundlessly asked for her hat and fur-lined jacket. She watched as Mrs. Ellis left the building, slamming the door behind her, and changed her appearance as best she could in order to continue her pursuit.

Outside she kept a distance of at least twenty feet, the hat pulled low over her eyes, and watched as the elegant woman marched into Sherwood's, likely for the first time. She hoped all she wanted was a stiff drink and not a secondary confrontation. Just in case, Heather gave it no more than two minutes before she entered through the back door via the beer garden and slipped into her favorite booth.

Nancy was at the bar talking to Bobby in a hushed voice. Bobby looked sorrowful, Savannah in a sling around his chest, and Nancy looked like a snake ready to strike. However, he didn't ask for her to leave, and as they talked, Nancy seemed to calm herself and took a seat on one of the worn, leather-topped stools. Bobby was a hard man to be angry at, and he quickly served her a large glass of wine with seemingly no charge.

THE CRASH

Nancy sipped the wine as the two continued talking, and she placed her head in her hands as Bobby looked near tears, not helped by the daytime drunks demanding his attention. Heather wanted to go and help, pour some beers, and let them talk. After all, the love of each of their lives had a baby together, and knowing who Savannah's father was and Amber facing jail meant it was a hard day for Bobby too. However, she knew she had to sit tight and view the scene without intervention.

When Nancy raised her head up again, she looked directly at Savannah before looking up at Bobby and asking him something. It was clearly a question to which he keenly said yes. He undid the sling and handed Savannah over the counter to Nancy. Heather tensed, terrified of what Nancy might do, before remembering that, above all else, this woman loved being a mother.

Nancy rocked the baby in her arms, soothing her instantly, and smiled at the gurgling baby. Heather had never noticed it before, but Savannah looked exactly like the baby pictures of Beau at the Ellis household. The same blotchy chubby cheeks, the same dark tuft of hair, and the same unmistakable blue eyes.

Nancy must've seen it, too, because as she held the baby close to her chest, she began to cry. Whether from nostalgia or acceptance of her husband's second life, Heather didn't know. Either way, it seemed like progress.

CHAPTER TWENTY-NINE

THE DETECTIVE

With Gabriel working late because of Operation Damage Control at the station, Heather had resorted to talking to herself as she perched on the dilapidated arm of the big, brown couch and exhaled her cigarette smoke out the window. She was on pack two of the day, and her tongue was starting to feel like an old rug, but she couldn't stop now. She was enslaved to the nicotine, and her cravings were only worsened by having swapped from coffee to whiskey.

She stared at the corkboard from her groove, muttering under her breath, running through her theories. The old lamp in the corner was doing a poor job of illuminating her shady surroundings, and the faces on the board leered at her through the haze. Amber, Pamela, Nancy, Roland, Beau, Lucy, and Francisco were reduced to sclera and teeth.

She shuddered and was unsure if it was from the nighttime chill seeping in through the window or if it was the seven faces staring at her. Francisco, in particular, made her uneasy. Though he was at a disadvantage considering his photo was a mugshot.

Heather shivered again, moved away from the window, and ended the unwinnable staring contest. She was sick of her own voice and bouncing ideas off herself, so she crossed her fingers and called Gene, hoping he was still awake.

The phone rang for a while, and Heather nearly hung up, not wanting to wake him and Karen, but just as she was about to press the red button, Gene answered.

"Hello? Wells residence," he muttered gruffly.

"Hey, Gene, it's Heather. Do you have a minute to talk?"

He took a beat to respond. "Yeah, all right."

"Am I interrupting something?"

"I was watching Columbo, but I suppose this is more important." He paused thoughtfully. "Is it?"

Heather barked a laugh. "It depends. What episode is it?"

"Étude in Black."

"Honestly, I have no idea what that means. I don't know how you can be a cop and watch detective shows. I need a break from my job when I watch TV."

Gene chuckled. "As if you ever sit still for long enough to watch TV."

"I can sit still!" Heather protested.

"What are you doing right now?"

Heather looked at herself in the hallway mirror and realized she had been pacing the length of her house for the last couple of minutes. She quickly sat down on the couch as if she'd always been there. For good measure, she also turned on the TV. The comforting imagery of the Home Shopping Channel was on and muted, as ever.

"I'm sitting," she said.

"Uh huh," Gene responded. "And I'm running a marathon."

"No, seriously, I am."

"Well, in that case, I'll join you."

Gene groaned as he lowered himself onto his recliner. The leather creaked and squeaked as he made himself comfortable, and Heather heard the rattle of ice in a glass of liquid. Gene slurped noisily, but she figured it was better than him drinking straight from the bottle. Not that she was in a position to judge even if he was.

Gene exhaled with pleasure, smacked his lips, and asked, "So, what's up?"

"Today has been crazy. Like really insane."

"Yeah?" Gene sounded intrigued.

"You haven't heard?"

"Nope. Woke up with a headache and spent most of the day in bed. Plus, Karen's at her sister's house, so if she's got any gossip, I haven't heard it."

"I don't know where to start."

"The beginning is usually your best bet, but go slow so I can listen and watch Columbo at the same time."

Heather had already heard Peter Falk fall silent in the background and knew she had Gene's full attention, but she humored him by delivering an abridged version of the day's events. First Beau's poisoning, then her visit with Nancy, followed by Amber's arrest, and finished off with the jail cell fistfight. She tossed in some of her theories and opinions for good measure, eager to know what Gene thought of them.

"You know what I think?" Gene asked.

"What?" Heather replied eagerly.

"I think you need to go to bed."

"Gene. Come on."

"Seriously, kid. That's enough for one day."

"People could be in danger. Who knows how much more cyanide-laced cocaine Roland sold before he died?"

"Well, that I can give you some advice on. Tell the FBI. This is above and beyond your pay grade and your jurisdiction."

"So, I'm just supposed to give up?"

"No, you're supposed to save lives, and that means sometimes knocking out your ego and admitting that someone else is better for the job. Keep investigating, find out who killed Roland, and figure out if Amber is as innocent as she claims,

THE CRASH

but you need to ask for help. Protect the town and the people in it. Let the feds protect the country."

"All right, all right. I'll tell Tina to alert the feds, but I'm not going to stop trying to solve this."

"No one's asking you to, but what Roland was caught up in—smuggling drugs over the border, running around with the cartel—is much bigger than the Glenville Police Department is equipped to handle. You're only one woman, and this is only a small-town police department."

Heather sighed. "You're right. I just hate feeling so... powerless."

"Kid, you are tougher than a two-dollar steak. Not just anybody could do what you do, but there's no point in being stubborn. I've been stubborn my whole life, but sometimes you have to admit when things are out of your control, or else, people can get hurt."

Heather thought about the long list of dead hikers killed at the hands of Dennis Burke; all the while, Gene stuck his head in the sand. Now it was tearing him up inside, and Heather knew she'd feel the same way if someone else died from the laced cocaine just because she was determined to solve everything herself.

She heard Gene refill his drink and knew it was time to change the subject. "Chilly tonight," she said, opting for the age-old classic. The weather. Luckily, Gene, being in his mid-seventies, could talk about the weather for hours.

"Tell me about it. Most of the remaining crops are gone on account of the frost. Least I've had a good run this year. It always happens eventually."

"Crap," Heather hissed.

"What?"

"The seeds you gave me," Heather lamented. "The ground is frozen over. Will they be dead?"

"Oh, didn't I tell you? You have to sow them in the spring."

"You did not, but I should've figured that one out on my own."

"Don't worry about it. Plenty more where that came from. I'll give you some more next time I see you, and then you can try again. That's all we can do as humans. Fail and try again.

Hopefully, next time will be better; if not, you just do it again anyway. Try not to get too discouraged."

"Thanks, Gene. Good advice."

"You don't get to my age without having a few pearls of wisdom up your sleeve. It's what us old folks are good for."

Heather chuckled. "I'll let you get back to your show."

"All right, Heather. Get some sleep and come over for lunch soon. Karen wants to test a new bread recipe on someone other than me."

"Looking forward to it."

Gene hung up, clearly eager to get back to drinking and watching comfortingly wrapped-up mysteries unravel. Heather stared blankly at her TV for a few minutes before growing restless again and resuming her never-ending list of things to do.

While calling Tina about contacting the FBI, she food prepped her lunches for the week and did the small handful of dishes that had been sitting by the sink for the past three days. She attempted to smoke at the same time, but her wet hands proved counterintuitive to the bad habit.

It was fortunate that Tina agreed with her assessment and had already considered involving the FBI, as Heather's multitasking abilities were stretched too thin to argue her case. Once their conversation ended, Heather cleaned out the coffee maker, dusted the kitchen, and sat back at the dining table with a final nightcap.

Though her mind still whirred and her knees still bobbed, the last double of whiskey of the night softened the intensity. Once finished, she decided to heed Gene's advice about getting some sleep.

Heather woke in the dark, knowing sleep once again hadn't tided her over until morning. She and her sheets were drenched in sweat, and the low temperature left her cold, damp, and clammy. Her nightmares returned to her. They'd been more vivid than usual.

THE CRASH

Dennis Burke had been in her house, dressed in skins and caked blood and filth. He'd whispered her name with foul, fetid breath as he crept into her room and perched on the end of her bed like a chimpanzee, his knuckles pressed into the mattress. The moonlight illuminated him in a sickly glow, and though she'd been terrified, she couldn't move a single body part. Not even her eyelids. He'd taunted her about killing Alice and that even in hell, he felt pleasure when he felt her soul pass on. He'd succeeded in killing her after all, and he was conscious of it even in the afterlife.

The idea made Heather sick, and she had no intention of trying to sleep again. So, she climbed out of bed and pulled on some track pants and an old college sweatshirt. After pacing some more along the dark hallway, she found that just being awake wasn't enough. She also needed to be out of the house. So, she added thick socks, a scarf, a coat, and a hat to her ensemble and headed out into the night with her gun in her pocket for peace of mind.

She initially didn't know where she was going, but her legs seemed to have some idea. The walk was enjoyable enough without a destination, so she tried to turn off her mind as she watched the snow fall. After about twenty minutes, she realized where her body was taking her, and with a heavy heart, she consciously continued toward it. It was time.

After fifteen more minutes, she reached it, and as she veered from the safety of tarmac streets and concrete sidewalks, she hesitated. Was she ready? She wasn't sure, but she wasn't going to turn back now. She trudged through the thick layer of snow covering the grass, reaching the duck pond at the center of Whitetail Park.

Alice had mentioned the pond a couple of times to Heather when they'd had the opportunity to chitchat. It was where she had liked to go when the isolation of the house got too much for her—which was fairly often. She said she'd always bring a bag of frozen peas for the ducks, a thermos of tea, and a good book for herself. It worked well as the thermos warmed the peas, defrosting them by the time she arrived.

When Alice died, Gene had suggested making a memorial for her, but with Paul and the Marshalls out of town, no one left behind knew her well enough to offer something suitable. So, Heather had suggested putting a plaque on the iron bench by the duck pond that Alice had so loved to sit on. Everyone agreed it was a great idea, and by the end of that week, the plaque had been etched and adhered. This had happened a little over three months ago, and despite it being her idea, Heather had never been to see the plaque.

She decided to sit and stare at the freezing cold and duckless pond. She wished she'd accompanied Alice when she'd been invited to eat sandwiches by the pond. She'd been too busy, of course, unknowingly trying to prevent Alice's murder. Still, it would've been nice. Now a bench was just a bench, and it was much colder without her.

Heather breathed into her hands and rubbed them together. Then she felt a cold tap on her cheek and wiped away a large snowflake that melted against her fingertips. She laughed tearily, her breath a thick cloud. She and Alice both loved the snow. They'd often talked about how they couldn't wait for winter on the particularly sweltering summer days. They'd said it made them feel like kids again. To her disappointment, it wasn't working this time.

Leaves crunched underfoot from the forest's edge behind her, and Heather spun, expecting to see someone approaching. There was no person, no animals, no footprints, but it didn't reassure her. Her heart pounded as it had when she'd looked into the trees bordering her yard and knew someone was watching her, just out of sight.

Dennis Burke was dead, so who was watching her now?

"Is anyone there?" she called out, standing and pulling her gun from her pocket.

She kept it by her side and rounded the bench, facing where she'd heard the noise, scrutinizing the undergrowth for movement. She knew they were still there. She could feel it in her bones. She put her finger on the trigger and backed away toward the road, frequently looking over her shoulder.

Once she was back on the pavement, she heard footsteps coming from behind her. She didn't look back this time, and unable to tell if they were approaching or getting farther away,

THE CRASH

she picked up the pace and ran home. She put her gun in her pocket, but her hand was still firmly wrapped around the grip.

CHAPTER THIRTY

THE SON

BEAU WOKE TO A QUIET, REPETITIVE BEEPING, AND AS HE opened his eyes, he saw a bright white light and a mess of surrounding machinery. He felt tubes in his nose and a cannula in his arm. Everything hurt, his skin most of all, and his mouth was dryer than it had ever been. With great difficulty, he peeled his lips apart and his tongue from his palate. It was similarly hard to keep his throbbing eyes open, especially with the comforting warmth of the blue blanket on top of him, but he forced himself to keep staring once his focus landed on another person.

"Mom?" he croaked.

THE CRASH

Nancy turned sharply, her coffee sloshing over the edge of the cup. She clearly was not expecting him to be awake yet. She placed her coffee and magazine on the mint-green linoleum and moved to his side, whispering urgently to someone out of view to get the doctor.

"You're awake," she said softly. "We weren't expecting you for a few more hours, at least."

He tried to laugh, but it hurt too much to breathe. "You know me, I hate to waste the day sleeping."

His mother looked unamused but combed her fingers through his matted hair and scratched against his sore scalp. It was the pleasurable kind of pain like a shiatsu massage, and her long nails, in particular, felt amazing. The action began to soothe him back to sleep until she spoke again.

"You've been out for twenty-four hours."

"Wow. That's a new record."

"I thought you were going to die," she whispered, her voice as hoarse as his.

"Can't get rid of me that easily."

"I don't want to get rid of you, Beau," Nancy said, already exasperated now that he'd returned to consciousness.

Beau grinned. "Wow, maybe you do love me."

"Of course, I love you." Her voice was clipped, the word unnatural coming out of her mouth, but Beau could tell she meant it.

The other person, who turned out to be a very angry-looking Lucy, and a doctor entered the room. The doctor cracked jokes that Beau was too tired to respond to, checked his patient's vital signs, removed the tube from his nose, and left Beau at the mercy of the others.

It took a minute for anyone to speak, but eventually, Lucy saw fit to. "What the hell is wrong with you? You scared us half to death and made me miss an exam *and* date night!"

"That must have been so difficult for you," Beau croaked. "I wouldn't know what it's like to suffer like that."

"Beau—" Nancy tried to cut in, but Lucy was already halfway through her riposte.

"It's your fault you're always ending up in situations like this. Maybe think about that."

This time he did manage a laugh. "Not exactly like I meant to ingest cyanide. I wouldn't talk to you like this if you got in a car crash."

"Not the cyanide. The cocaine," Lucy growled. "Where do you get off roleplaying as some sort of impoverished junkie with all the privileges you've been offered? You're well educated, you have a supportive family that bails you out, you're clearly smart, people seem to enjoy talking to you when you're not being a prick, and you're not ugly. So, what's the deal?"

"Can you piss off?" Beau asked. "Go do your precious exam or screw your big shot boyfriend."

"I'm not going anywhere until you answer my question," Lucy insisted, arms folded.

"Lucy, he's just woken up," Nancy scolded.

"Perfect. That's supposed to be the best time to get the truth out of people. Haven't you seen all those wisdom teeth removal videos?"

"Fine," Beau said. "You want to know what my problem is? It's you, and it's Dad, and it's him leaving. It's all our messed-up family stuff."

Lucy scoffed. "He left me too, and you don't see me acting like this."

"It's different. You were too young to remember. You don't remember the affair, the screaming, the crying, followed by the radio silence. I thought he was dead, but I couldn't grieve because, officially, he was still alive."

Lucy chewed her lip. "You know, I might've been young. But I remember most of it. The difference was I coped by staying busy, and when I got old enough, I went to therapy. I got my shit together. You can only excuse your problems for so long before you need to take responsibility. You're not a victim, Beau. It's not everyone versus you. You're just too lazy to get better. Being a drunk loser who lives in a van is easier than making something of your life."

"Lucy," Nancy warned.

Beau tried and failed to shake his head. "No. She's right. Maybe not about all of it, but she is right."

"I know I am," Lucy said. "I know Dad walking out sucked; I know thinking he was dead sucked more; I know Mom was mean to you; I know I was the favorite. You're not smarter, more sensitive, or more observant. We all know how it is and how it's been, and maybe you're owed an apology, but you owe us plenty in that regard."

Beau closed his eyes. "I'm sorry. For scaring you."

"You should be," Lucy snapped.

"Lucy," Nancy hissed, reaching the end of her tether. "Thank you for apologizing, Beau."

"I'm going to get better," he promised. "I know you don't believe me, but wow, nearly dying is one hell of a wake-up call."

"Oh, so the other four overdoses weren't close enough to death for you?" Lucy asked, her voice quaking with anger.

"Lucy, I think you need to leave the room," Nancy said softly.

"Seriously? Fine. This is why he's like this. You two would kick his ass up and down the street about bad grades, but you look the other way when he tries to kill himself with drugs. Well, I won't be complicit in this." She loudly gathered her things, and Beau watched as she opened the door and looked back at him. "If you really do get better, you have my number, but I imagine I won't be hearing from you."

She slammed the door behind her, and both Beau and Nancy recoiled at the sound. He closed his eyes again and swallowed hard. Lucy's words had cut deep.

"I really am going to get better," he whimpered insistently. "I've got the money now. I'm going to get rid of the RV and build a real house. I'll start my own business too—legally, I mean—not just shady deals with the guys at Pacific Silver."

"That sounds like a great start, Beau," Nancy replied, her voice distant.

"I'll go to AA too. And Heather gave me a list of contacts who do drug counseling over the phone. I've never tried any of that stuff before. It's really going to be different this time."

"Of course, it will," she said kindly, though he could tell she didn't believe him. At least Lucy was honest.

He sat back in frustration, trying not to cry. "I think I want you to leave," he croaked.

Nancy removed her hand from his head and frowned. "Are you sure?"

Beau nodded, unable to speak because of the knot in his throat.

"Okay. I'll see you soon."

Beau swallowed hard and looked up at the ceiling. Nancy sighed and quietly exited the room. A few minutes later, the door creaked open again, and from the hardness of the shoe sole, he could tell it wasn't his Crocs-wearing doctor. Beau groaned, aggrieved by his family always having to have the last word.

"I thought I told you to leave me alone?" he asked his mother, struggling to keep the frustrated wobble out of his voice.

"Sorry, I can leave."

The voice didn't belong to Nancy or Lucy, and Beau opened his eyes to see Heather standing nervously in the doorway. She offered him a small wave before turning away, the door still half open.

Beau propped himself up on his elbows and called out weakly. "No, stay, please."

Heather turned back and quietly said, "Okay."

Beau flushed at how desperate he'd sounded, and his ears grew pink as Heather shut the door behind her and approached. She looked to the foot of the bed questioningly, and he nodded.

She sat down and frowned. "Jesus, this bed sucks."

"You should try the food. They serve it to you in a tube," he joked.

"Wow, I've always wanted to try experimental dining."

"Sorry to say, but it's a little overrated."

"Ah, well. Out of my price range."

Beau chuckled. "Yeah, I reckon this will set me back about thirty large. Think I'll stick to Luigi's."

"Yeah, me too." She paused. "Sorry if I upset you."

"You didn't. I thought you were my mother."

"Oh, is she here?"

Beau tried to shake his head again and winced at the stiffness of his muscles. "No, I told her and Lucy to leave."

"Why?"

"Because they didn't believe me about getting better. Buying a house, getting clean, and all that." Heather didn't respond, so Beau prompted her. "Do you believe me?"

He wanted a resounding yes and waited expectantly for it. It didn't come. Instead, Heather said, "I don't know, but I really hope that you will."

"I promise I am." He raised an arm shakily and stuck out a long pinky finger.

Heather smirked and wrapped her much small finger around his. "Pinky promise?" she asked.

"Pinky promise," he guaranteed.

"Okay, I believe you," she said, still smirking. "But I'm going to swing by AA once a month at random to check that you're going every week. No excuses, okay?"

"All right. Deal. But what happens if I don't go?"

"Then I pay you a visit."

"That's not much of a threat."

"It will be if I kick your ass."

"I don't know. Maybe I'm into that."

Heather rolled her eyes. "Here we go again with the flirting."

"It would be better if you flirted back."

"Beau," Heather warned.

"Seriously, why don't you like me back?" he asked, propping himself up, much to Heather's disapproval.

"Don't do that. Lay back down."

"I will when you answer me. Come on, please. I'm sick."

Heather rolled her eyes. "You're too young for me, for starters."

"It's because I'm a fuckup, isn't it?"

Heather hesitated. "No. I used to be a fuckup too. Still am, actually, and we've both got a lot of healing to do before we inflict ourselves on other people."

"And if I get my life together?"

"Don't hold your breath. To be honest, Beau, you're just not my type."

Beau cracked up, even though it hurt to laugh so hard, and Heather joined him less enthusiastically. He wiped tears from his eyes. "Wow. You really don't mince words, Detective."

"Sometimes I do, but I don't think lying will do you any good. I'm sorry if I gave you the wrong impression. Hanging out at your place was really unprofessional of me."

"Hey, your unprofessionalism saved my life. Holly Warren's, too, and a whole bunch of others."

Heather looked away. "Well, at least there's that."

"Seriously, though, I've been on enough self-improvement kicks to see when someone is doing the same. So, straighten up and fly right or whatever, but don't lose everything by turning into something else. Because I really like you, Heather Bishop."

Heather smiled warmly and reached forward, taking Beau's hand in hers. She squeezed it gently.

"See you at AA next week," she said.

"I thought you said it would be a surprise."

She stood and stretched. "Not this time. As you said, you're not the only one who needs to get their act together."

Beau still felt the phantom touch of Heather's hand squeezing his long after she left, and he imagined a better life set to the harmony of hospital equipment. Bonding in AA, getting sober, starting to date, building a house for two, her dogs getting lashes from Sid's vicious paws, and having a wedding in the woods. It was something he knew he'd only obtain in a parallel universe, but it soothed him to sleep anyway.

CHAPTER THIRTY-ONE

THE DETECTIVE

On the drive back from the hospital, Heather decided to take the scenic route back to her house. She had a lot to think about, and her home was as unwelcoming as it had been toward the end of the Warren case. She hoped for her sanity that it meant the Ellis case was nearly done, too, but it felt like there was plenty left to unturn.

Besides the mass of trees and a great view of the sprawling lake—a significant aspect of the longer route—was seeing a section of suburbia that she didn't often visit. It was primarily inhabited by the elite who had little to do with the rest of Glenville: the city folks, the nouveau riche families, the wealthy retirees, the tech geniuses, the landlords, the Airbnb industrialists. Heather didn't know any of them except for the Marshalls, whom she occasionally glimpsed during summer. At this time of the year, most of the houses by the lake were abandoned, which allowed Heather to crawl past at a snail's pace and marvel at all the money that had gone into building these modern palaces.

All of them were new—the oldest ones only a few decades old. Some were designed to look historical—log cabins, colonial revivals, cape cods—and then some didn't give a damn about blending in at all. Those were the ones that caught Heather's attention the most: the blocky smart homes with their palm trees imported from California and garages full of luxury sports cars. These infrequent occupants of Glenville were vital to the economy, but Heather often wondered, why here? She had grown to love Glenville, but it was hardly a mecca of entertainment or recreation. She presumed the only logical answer was that building in a town with so much tragedy must be cheap.

As she inched along the street, she caught sight of someone walking on the opposite side of the road to the waterfront. He was behind the trees that acted as a screen between the rich and everybody else, mostly obscured from sight. It was as if he wasn't trying to be seen, but if that was the case, why not stop walking? It almost felt like he was trying to stealthily follow her.

She tried to get a good look at him and received an opportunity as he passed an extensive gap between two Western Hemlocks. Her worst fear came true when she realized it was the man who had been filming Amber—the one with the long face, thinning hedgehog hair, and blue tattoos. As she watched, she wrote a description in her head: male, around 6'3", wiry, tattooed, likely of Hispanic heritage. She'd need it for the APB if her next step didn't go to plan.

She made a move, and swerved to pull over, but as she did so, her cell phone started ringing at full volume, alerting the man to her movements, and he took off running. She knew the pursuit would be hopeless even if she jumped out now. She cursed louder than her ringing phone and parked before placing her forehead hard onto the padded wheel.

She answered the phone without checking who was calling and was surprised to hear Julius on the other end.

"Hi, Heather. Is this a good time?" he asked.

It wasn't, really, but the guy was already long gone, so what could she do? "Yeah, what's up?"

"So, I've got a body. The FBI has already taken a look at him, but I was wondering if you wanted to come and examine him for yourself before he's out of my hands."

"I know I said I was interested in your cold cases, but I don't have time to solve any other deaths right now."

"You misunderstand me. This guy died of cyanide-laced cocaine too."

Heather's heart sank, her worst nightmare realized. The epidemic was already spreading.

"Wait, what?" she asked.

"Yeah, we've IDed him as Luis Sabado. He's heading back to Mexico tomorrow. As far as we've figured out, he crossed the border illegally but didn't seem to be living here."

"What else have you figured out?"

"Come up to Seattle. I'll show you Mr. Sabado, my autopsy report, and what our guys have figured out regarding his death."

"Julius, come on. I don't have the time. Just tell me. Send me an email."

"It's an hour's drive to look at something case related," he countered.

"Please don't try and bribe me into hanging out with you," she said, regretting it as soon as it left her mouth.

Julius sighed. "I'm not bribing you, Heather. I'm helping you. Not everyone has some dark ulterior motive. I just don't feel comfortable sharing this information—information that the FBI has made classified—over email. Of course, we'd all love to see you again, but I'm not luring you with a dead body."

"God, that makes me sound like a freak."

"Well, if a homicide is what it takes to get you to see your friends and family, maybe you do have a problem worth looking at," he replied coolly.

It was the meanest thing he'd ever said to her, but like Beau, maybe an ass-kicking was what she needed. Gene had gone soft on her, and Tina was harsh in all the wrong ways. What she needed was someone who wasn't afraid of honesty.

"Fine," she relented. "I'll come up today, check out the body, and head home."

"And visit your parents."

Déjà vu would've bowled Heather over had she been standing. "You just sounded like my ex."

"I'm sure. Though apparently, he's stopped answering your parents' calls, so they've turned to me instead. I told them I've only seen you once in the past three years, but it hasn't stopped them from asking me to trick you into visiting. I don't like tricks, so I'm asking you—can you please visit your parents?"

"Fine. I'll visit them afterward."

"What about a coffee in between?"

"I'm really starting to miss the times when everybody hated my guts. There was a couple of months before I left Seattle when even you weren't interested in grabbing a drink."

"I didn't hate you, Heather."

"You didn't like me either."

Julius clicked his tongue. "Well, I like you well enough now."

Heather snorted. "Thanks. I'll see you in a couple of hours. No coffee."

"Sure. See you then."

After they hung up, Heather's mind was spinning so fast that she hardly noticed the movement coming from behind a bush in someone's front garden, but her instincts never let her down. She knew it was him. Watching her. Waiting for something.

With her gun strapped to her hip, she jumped out of the car and ran toward the bush. A few feet before impact, the man leaped up like an actor in a haunted house and darted toward the nearest alleyway.

He was fast, slender, and agile despite his height. More than that, he seemed to know the area well. It was as if he'd been casing it. Was he a robber? A killer? Another piece to the Ellis puzzle or the start of something different altogether?

Heather had no idea, but with her baton in one hand, and her other hand on her gun holster, she called out after him, "Stop! Police! You're under arrest!"

While the threat stopped most people, it didn't deter him. Neither of them slowed, and she pursued him down alleyway after alleyway, dodging trashcans, piles of snow, and ice patches.

THE CRASH

She kept expecting him to jump out and attack her from behind cardboard boxes or other mounds of trash, but it never happened. Instead, he disappeared without a trace.

Lost in a maze of unfamiliar bricks, Heather had no idea which way was back or which way he could've gone. What she did know was that whoever he was, he was definitely trouble, and Amber was right to warn her. No one ran like that if they didn't have something to hide.

As she tried to make her way back, she called Tina and put out an APB. She also told her to tell the entire department about the man and his description and that she wanted everyone available to patrol the streets. They were to apprehend him immediately for resisting arrest and evading the police. She knew she sounded crazy, especially being so out of breath, and though Tina's tone reflected that, she reluctantly agreed to do as Heather asked. The last thing Glenville needed was more run-ins with strange and dangerous men.

As the call ended, Heather knew more months of recuperative desk work awaited her, but it was all worth it to keep Amber, the Ellis family, and the town—if not the state—safe.

Eventually, she escaped the suburban labyrinth, got back into her car, and began her drive to Seattle, all the while keeping an eye out for the strange man in the all-black outfit... which, in rural Washington, meant her journey was filled with terrifying double takes.

CHAPTER THIRTY-TWO

THE DETECTIVE

HEATHER REACHED THE WALL OF TRAFFIC THAT HALOED Seattle in just under an hour, but it hadn't felt like it. She'd nearly turned back a dozen times, but as the cars moved and the green sign welcomed her into the unforgiving belly of Emerald City, it was too late. There had been something abnormally eerie about the man in the bushes, and abandoning the people of Glenville while he walked among them felt akin to letting a toddler wander through bear country smothered in pâté.

There was a possibility that she and Amber were wrong about him and that he was harmlessly strange or perhaps mentally unwell, but deep down, she knew her first instinct was the right one. She just hoped that Tina, Gabriel, and the rest of the department could hold down the fort until her return.

At first, she'd tried to distract herself during the drive with music and the news, but all the sounds and voices were too noisy for her already overwhelmed brain. So, she spent the remainder of the journey in silence, which was not much of an improvement. It provided a void for her paranoid brain to fill with things that weren't there. Strangers hiding among the trees and suspicious cars haunted her, and she spent so much time looking in the rearview mirror that she nearly ran a red light.

As her anxiety mounted, she even worried that Julius had called her under duress. He was the bait to lure her out of Glenville so that evil could strike. Or worse, that he was part of whatever was going on. She knew it wasn't true—she wasn't living in an early-aughts action movie—but the fear still niggled at the back of her skull as she finally arrived at her destination.

Deciding to get it out of the way, she pulled into the parking lot of her parents' condo complex before heading over to the crime laboratory. She'd hoped that seeing the historic red brick building—where she'd spent much of her teen years—would provide some comfort, but almost everywhere in Seattle now carried bad memories. The Paper Doll Case had spread through her life like a sickness, infecting everything she'd once held dear. Now the russet walls looked like scabs not yet healed. She supposed it was better than a fresh wound, and so long as she didn't scratch, it wouldn't bleed.

Though unpleasant recollections had lingered, she couldn't remember anything as helpful as the entrance code and smoked outside to unwind until someone left. The soft-close door shut slowly, allowing her to sneak inside unnoticed.

The out-of-order elevator forced her to take the stairs to the third floor. Fortunately, she could remember that much and was guided to unit two by the autumnal wreath of plastic flowers. Her mother had one for every season, and considering all the other doors were blank, it was easy enough to deduce which one belonged to her parents.

She knocked and waited with bated breath. It didn't take long for an answer, and the door opened to reveal her mom, Sima. She was a petite, dainty woman with a heart-shaped face, a glossy black braid of hair, and jowly cheeks. Heather wouldn't have ever noticed the latter had her mother not complained about needing a face-lift so frequently. She was dressed to go out, wearing an emerald sari, freshwater pearl earrings, and a full face of beautifully applied makeup—something that Heather never had gotten the hang of.

It took Sima a full thirty seconds to believe what she was seeing, her face lacquered in shock as if she'd seen a ghost. Heather thought that a literal full-bodied apparition might be a less surprising visitor at this point, though she hoped not a more welcome one.

This fear was quickly dispelled as Sima lunged forward, wrapping her arms tightly around Heather's waist and immediately bursting into tears. Heather rubbed her back and rested her chin on her mom's perfect center parting.

"Sima, darling, who is it?" Heather's dad, Adrian, called from some remote alcove of the luxurious condo. He sounded concerned, considering his wife's silence since opening the door and, upon receiving no reply, strode quickly to her aid.

His shock wore off much quicker upon seeing his daughter and was soon replaced with beaming joy as he wrapped up the pair in a group hug. The hug lasted for much longer than Heather was comfortable with, but she had anticipated it happening. Her parents were affectionate, demonstrative people—especially with each other, which had embarrassed her to no end during her younger years.

"Oh, Heather!" Adrian exclaimed, his accent still unwaveringly English.

He squeezed her so tightly with his lanky arms that she could hardly breathe, and when he pulled back, she could see that he was also wearing one of his favorite outfits. It was a brown tweed suit—complete with elbow patches—and his favorite, but rarely worn, horn-rimmed glasses that hurt his prominent ears if worn for too long.

"You two look nice," Heather wheezed, somewhat winded, her mother still wrapped about her chest.

"Ah, yes, we were about to grab a late lunch and a couple of drinks," Adrian said, looking down fondly at Sima, who was at least a foot shorter than him.

"Special occasion?" Heather asked.

Sima unraveled and backed inside, beckoning Heather to come with her. "Yes, our thirty-fifth anniversary," she said softly, with a smile.

Heather's face burned hot. "I totally forgot. I should've sent a card."

"Psh," her mom said, waving her off. "What child cares about their parent's anniversary?"

"No, really. I'm thirty-two, not eighteen. I should be better with important dates. I'll put it into my calendar right now."

"I suppose we should tell you everyone's birthdays while we're at it," Adrian teased.

"Don't you worry your sweet head, my princess," Sima said, narrowing her eyes at Adrian as she led the group into the living room.

"I can piss off if you two have plans," Heather said, accidentally adopting one of her dad's favorite phrases. It sounded strange. Any hint of accent she had acquired as a child from either of them was completely gone.

"Don't be silly," Adrian replied. "We can just go for dinner instead. The best present we could ask for is seeing our only daughter."

Only child, Heather thought guiltily, wishing she had siblings to fill the Heather-shaped hole she often left behind.

"Coffee?" Adrian asked, and disappeared to the kitchen before getting confirmation.

Sima sat on the brocade couch and patted the place beside her for Heather to sit. Once she had, Sima turned to examine her daughter in detail. She brushed the hair from Heather's face and reached for her daughter's restless hands, grabbing them both in her tiny soft ones.

"You look tired, princess. Your eyes..."

"I'm fine. Just working hard as usual," Heather replied, avoiding eye contact.

"Working too hard," her mom scolded. "You know me and your father met a lovely man we think could look after you. You could work part-time instead. He makes a lot of money. Could look after you the way you deserve."

"You know I can't quit my job, Mom. I love what I do."

Sima frowned. "I just don't understand why you want to do something so horrible."

The usual lecture had arrived early, and Heather was too tired to argue, so instead, she stayed silent and allowed her mom to say her invariable piece.

"We saw you on the news. The Warren family and that horrible man in the woods. I want you to know we're very proud of you, my love. You're a hero. You've saved so many lives, and we know how important that is, but you have to understand that you're our child. I carried you inside of me for nine months. You're my priority. Not anybody else. And we worry about you. Maybe you've done enough for the world, and it's time to take care of you. Even if it's just temporary."

Heather smiled tightly. "I'll think about it. Maybe after this case is over, I'll take a break."

They both knew it wasn't true, but Sima seemed sated by the lie.

"At least come up for Christmas," she requested. "It's not the same without you here."

Heather hesitated, not wanting to make promises she couldn't keep, but nonverbally agreed to keep the peace. With the rest of their family in India and England, it would be an awfully small Christmas for two people who loved the holiday so much. Her guilt grew as it always did when visiting her parents, and each gap between social calls only made the monster grow stronger.

"I'm seeing Julius later," Heather said for lack of other topics.

Her mother beamed. "Oh, Julius. What a lovely man. See, there's a man who could look after you."

"Mom."

"I know—I know. Though he is single now. Did you know that?"

"I did."

Sima tutted. "I can't believe what his wife did. I saw her the other day. She was wearing an engagement ring—can you believe it? It was a horrible, tacky thing. Nothing like yours. Very blingy."

Heather's stomach roiled for Julius, knowing how much it must hurt seeing the woman he loved marrying another man.

THE CRASH

Sima continued before Heather had a chance to conjure a reply. "Are you meeting him for business or pleasure?"

"Business," Heather replied. "There's a body he needs me to look at."

Sima pursed her lips. "You know I don't like hearing about that stuff."

"Yeah, I know. Sorry."

"Don't worry, princess," Sima said, rubbing Heather's back before changing the subject to neighborhood gossip. Heather absorbed little of it, and her relief when Adrian re-entered with coffee was brief as he quickly joined in. The pair complained viciously about their new neighbors in 301. Something about vacuuming past 9:00 p.m. and leaving trash in the hall. Heather was envious of their grievances, wishing she lived a life so devoid of drama that she even noticed what her neighbors did. Or knew their names.

"You can smoke in here, you know. Adrian does," Sima said sweetly, gesturing to a French-style table and chairs by an open window.

Heather meandered over, knowing there was no use in pretending she'd quit with the stench sticking to her clothes, and joined her father at the table. Adrian rolled up a thin cigarette as she pulled one from the pack and held out a lit Zippo for her to lean into.

Her dad didn't speak as much, leaving the lectures to Sima, and simply observed the renovations quietly with his daughter as Sima busied herself with unnecessary cleaning.

It looked much the same as it always had, but she noticed a new set of shelves had been added. The bottom rows held Blu-rays of classic Western movies, while the top rows sported DVDs and VHSs of English period dramas. Heather noticed the TV was paused on one such show. She didn't recognize it, but the ladies in corsets and bustles gave the genre away.

She looked at her mom and noticed her pearl earrings matched those of the older lady on screen. It was funny, she thought, how much her parents had assimilated. Sima to England—where they'd met and married—and Adrian to America, where he'd moved them for work reasons before Heather was born. Heather had none of their love for any country; she simply was where she was and was happy to have somewhere to rest her head.

Her eyes wandered to the framed photos on the wall and noticed that her wedding photos were still up. She hardly recognized the younger woman immortalized by them as herself. Her makeup and hair had been professionally done, and she was dressed in an ivory and powder blue sari, complete with a traditional silver jewelry set and maang tikka. Heather, who tried to think as little as possible about her appearance, had to admit that she had looked beautiful.

Adrian must have noticed her looking and said quietly, "He asks about you, you know."

"How is he?" Heather asked.

Adrian hesitated, removing his glasses and cleaning them with his jacket. "I think it's best you talk to him for yourself."

Heather turned and looked at the somber profile of her rarely serious dad and asked, "Why? What's going on?"

"As I said, it's not my business to say. Sorry, sweetheart."

Heather returned to the photo. She remembered meeting her ex-husband so vividly. It had been in a bar—which was much too cool for her—while she waited for a friend that was also too cool for her. She'd sat alone at a small table, her eyes bugging out at the bar snacks—quail eggs, oysters, black caviar—when a man approached her. He was tall, dark, and handsome with a deep, soothing voice, and she'd been head over heels from hello.

She had no idea that four years later they'd be having their last argument—a particularly nasty blowup with a lot of things said that couldn't be unsaid—and that he'd walk out the door for the last time. It was unexpected, the end of it all. They'd always been the best couple in their group and delighted in complaining about their friends' terrible new boyfriends and girlfriends. They hadn't realized that they weren't untouchable and that trouble in paradise would soon turn into just trouble.

"Maybe we should take those down," Adrian said.

"No. It's okay. If you like them, you can keep them up."

"I just like how happy you look in them."

"Yeah... me too."

CHAPTER THIRTY-THREE

THE FATHER

2021

Roland wandered back to the table with two Blue Lagoon cocktails topped with glace cherries and a juicy slab of lemon. He forced a smile as he approached Pamela from behind. Just as he'd left her, she was still staring despondently at the cerulean ocean, her shoulders slumped. It didn't seem to matter if the sky was blue or gray for her lately; all of it seemed to tire or bore her, and Roland was trying hard not to grow tired of her melancholy.

Zealously, he sat down and placed the drinks on the table. He pushed hers toward her before slurping down a quarter of his drink through a spiral straw. He gestured enthusiastically as if it were the best thing he'd ever consumed.

"Mmmm. This is good. You have to try this," he said.

"Yeah, okay," Pamela replied. She took a small sip and offered a weak simper in agreement. "It is pretty good."

"See? I told you getting out of the house would be good for you."

"I like the house. I feel safe there."

Roland frowned. It had been seven years since he'd shot what had turned out to be Francisco's youngest nephew, and Pamela was still unwaveringly fearful of being caught. She'd become a complete recluse for the first two years, but slowly Roland managed to somewhat coax her out of her protective shell.

Roland had none of the same fears as his accomplice. For one thing, he knew it would be nearly impossible to recognize either of them. First, Pamela had dyed her hair a mousy brown, and then she stopped wearing high heels and eye-catching outfits. Instead of her usual glamour, she spent most of her time wearing patchwork shawls, harem pants, and leather sandals. Roland thought she looked like the crunchy holistic owner of a crystal shop but would never say as much.

Roland, on the other hand, had embraced the look of the men who often occupied the local resort. He'd gained weight, remained constantly sunburned, and wore oversized Hawaiian shirts, cargo shorts, and flip-flops as his daily attire. He liked going to the resort. Everyone was American, and the staff spoke fluent English. It made him feel like he was on vacation instead of stuck in an arid, nowhere town.

He often expected to be recognized—knowing his face had been on the news a few times back home—but it seemed not as many people cared about small-town mayors as he'd thought. The shaggy hair and thick, black beard helped too. Add sunglasses to the combination, and he was just any other loud-mouthed American tourist who spent ninety percent of their vacation by the hotel pool.

THE CRASH

Roland reached out and squeezed Pamela's hand. "I'm always going to keep you safe."

She gave a quick squeeze back before retracting her hand. He wished she'd put her sunglasses back on so he wouldn't have to see how dull her hazel eyes had become.

"What about if you go back to your wife and family?" she asked. "Will you even give two craps about me?"

Irritated by last night's argument being dredged into the daylight, Roland raised his voice. "I was just thinking out loud! I'd never go back to Nancy romantically, but I would like to return to Glenville and have a relationship with my kids. Think about it, no one in America thinks we've done anything wrong aside from having an affair. We'd be actually safe there. No more hiding."

"No more hiding does sound nice."

"I could divorce Nancy, and we could get married for real."

Pamela fiddled with her wedding band. "If I felt like any of that were true, I'd agree to go, but I think you're just bored of this life. You're getting old. You had your adventure, and now you want to go back to money and comfort. You'll leave me in the dust in six months flat—find some new blonde to screw while you make nice with your wife."

Roland rubbed his forehead. "How can you think that about me? I've been with you longer than I was with Nancy. I still love you, I'm still attracted to you, and I still want to be by your side all day, every day. Is that not enough?"

"I wish I could believe you. I wish I could open up your chest and see that the love is there because, at the moment, it only feels like a bunch of words in the breeze." Pamela paused. "What about if I stay and you go?"

"Pamela. You know I can't leave you behind."

"Well, then, I can't win. I either keep you tethered here while you're dying for something better, or I go with you, and you leave me."

"I won't leave you there either!" Roland exclaimed in frustration, his fists clenched.

"There's nothing to tie you to me. We're not married, and we never had kids," she said, her voice cracking on the last word.

Roland frowned and looked out at the children playing on the beach. "I know we've had some hard times over the past few years, but that doesn't mean I'm going to throw what we have away."

Pamela cleared her throat with a sip of her drink. "Nancy is your wife and the mother of your children, and I suspect you love her a lot more than you let on. Or at least you love the life she gave you. You miss being a *somebody*. Being a nobody in the middle of nowhere is only fun when you're young."

"You're wrong," Roland insisted.

Pamela laughed coldly. "Fine. Then prove me wrong. Let's head back to America and see if you follow through on your promises."

"What happens if I don't?"

"Then you'll have to live with the fact that I was right about you for the rest of your life."

Roland swallowed hard. He barely recognized her. She was a kicked street dog, hungry and quick to bite. Long gone was her sweet-as-apple-pie voice and manner, and Roland missed the girl he used to know. He hoped that Glenville would bring her back to life and lay this husk down to rest.

Roland stood. "I'll get us some more drinks."

"Sure. You do that."

Not looking where he was going, Roland walked straight into a tall, wiry man with a long jaw and dimpled chin. In the collision, the man had spilled beer onto himself and looked down at Roland with darkened eyes and heavy brows.

"God, I am awful sorry about that," Roland said, backing away from the intimidating figure. "I'm just heading to the bar. Let me buy you a round."

The man surveyed Roland for a very long time. Examining his face, looking his body up and down. Slowly his face melted into a leering smile. He clapped Roland on the shoulder with a large hand.

"Do not worry. Just an accident," the man said.

The man spoke with a thick Mexican accent, which was unusual for the resort despite its location, but Roland shrugged it off, happy to escape with some extra dollars in his pocket and all of his teeth intact.

THE CRASH

They were drunk when they arrived home, and Pamela's alcohol-induced mood swings were in full effect. At first, they practically fell through the door as she couldn't keep her hands off him. She tried desperately to undress him and soon stripped down to her underwear herself. She began to dance around the living room, looking for more alcohol. He chuckled, less drunk than she was but glad to see her in a happy mood.

That was until she sidled up, a glass of wine in hand, and kissed his neck. "Let's try again," she begged. "This time, it'll stick. I can just feel it."

"Pammy, baby," he whispered in her ear, hugging her and rocking back and forth. "We can't. You know you'll just end up heartbroken all over again."

"You don't love me anymore," she whispered, fighting him off, her eyes brimming with tears. She backed away as if afraid of her realization—or him.

"Pam, please. Let's not do this again," Roland said sternly.

She shook her head. "Don't lie to me. You don't love me anymore. Admit it."

"You're drunk," Roland said, stepping toward her, aiming to snatch the glass of wine away and send her to bed.

She stepped back again, getting dangerously near the balcony doorway. Envisioning a potential accident, Roland held out his hands and retreated.

"Baby, come here. We'll try again—whatever you want. Just calm down. Let's smoke a joint, drink some wine, and go to bed. Just like the old days," he said, using all his politician charm.

"That sounds nice," she slurred, finally pausing her withdrawal onto the second-story balcony.

"Yeah, it does. Just come back inside, and we can do whatever you want."

"Am I outside?" she asked and looked around. She laughed loudly as she looked up at the star-speckled sky. She turned toward the balcony's edge, leaned over, and asked, "Do you think it's high enough to kill me?"

"Pamela. Come back inside. Please, baby?"

"Oh, all right," she giggled, blowing him a kiss.

Bang!

The kiss never reached him, and Roland closed his eyes at the awful sound.

He felt it in his bones and teeth. It was the sound of something terrible, but not a body hitting the concrete below. It was a gunshot.

He opened his eyes and watched as Pamela staggered backward into the room, clutching her throat. She turned, and rivulets of alcohol-thinned blood poured out between her fingers. So much blood. Too much blood. The color rapidly drained from her face, and she fell to her knees, silently pleading before collapsing onto her side. She reached out for Roland, but by the time he was able to move, the door was kicked in, and two more guns were pointing in the direction of his head.

"Don't move," came a familiar voice.

Everything inside of him broke so harshly that all he could do was ask numbly, "The guy from the resort? Have you been following us?"

"Yes and no. I'd heard of a guy who looked like you in the area, so I figured why not have myself a little trip and keep my eyes peeled at the same time. Who knew I'd run into you on day one. I almost didn't recognize you, old man."

Pamela gurgled, and Roland impulsively threw himself to her side regardless of the guns.

Bang!

"Arghhh!" Roland screamed, reeling back and clutching his quickly dampening arm.

"I told you not to move," said the deep-voiced man. "Don't worry. I didn't hit any arteries."

Roland fixed his gaze on Pamela and watched her hazel eyes turn gray. He was too stunned to cry, blink, or swallow. His whole body felt both heavy and empty at the same time. He watched her beautiful face patiently, waiting for her to wink as if this were all part of her plan.

"Baby…" he whispered.

She didn't wink, didn't move, didn't breathe. Still, he kept waiting until his world went dark, and as he was dragged into

THE CRASH

a vehicle by the zip ties around his wrists, he didn't struggle. Whatever was waiting for him, he was sure he deserved.

CHAPTER THIRTY-FOUR

THE DETECTIVE

Heather knew that seeing the Seattle Crime Laboratory again would be somewhat uncanny, but she was wholly unprepared for the profound effect it would have on her. As soon as she laid eyes on the ultramodern glass building, she completely froze. Her car rolled to a steady stop at an awkward angle, much to the dismay of those trying to enter and exit the parking lot. When the beeping started, she waved apologies to the aggravated doctors and scientists and parked in the farthest spot away from the entrance.

It was arguably a pleasant building to behold, but it was more haunted than The Winchester Mystery House, The Lizzie Borden Bed & Breakfast, The Sallie House, and the Ellsworth

THE CRASH

Family Funeral Home combined. Not that Heather entirely believed in ghosts, but that didn't seem to matter much to the dead. They plagued her regardless, even if only in her mind.

She always used to avoid the SCL whenever she could, and as she sat with her back to it, she felt *it* and remembered why. That same heavy presence that one might feel at a loved one's grave or a war memorial overwhelmed her. It seemed to her that death had a weight to it when crammed into one area and that those who worked at the SCL daily were essentially heavyweight champs.

The SCL dealt with the most restless, aggrieved, and tormented souls. Not only were there those who had done enormous wrongs but more commonly, there were those who had been wronged on the slabs. There were the Jane Does, the neglected children, the battered wives, the brutalized hitchhikers, and countless others wandering the endless halls, and Heather shivered as if one had passed through her.

She remembered the last time she'd been in this parking lot. Not much had changed physically since then. She'd been sitting in the same car—though its footwells hadn't been filled with spare shoes and drive-through wrappers back then—and the building had been identical aside from the recently repainted parking space lines. She, too, hadn't physically changed much, though she no longer wore her hair in a thick braid like her mother, and she'd been notably thinner. Too thin, as many had said, her work clothes draping off of her overexercised and underfed frame.

She'd been sitting in silence, as she did now, avoiding moving because she couldn't bear to go inside and face what she knew she must: Julius had been waiting for her back then, too, the body of a murdered eight-year-old girl on his table… and the longer she stayed frozen, the guiltier she felt for abandoning him with something so horrible.

After that day she swore she'd never abandon him again, so she forced herself out of the car, turned, and walked toward the towering building.

Inside, it was much the same as it had always been, but there were enough differences that she wasn't swallowed headfirst by the maw of the past. The receptionists were new for one thing, as was the technology on their desks. The worn-out linoleum had been replaced with glossy, white epoxy resin that made the building almost too bright.

Squinting, she asked the young man at the desk where she could find Dr. Tocci, and he enthusiastically informed her to head to the basement morgue. It was an odd sentence to deliver with a sunny expression, but she supposed, like her own job, you become numb to what others find unpleasant.

Despite only going one floor down, the elevator's decent felt like she was plunging through earth's crusts and heading straight toward hell. With a ding, the doors opened, revealing a hallway that had not received the same makeover as the lobby. The old linoleum was still there, and fluorescent ceiling tiles still flickered and buzzed.

She hurried down the length of it, pushed open the swing door at the end, and entered a room occupied by multiple bodies hidden beneath sheets aside from their toe-tagged feet.

Julius turned as he heard her approach, his expression even more tired than her own. She wondered when he'd discovered his ex-wife's engagement and feared it may have been recent. She hoped it hadn't been her prying mother who'd revealed the big news.

"Hey," she said.

"Hi, Heather. It's good to see you," he replied, tilting his head toward the covered body on the gurney before him.

She approached tentatively. "So, this is him?"

"This is him. Luis Sabado. Twenty-seven years old. Married with two kids back in Mexico. I've written up the death certificate so he's ready to be transported as soon as we're done here."

"God, that's so young," Heather murmured sadly, looking at the cotton cast of the husband and father.

Julius nodded solemnly. "About the age you were when you were last here."

"Wow, maybe I do need to visit more often."

"I'm sure your parents would agree. They texted me after you left. The visit made them very happy."

"Thanks for pushing me."

Julius looked pleased. "You're very welcome."

THE CRASH

"It was weird though. They still had my wedding photos all over the place."

"Hmm," Julius hummed as if he wasn't really listening. Or wanted to change the subject.

Heather furrowed her brows. "What aren't you guys telling me about him?"

"Nothing, nothing. Just... he's gotten himself into a bit of a pickle."

She could tell he was putting it lightly. "What sort of pickle?"

"Why don't you ask him yourself?"

"Julius," Heather groaned. "We haven't spoken since the divorce. I can't just ask him about his woes out of the blue."

"Sorry, Heather. It's not my place to say."

"Whatever. Let's get on with this and send this guy back home."

"Of course."

Julius unveiled the ashen body of Luis Sabado, who looked even younger than twenty-seven. Aside from the blue tinge and rigor mortis, he was still in good condition and looked much more peaceful than Roland had, which made the examination somewhat more bearable.

She circled the gurney, pulled out her notebook, and jotted down any observations she thought might be useful. Not much stood out until she reached Luis's right arm and noticed a familiar tattoo among the numerous others.

It was a harpy eagle, the words *las águilas arpías volarán para siempre* written underneath. It was identical to Roland's sole tattoo. She looked up at Julius, her mouth hanging open.

Julius nodded again. "Yeah, I noticed that too. I guess they were in the same gang."

"And they both died from acute cyanide poisoning." Heather flipped through her notes. "Clearly, both of their deaths are connected. Maybe hits arranged by a rival cartel?"

"As usual, I have no idea, but I've watched enough documentaries to think that you're on the right track."

"What about the FBI? Did they say anything?" she asked.

"Nope. Zero insight from them."

"And the officers that brought him in?"

"Now, there's something I can help with."

Julius looked around to check they were alone before pulling a file from the inside of his white lab coat. He handed it to Heather and spoke in a low voice. "Take a look at this. He was with some other guy at a bar. CCTV caught them entering around seven with a huge suitcase."

"Full of cocaine, I imagine."

"Or money. Either way, they leave again at eight and return without the suitcase, but they're loaded with cash. Check out the third picture."

Heather did so, the men's backs to the camera, leaning on the bar, wads of rolled-up cash in hand.

"Okay, so they did a deal and decided to party with their cut of the profit."

"Seems that way. They ordered rounds of shots and moved to a table full of young girls. One of those girls has given a statement and said these two guys were trying to get her and her friends to come back to their room to 'party,' if you catch my drift. The girls refused, and eventually the bouncer kicked them both out. There was a small scuffle in the parking lot, and then they headed back to the motel they were staying at. There were some noise complaints throughout the night—loud music and banging sounds—and then at 6:13 a.m., Luis Sabado's 'friend' checked out and left in the car they both arrived in. The maid then enters the room two hours later and finds Mr. Sabado on the floor in the bathroom. He'd been dead for roughly six hours by the time the cops arrived."

"Maybe the other guy is the hitman in question. Either double-crossing the gang or doing a favor for the big man in charge."

"Makes sense to me, but it seems like a weird way to kill someone. Expensive, too, wasting the product."

"That's what I don't understand either. I guess it's less messy than a bullet."

"And it's untraceable," Julius agreed. "Even so, why tamper with the drugs instead of poisoning a drink?"

"Yeah, and in Roland's case, why poison the entire batch?"

"Well, I hope when you find out, you'll let me know."

"You got it."

Once Julius had covered the body, Heather moved to hand the folder back to him, but he shook his head.

THE CRASH

"They're copies," he clarified, his voice still faint and his eyes darting. "But if anyone asks, you didn't get them from me."

"Thank you, Julius. I really owe you one."

He waved her off. "Don't think of it as a favor. Just think of it as help from a guy who believes you can do more good with this information than anybody else."

"Still, thank you."

"Anything for you, Heather. And hey, if you really do want to repay me, I'm off in fifteen if you want to grab that coffee."

"Maybe, I—" Heather stopped dead as she flicked through the CCTV images in the report.

The photo in question was the clearest one of the bunch and detailed the two men, their hands laden with drinks as they made their way back to the table of young women. One of them was Luis Sabado, who lay dead in front of her, and the other was the man she'd seen earlier that day in Glenville. His smirk was crooked, and his eyes were predatory as he prowled toward the group of innocents. There was suddenly no doubt in her mind that he'd been the one to kill Luis and was likely responsible for Roland too.

"No coffee today," she said, looking at Julius, breathless from the shot of adrenaline coursing through her system.

"What's going on? What do you see?"

"The other guy. I've seen him around Glenville. He was following me today, and when I tried to arrest him, he vanished. I have an APB out on him already, but I need to get back. I think he's there to hurt somebody."

Julius frowned. "What if he's there to hurt you?"

"Then I need to be there to lure him out."

"Heather."

"I'll be fine."

"Heather," Julius repeated.

"Seriously. I'll—um—I'll call you," she said, stumbling over her words and feet as she backed out of the morgue, leaving a bewildered Julius in her wake.

She tried and failed to catch her breath as she tore out of the parking lot and called Tina once again. The Sheriff sounded as concerned as Julius had, but she couldn't worry about that. Glenville needed her. Maybe more than it ever had.

CHAPTER THIRTY-FIVE

THE FATHER

2021

TWO WEEKS AGO, THE CONCRETE CELL HAD BEEN COMpletely bare aside from Roland and some cockroaches... though even those quickly abandoned him in his squalor. There had been no windows, bed, pillow, food, or water, and where the toilet should've been was a small circular pit. Then after a few days, once Roland had ceased insulting everyone he saw and screaming for help, a man dressed in black brought him a bucket of water and a plastic cup. The next day the daily feedings started—if you could call the mush they served food—accompanied by a thin mattress. It was unpleasant and uncomfortable, but the dirty water and bland food kept him alive while his bed soothed the bruises acquired from sleeping on the hard ground.

It flatlined after that for another week. Bucket, gruel, and the dirty mattress were his only kindnesses, and the only human interaction he received was from the silent men with automatic weapons. Desperate to stay sane, Roland began to work out as best he could, attempting alternating sets of push-ups and sit-ups, and when his body became too tired to stand, he'd lie on his back and play solitaire or chess in his mind. He frequently lost his internal voice, becoming increasingly mean-spirited and uncooperative.

Then, fifteen days after Pamela's death, according to the tally marks on the walls, Francisco appeared in the cell's doorway wearing a gaudy silk shirt and an even more exaggerated expression. He stuck his bottom lip out as he entered the room. Roland pretended to ignore him, still lying on his back, as he heard dress shoes approach. Francisco kneeled by Roland's bed, grabbed his captive's chin with strong fingers, and turned his face toward his own. He then recoiled from the filth and wiped his hand on his pants in disgust.

"You disappoint me, Roland," Francisco sighed.

"You killed Pamela," Roland replied, reflecting Francisco's sentiment.

Francisco's cartoonish expression twisted into something natural. "*Sí*. A very unfortunate business. I didn't mean for either of you to get hurt. But my men, they get overexcited, especially after seven years of hunting. You know, if you think about it, you were the one who killed her with your actions."

Roland propped himself up, not even able to muster up the emotion to fight back. "How do you figure?"

"What is that American phrase? Play stupid games; win stupid prizes?"

"That's the one."

"Well, I think it's safe to say we both have blood on our hands. Which, in a way, makes us equals."

"We're not equals."

"Perhaps not now. But I would like to be."

"Not interested," Roland said, lying back down.

"Well, if you want to stay in the cell forever, be my guest. But I have something I'd like to offer you. A little present."

"Hmm."

"I'd like to let you go back to your old life, as a way of apology for ruining this one. And in return, you don't say anything about where you've been or what you've seen. Two powerful men with terrible secrets. See? Equals."

Roland exhaled. "Okay. I'm interested."

Francisco clapped. "¡Excelente!"

"Great," Roland said flatly. He moved to stand up and move toward the open door, but Francisco placed a hand on his chest and kept him in place.

"Ah, ah, ah. Not so quick. First, we need to rebuild some trust. Don't you think?"

"I—"

"Roland, *amigo*. You killed my nephew. You stole from me. You hid from me for seven years. You put my beloved Pamela in a situation that got her killed. Most men in my position would put a bullet in your head."

"I didn't take you for such a benevolent god."

Francisco laughed. "Benevolent? Yes. A god? No."

"How can I trust you to follow through?"

"I'm a man of my word. Cross my heart, and hope to die." Francisco crossed his heart with a gleeful expression.

"What do you want me to do?"

Francisco clapped him on the shoulder. "¡Qué magnífico! All you have to do is a series of jobs. Once you're done with them, then I'll let you go."

"How long will that take?"

"It takes as long as it takes."

Realizing he had no other choice, Roland sighed and asked, "What's the first job?"

"The first job is an easy one. I want you to clean all of the floors of my new house with a toothbrush."

"Seriously?"

"Oh yes. I'm afraid the mop just doesn't cut it on the tiles. Then, if you do a good job, I want you to fly to Texas to drop off a special shipment for me." He put on an exaggerated Texas

THE CRASH

accent. "Maybe you can say hello to Maw and Paw if they're still alive."

They weren't, and he knew that if Francisco had done his research, he knew that they were both long dead. All Roland could do was oblige and agree to the terms laid out. He just prayed that the duration of his punishment would be short enough that he'd be back home by Christmas.

―――

The flight to Texas was short and simple, but the empty passenger seat left Roland cold despite the overbearing heat. The drop was close enough to his old family homestead that he decided to land in one of his parents' fields and then borrow his dad's old truck to transport the shipment into town.

The location was strange in and of itself. It was a small town for such a massive quantity of drugs. Weirder still, Francisco had told him to not expect any money to change hands. Supposedly, it was coming at a later point. None of it made sense, but at this point, Roland no longer questioned Francisco's methods.

The field he landed in was overgrown and unrecognizable, painting a painful picture of how long it had been since he'd been young. He wondered why none of his siblings had taken over the land, but looking around at the sheer expanse, he understood why they'd want an easier life than their parents had had. He wondered if his brothers and sisters were all still alive. They were all older than he was, and he was crossing over into his fifties. Several things could've gotten to them in the past thirteen and a half years. There were the two major suspects: cancer like their mother or liver disease like their father—but there were also road accidents or any number of other possibilities.

He checked the cargo in the plane and noticed there were twenty-six bricks instead of twenty-five. After careful deliberation, he decided it wasn't a test. Mistakes had been made before, and though he knew he'd get brownie points for bringing back the excess, he decided to stash it beneath the passenger seat for a rainy day.

Then, leaving the plane and stash behind, he stalked toward the house to see if any cars remained and if they were still in a fit state for driving.

The big farmhouse was in worse shape than the fields. The windows were broken, the white walls were covered in spray paint, and the front porch was littered with beer bottles.

"Damn kids," he muttered, making his way to the shed where the trucks were kept.

To his surprise, two of them remained, as did several jerry cans of fuel and a few car batteries in the cupboard. His dad had been somewhat of an end-of-the-world prepper, even before that was a thing. The family had teased him for it back then, but now Roland looked up to the heavens and thanked his late father for being so prepared.

He got to work on the pickup truck, and it was road ready within thirty minutes. He didn't bother loading the shipment as the meeting wasn't until four in the morning. Instead, he decided to enjoy his temporary freedom and drove into town to scope out the local bars.

A pit formed in his stomach as he drove through a section of what had been his whole world as a child. He'd been to livelier ghost towns and worried the liquor store would be his best option before spotting a chalkboard sign outside the motel. Supposedly it was the only bar for more miles and boasted a 7–9 p.m. happy hour that he was just in time for. He knew it would be overpriced regardless, but Francisco had provided him some 'pocket money,' so he parked and wandered inside thirstier than ever.

The bar was so tiny that even the five tables and roughly a dozen chairs were crammed together. It had clearly been one of the motel rooms at some point, considering the single unisex bathroom in the corner.

To his surprise, the room was dominated by young women and hardly any truckers. He supposed it was early yet, but he was still confused by their presence in the middle of nowhere until he observed them and their attire more closely.

Lot lizards, he thought, as his father used to say. They weren't uncommon in these sorts of areas, which used to aggrieve his parents to no end. Honestly, Roland was just happy to be in the presence of attractive women, and considering his line of work, he wasn't one to judge.

One woman, in particular, stood out to him. She was sitting with her back to the door wearing denim shorts and a crochet crop top, her starchy blonde hair piled high.

She was laughing with the group of women and held a cigarette in one hand—despite the indoor smoking laws—and a beer in the other. His heart stopped. He knew it couldn't be Pamela, but she bore such a resemblance to her that he drifted toward the lively group despite the bartender asking for his order.

He stood next to the woman, and she swiveled, looking up at him in confusion. She wasn't as pretty as Pamela. A lifetime of hard rural living had roughed up her edges, but when she looked him up and down with a smile, her dimples were exactly the same.

"Well, hello, stranger," she cooed.

"Can I buy you a drink?" he asked with all the charm of a robot.

She laughed. "Well, sure. I could do with some fresh meat and conversation."

The girls around her tittered disapprovingly at her rejection as the woman stood from her seat and moved them over to a quiet two-seater in the corner.

"What's your name, handsome?" she asked.

"Dallon Riles," he said.

"Dallon Riles, huh? Well, I'm Amber Horton."

He wondered if it was her real name, but once again, he was in no position to judge. "Pretty name," he said.

"Thanks. I'm on a girls' trip with my gal pals across Texas."

Roland glanced back at the women and went along with the lie. "What do you want to drink?"

"Beer or whiskey is fine with me."

"Girl after my own heart."

Several beers and whiskey shots later, the two excused themselves to her motel room, and though Amber was sweet and pretty enough, his drunken mind reimagined her as Pamela. Once he did, all of his charisma—tamped down by weeks in a cell and the death of the love of his life—came spilling out, and he could see this young woman falling for him like watching a morning glory bloom.

When it was all over, they drank from Amber's mini fridge supply, and the pair exchanged troubles as if they were funny first-date-friendly anecdotes. He confessed his recent loss of Pamela to her, and she consoled him like a mother or a therapist. He was grateful, warm, and comforted, but it couldn't last forever. She begged him not to go, but he said his goodbyes and returned to the farmhouse, wishing he'd stayed in her bed.

The next day, when he landed at the strip in Mexico, Francisco was there to greet him with open arms. He congratulated him on making the drop, clearly pleased that he hadn't tried to run away. Apparently, his friends in Texas—who bore the same tattoo that Roland had been branded with twelve years ago—were pleased with his professionalism. A black car was waiting for them, and Francisco sat in the back with Roland and babbled about his operation and love life woes as if they were colleagues once more.

At headquarters, Francisco left without a word, and a bodyguard escorted Roland back to his cell. Once more, he was locked inside the windowless walls, but Francisco's jubilation over the first job's success was evident. The mattress had been replaced by a king single and cotton bedding, the water bucket had been replaced by a cooler, there was a toilet where a toilet should be, and the food set on the one-seater dining table smelled more than edible. Best of all, a postcard of Glenville was taped to the wall at the foot of his bed as motivation for the upcoming toil.

THE CRASH

For the first time in weeks, months, and perhaps years, Roland felt hope for what would become of his remaining life span.

CHAPTER THIRTY-SIX

THE DETECTIVE

When she opened her eyes, Roland Ellis's waxy face was staring at Heather from her laptop screen. She'd fallen asleep looking at the photos Julius had taken of Roland Ellis and Luis Sabado to see if anything other than the tattoo tied them together. She'd gone over the unpleasantly high-definition images and the accompanying reports with a fine-tooth comb but found nothing.

She reached out to shut the lid, but the coffee table was too far out of reach. Groaning, she sat up, her head spinning and her clothes smelling like an ashtray. She glared at the half-empty bottle of whiskey and the crumpled packet of cigarettes with

THE CRASH

revulsion. She hadn't been this hungover in over a month, and it didn't feel good to be back in the trenches.

When she'd arrived back in Glenville yesterday afternoon, she'd spent the first several hours patrolling the streets and loitering around the station in anticipation of danger. When nothing happened, and the man didn't materialize to strike again, Heather was encouraged to head home and rest. She'd railed against Tina's urgings for another hour before admitting defeat around nightfall, but only under the condition that they'd allow her access to the holding cell CCTV.

Once home, Heather had watched the live footage intently until Amber fell asleep under the watchful eye of two officers. Once she had, Heather left the footage on—much to the displeasure of her overheating laptop—and glanced at it for reassurance as she went over the case.

In retrospect, she should've gone for a run to expel the anxious energy, but she'd been too bone-tired for any form of exercise. So, instead, she'd turned to her old reliable to take the edge off. It was evident now that she'd overdone it, and she cursed at her drunken evil twin for not knowing when to stop.

She leaned forward toward the laptop and exited the layers of autopsy images until she reached the CCTV footage of the holding cells. It was angled into Amber's cell as requested, but not only were the two guards no longer there, neither was Amber.

Heather looked around for her phone and was only able to find it when it started ringing from somewhere within the couch. She fished around in the gritty crevices until she felt the vibrations against her fingertips. Eyes still on the open cell, she answered without looking at the screen.

"Hello?" Heather asked.

On the other end, a woman was breathing frantically, and Heather began racing through possibilities as to why. Was she running? Having an anxiety attack? Mortally injured? It was impossible to tell, but from the sounds of the singing birds, Heather knew she was outside in the cold and terrified.

"Heather?" the caller replied in a hushed voice. It was Amber.

Heather's blood froze over. The chill sobered her up, and she was wide awake and on her feet. She balanced her phone on her shoulder as she pulled on clothes that were littered across the living room floor.

"Amber? What's going on? Are you okay?" Heather asked.

"Something feels wrong."

"What's happening? Where are you?" Heather implored, trying to keep her voice steady.

"I'm outside the bar. By the front door."

"When did you get released?"

Amber fell silent again as Heather zipped up her boots and clipped on her police belt. Not wanting history to repeat itself if worse came to worse, she checked that her gun was loaded and operational. It was, and with a swill of mouthwash, so was she.

"About half an hour ago," Amber finally whispered, clearly listening out for something. "According to one of the officers, Bobby showed up, paid my bail in cash, and told them to tell me to meet him here. I don't know why he wouldn't just wait for me at the station. It just doesn't feel right."

Heather agreed. It didn't feel right. Not at all. She jumped into her car, put the key in the ignition before the door was shut, and put her foot on the accelerator before buckling in. Her car ground its gears as she bounced up and down in her seat, cursing the cold. When it finally revved, she put the pedal to the metal but kept her siren silent.

"I'm on my way. Whatever you do, don't go inside the building. Go back to the police station and tell Tina what's happening."

"Tina isn't there. There was an explosion at some nearby farm, and now there's a big forest fire. It's an all-hands-on-deck situation, apparently. Doesn't seem like there's a soul in town."

A distraction, Heather thought.

"That's okay. Doesn't matter. Go back anyway. Somebody will be there."

Amber hesitated and fell silent again.

"Amber, please listen to me. Go back to the station. Everything's going to be fine. Just don't go in the bar," Heather pleaded.

Savannah began to scream in the distance, and both women drew sharp breaths. The baby sounded as if she was in terrible pain, and Heather knew that Amber would never go back to the

THE CRASH

station now. Regardless, she continued to beg, desperate to buy herself some more time as she drifted around on the icy roads.

"Amber. Savannah's teeth are coming in, right?"

"Yeah."

"That's why she's crying! She's crying because her teeth hurt. Everything is okay. Just stay right there."

"I can't, I—"

"Amber. It's a trap. I'll be there so soon. Please don't go in."

"I know. I know," Amber wailed. "But what if they kill her before you get here?"

"That's not going to happen. I'm only a couple of minutes away."

"I'm sorry, Heather. I can't abandon my daughter."

Heather heard the opening of a door and held her breath. There was nothing else she could do but keep quiet and keep driving. It was silent for thirty seconds, and just as Heather was about to ask if she was okay, Amber released a deafening scream. Then came the bang of Amber's phone hitting the floor hard, followed by the line going dead.

"Shit. Shit. Shit," Heather hissed as she pulled up outside Sherwood's.

As quietly as she could, she jumped out of the car and entered the front door, bracing herself for another Alice Warren—another dead woman, another grieving partner, and another motherless child. It was all happening again.

Don't think like that, she told herself firmly, but the thoughts wouldn't stop coming.

She looked around the seemingly empty bar. There was no man, no Amber, and no blood. Then Savannah cried, and Heather moved toward the sound and peered over the bar, terrified of what she might find.

She was relieved to see that Savannah was unharmed and swaddled in her baby carrier. She was unhappy, likely on account of her cold nose and ears, but despite all of her fears, the baby was unharmed. At least there was that.

Bobby, on the other hand, didn't look so good. He was propped up against the wall, completely motionless, his skin sallow and pale. She was sure he was dead until she saw his chest rise and fall. She continued to watch his chest, worried her mind was playing tricks on her.

Just as she was about to hop the bar to check his pulse, she heard Amber scream again in the distance. Pointing her gun in line with her line of sight, Heather saw that the back door was open and blowing in the wind. Promising Bobby that she'd come back for him, she took off in pursuit of the fearful sound.

The beer garden was a disaster. Chairs, tables, umbrellas, and rope bollards had been knocked over in what looked like the results of a violent altercation or an effort to slow down a pursuant. Heather prayed for the latter.

Amber screamed again, and Heather saw two people run across a main road and down an alleyway in the distance. The man from the bushes, the one who'd killed Luis Sabado and likely Roland, too, was chasing after Amber at full speed.

Heather joined the chase, ignoring the honking cars as she dashed across the road. Her lungs burned, and her hangover broiled, but her recent running had paid off. Her legs pumped like a well-oiled machine, and she closed in on Amber's would-be attacker in mere seconds.

The man was so focused on Amber that he didn't even seem to hear Heather coming until she was right on top of him. He glanced over his shoulder, shouted a series of what Heather assumed were Spanish curse words, and drew his gun. It was prettier than Heather's black Glock 22 and featured a gaudy gold and diamond-encrusted grip that glittered in the light. Heather considered herself a good shot, but this man handled his weapon in a way she could only dream of.

She anticipated receiving a bullet—maybe in the knees to slow her down or perhaps turn her lights out forever—but she moved forward unwaveringly. She'd let Alice Warren down and refused to let it happen again to Amber.

However, the man didn't shoot her. Instead, he turned toward Amber, who was hurtling along the alleyway at Olympic speeds, and before Heather could reach him, he took aim and fired. The shot landed, and Amber fell over hard onto the rough ground. The speed at which she was going, combined with the height of her shoes, propelled her forward, grinding her exposed skin and face against the gravel for several feet.

THE CRASH

"No!" Heather screamed.

Confident his prey could no longer escape, the man turned and pointed his gun at Heather's throat. In the same second, she propelled into him and tackled him to the ground. She snatched the gun from his hands and threw it like a frisbee as far as she could. Another shot rang out as it hit the wall, the bullet embedding itself in a trash can.

Straddling his stomach and holding him still with her muscular thighs, she pointed her gun at his sun-lined forehead. She wanted to pull the trigger but forced her finger steady.

"Who the hell are you?" she barked.

The man raised his hands in surrender and offered a toothy grin that seemed to stretch painfully far. His pure black eyes were dull and beady like a shark, and his face was covered in distorting scars.

She kept the gun trained on him with one hand as she reached for the cuffs by her back pocket. Just as she unclasped them, the man's smile turned into a snarl, and he flipped his lower half up. With his knees in her pits, he slammed her hard into the wall and slid out of her grasp.

Her cheek and temple smacked against the brick with a dull thud that felt anything but. The impact was enough that she nearly lost consciousness, but she somehow stayed awake. As her vision returned, the pain seared through her right side, and she was sure she'd shattered her cheekbone. She tasted blood, but after tonguing around the area, she found all her molars intact.

She struggled to turn, but managed to twist, and saw the man walking away at a leisurely pace. He was leaving her to die, she realized, and she crawled toward him along rough gravel before getting to her feet, her gun still in her hand. She pointed it at his back, but still didn't shoot.

"Hey!" she rasped.

He turned around, bemused as if she were a child who'd just said something inappropriate. The shock over her consciousness was evident, and though she detected a note of respect among the surprise, he kept his gun by his side as if he didn't believe her to be a threat.

"Tough girl," he said with a thick accent. "Stupid too."

He charged before she got the chance to respond, and still dazed, she didn't move in time to avoid being pinned to the wall. His muscular forearm pressed into her throat as she pressed her gun into his gut. It didn't deter him. He knew as well as she did that she wouldn't shoot. She needed answers, and he was probably the only person in the world who could give them to her. So, instead of a shot to the stomach, she brought her knee up as hard as she could into his crotch. He staggered back, and she took the opportunity to punch him as hard as she could in the jaw.

It seemed to hurt her hand more than his face, and he quickly countered by busting her lip. Enraged, she tackled him again by wrapping his arm around his waist and using her weight as an anchor. As she fought to pin him, she was forced to holster her gun. Once she had his wrists, she attempted to cuff him, but he was too strong for her to keep still. He wrapped his own hands around her wrists and twisted sharply, causing her to yell out in pain.

"Give up, little girl," he soothed. "Before you get really hurt."

Heather spat blood in his face, and his expression darkened; all his cat-and-mouse joy vanished, and he swapped their positions, flipping her onto her back.

The man moved his strong hands to her throat and pressed down even harder than before. After ten seconds, he released her, and just as she was halfway through inhaling, he returned his grip. He did this over and over. He allowed her just enough oxygen to live so he could watch her suffer and cling to life as she faded away. The fear of death was like a drug to him, and pleasure washed over his features as if injected with morphine.

Heather reached carefully for her gun, black spots appearing in her vision. She didn't care about answers anymore. She just wanted to live. She wanted Amber to live. She wanted Glenville to go back to normal. She wanted this man dead.

Bang!

A deafening gunshot whistled through the alleyway, and the man released his grasp, looking to his left where the bullet had grazed his ear. Heather saw her opportunity and headbutted the man hard, and as he reeled back, she pressed her advantage and landed one, two, three blows to his face, sending him crashing

THE CRASH

to the ground, and then she reached for her gun, planted a knee firmly on his back, and held it against his head.

Whoever had fired the shot jogged toward her, and she looked up to see Gabriel, his weapon also trained on the suspect. Heather nodded at him, and as Gabriel pinned the man against the wall and cuffed him, her gun never wavered. For good measure, Gabriel delivered a blow to the man's stomach that brought him to his knees.

"Keep him here," Heather said.

"No problem."

"And call an ambulance. Bobby's inside in bad shape, and Amber..." Heather drifted off as she looked at Amber's unmoving body and took off running.

She collapsed onto her knees and into a pool of blood. Amber's pulse pounded against Heather's fingertips, and Heather let out a sob of relief. She brushed the bloody blonde hair from the woman's face and watched as she slowly returned to consciousness. Amber opened her mouth to scream in fear, but Heather shushed her.

"It's okay. I'm here. He's in handcuffs. Everything is going to be okay."

"Heather?" Amber croaked.

Heather smiled. "Hi. I want you to stay calm for me and not move. Can you do that?"

Amber nodded weakly.

"Okay. You've been shot, but you're going to be fine. The ambulance is on its way."

Amber stayed very still, clearly in too much shock to feel much pain, and Heather began looking for the bullet hole. It was hard to find amongst the swathes of black denim, but as a cloud passed, she saw a gleam of blood in the sunlight. It was on the left side, and how the oversized jacket had swung as she ran meant that the bullet could have landed anywhere from her lung to her gut.

Heather cautiously peeled the jacket away from the light gray T-shirt beneath and nearly collapsed when she saw the bullet-shaped slit on the woman's side. The man must have wanted her alive and missed every major organ.

"Are Bobby and Savannah okay?" Amber asked.

"Yeah. You're all going to be okay."
For once, it didn't feel like an empty promise.

Heather, Gabriel, and Tina supervised the scene until everyone was gone. The suspect was to be placed in a holding cell with guards on twenty-four-hour watch, Amber was being taken to the hospital for her gunshot wound but was in stable condition when she left, and Bobby was with the local doctor being supervised while his mild concussion wore off. A family member—one of the endless Sherwoods—was looking after Savannah while the pair recovered.

Tina looked at Heather fondly. "You did well today, Detective Bishop."

"Thanks, Sheriff," Heather rasped, her throat still throbbing. It wasn't the only thing that hurt. Nearly everything on her body ached: her cheek had been freshly stitched up, large raised bruises were already starting to form, and whatever she'd done to her ribs on the day of the crash had returned. She desperately needed some painkillers and her bed. She was dying for a drink, too, but her hangover nearly costing Amber's life had significantly stripped her love of liquor away.

Maybe just one, she thought, unsure if she could stomach even that.

"Seriously, Heather. You saved lives today, and I barely had any idea any of it was happening. You're a hero," Tina enthused breathlessly before turning to Gabriel. "You are too."

Gabriel shook his head. "No. It's all Heather. I'm just glad I could help."

"If you say so. Please call me if either of you needs anything," Tina said as she walked toward her car, clearly understanding that the two of them wanted to be alone.

Once she was gone, Heather pulled Gabriel in for a tight hug, resting her chin hard on his shoulder. She felt him relax, so she held him longer than she had ever voluntarily hugged anyone.

"You saved my life," she whispered.

"I heard gunshots and went to look and saw him... on top of you," Gabriel murmured.

Heather realized how horrifying it must have been seeing her bloodied and pinned beneath a deranged and dangerous man. She wondered if he pointed the gun at the man's head as he had with Dennis Burke before firing the warning shot. Or had it even been intended to be a warning shot, or had the man survived because of the error of shaky hands? She didn't ask him. They could talk about it another time.

They broke the hug, and Heather looked at him, his curly hair hanging in his face, his body slumped. "Tina was right. You are a hero."

"I was just lucky," he said.

"No such thing. You listened to your gut, and you saved Amber and me."

"*You* saved you and Amber."

Heather chuckled weakly. "Let's just say we made a really good team today."

"Yeah, we did," he agreed.

Heather looked around at the darkening alley. "I think it's safe for us to go home. You want a ride?"

"My mom is coming to pick me up. Do you want to come over for dinner?"

"Not today. I think I—"

"No need to explain. It's been a long day."

Heather patted his shoulder gratefully as they walked opposite ways down the long, dark alley. At the end, illuminated by the headlights of cars on the road, they turned and waved goodnight to each other.

CHAPTER THIRTY-SEVEN

THE FATHER

2023

IT HAD BEEN FIVE HOURS SINCE ROLAND CROSSED THE BOR-der and a little over three since he'd decided he wouldn't be returning. Francisco had promised him that it was the last job he'd ever have to do, and though Roland believed he was telling the truth this time, the previous dozen 'last jobs' had left him skeptical of his boss's sincerity. Roland could take the beatings, the windowless cell, and the indentured servitude, but he could not stand being a donkey chasing a carrot on a stick for the rest

THE CRASH

of his life. If Francisco was going to dangle his freedom in front of his face, he would take it by force.

As with every other job he'd carried out over the last eighteen months, he was supposed to take the shipment to Francisco's contact to a new location in North America. The receivers were always Mexican, dressed in black, and never offered any payment in exchange for the shipment. It seemed to him as if they were just looking after the drugs rather than selling them. He never asked because he knew they'd never answer. However, he had a plan that he could squeeze a very respectable chunk of cash out of.

He was still going to go to Seattle as promised, but instead of handing the drugs over to Francisco's men in some shady motel alleyway, he was going to meet with Pamela's American contacts. The ones Francisco had betrayed many years ago.

They didn't know Roland was coming, but with the amount of product on board, he knew they wouldn't care about the imposition. Moreover, they still despised Francisco and would undoubtedly be eager to help Roland double-cross him for a second time.

However, Seattle would come later. The first part of the plan involved landing in Glenville, apologizing to his wife and children, and then driving to Seattle in a pickup truck that Francisco and his men would never recognize. They'll be too busy watching the skies anyway.

Maybe I should wear a disguise, he thought, rubbing his freshly shaved face.

He knew he'd once owned a variety of high-quality Halloween costumes and accompanying supplies but feared that his party regalia had been likely the first things to go once Nancy realized he wasn't coming back. She'd always loathed Halloween and refused to participate, even for the children's sake. Still, Roland was confident in his ability to make something out of nothing.

However, despite his belief in his plans, as Glenville appeared on the horizon, he found himself wracked with anxiety. Who knew what he was about to discover after fifteen years of abandoning his town and his family? The place could've burned down. Nancy might've declared him dead and remarried. His children would be adults, and neither he nor they would recognize the other. But he could fix it. He hadn't run into a problem yet that he couldn't solve with a little bit of creative thinking. He hadn't gotten this far in life without learning to roll with the punches.

His palms grew sweaty, and a burning heat formed at his collar. He was panicking. That much was certain. And one crucial thing you could not do as a pilot about to land was panic. So, he opened a secret compartment in the floor and retrieved a brick of high-quality cocaine. He hadn't had any since Pamela had died. Having fun without her felt wrong, but he needed a quick solution and knew she would understand.

He blew a kiss to the heavens, slit the plastic wrap, and then pulled the knife to his nose and inhaled before licking the remnants off. As it had the first time, the euphoria washed over him, and he whooped and hollered with joy as he finally reached Glenville.

At long last, he was coming home.

CHAPTER THIRTY-EIGHT

THE DETECTIVE

HEATHER LIMPED INTO THE POLICE STATION EARLY THE next day to boisterous applause from her peers. There was a bouquet of flowers, a card signed by everyone, and a bottle of champagne waiting for her on her desk. She thanked everyone as warmly as she could, waving off their well wishes with her one good arm. That's when their joyous expressions turned into sympathetic ones. She hated being pitied but could understand their concern.

Her right arm was supported by a sling fashioned out of old bed sheets, and her face was puffy and purple. She wore a pajama top, cardigan, and paint-stained sweatpants tucked into thick winter socks and sneakers. Almost no one in attendance had seen her outside of work and were clearly shocked by not only her injuries but her informality.

Her hair was also down, which was probably the most startling aspect of her appearance for her colleagues. It turned out that tying a ponytail with one good arm was nearly impossible. She hadn't realized last night, but when the man had thrown her, she'd torn a muscle, and when the agony woke her up at three o'clock in the morning, she knew something was wrong.

The doctor said it'd be fine in a few days, same for her ribs and the rest of her contusions and injuries, but she just had to take it easy. That she could do. There was just one last thing before everything was tied up with a bow.

She walked toward Tina and asked, "Has he spoken?"

Tina nodded, her expression tight. "Yeah, I can't get the asshole to shut up. Seems like the type of guy who likes the sound of his own voice. Cocky and possibly high as a kite." Tina looked over her shoulder through the small window in the interrogation room door. "Okay, probably high as a kite."

"Crap. A defense lawyer could have anything he says thrown out if they find out he's high."

"Hey, it's fine. We're just going to talk to him for our own purposes. He belongs to the FBI now. They'll get the important stuff out of him."

"Yeah, you're right."

"You ready to get your answers?"

Heather nodded and placed her hand on the door. Just before pushing it open, she stopped and asked, "He got a name?"

"Yep. Shared that enthusiastically too. Gustavo Molina. He's an American and Mexican dual citizen. Was an inmate at Texas State Penitentiary from 2001 to 2007 for aggravated assault and possession. Once he was released, he broke parole and supposedly crossed the border."

"Huh," Heather said, scratching her head.

"What?"

"Nothing, it's just this guy who knew Pamela Bennet was also an inmate at Texas State Penitentiary. He was released in 2005, broke parole, and headed to Mexico. Seems like a weird coincidence."

"No kidding."

"Let's see what else he can tell us."

Heather said the name back and entered the room. The man surveyed Heather with amusement as she and Tina set everything up. Cameras were on, the tape recorder was documenting every sound, and the date, time, suspect, and crime had been announced out loud. Though it would likely be thrown out, it was important to keep everything above board.

Heather and Tina sat opposite him, and the man continued to grin.

"Something funny?" Heather asked.

"Have you looked in a mirror this morning?" Gustavo's replied, circling his own countenance. His accent was thick, but his English was perfect despite him having pretended otherwise. That made things easier.

"Yeah, I guess my face is pretty funny. But you know who won't think so? The FBI. Attempting to murder an officer of the law is a pretty big deal."

The smile stayed put on Gustavo's lined face. "You don't have to play bad cop with me, Detective. I'll tell you exactly what I want to tell you. No more, no less. No matter what you do or say."

"Yeah, Sheriff Peters was telling me that you're quite the conversationalist. We appreciate that you've been an open book so far, but I'm just wondering why that is?"

"Is there a reason I shouldn't speak?"

"No. But most guilty people prefer not to. Serial killers brag sometimes, but you're running an entire trafficking operation. You surely don't want to blow up all your hard work."

He gave her a smug, satisfied smirk. "Running it? That's quite the compliment, but I'm afraid all the credit goes to The Harpy."

"The Harpy?"

"My boss."

"That's why you all have those tattoos?"

Gustavo nodded.

"Got anything else to share about him?"

"Not today. Not that it would matter if I told you everything. No amount of chitchat can stop it now," Gustavo purred, leering at Heather's injuries with dilated pupils.

"Stop what?" Tina asked, looking around as if a hidden bomb might go off any second.

Gustavo grinned but didn't answer. Clearly, that question belonged in the 'refuse to talk about' column.

Heather rubbed her face and winced. "Let's circle back to that. What I really want to know is whether you killed Roland Ellis?"

A wild howling laugh burst from Gustavo's mouth that made Heather and Tina recoil as if someone had just unleashed a rabid wolf into the room. Heather looked at the chains binding him to the table to reassure herself that he wasn't about to lunge forward and rip her jugular out. His teeth looked sharp enough to get the job done.

"Answer the question, Gustavo," Heather said firmly.

Gustavo wiped tears from his dead eyes. "No. I didn't kill Roland Ellis. A smart girl like you—I'm surprised you even need to ask."

"I like being thorough."

"Roland's death was an accident. Imagine wasting a million dollars' worth of cocaine to take out an imbecile like Roland Ellis?" Gustavo shook his head. "No, he was supposed to take that to our contact in Seattle. He'd been a good boy about not skimming off the top, so we trusted him to leave it alone without having to tell him about the cyanide."

"And what about Luis Sabado? Did you mean to kill him?"

"Ah, Luis. Poor kid. He and I were sent to Seattle a week in advance to make a drop of our own. It was a small amount for such a long trip, but it was important to The Harpy to spread as much product across America as possible. So, we made the delivery, and then the boss called me and said he had two jobs for me. Kill Luis, and then hang around, enjoy myself, and when Roland lands, kill him too."

"Why?" Tina asked, making frantic, scrawling notes in the absence of Heather's right hand.

"He was done with both of them. Luis had stolen one too many times, and Roland... Roland was not the man this town thought he was. He betrayed us all and killed the boss's nephew in cold blood."

"He killed The Harpy's nephew?"

Gustavo nodded forlornly, looking away for the first time. "That poor boy's body. Resting forever in Panteón de San Antonio in a town he never got to leave."

"Where is Panteón de San Antonio?" Heather asked.

"You won't have heard of it," Gustavo replied confidently.

"Still. I'm curious."

"Valle de Bravo. It's a town not unlike this. Surrounded by woods with a lake at the center."

"Sounds lovely," Heather said, keeping her expression neutral.

She knew all about Valle de Bravo. She had a map of it pinned to her corkboard at home with a red pin stuck into the villa where Pamela's body had been found.

"Can you tell me anything about Pamela Bennet?"

"Pamela... Pamela... Pamela. Oh! I remember. Roland's little girlfriend. What a pity. She was a beauty."

"What about Francisco Medina? Have you heard of him?"

Gustavo looked at her blankly. "Doesn't ring a bell."

"He knew Pamela. Dated her, actually."

"I didn't really know Pamela very well. Only that she helped Roland betray us all and that doing so ended very poorly for her."

"So, why kill her in May 2021 and keep Roland around until November 2023?"

"We needed him—his plane specifically—and my boss felt he deserved a more elaborate punishment," Gustavo enthused. "What better way to punish Roland than to tell him he was free to go, only for him to eat a bullet at the finish line?"

"You're right. That is cruel," Heather said coolly. "Okay, so back to the story. You kill Luis, I'm guessing, by tricking him into snorting laced cocaine?"

"Correct."

"And then you're hanging around waiting for Roland, see that he's died in a plane crash on the news, and head down to Glenville. Why? He's already dead. The poison did your job for you. Surely you didn't think you could salvage any of the cocaine?"

"Actually, I was here before the crash," Gustavo replied smugly, leaning forward as if telling a secret before returning to squirming and grinding his teeth.

Heather furrowed her brow. "How did you know he was going to crash here?"

"My boss called the day before the drop, told me he knew Roland was going to betray him and told me to find out where he would go instead. I believed him, which gave me twenty-four hours to figure out where in the world he would go to hide from us."

"Okay, so how did you figure it out?" Heather asked, unable to pretend like she wasn't curious.

"I thought back to a year and a half earlier. I was tailing Roland in Texas—keeping an eye on him while he ran errands. He spent hours in a room with the trashy blonde you know as Amber. Then a few months later, they meet again, and she's carrying his child. After that, I kept tabs on her on social media, just in case he'd spilled any important beans during their lovemaking. She never did, but I still checked in occasionally and remembered that I'd seen her tagging a town called Glenville. So, I use the magic of the internet to combine Roland Ellis and Glenville together, and boom. Turns out my fugitive was the mayor of said shithole little town, and his family still lived there. So, I drove down to Glenville, got myself a room at The Black Bear Motel, and waited. I stalked all of them. The tall skinny woman and her loser of a son. Amber and her adorable family. You."

Heather felt a shiver run down her spine. "Okay, so you get here, and then Roland crashes, and we confiscate the cocaine. Why stick around to stalk Amber?"

"Oh, so you think this is about Amber?"

"Considering you shot her, yeah." Heather was becoming exasperated and grew tired of Gustavo's riddles.

"Oh no, Detective. This is about you. I chose Amber because I'd considered killing her for years, just in case, but really it could've been anyone in town."

"You wanted to be arrested?" Tina asked.

THE CRASH

Heather looked at her with surprise and then back at Gustavo and realized she was right. "Why?" she asked, her eyes wide.

"Do you know what a green light means?" Gustavo inquired.

"I—" Heather stammered.

"It means go," he said.

"Go?" Tina asked. "What do you mean?"

His grin was so wide it nearly split his face open. "Oh, you'll see."

"What will we see, Gustavo?" Heather asked, fearing the answer.

Gustavo stretched, yawned, and cracked his neck. "I think I'm done answering your questions now."

"That's great, because I'm done asking them," Heather snapped, standing up.

"Thank you for your time, Mr. Molina," Tina said, trying to sound as professional as possible, though her dislike was visible.

"Bye, ladies. It's been a lovely chat," he replied, getting the last word in before the door shut.

On the other side of the door, Heather groaned. "When is the FBI getting here?"

"In an hour. Then none of this will be our problem anymore."

"Good," Heather said, though she mentally tugged at the loose threads of the case in irritation. "I'm ready to pass this one on to the big dogs. It's officially become above my pay grade."

Tina nodded. "Tell me about it. I'm good with looking after the county."

"Hey, I'm good with just looking after Glenville."

"Well, you're doing a great job at that."

"You are, too, Sheriff."

Tina looked pleased and rubbed Heather's good shoulder. "Thanks, Heather. Now go enjoy a day off. Rest. Get some sleep. Heck, take the whole week off."

"I can do a long weekend."

"Deal. See you on Tuesday."

CHAPTER THIRTY-NINE

THE DETECTIVE

Heather spent the following twenty-four hours half asleep, curled up with her dogs, with her phone on silent. Though, as she always did when resting, she grew restless and ended up venturing to the grocery store in search of microwave meals to get her and her arm through the following week.

With an array of various frozen curries and pasta in the trunk, she pulled up to her house and saw Gabriel waiting for her on the porch step. Next to him was a six-pack of cheap beer and a bottle of Wild Turkey, and in his hands, he held a white bag full of what she guessed was Chinese food and a short stack of DVDs he'd brought over from his parents' house. He waved these items at her sheepishly as she pulled up.

He got to his feet as she exited the car and approached, and she laughed at his sheepish expression.

"What's all this for?" she asked.

"Congratulations... and an overdue apology."

"Overdue apology? Gabriel, you have nothing to be sorry for."

Gabriel shifted awkwardly. "Can we go inside?"

"Sure. I think you've more than brought enough to afford a ticket to Casa de Bishop. Step right up."

She unlocked the door, and they both shuffled in, much to the joy of her three dogs, who bounded around Gabriel as he laid his offerings on the already cluttered coffee table. He held up the bottle of whiskey, his hand at its throat.

"May I?"

"Go for it," Heather replied, grabbing two mismatched glasses and holding them out.

Gabriel poured them each a double, they clinked, and down the hatch it went. It seemed to do the trick for Gabriel, who sat on the couch and made himself at home, his tight expression softening.

Heather sat in the armchair to his left so that she could look at him without straining her neck. She leaned forward, one elbow on her knee like a parent talking to a troubled child. "So, what are you apologizing about?"

Gabriel sighed. "I've been distant lately. I'm sure you've noticed."

"Distant? You? I don't know what you mean," Heather teased.

"And things have been awkward between us."

"They've been improving."

"Sure, but I still want to talk about why things have been the way they've been. My therapist thinks if we talk about why things have been weird, they'll stop being weird."

Heather shrugged. "Okay, let's give it a shot."

"I think I've been distant because of the Warren case. It affected me more than I let on, and being around you or our coworkers just reminded me of it. I was seriously thinking about quitting, and then I met Briana, and she saved me. She gave me a space that wasn't..." He drifted off.

"Tainted by death?"

"Yeah. That. She doesn't watch the news and hates all things morbid. It was like choosing between a graveyard and Disneyland."

"Right. And I'm the graveyard?" Heather asked.

"It sounds bad when you say it like that, but yeah. Sorry."

Heather shrugged. "It's fine. None taken."

"Anyway, so I start going to Disneyland every day because I can't bear the sight of tombstones, but my therapist says that's just slapping a bandage on the issue, and I need to actually work on my trauma, not just run away from it."

"Smart woman."

"You'd like her."

Heather simpered. "Maybe. I'll think about it."

Gabriel paused to sip his drink and grimaced. "I think I have to break up with Briana."

"Why?"

"I think I hate Disneyland?"

"Gabriel," Heather scolded, trying to hold back her laughter.

"Okay. Not hate. But I think I've been using her as an emotional distraction, and she's been using me as an accessory to show off to her friends. She even dresses me before we go to the mall up in the city. And I think she likes me more than I like her, which isn't fair, and I need to work on myself some more before getting serious. Clear some of the emotional baggage out of the attic, ya know?"

One word—baggage—and it all came flooding back. The funeral. The wake. The drinks. The taxi ride home. The drinks. The smoking. The meaningful conversations. The confession.

"That's why I turned you down. My baggage," Heather said.

Gabriel flushed and stuttered. "You remember?"

Heather sighed. "I do now. I think I blacked it out at the time."

Gabriel looked at his hands. "I'm not like, in love with you or anything. I was just really drunk and sad. I had a little crush, but I'm over it now."

THE CRASH

"You don't have to be over it, but it's important that you know it's never going to happen. Not only am I too damaged to date anyone, but I'm definitely too damaged to date you. You need someone stable and easygoing. Someone with their shit together."

"You deserve that too."

Heather laughed. "I don't think anyone can handle my baggage. It must weigh several tons by now."

"Someone strong will come along," he assured her.

Heather looked down at her bruised knuckles. "We'll see."

"So, if neither of us had baggage, would you be after all of this?" Gabriel teased, gesturing up and down at his body, which Heather noticed was dressed in fleece Elmo pajama bottoms and a coffee-stained band T-shirt.

Heather chuckled. "Gabriel, I love you, but like an annoying little brother or a best friend."

"Oh, I see how it is. You think I'm ugly!" he exclaimed in amusement.

"I didn't say that!"

"Okay, so what's wrong with me? Too short? Too shockingly handsome and muscular?"

"You're too... cute," Heather decided.

"Cute? I'm not cute." Gabriel began unbagging the food, then looked at Heather and tutted. "I'm not cute."

"If you say so, kiddo."

"Oh, please, God. I've been punished enough. Do not start calling me kiddo like I'm your sidekick in a comic book."

"Alright. Buzzkill. So, how are you feeling after yesterday?" she asked hesitantly, not wanting to open a can of snakes disguised as worms. Gabriel shrugged, but his face gave him away. Heather cocked an eyebrow.

"I've been better," he admitted.

"Me too," she agreed.

Gabriel looked at her bruised face and rubbed his mouth with his hands in distress. "Jesus," he muttered.

"Oh, come on, it's not that bad!"

"If I'd been a better partner and kept up to date with you and the case, maybe I would've been with you for the chase, and none of this would've happened."

"Hey! You take those 'what ifs' out back and bury them in the dirt. They don't change anything, and I won't have them in the house."

Gabriel ruefully smiled and cracked a beer. "It reminded me of Alice. I think about her a lot."

"Me too," Heather admitted before noticing his remorseful expression. "You were the one at her memorial bench!"

"Yeah. I didn't mean to scare you."

"Why didn't you call out?"

"I didn't want you to know I was there. Didn't want you worrying about me. Didn't want you to feel awkward about it either."

"You scared the crap out of me."

"Sorry."

She waved him off. "It's fine. I get it. I'm just glad it wasn't Gustavo."

Gabriel ran his eyes over her injuries and said solemnly, "Me too."

"Do you go there a lot?"

"Yeah. Once or twice a week," he replied. "I struggle to sleep occasionally, and the walk does me good."

"I don't sleep well either."

"I can tell, dude. Your eyes look like they've been through some shit."

Heather chuckled. "Oh, they have. They've been put through hundreds of hours of the Home Shopping Network."

"Oh, that explains it," Gabriel said, looking around.

"Explains what?"

"Why your house looks even more like an old lady's house."

Heather looked around at her Snuggie, her foot spa, her Shake Weight, and the variety of other purchases made while sleep deprived.

"Okay, I see your point. Turns out that I'm an old lady at heart."

"I could've told you that."

"Don't push your luck, buster. You're the one with a crush on an old lady, you weirdo."

"Buster!" Gabriel exclaimed, shaking his head. "You know what? I could do with some useless inventions too."

THE CRASH

He turned on the TV, and Heather expected to see the Home Shopping Network, but instead, the news was on. She remembered it was the last thing she'd watched in fear of more cyanide-related deaths.

A Seattle reporter was standing on the steps outside the Seattle Police Department, her back to a man being escorted by heavily armed police officers into the building. The man was pale with a shaven head and arms covered in tattoos. Underneath the scene, a banner read, "Russian drug lord, Alexsei Volkov, arrested on suspicion of a string of countrywide cyanide poisonings."

"Russian?" Gabriel asked, as dumbfounded as Heather.

"Unmute it."

The previously silent reporter informed them, "Volkov was arrested earlier today after almost one hundred cyanide poisonings have swept the country. The method? Laced cocaine. Those who have survived have pointed to Russian gangs as the source, with Volkov as the mastermind behind the plot. Is this an attempt at terrorism or simply narcotic manufacturing gone wrong? More at six on CNN. I'm—"

Heather paused the screen as another banner popped up at the bottom of the screen, reading, "Gustavo Molina, arrested in Glenville on suspicion of the murder of Luis Sabado and the assault of police officer Heather Bishop."

"Green means go," Heather whispered.

"What?" Gabriel asked.

Heather jumped to her feet and moved toward her corkboard. She whipped around with a manic look in her eyes. "I couldn't figure it out. The cyanide-laced cocaine—why they were moving so much poison around, ruining expensive goods. It's a setup! They must've been sitting on piles of this stuff all over the country, and at the signal, they sold it to the Russians. They want to start a war."

"Or wipe out the competition."

Heather nodded. "And that's what Gustavo is. He's the signal. His arrest unleashed chemical warfare."

"This is crazy."

Heather looked back at the TV, her corkboard, and then back again. Her blood ran cold as she slowly padded toward the flat screen.

"No fucking way," she hissed, getting out her phone to take a picture.

"What?"

"It's him," she said, moving out of the way to let Gabriel see. "It's Francisco Medina."

Gabriel squinted before raising his eyebrows. He, too, looked at the mugshot on the wall and nodded to confirm that Heather hadn't lost her mind. "You're right. It's him. What the hell is he doing in Seattle?"

"He's gloating. Press play, but keep it on mute. I have to make some calls."

"Do you think he's The Harpy? The guy Gustavo wouldn't shut up about?"

"I think so. And if we're right, we can tear his whole operation down."

Heather sat down beside Gabriel as he muted and pressed play. She watched in awe as Francisco stood in the background, looking directly into the camera, cigarillo hanging from his cocked lips. The smog it produced looked toxic, and the crowd kept their distance from the fumes.

"I've got you," Heather whispered as she pressed the call button.

As Tina picked up, he sunk back into the crowd. It didn't matter. Gabriel was recording him, and she knew where he and his operation were located. Soon enough, The Harpy's wings would be clipped for good.

After telling Tina everything the FBI needed to know about Francisco, the drugs, and Valle de Bravo, she hung up and sent the video that Gabriel had taken. They stared at the spot in the crowd where Francisco had stood until the footage changed.

"You want a cigarette?" Gabriel asked.

"No thanks. I quit."

AUTHOR'S NOTE

Thank you for reading *The Crash*, the second installment in the Glenville mystery series! It means the world to me that you have chosen to embark on this journey with Heather and explore the mysteries of Glenville.

One of the most exciting aspects of writing this series is exploring the mystery from multiple perspectives. Each viewpoint provides a unique piece of the puzzle, allowing me to delve deeper into various settings, subplots, and themes. I hope that this approach has added texture and richness to Glenville, captivating your imagination and enticing you to explore its streets alongside Heather!

As an author, I put everything into my writing, and I'd love to hear your thoughts on The Crash. If you have a minute, please consider leaving a review or sharing your thoughts with others! Your reviews and word-of-mouth recommendations help me continue pursuing my passion for writing and storytelling.

I'm already hard at work on Heather's next adventure, so don't worry! You won't have to wait too long before you can join her on another thrilling journey. Up for another mysterious and thrilling adventure right now? Be sure to read Book 1 of my other series set in beautiful Hawaii - *Murder in Paradise*.

Warm regards,
Cara Kent

P.S. I will be the first one to tell you that I am not perfect, no matter how hard I try to be. And there is plenty that I am still learning about self-publishing. If you come across any typos or have any other issues with this book please don't hesitate to reach out to me at cara@carakent.com, I monitor and read every email personally, and I will do my very best to rectify any issues that I am made aware of.

Get the inside scoop on new releases and get a **FREE BOOK** by me! Visit *https://dl.bookfunnel.com/513mluk159* to claim your **FREE** copy!

Follow me on **Facebook** - *https://www.facebook.com/people/Cara-Kent/100088665803376/*
Follow me on **Instagram** - *https://www.instagram.com/cara.kent_books/*

ALSO BY CARA KENT

Glenville Mystery Thriller

Book One - *The Lady in the Woods*
Book Two - *The Crash*

Mia Storm FBI Mystery Thriller

Book One - *Murder in Paradise*

An Addictive Psychological Thriller with Shocking Twists

Book One - *The Woman in the Cottage*
Book Two - *Mine*

Made in United States
Troutdale, OR
03/02/2024